Captain of my Heart

Brendan swallowed and looked away, still shivering. Without further deliberation Mira reached over, found the buttons of his lapel, and one by one, undid them. Still, he didn't move, only stared into the fire with his jaw set and his knuckles showing white with the effort it took to contain himself.

Gathering her courage, Mira pressed her lips to his temple, and put her tongue against his skin.

"Why are you doing this, *Moyrrra?*" he said in an agonized whisper.

"Doing what?"

"Driving me insane. I can't take much more of this and still behave like a gentleman."

"I do wish you'd *stop* behaving like a gentleman. I'm beginning to find it quite boring."

"Faith." He shut his eyes once more.

"The world is full of gentlemen and rakes. You've already proven to me that you can be a gentleman. Prove to me now that you can be a rake . . ."

Captain of my Heart

Danelle Harmon

AVON BOOKS ◆ NEW YORK

CAPTAIN OF MY HEART is an original publication of Avon Books. This work has never before appeared in book form. This work is a novel. Any similarity to actual persons or events is purely coincidental.

AVON BOOKS
A division of
The Hearst Corporation
1350 Avenue of the Americas
New York, New York 10019

Copyright © 1992 by Danelle F. Harmon
Inside cover author photograph by Thomas F. Keegan
Published by arrangement with the author
Library of Congress Catalog Card Number: 92-93073
ISBN: 0-380-76676-0

First Avon Books Printing: October 1992

AVON TRADEMARK REG. U.S. PAT. OFF. AND IN OTHER COUNTRIES, MARCA REGISTRADA, HECHO EN U.S.A.

Printed in the U.S.A.

RA 10 9 8 7 6 5 4 3 2 1

CAPTAIN OF MY HEART
is dedicated to four very special people:

my sister, Jody
her husband, Brian
and my mom and dad

God bless you all
Let's hope this one brings me back home

Acknowledgments

I would like to extend a very heartfelt thank you to my agent, Pesha Rubinstein, and my editor, Marjorie Braman.

I'd also like to acknowledge Christine Zika and Karen Gudmundson at Avon Books, as well as those individuals who contributed so much to me during the writing of CAPTAIN OF MY HEART: Reverend Edwin Trench, Jr., Bruce Harmon, Rochelle Alers, Ken Kinkor, Lynne Leathers, Helene and Jim Chadwick, Rod Cambre, and the faculty, residents and staff at Tufts University School of Veterinary Medicine—especially Sandy for Fridays, Barbara for bulletin boards, and Karen and Trena for reading the first draft; Mark Hayden for his help in naming the schooner; Sarah Truitt for hers in tracking down the "real" Brendan; Siobhán, Feidhlimidh, Cionaodh, Cairellán, Deasún, Chríostín, *agus* Maitiú of the Worcester Irish Club's *Ár dTeanga Féin* class; Paul, Fred, Ernie, Jim, and all the members of the Menotomy Minute Men who not only taught me how to fire a flintlock, but gave me inspiration for this book and the next; Captain John Foss and the crew of the *American Eagle;* Captain Bert Rogers and the crew of the *Spirit of Massachusetts;* and last—but certainly not least—the memory of the original *Pride of Baltimore*, which visited Newburyport so long ago and was the inspiration for my own little *Kestrel.*

Oh, and no thanks at all to Roscoe and Dixie. You provided the model for the dog and cats, but between ingesting the corn cob, ransacking my things, chewing the antiques, and conspiring to drive me crazy, you made it awfully hard to get any writing done. . . .

But I love you anyhow.

FOR LOVE AND LIBERTY

That seat of Science, Athens, and Earth's proud mistress Rome;
Where now are all their glories? We scarce can find a tomb!
Then guard your rights, Americans, nor stoop to lawless sway;
Oppose, oppose, oppose, oppose, for North America.

We led fair Freedom hither, and lo, the desert smiled!
A paradise of pleasure was opened in the wild!
Your harvest, bold Americans, no power shall snatch away!
Preserve, preserve, preserve your rights, and free America!

Torn from a world of tyrants, beneath this western sky,
We formed a new dominion, a land of liberty:
The world shall own we're free men here and such we'll ever
*   be;*
Huzzah, huzzah, huzzah, huzzah, for Love and Liberty!

Lift up your hands ye heroes, and swear with proud disdain.
The wretch who would enslave you shall spread his snares in
*   vain.*
Should Europe empty all her force, we'll meet them in array,
And shout huzzah, huzzah, huzzah, for brave America!

"Free America"
—DR. JOSEPH WARREN, 1774

Prologue

July 1775

Unwilling spectators to yet another whipping, a trio of pigtailed seamen in blue jackets and striped ticken trousers stood by the rail of His Majesty's Ship *Halcyon*. Their attention was not on poor little Dalby, strung up to the gratings with his stooped back already blistering in the merciless sun. It was not on Captain Crichton, tapping his foot in impatience as he waited for the boatswain's mate to begin the punishment.

It was on the barge that had set out from the big seventy-four-gun flagship *Dauntless*.

"He's coming," said one, in a low, reverent whisper. "I knew he would."

"We all knew. Our Brendan would never let us down."

"Aye, just because he's been promoted to flag captain doesn't mean he's forgotten us."

They stared at the barge, watching as it cut its way through gentle swells that danced and glittered in the summer sunlight. Then Crichton turned, saw it, and paled. Swearing, he barked off a string of commands. Marines were hastily mustered. Officers in blue and white coats scrambled to receive the esteemed visitor. Uniforms were straightened, pipes shrilled. And then the barge was alongside, bumping against the frigate's hull as its crew tossed their oars.

As usual, the flag captain had arrived unexpectedly—and with his usual disregard for the fanfare the Royal Navy insisted upon giving him.

Crichton was furious.

"Boat ahoy!"

"*Halcyon!*" roared the flag captain's coxswain, Liam

1

Doherty, a strapping, blue-eyed Irishman with a beam-to-beam grin and a shock of spice-colored curls. "Stand by t' receive Cap'n Merrick!"

Orders were passed. The bosuns' pipes pierced the air.

"Imagine," whispered one of the seamen, "troublin' himself with the likes of us. Ye don't really think that's why he's here, do ye, John? 'Cause of us?"

"Oh, aye. No doubt about that," the first seaman said. He gazed at the purple hills that rimmed Boston Harbor. "We all signed that appeal to Sir Geoffrey to do something about Crichton, didn't we? The vice-admiral's got a good heart, and a wise head on his shoulders, picking our own Brendan Merrick to be the new flag captain. Just think of how easy things were when Captain Merrick commanded *this* ship—he never once had a man punished, not once, mind ye! And he's not going to like how bad things've gotten here!"

"Bad? By the saints, poor ol' Dalby's the second man Crichton's strung up to the gratin's for punishment this mornin' alone, and that ain't countin' the three from yesterday!"

"There were four from yesterday, Zach, not three. . . ."

At the rail, smart, red-coated marines snapped to attention. A final drum rolled on the wind. The pipes quieted, the seamen held their breaths, the tension built. They heard him coming up the ladder. They saw his gold-laced hat appear in the entry port. And then *he* was there, resplendent and handsome, the sunlight glinting with blinding intensity off his epaulets and picking out every gold button on a coat as blue as the sea that rolled behind him. Doffing his hat to the quarterdeck with a solemnness befitting the gesture, he turned, met their gazes—and grinned, for he had last walked among them as *their* captain, and he knew every one of the 150-man crew by name.

"Mr. Burke! *Ce'n chaoi bhfuil tú?* You're looking a wee bit on the jolly side this morn! Been in your cups again, laddie?" The same thought was almost visible on every man's face. Promotion to flag rank hadn't changed him a bit; he was still their same old captain, not above using the old *Gaeilge* when addressing an Irishman, not above caring about the welfare of everyone on the ship. "And Mr. Howes! You keeping your hands off my little sister?

Where is the lassie, anyhow? Faith! A half mile through spray and wave in that damnable barge and the least that Eveleen could do is come topside to greet me, eh?''

Still grinning, he winked at one of the drummers, a pale, scrawny little tyke who blushed and bobbed and dropped his drumstick under the attention. Captain Brendan Jay Merrick merely laughed and handed it back to him, oblivious to the way the boy clutched it to his chest as though it had been blessed. He was nothing like Crichton, the men thought with a mixture of pride and bittersweet relief, nor those who'd held the coveted post of flag captain before him, dour-faced, cautious men who'd reeked of protocol and the stuffiness so inherent in those of their station. No, their Brendan had always been carefree and gallant, with a face to turn a lady's head and the charm to win her heart. Elegance lay in the span of his shoulders, the shape of his hands; mirth danced in his eyes, and laughter in the swiftness of his grin. But beneath his jocular manner, he was strong and capable and a clever tactician, and no one in the King's Navy knew ships as well as he. No one before or since had been able to make the *Halcyon* frigate dance through sea and spray as he had done; no one had had the deck a-hopping to Irish jigs as they'd gone into battle; and certainly, no one had stood on the quarterdeck sketching the enemy's ships while iron flew overhead and the deck thundered beneath the might of *Halcyon*'s thirty-two guns. . . .

Someday he'd be an admiral as his English father had been before him. No wonder his dash and derring-do had caught the attention of his superiors back in London. No wonder sir Geoffrey Lloyd had promoted him to flag rank. No wonder the seamen were all ready to mutiny under Richard Crichton's iron rule, whereas they looked upon their "Captain from Connacht" as a god.

No wonder they looked upon him now as their savior.

And as Crichton came forward to greet him, the marines stepped back and Captain Merrick got a clear, unhampered view of Dalby O'Hara at the gratings, his head hanging between his frail shoulders, the rope that bound him leaving bracelets of angry red flesh at his swollen wrists.

Instantly the mirth faded from his eyes.

"Captain Merrick, how nice it is to have you grace my humble command," Crichton said tightly, with a quick salute that was more mocking than respectful. Sarcasm stained his words, and any sincerity he thought to convey was belied by hard, naturally red-rimmed eyes whose irises were the color of milk allowed to go bad. Obviously Crichton was still furious that Sir Geoffrey had put the young half-Irishman in command of his flagship and not him, a fact he tried, unsuccessfully, to hide beneath the veil of hospitality. "Perhaps you'd care for some tea in my cabin? 'Tis dreadfully hot out here on deck. . . ."

Brendan, staring at Dalby, didn't give a damn about Crichton's sarcasm, his hatred, or, for that matter, his tea. It was hot, all right; brutally so. The sun beat down upon Dalby's sunburnt back and pulled blisters from the angry flesh. It baked the planking beneath his shoes, melted the tar between the deck seams, and made the sweat run down Crichton's pale face.

And Crichton was offering him tea?!

Furious, he tore his gaze from Dalby and swung around, his jaw clenched, his fingernails biting into his palms. Out of the corner of his eye he glimpsed the flagship, anchored in shimmering haze a half mile distant, where Sir Geoffrey's flag floated on the wind and tickled the pale clouds above. He would not let his admiral down. He would not let that flag down.

He would not let his *men* down!

"Captain Crichton—"

"If not tea, sir, then how about a cup of coffee?" Crichton sputtered, sensing his superior's rage and nervously fingering the hilt of his dress sword. "I'm sure Miss Eveleen has it all poured for you. She really is a most unusual young woman, and thoughtful, too! Doesn't matter how hot it is, every morning she hauls her paints and canvas topside and sits out on deck painting the men's portraits; why, she even gives them away afterward! Must run in your family, this talent for the fine arts! I needn't tell you how popular she is with *Halcyon*'s people—" sweat ran from Crichton's temple as Brendan's gaze went once more to Dalby "—and how we all consider it a blessing that she's chosen to accompany you here to Boston.

And while I'm not accustomed to having a woman traveling aboard my ship, I daresay her presence has been a most enjoyable one—"

"Captain Crichton, I did not come here to discuss my sister!"

"But of course not, sir, though she *did* see your barge coming across and is probably expecting you—"

"I came here to address complaints made to me and our admiral regarding your unnecessary brutality!" Brendan continued, as if Crichton had never spoken.

A hush fell over the ship, the slap of waves against the hull breaking the sudden, strained silence. Somewhere overhead a gull cried.

"My—my *brutality?*" Dark, angry color suffused Crichton's fair face. "Why, that's preposterous! Who would dare lodge such a ridiculous complaint, anyhow?!"

"Your crew. And *I*, after observing your actions over the past several moments."

Crichton followed the young flag officer's gaze and waved his hand in a dismissive motion. "What, are you talking about Dalby O'Hara? Why, he deserves everything that's coming to him! Lieutenant Myles caught him stealing bread just this morning from the purser's stores. Surely you don't think I'm going to let such atrocities go unpunished—"

"Captain Crichton, the only atrocities I see here are those committed by *you*. Do you think a man can subsist on moldy bread and watered-down rations *and not be hungry?!* Cut him down now and send him to sick bay until he is well enough to return to his duties. And after you've done so, I would like a word with you!"

"A word, sir?"

Brendan drew his admiral's orders from his pocket and said tightly, "I am taking over command of *Halcyon* until Sir Geoffrey's faith in your competency as a captain can be reestablished."

Crichton stood as if stunned. His upper lip quivered, his nostrils flared, and the trickle of sweat that ran from his temple seemed to freeze in place.

"I said, *cut him down*," Brendan snapped.

"But that man is guilty of numerous crimes, and by thunder, he'll get the punishment he deserves!"

"That man will be cut down *now* or so help me God, 'twill be a court of inquiry you find yourself facing, not just Sir Geoffrey's wrath! Now, *do* it!''

The seamen, the officers, and even the marines gaped, for never had they seen their former captain show anything but blithe good spirits. Even the wind, humming through tarred shrouds and luffing, salt-streaked canvas, held its breath. Crichton remained unmoving, blatantly defying the order; a moment passed. Two. Then Brendan shoved the dispatches back into his pocket and strode toward Dalby himself, his shoulders rigid with fury, his stride purposeful, his mouth tight and hard.

Crichton, they all knew, had just sealed his fate.

Hearing his approach, Dalby dragged his head up. "Oh, sir, I *knew* you'd come! You'd never have let anyone treat us like this! Crichton's a demon, sir, a demon! 'Twas just some biscuit I took, I didn't do anything bad, sir, honest, I didn't—"

"I know, Dalby. Rest easy."

"He barely feeds us enough for a rat to live on and then expects us to work like dogs! Just yesterday little Billy fell from the rigging and drowned because he was so weak from lack of food! Oh, there's good grog and plenty of fresh meat, but it all goes to Crichton and his officers! And all I took was a piece of moldy biscuit, sir, just one little piece. . . .''

"I know, Dalby. And we can't have you eating biscuit when everyone knows the salt beef's far better, now, can we?" he joked, for it was a well-known fact that the beef was far worse than the biscuit could ever be. "Faith, at least there are no worms in it!''

But Dalby didn't notice that Brendan's words came through tightened lips, nor that his grin didn't quite light his eyes. All he knew was that his captain had come to save him. All he heard was the musical lilt of his voice, its Connemaran cadences still wonderfully vibrant despite a British father and fifteen years in the Royal Navy. Dalby sobbed in relief, unwittingly setting the spark that inflamed the crew to mutiny.

"No worms, aye, but 'tis hard as bloody leather!" someone shouted.

"And tougher than nails!"

"Cut him down, Captain!"

"Aye, cut him down! Cut him down!" It became a chant, gathering force and momentum and thunder, rolling through the ranks like a comber in stormy seas. *"Cut him down!"*

"Sir, I will not tolerate this!" Crichton roared, above the din. "Do you hear me? *I will not tolerate this!*"

Brendan grinned and began cutting.

Crichton stepped forward, and all hell broke loose.

A seaman broke from the crowd with an unholy yell, his eyes maniacal, his knife raised as he charged toward Crichton. Someone screamed. Someone else cheered.

The reports would say that it had been an accident, and that the shot had been fired in self-defense, for with officers and marines trying frantically to regain control over the rioting crew, no one knew exactly what happened. But Dalby, turning his head, saw it all: a lieutenant knocking the knife-wielding seaman aside; men storming the quarterdeck; and Crichton, calmly drawing his pistol and taking careful aim—not at the seaman, not into empty space, but at Brendan, the man who'd come to save him, to save all of them—

Dalby screamed.

The explosion rent the air and stunned the decks into silence. And when the echoes died and Dalby opened his eyes, he saw that the flag captain was down, lying on his back and blinking up at the white sails and hazy sky, his mouth tight with pain, his rich chestnut curls bared to the sun. His tricorn lay upside down beside his shoulder. A dark rose bloomed on his chest, spreading over his snowy shirt and fine new coat. He coughed, once, twice, and a bubble of blood broke from his mouth and ran down his jaw. And then his eyes began to close. . . .

"Brendan!" A woman charged through the stunned crowd, her paint-smeared skirts and petticoats flying, her golden hair streaming behind her. "Brendan! Oh God, Brendan, *noooooo!*"

The young flag captain opened his eyes. Weakly, he turned his head, trying to muster a grin. And then Dalby saw those pain-glazed eyes widen in alarm, for Crichton had reloaded, was bringing the pistol up once again, and Eveleen was running directly into its path. . . .

Brendan staggered to his feet. *"Eveleen!"*

The bark of the pistol; the girl crying out and clutching her hand as she fell; her brother reeling forward. And Crichton, smiling now, as he narrowed those pale, red-rimmed eyes and raised a second pistol to finish a task left undone. . . .

The ball caught the flag captain in the chest, spinning him around and flinging him backward. Through the blur of tears, Dalby saw him flounder, saw the brief flash of sunlight against his epaulets and gold buttons. Then his legs hit the rail, and staggering, he tumbled over it, falling down, down into the sea below. . . .

Silence.

The wind sighed through the shrouds above. A mast creaked. On deck, the crew stood frozen in shock, horror, and fear.

And Crichton, in command once more and hopeful candidate for the now vacant position of flag captain, smiled, tucked his pistol in his belt, and met the gazes of his faithful lieutenants. Their expressions were carefully veiled, their drawn pistols holding the stunned and horrified crew at bay once more. His officers would not disappoint him. They'd allow no more reports to get to Sir Geoffrey. And what they'd seen today would go no further than the wardroom.

He'd make sure of it.

The girl lay in a crumpled heap, her shattered hand clutched to her breast, her frilly white petticoats sopping up the young flag captain's blood. Ignoring her sobs, Crichton picked up the whip and handed it to the boatswain's mate. Dalby was still lashed to the gratings, his face paler than death. Smiling, Crichton nodded to his officer.

"You may proceed," he said coldly.

The mate smiled back and the whip slashed down, again and again and again.

And this time, there was no one to come to little Dalby's aid.

No one at all.

Chapter 1

Newburyport, Massachusetts, 1778

Three years had elapsed since Captain Brendan Jay Merrick had fallen off the frigate *Halcyon* and, subsequently, out of the Royal Navy. The American colonies had made good use of those years; they'd declared their independence from Britain, they'd won many fine fighting men and sea officers—including Captain Merrick—to the American cause, and they'd been busy infecting themselves with healthy patriotic fever.

The town of Newburyport had no trouble taking up the fight for liberty, for its people had been independent even in the days *before* the struggle for independence. Situated at the mouth of the mighty Merrimack River some forty miles north of Boston, the town depended only on the sea for its survival. Salmon, herring, striped bass, and bluefish migrated up the river. The ocean provided cod, mackerel, and other fish, as well as oysters, lobsters, and scallops. Clams grew fat in the tidal flats of nearby Plum Island; ducks were plentiful. A few wooden fish flakes dotted the riverbanks to dry the great catches of cod, but Newburyport, unlike Gloucester and Marblehead to the south, had never relied on the fishing industry to support itself to the extent that they had. Commerce was its lifeblood.

Not so many years ago, it had been a common thing to see great oceangoing ships tied up at the wharves unloading cargoes from distant lands. Farmers had come from the inland towns of Haverhill, Amesbury, and Bradford to trade vegetables, corn, barreled pork, beef, and flour for staples—rum, coffee, sugar, and molasses—as well as extravagances: silk from the Orient, and grapes and oranges from Spain. The docks had bustled with activity, and the shops in Market Square had boasted linen, wool, and porcelain from England, wine from Madeira, broadcloth and satins, iron, paper and glass, nails and gloves and just about anything anyone could want that Newburyport didn't make or supply itself.

The farmers still came. The docks still bustled with activity. But the ships that were now tied up at those wharves were of a very different breed from the ponderous, wallowing vessels that had come before. This new breed was leaner. Battle-scarred. Sharp-toothed, toughened, and hungry—and as independent as the town that spawned them.

These vessels were the privateers.

And Newburyport couldn't turn them out fast enough to meet the demand.

For if commerce was the town's lifeblood, then shipbuilding was its livelihood.

Along the Merrimack's banks, new shipyards sprang up seemingly overnight, and existing ones grew in size. Each was as self-sufficient as Newburyport herself. Each had its own blacksmith shop, sawpit, mast pond, and mast houses. Each had its own sail loft, where bolts of heavy linen were destined to hold the wind as foresails, mainsails, topsails, and jibs. And each had access to the town's rope walk, where hemp fibers were combed out, spun into yarn, and formed into rope that would see service as rigging in those predatory vessels that called Newburyport their home.

Prosperous merchants and shipowners who'd gained their fortunes through commerce, rum manufacturing, and the blatant ignorance of England's Navigation Acts now invested in the privateering boon. On High Street, handsome three-story Georgian houses surrounded by elegant gardens and furnished with fine Chippendale and Hepplewhite furniture, reflected the affluence of those who were successful at it. In the spirit of liberty, the men abandoned their silks, velvets, and fancy powdered wigs for clothes of native wool and homespun; the ladies burned their English tea and brewed their own from ribwort and other plants instead.

Newburyport was as independent as ever. And its patriotism was reflected in every citizen, young and old, male and female; in its militia, in its naval men, and in its privateers. . . .

Enclosed by woods and a haphazard fence, Miss Mira Ashton's School of Fine Horsemanship was nothing more than a field that smelled of clover and wet grasses and the fresh pungency of newly churned mud. Birds twittered in the nearby trees; it had rained the night before, and now moisture dripped from the many oaks, maples, and pines, pitter-pattering down through branches and shimmering leaves that quivered beneath the extra weight. Drip, drip, pitter, patter, on and on until the entire woods surrounding the field were alive with the soft sounds of falling rain. Yet the sky above the treetops was cloudless and pale, and sunlight stabbed through the branches, glowing pink and gold through the mists and sending vivid rainbow colors twinkling off the bent grasses like stardust on a fairy's crown.

It promised to be another scorcher of a day.

Sounds broke the tranquillity of the new morning: the steady thud of a horse's trot; the snap of a whip licking the air; the snort of a dappled colt whose chiseled head and short back spoke of desert blood and whose color was so pure a gray as to appear almost blue; and from the slight figure in the middle of the field, around whom that colt trotted in a doughnut of deepening mud, an exuberant voice raised in song:

"Fath'r and I went down to camp, along with Captain Good-ing! And there we saw the men and boys, as thick as hasty pud-ding!"

A quarter mile away, Ephraim Ashton, shipbuilder, sat down to breakfast and the *Essex Gazette,* a pot of strong black coffee at his right elbow, a basket of hot buttered corn muffins at his left, and a jug of New England rum before him, blissfully unaware that his dainty daughter stood heel-deep in mud with her head thrown back, her chest puffed up, and her dulcet voice belting out a song with all the lusty fervor she might've lent her favorite fo'c'sle chanty:

"Yankee Doodle keep it up! Yankee Doodle, dan-dy"

Rigel flicked an ear but knew better than to slow his stride.

"Mind the music and the step, and with the girls be han-dy!"

But then, there were a lot of things Father was unaware of; he didn't know about Rescue Effort Number Thirty-One, he didn't know that she was going to ride Rigel for the first time tomorrow, and he didn't know that she had a bet going with her brother, Matt, that she could sneak aboard Matt's privateer, *Proud Mistress*, at least two more times before Father caught her at it—again—and flew off into one of his rages. No, Father would be reaching for one of those muffins just about—Mira squinted up to look at the sun's angle—*now*, dipping it in maple syrup, and shoving the whole sticky mess into his mouth as he thumbed to the newspaper's Marine News section, where he would scrutinize each and every word until he found mention of an Ashton ship. He might get a smudge of syrup on the top right corner of the page—but not on the Marine News section. Heaven forbid. And it would take him exactly one third of the hour he allotted to the paper to study that section, snowy brows curling out over his beak-nose like fishhooks and throwing shadows across the page, his eyes searching for mention of an Ashton-built ship, and his fist slapping the table with a good hard wallop when he found what he was looking for. And then he would hoot and holler, and heaven help the neighbors if they were still abed, for they'd be asleep no longer.

"And there we see a thousand men, as rich as Squire Da-vid, and what they wasted ev'ry day, I wish it could be sa-ved! Yankee Doodle, keep it up, Yankee Doodle Dan-dy . . ." She sucked in a great gulp of air and shouted to the treetops, *"Mind the music and the step, and with the girls be han-dy!"*

Hers—like her father's, her brother Matt's, and New-buryport's itself—was red-hot rebel's blood. Yet Mira's patriotism didn't end with a mere song, nor the limitations of her sex, though she'd shunned English tea, donned native homespun, and worn her dark hair in thirteen braids, one to represent each colony, as the other women had. As she was a sea captain's daughter who'd come into the world some one hundred forty leagues east of Newfoundland in the middle of a raging gale, with a pitching, yawing ship her cradle and a piece of sailcloth her first blanket, the role she took in the defense of liberty was a bit more . . . active. But it was damned hard to man a cannon—and win a wager—if Matt kept sneaking off on *Proud Mistress* without her, which was the only reason she was standing here in the muddy field this morning and not beside him on the brig's stout decks!

"And there we see a whopping gun, as big as a log of ma-ple, mounted on a little cart, a load for father's cattle! Yankee Doodle, keep it up . . ."

She bawled out the rest of the verse, then hummed the next one through her nose, pacing the song to Rigel's hoofbeats and plotting, as she'd been doing all morning, the best way to sneak the latest cat—Rescue Effort Number Thirty-One until further named—into the house without Father's knowledge.

She could hide him in the stable and wait till Father left for his shipyards, which he would do at precisely one o'clock. She could smuggle him in through the back door. Or she could simply put him in the front hall and hope he mingled well enough with the other Rescue Efforts that Father wouldn't notice him.

But whatever she did, she'd have to be careful, because Father was in one of his Moods this morning, and with good cause.

The client—not just another client, but *the* client, whose drafts for a fine new schooner would've pulled the Ashton Shipyards out of their slump and made Ephraim's name famous—had never shown up last night.

So much for all their efforts to make a favorable impression on this naval architect whom only Matt had met, and then, several months ago off Portsmouth. But these drafts of his had so impressed her brother that Ephraim, stopping to listen to him for once, had finally posted a letter to this Captain Merrick fellow and invited him to Newburyport in the hopes of snaring his business. And the preparations they'd gone through to make sure they got it! Abigail cooking up a supper that could've fed the entire town. The servants beating the rugs, rubbing the table with beeswax, polishing the silver till it shone. Mira had even donned a gown and put her hair up under a little laced mobcap, managing to look demure and ladylike enough to please even Father, who'd been just coming up from the cellar with several bottles of his finest Madeira when he'd spotted her uncharacteristic appearance and almost dropped them on his toe.

But it had all been for naught. Just like Matt's dire warnings to mind her behavior, now dancing through her head like singsong verses from a nursery rhyme, shaping themselves to the tune of "Yankee Doodle" and filling the morning with sound:

"Don't race El Nath down High Street, the client mi-ight see you! Stay at home and mind yourself, and please try to be go-od!" Laughing out loud, she threw her head back, let the sun splash across her face, and belted out, *"Mira Ashton, you're a brat! Mira, you're naught but trou-ble! All boldness and all brazenness, and don't feed Luff beneath the table!"*

Hmm. That last phrase didn't quite fit within the confines of the tune; she'd have to work on it a bit, then bawl it out on the fo'c'sle the next time Matt took *Proud Mistress* to sea. Nice and loud, loud enough to send the company into a fit of guffaws and Matt into teeth-gritting anger. She could already envision him going as red as his hair, his spectacles steaming up, his lips thinning out the way they always did when he was particularly annoyed about something. . . .

Her laughter, fresh as the sea wind that drove across the marshlands and dunes of nearby Plum Island, soared up to the hazy blue sky above, for the rest of his silly warnings didn't have a prayer of fitting within the confines of "Yankee Doodle":

No climbing Mistress*'s masts just to prove you can do it faster than anyone else!*

Watch your language, and don't show up at the supper table wearing those trousers and smelling like horses!

And for God's sake, please *find a place to hide that cat you snuck home off the docks! When Father finds out, he's going to have a damned fit!*

"A fit, Rigel!" she cried. "Think I ought to be *scared?!*" The colt flicked his smoke-colored tail, arched his neck, and shook his head as though he found the thought amusing, too. But Ephraim's dark warning, delivered in the tone of a judge at a murderer's trial, stuck in Mira's mind despite her best efforts to laugh it off, and she shivered, feeling as if a cloud had just stamped out the sun.

"One more time, Mira!" her father had roared after Rescue Effort Number Twenty-Nine had leapt onto the last prospective client's leg, spilling the gravy boat's contents into his lap and sending him fleeing the Ashton house as though the hounds of hell were at his coattails. "You make me lose one more client and by God, I'm gonna have to take drastic measures about these confounded, god-damned, pain-in-the-ass animals, *do I make myself clear!*"

She'd bowed her head, more to hide her smile than to paint a picture of demure obedience, although in that, she'd been convincingly successful. "Aye, Father," she'd replied, having no intention of obeying him then, and certainly none of doing so now. Besides, it wasn't as though she *kept* all of the Rescue Efforts. . . . She *did* place them in good homes after getting them back on their feet! So what if the number was up to thirty? It was a cumulative count, anyhow; there were actually only *nine* cats presently living at, in, and around the Ephraim Ashton household.

Well, ten. She'd forgotten Rescue Effort Number Thirty-One, a scruffy ball of orange fur watching her from atop a fence post and wondering, no doubt, just *how* she intended to get him into the house and past Ephraim without all hell breaking loose. She'd planned it for yesterday; having this esteemed Captain Merrick around would certainly have diverted Father's attention long enough for her to get the cat in and placed safely among the others roaming the house. And just to make sure that nothing, absolutely *nothing*, happened to scare *this* client off, she'd even gone so far as to lock every cat she owned in her bedroom with a chair snugged up against the door, just in case.

But it had all been for naught.

For the gallant captain of the American privateer *Annabel*, who'd outfoxed a British frigate last night, had been swept overboard during the ensuing sea fight and was, by all reliable accounts, presumed dead.

No wonder Father was in one of his Moods this morn. That privateer captain had been the esteemed guest they'd all been waiting for.

She sighed and squinted up at the sun, just beginning to burn through the haze. Right about now Father'd be reaching for his third muffin and hollering for his second pot of coffee, laced with a generous dose of rum to "wake him up." And any time now, she predicted, with that strange intuition that binds sibling to sibling, Matt would come home with another brave deed under his belt to make the ladies sigh, the young boys idolize him, and the other privateers go green with envy. His name would make the *Essex Gazette*, of course; Ephraim would have something more to brag about when he met with his cronies down at Davenport's Wolfe Tavern on Saturday night; and perhaps he'd cool off about the loss of the client whose business he'd been so eager to land, a client whose loss had not been because of *her* this time. . . .

Just then she heard the distant, dull thump of a cannon down in the harbor as a ship was welcomed in from the ocean and into the Merrimack River. The report was followed by a steady succession of twelve more, totaling thirteen in all, one for each colony. It was a jubilant salute, repeated by every vessel in the harbor and the great field battery guarding Newburyport at the tip of Plum Island. Finally the reverberations faded, leaving only the distant screams of gulls and wild cheering from the wharves and shipyards lining the riverfront in its wake.

Matt was back, all right.

She pictured him standing tall and proud on *Mistress*'s quarterdeck as the brig glided past the smoking field battery and up the river, his spectacles hazed with dried spray, his coattails flapping in the wind, his red hair whipping about his freckled face as he considered which woman to choose from among the throng who would be waiting to pounce on him at the wharf. It would probably take about an hour for him to drop anchor, make that decision, claw through that throng, and find his way up High Street and back to the house in time for breakfast.

Mira would be waiting for him, of course—but the greeting she planned for him would not be as sweet as the one he'd get down on the wharf!

A mosquito bit through her trousers (which had been Matt's before she'd raided them from *Mistress*'s cabin) and she reached down, slapped her leg, swore in a way that would've made Father proud had she been his son and not his daughter, and wiped the sweat from her brow with the back of her sleeve, when she heard the commotion coming from the house. Was Matt home? *Already?*

Mira could hear Luff's insane barking, mingling with the frightened whinny of a horse. Above it all came the sound of male voices raised in greeting, or, as one of them was Father's, more likely battle.

Already.

By the time Mira had cooled Rigel down and led him back to the stable, the argument was loud enough to be heard clear across the street, across the town, and across the river in Salisbury. Standing outside in the house's palisaded doorway, she traced its progress as it moved, at what sounded like dizzying speed, from the upstairs, the hall, the parlor, the dining room; Matt shouting at the top of his lungs; Father bellowing ferociously; Matt again, his voice suddenly muffled as he no doubt shoved one of Abigail's muffins down his craw. Counting the seconds, Mira waited for the hollering to fade toward the back of the house before tearing the front door open. With Number Thirty-One tucked in the crook of her arm, she kicked off her muddy boots and, on bare fairy-feet, darted across the thick carpet.

"I'm telling you, Father, he's *not* a Brit! How many blasted times do I have to repeat myself?! He's not a Brit! *Not a Brit!*" Something crashed violently against a wall.

"For Christ's sake, he was wearing an *American* privateer's coat!''

The argument was approaching the parlor now, fading behind wainscoted walls painted in strong shades of blue-gray, rounding entranceways, and bouncing off high ceilings as Mira listened with amused curiosity.

"That don't make him American!" Ephraim bawled.

"What about the missing client, huh? What about the *drafts*?!''

"*What* drafts?! I ain't seen no bloody drafts!''

"That's because they were destroyed by seawater, damn you!''

Father's gale-force roar made the walls shake. "Don't gimme any of yer lip, Matt! I know a damned Englishman when I see one! Ye come to me with some cockamamie story about Merrick surviving a sea fight with a British frigate, and then a night alone on the open ocean?! Whaddye take me fer, a damned idiot?! That rascal upstairs ain't my client! Why, I'll bet ye my eyeteeth he's a British deserter off that same bleedin' frigate! *Christ!* Now, get him outta here, damn you! Cart him down to Davenport's tavern, let them take care of him! I want no part of him, ye hear?!''

"Damn you, he's *our* responsibility, *our* client!''

"*My* client died a gallant death aboard that sloop!''

"Your client'll die upstairs unless you show him some proper American compassion!''

"He ain't my client, and I ain't showin' nothing to no goddamned Brit!''

"Damn you, get it through your thick skull he's *not—a—Brit!*''

Mira ducked behind the staircase, flattening herself against the fine paneling of Santo Domingo mahogany and thanking God for the camouflage of the dark wood. She held her breath as the two stormed into view, Matt with so much steam on his spectacles, she wondered how he could see. Behind them the housekeeper, Abigail, trailed like bubbles in a warship's wake, flour breezing from her skirts, and the scent of spices and kitchen smells chasing her madly. "Christian charity, Ephraim!" she pleaded. "What if Matthew's right and he *is* the captain of the

American ship *Annabel?* And if not, what difference does it make? So what if he's British? You can't just abandon the poor fellow like so much garbage!''

''All Brits are garbage!''

''Dammit, Father!'' Something else crashed against a wall.

''Ephraim, *please* listen to your son—''

''Abigail, you stay outta this! And, Matt, you throw one more thing and I'm gonna take a stick to yer hide! Don't think I'm too old to do it! I'm still yer father, and what I say goes! Now, git that bloke outta here by the time I count to ten or you can damn well fergit ever making another cruise in that brig again, is that clear?!''

''You can't threaten me, damn you!''

''I'll threaten all I like!''

''Over my dead body!''

Something else shattered.

They were storming into the dining room now, Father's silver-buckled shoes just disappearing behind the doorway. Thanking God for the argument, for it was the perfect chance to get Number Thirty-One safely inside, Mira darted out from behind the staircase.

Matt turned—and saw her.

She leapt for the stairs.

''Mira! You stay out of the east bedroom, you hear me?! *Mira!''*

He couldn't have issued a better invitation. Taking the stairs three at a time, she careened around the landing, leapt the rest of the steps in two bounds, charged down the hall, and bolted for the closed, paneled door. Downstairs she heard Matt sliding to a stop, his pursuit halted as Ephraim lit into him once more.

Her hand hit the latch. Without a second thought, she burst into the room.

Chapter 2

B ehind her, the door swung shut with a click she never heard.

A man lay in the big four-poster tester bed, a handsome, nearly naked man, with damp knee breeches pasted to his well-muscled thighs, long legs sprinkled with auburn hair, and bare feet that stuck out over the footrail by a good ten inches. There was sensitivity in the shape of his face, elegance in the slant of his brows, artistry in the way his cheekbones stood above the faint hollows beneath them. It was a handsome face, even in sleep; the jaw firm, the lips sensual, the mouth and eyes framed by laugh lines that appeared to get much use. His hair, dark against the white pillowcase, tumbled rakishly over an intelligent brow and was the color of September chestnuts, rich and glossy and curling at the ends where it had begun to dry. He was by far the best-looking specimen of his gender Mira had ever seen, and she was seized by an unexplainable urge to lay her finger against his parted lips, to touch his rough, shadowed jaw, to trace the sunburst of white scar tissue between the cleft of his chest muscles, just to see if he was real. She swallowed tightly, wondering why she suddenly felt all hot on the inside, all shivery on the outside; and as her gaze traveled down his throat, his hard-muscled shoulders, his long arms, and sinewy chest where a T of auburn hair gathered and led down a rock-ribbed torso before disappearing into those damp breeches, she flushed hot beneath her mud-stained shirt with the jolting knowledge of just *who* he was. It wasn't the damp blue breeches that gave him away. It wasn't the dried sea salt that glazed his elegant brows, nor even the fact that his hair was still

20

wet. It was his hands; the hands of a musician, an artist
. . . a naval architect.

The client.

Good God. She stepped closer, staring. Beneath swollen lids rimmed with long, pale lashes, his eyes were moving slowly, as thought he was caught in the throes of a dream. She saw his fingers twitch, heard his soft intake of breath, watched his head move on the pillow and his handsome mouth fall open.

But Brendan never knew she was there. For him, time had rolled back to the night before, and he was once again commanding *Annabel*'s desperate flight from the sea, the rebel town of Newburyport approaching off their bows, HMS *Dismal* in hot pursuit, and the schooner's drafts spread out over his knee and fluttering in the breeze.

"Brendan!"

Liam's voice, desperate and wild.

"Bren-*daaaaan!*"

Faith, where was their confidence in him?

Sure enough there was Liam, all strapping two hundred pounds of him, shoving his telescope into a seaman's hand and hurtling toward him at breakneck speed. Blue eyes bulging, he slid into the deckhouse where Brendan was sitting, nearly tripping over a ringbolt as he grabbed desperately for his arm.

Brendan didn't bother to look up. "Honestly, Liam, as an officer, you really *should* try to set a wee bit better example for the people. Racing across the deck like that—"

"God Almighty, Cap'n, it's *Crichton* commandin' that frigate!" Liam had his arm now, nearly ripping it from its socket; the drafts jumped in the wind, and Brendan grabbed them just in time. "D'ye hear me, Brendan?! *Crichton!*"

Behind them, the British frigate drew closer, determined to prevent them from reaching the Merrimack River and the safety of Newburyport. Water thundered and creamed from her bows. Drums rolled ominously upon the wind. Pipes shrilled. Gunports were yawning open. . . .

While forward in *Annabel*'s bows, Dalby O'Hara

crouched miserably, a gnarled hand clamped over his belly, and his face the color of oatmeal as he remembered his own treatment at the hands of that frigate's captain, three years ago.

At his elbow, Fergus McDermott, an atheist who'd adopted religion as of thirty seconds ago, recited the Twenty-third Psalm over and over in a mindless chant.

Brendan held up the schooner's drafts so that Liam could see them better. "Y'know, Liam, I've been thinking. . . . Maybe I ought to give the bowsprit a wee bit more steeve. Other than that, I think she's going to be perfect. Sharp in the topsides around the bow, lean in the stern, and lots of rake in both. Not only will our new privateer be as swift as the wind, she'll sit so low in the water that her profile will be all but invisible from a distance! And with this hull shape, she'll be *perfect* for windward sailing, since it'll reduce windage in proportion to hull size, and therefore enable us to carry a greater press of sail than the more traditional short, high-sided ship would allow. That means, of course, that we can also fly topsails and topgallants if we've a mind to—"

"Brendan—"

"Too little beam and she'd be fast but unstable. Too much and she'd be a laggard. Too fine at bow and stern and we'd sacrifice weight-carrying ability fore and aft. That means *guns,* Liam! And in a privateer, that won't do, now, will it?" Beyond *Annabel*'s desperate bowsprit the sunset smeared the sky in brilliant tones of red and purple, reflecting against the water as it changed from sea-chop to rippling cat's paws of current. Any moment now, Newburyport would be coming into view. "Ah, Liam, if we had this schooner right now, we'd leave that beast back there lumbering in her own bow-wake. If we had the schooner—"

"Dammit, Brendan, we're not goin' t' 'ave no schooner if ye don't *put down those bloody drafts and listen t' me!* It's *Crichton!*"

Brendan glanced up, his rich chestnut hair blowing about his face, his eyes alight with mirth, and his mouth set in that same quirky grin that was as reckless now as it had been when he and Liam had spent their childhoods exploring the rocky shores of Connacht. It was a grin that was sure to drive poor Liam mad. "So anyhow, I've decided that if I have this Ashton fellow build her exactly to my specifications, just a bit shy of ninety feet on deck, twenty-three feet and eight inches on her beam—"

Dead astern, the frigate's sails shook and boomed as she leaned over onto a new tack, the guns that stabbed from her forecastle glinting blood red in the setting sun.

"—and with a depth of nine feet ten inches in the hold— Faith, Liam, will you *please* let go of my sleeve?!"

"But it's *CRICHTON!*"

"I *know* it's Crichton, and I imagine I've known so for a sight longer than you have, given the fact you were boozing it up belowdecks for the better part of the afternoon. I also know there's a squadron behind him and Sir Geoffrey Lloyd's flag on the seventy-four. Three years ago that was *my* ship, remember? And Sir Geoffrey *my* admiral? Ah, there's an august old gent if ever there was one. . . . Used to take tea with him, in fact!" He grinned, as though the memories brought him no pain, and glanced around Liam's brawny shoulder. "A point more a'larboard, Mr. Keefe! Aim her right toward that big tree sticking up above the others!" Dropping his gaze to the drafts once more, he added conversationally, "They call that the Beacon Oak, Liam, because it's a landmark to guide mariners in from the sea. In his letter, Ashton said to watch for it—"

"If ye don't get yer head out o' th' clouds an' stop thinkin' o' that bloody schooner, none o' us'll live long enough t' see her built, let alone sail her!"

"Now, Liam." Brendan elevated his brow and gave his friend a patient look. "My head is *not* in the clouds, but set properly atop my shoulders, just where it should be and just where I intend it to remain. Faith and troth, I *do* wish you would all stop pestering me so."

"But yer leadin' him straight int' th' river!"

"Precisely." He grinned, his russet eyes dancing with raillery, his jaw dimpling, and his expression one of false innocence. "Now, stop worrying, would you? Do you see *me* worrying? Faith! Newburyport's a rebel town, Liam; they simply *despise* the British! Not only did they stage their own tea party four years ago, they've even sunk a pier and some old hulks across the mouth of this river just to keep them out! Hidden, of course, but combined with the currents and shifting sandbars just beneath this placid-looking surface, I do believe one of them will stop Crichton.''

''One o' them'll stop *us!* Ye haven't th' foggiest idea where yer goin'! Ye've never been up this damned river in yer life!''

''First time for everything, eh?'' Grinning, Brendan returned his attention to the drafts.

The frigate was so close now, they were almost riding her bow-wake. Carriages squealed as her mighty guns were rolled into position. Musket fire cracked from her tops, and a ball whizzed past Liam's ear, parting a stay. Another holed the speaking trumpet beside Brendan's hip and flung it to the deck. Forward, *Annabel*'s men began to shout, to yell, and some of them, to sob, while Fergus's chanting rose to a desperate pitch: ''The Lord is my shepherd, I shall not want. . . .''

Shots pinged against a nearby cannon, tore another chunk from the deckhouse, drove into the mast.

''He maketh me to lie down in green pastures; he leadeth me beside the still waters—''

Another shot ripped the tricorn from Brendan's head.

''Yea, though I walk through the valley of the shadow of death, I will fear no evil—''

Brendan spared a glance up, his expression puzzled. ''How odd, all this time and I never knew Fergus to be a religious man. . . . Oh, Liam, would you fetch my hat, please? I seem to have lost it! Faith, what would Ashton think if I showed up for dinner half-dressed?!''

''—*for thou art with me; thy rod and thy staff they comfort me!*''

''I *do* hope I can find this place, Liam. Ashton says I'm supposed to look for a big, handsome Georgian house when I get into town, white with green shutters and an anchor out front. Newburyport's a sea town, Liam. I'll bet *everyone* has white Georgian houses with green shutters and anchors out front. Think I'll have any trouble finding it?''

Pop. Crack. More musket fire. Pieces of wood exploded

from the boom above their heads. Liam buried his face in his huge hands.

"And do you think Ashton'll have the table all set?"

Liam's head jerked up. *"What?!"*

Brendan folded the drafts with precise care, slipped them into his pocket, and grinned. "Why, I could just kill for a nice, savory neck of mutton, a wedge of fine cheese, hot boiled potatoes, and some of that Indian pudding, drenched in that maple syrup these laddies hereabouts are so fond of. . . ."

"Dammit, Brendan, how can ye even think o' supper at a time like this!"

"And why not? 'Tis seven o'clock, precisely the time I *should* be thinking about supper, as it is when I usually dine. Oh, Mr. Keefe! You might let her fall off another point; we don't want that broadside staring us in the face. . . . Liam? Liam, are you *listening* to me?"

"Jesus, Brendan, *Jesus*—"

"Well, please do, because if I should fall today—which I've no intention of doing, of course—you *will* remember your promise to get these drafts to Ashton, won't you? Have him build the schooner and use her as the privateer I've designed her to be. And as for the steeve in the bowsprit, I've decided that more *is* better, after all. . . ."

But Liam wasn't listening; he was staring, transfixed, at *Dismal,* his mouth opening and shutting like a gasping fish as he caught sight of the haughty, triumphant figure on her quarterdeck. "B-Brendan," he choked out.

"And if Crichton should take us—again, I vow he shall not—then, and only then, rip the drafts up. Toss the pieces over the side. Destroy them, burn them, *swallow* them if you have to, but do not, I repeat, *do not* allow them to fall into British hands. If the Admiralty manages to get a hold of them, 'twill be a terrible mess. . . . Why, Dalby!" Brendan glanced up to find the terrified little sailmaker standing before him, his Adam's apple bouncing up and down amid the cords of his birdlike neck. " 'Tis kind of you to join us, but I really *would* like a good eye up in the bows—"

"Those sunken piers are beneath us, sir, I just *know* it! And I can't see a thing with all this glare on the water!"

We're going to hit one of them, and it'll be my fault! *All my fault!*''

"Calm yourself, Dalby. I have things well under control.''

"But, Captain, I'm going to be sick, *sick—*''

"Please don't get sick now, Dalby; wait till we reach port.''

"But, Capt—''

"Liam!'' Brendan grasped his lieutenant's arm, jerking him from his terrified reverie. Newburyport was approaching fast; Brendan could hear the church bells ringing now, guns firing, dogs barking as the alarm was raised. "Please take Dalby forward and watch for those piers, would you?''

"Aye, Cap'n!'' he shouted. " 'Bout *time* ye got serious!''

Liam was already hauling Dalby forward at a dead run, his shirttails billowing behind him, his spice-colored curls blowing madly. Brendan grinned, and in his best quarterdeck voice, called, "And glazed almonds and minced pie, and pear tarts smothered in sweet, fresh cream . . .''

He heard Dalby's wheedling voice: "Liam? Liam, why's the captain talking about food at a time like this?''

But Liam only ran faster, hauling Dalby over debris and deck furnishings alike.

"Haven't had fresh cream in *ages!* Faith, must be at least three, four years now! How 'bout you, Liam? Getting sick of pork souse and hardtack?''

Over his shoulder Liam shouted, "If I ever get t' see pork souse an' hardtack again, I swear, I'll get down on me knees an' kiss yer goddamned feet!''

Brendan, grinning, glanced up at *Dismal*'s bloated spritsail. ". . . And custards and jellies, apple cider, cold glasses of milk—run out the starboard guns now, would you, Mr. Saunders?—sauces and gravies and piping hot bread, fresh from the oven and just *oozing* butter . . .''

"And your bloody toes, too!'' Liam bawled.

Brendan laughed. "Double-shotted, Mr. Saunders!''

"In the *bread*, sir?''

"For heaven's sake, Mr. Saunders, in the *guns*. What in God's name d'you *think* I'm talking about, eh?''

"Aye, sir! Right away!''

"And lively, Mr. Saunders!"

They were well into the river now, the current slamming against their bows and trying desperately to drive them back toward the sea. Abeam, marshlands and riverbanks thick with yellow grasses shot past at dizzying speed. To larboard, Newburyport swept into view; fine homes of brick and white-painted wood looked out over the riverfront, their windows glinting with orange sunset. Thick meadows were dotted with cattle and sheep. Wharves stretched into the harbor, and a church thrust a spire, painted purple with sunset, toward the sky.

Dismal, just beginning to overtake them, maneuvered her mighty broadside into position.

"Stuffed mutton and Indian pudding . . ." Retrieving his speaking trumpet, Brendan dusted it off with his elbow, heedless of the fresh musket hole that stood out like an eyeless socket in the metal. "Though I *could* pass on the green beans, if Ashton's serving them!"

He peered over the side, staring down into the black, swirling depths, not thinking at all about the supper he was determined not to miss, but about those sunken piers that Dalby and Liam would probably never see, the sunken piers that were probably approaching just . . . about . . . *now*—

"Hard a'lee, Mr. Keefe!"

The helmsman shoved the tiller over so violently that men lost their footing, shot spilled across the deck, and the topsail yard stabbed down like a harpoon. Striated bars of sand swept beneath them, broken here and there by the fuzzy, ominous hulk of the sunken pier just beneath the river's surface. As one, the crew held their breaths, cringing. But their captain knew what he was about. A sigh, a whisper, and they were safely through the channel. Another sigh and they looked up to see brigs and sloops, schooners and cutters, some anchored, some docked, and some flying toward them at desperate speed—

Brendan leapt onto the deckhouse, waving his speaking trumpet and jumping up and down in wild excitement. "Steady, Mr. Keefe, steady, steady, *steady!*"

Crichton wasn't as clever. With an agonized shriek of grinding timbers, *Dismal* struck the sunken pier, her broadside flashing out simultaneously and lighting up her entire side in fiery tongues of orange against black. Thunder split the air with an unholy, deafening roar. Iron slammed against *Annabel*'s sides and whined overhead. There was an awesome crack, like a lightning bolt hitting too close, and the mast teetered wildly. Men screamed, stays and shrouds split with a noise like gunfire, and the deckhouse fell out from beneath Brendan's feet.

Air whooshed past his neck. A cannon belted him across the shoulders, red sky flashed beneath his shoes, a piece of railing shot by his face. He hit the deck on his back, careened across it on his coattails, and slammed into the truck of a gun so hard that his sword split in two. He lay there for a moment, stunned, the fact that he was too dazed to even wonder if he was dead assuring him that he was not. Smoke caked upon his tongue, burned his throat, seared his lungs—and through it he saw the ghost gray shapes of Crichton's guns, running out once more.

He lurched to his knees, raised his half-sword, and choked out, *"Fire!"*

And then the deck itself seemed to open up and fall away. Grabbing frantically for a line, he was aware of someone yelling his name, and then nothing but weightlessness, space, and the dizzying rush of air against his face, his arms, his legs, before he hit the sea with a stunning slap. . . .

Not again.

He clawed toward the surface, grabbing a piece of flotsam and fighting to stay afloat as the river's mighty current swept him past the smoke-wreathed frigate, the point of Plum Island, and into the cold, open Atlantic. Powerless, he watched the thick black cloud that hung over the two ships diminish in size as the outgoing tide took him further from his ship, saw a few stabs of orange as fire was exchanged. And then there was nothing but vast, empty space beneath his feet and a sea bottom that lay a hundred feet down, maybe more. And still the current, drawing him farther and farther out.

Sunset came and went. Gloom snuffed out the smudge of land that was Plum Island, distant now and growing more so, until even the lights that marked it sank below the horizon. The flotsam was cold and slimy beneath his cheek, the constant slap of the waves filling his nose and mouth and sinuses with every rise and fall of the sea beneath him. Up and down . . . up and down . . . The stars came out and glimmered on the waves. The moon rose to stand guard over him, sheeting the ocean in silver and picking him out as a speck of life in a vast and starlit emptiness. He locked his arms around his float, laid his cheek atop the wet wood, and despite the biting chill of the ocean, fell asleep.

His Irish luck held. Dawn found him still alive, paralyzed with cold and barely able to open his swollen eyes when the first rays of sunlight poked over the horizon and nudged him out of his stupor. His waking thoughts were of neck of mutton, and Indian pudding dripping with sweet maple syrup. . . . Groaning, he dug at his burning eyes with a white and wrinkled fist. Sunlight lanced his pupils and sent a shaft of pain straight into the back of his skull. Spitting out seawater and squinting against the glare, he managed to focus on that blinding ribbon of sea that marked the eastern horizon.

He blinked, squinted, blinked again. For there, etched as dark triangles against the white glare, were the sails of a fine and lovely ship, a ship that saluted the morning and heralded its arrival upon her proud pennants and the highest reaches of her sun-gilded masts. A curl of pink light sparkled at her bows, along her sides. Her canvas and shrouds sang in the wind. She was glorious. She was beautiful.

And she was coming for him.

He wondered if he was dead and this was his just reward, for there was no feeling left in his limbs, no reasoning left in his brain. Just . . . existence. Fogginess. Thick and swirling haze, pierced here and there by sounds; the protests of spars and canvas as the brig hove to, the keen of water dying beneath her bows. Frantic shouts above him, splashes nearby, the thunk of oars against a hollow hull. Gentle hands worked around and beneath him. Rope, swathed in sailcloth to lessen its bite, was passed beneath his arms and chest, tightening until the pressure between his shoulders and against his ribs became blinding pain. Water sucked at his legs in a last desperate attempt to hold him as he was hauled free of it, and through the slits that were his eyes, he saw the sea, slowly revolving beneath him, sparkling, blinding, as he was hoisted higher and higher.

A rail brushed against his knees. Hands supported and guided him as his feet touched upon a solid deck, his legs crumpled beneath him, and he was eased down to warm, dry planking that smelled pleasantly of sunlight and vinegar beneath his cheek. Dimly he was aware of someone tugging at his stock, loosening it and tearing it free.

"Easy, now, careful with him. The poor fellow's been through enough. Joey, fetch the surgeon, would ye? And Jake, stop gawking and go get me a bucket of fresh water from below. Blankets, too, while you're at it, lots of 'em. Hurry, now!"

Brendan coughed, and tried to sit up.

"Easy, there, fellow," came that Yankee drawl again. Firm hands pressed against his chest, pinning him against the sickeningly solid deck. Brendan saw a pair of boots three inches from his face, smelled their worn leather, and felt shadows cooling his cheeks as someone leaned over him. "Mr. Malvern's on his way to see you now. Some hot gruel and a few warm blankets and you'll be on your feet in no time, guaranteed."

He tried to open his eyes, for there was something familiar about that voice . . . something very familiar.

Something connected to the drafts.

It hit him with choking horror. *The drafts.* He'd never given them to Liam! They were still in his pocket, and he'd just spent the night in the open Atlantic—

He clawed upward into the blinding brightness. His fingers brushed a hat, knocked it awry. A rough cheek, someone's nose, a light object of wire and glass. *"The drafts!"*

He eyelids parted like ripping cloth. Through a wall of pain he saw a reedy man in a slapdash, half-buttoned coat bending over him and blocking the sunlight, the sea of faces peering down at him, the proud pyramid of sails rising high above his head. Hair so red, it hurt his eyes to look at it. Dense patches of freckles sprinkled like cinnamon over a narrow nose down which a pair of spectacles was slowly sliding. The man raised his head, presenting the underside of his red-stubbled jaw, but Brendan had seen enough to know who he was.

"Ashton!" he gasped, lapsing into a fit of choking.

"That water, Jake, give it here!" the man yelled. Moisture trickled between Brendan's teeth and across his swollen tongue, dragging pain down his throat and into his writhing stomach. The world tilted and swam as he rolled his head and stared up past that hanging stock, the shadowed chin, the spectacles beneath the wild red hair.

"Ashton . . ." he rasped, trying again. "The shipbuilder . . ."

"My father," the man said simply, reaching impatiently for the wooden pail. "Goddammit, more water, Jake!"

The water was coming too fast for him to swallow, most of it splashing down his chin, and the rest of it making him cough and gag. Choking, Brendan twisted away, groping blindly for Ashton's hand. He sucked in a lungful of air, willed himself not to be sick, and gasped, "And you're Matthew, his son!"

Instantly the water stopped coming.

"Nice . . . to meet you again, sir. I trust—" Brendan's swollen lips cracked in a grin "—you have the table all set?"

Ashton gaped at him. *"What?"*

"He's out of his head," a seaman muttered.

"And British, just as we thought," another said darkly. "His Majesty's finest. Told ye he was off that frigate!"

"British? Sounds Irish t' me!"

"Idiot, he's as British as tea 'n' crumpets!"

"Irish, damn ye! And as full of blarney as a four-leaf clover!"

" 'Bout as lucky, too!"

But Ashton was peering speculatively at him, the pity and compassion in his kind brown eyes magnified by the thick lenses of his spectacles. Didn't he recognize him?! Didn't he remember their meeting off Portsmouth?! *Faith!* But no, the Yankee was already standing up, thoughtfully biting his lip and pushing his spectacles up his nose with one freckled finger. "I, uh, think we'd better take you below, good fellow. My surgeon is most competent, and perhaps some rest would do you good. You've obviously been through quite an ordeal.''

''No, please, you must understand! I am not . . . unhinged.'' Brendan shut his eyes, too sick, too weak, to protest further. ''I know fully well what I'm about . . . but I see that my delay in introducing myself has . . . led to some confusion about my identity . . .'' He opened his eyes and stared desperately up into the Yankee's freckled face. ''You are Matthew Ashton, American privateer. Your father is Ephraim Ashton, shipbuilder—'' he took a deep breath and tried to grin ''—and I am Captain Brendan Jay Merrick, late of His Majesty's Royal Navy, late of the sloop *Annabel,* and late—very late, I'm afraid—for dinner.''

''Good God,'' Ashton expostulated, and dropped the water pail.

Someone wrapped a blanket around him, the wool chafing his sea-raw skin. Hands drove beneath his shoulders, his arms, his legs. The deck fell away beneath him and he opened his eyes to dizziness, nausea, and the sight of Ashton's stunned face, spinning in a blurry mass of freckles, red hair, and spectacles. Didn't Ashton believe him? Did he look so bad he didn't recognize him? Panicking, he began to struggle wildly.

''Hold still, ye bugger!'' a seaman growled. ''Ye wanna make us drop ye?''

''Won't be no big loss, I tell ye!''

''Only t' Georgie's bloody navy! He's lyin', I tell ye! He ain't no American!''

And then, Ashton's quiet voice. ''You drop him and you'll be going to England in his place.''

''But, Cap'n, 'e's a *Brit!*''

''*I said be easy with him!*''

But one last, fading look at Ashton's uncertain face told Brendan the Yankee was unconvinced. He had to make him believe him! Already hands were lifting him up once more, driving beneath his legs and arms, his shoulders and head. And as his dripping blue coattails brushed the deck, and a blessed, pressing darkness began to dim his vision, he remembered.

The drafts.

He drove his hand beneath the wool blanket and along the coarse, sodden cloth of his coat.

"Hold still!" someone yelled.

His hand plunged into his pocket. His fingers found—and sank into—a sopping, squishy mess of pulp that instantly disintegrated between them. With something like a sob, he drew it out.

Motion stopped. The back of his head lurched against someone's chest, slamming his teeth down hard upon his swollen tongue. He choked back the flood of nausea and let his head roll, until Ashton's face appeared within the circle of his spinning, darkening vision. The Yankee still looked dubious, unsure, his kind brown eyes confused behind the thick lenses of his spectacles. And then he looked down and saw the sodden ball of pulp that dripped, in pieces, from Brendan's fingers.

Brendan shut his eyes as Ashton reached out and took what remained of the sad lump, hearing his own voice coming from further and further away. . . . "The drafts . . . for the schooner . . . your father was to have . . . built . . . for . . . me . . ."

And then that freckled face faded, the darkness swept in, and the nightmares that had been his for three years now came surging back. *Halcyon*'s sunny deck. Crichton's ball ripping through his back, another plowing through his chest. And Eveleen, oh God, Eveleen . . . He struggled, knowing it was a dream, fighting to wake up but unable to.

The drafts.

Please God, no—

The drafts! For God's sake, Ashton, don't let Crichton get his hands on the drafts!

Panicking, he went wild, clawing desperately toward consciousness—*wake up, wake up, WAKE UP!*—and then his own screams jolted him rudely awake.

Wild-eyed, he threw off the dream and bolted upright in the bed.

Chapter 3

His heart thundered madly in his chest. Blood roared through his head. His lungs heaved, his legs were trussed up in a tangle of starched sheets and a butter-colored counterpane, and rivulets of sweat ran down his chest. Dazed, it took him a moment to realize he was not on a ship, not in the sea, and certainly not drowning, but lying on a handsome Heppelwhite field bed whose tall, curved posts rose majestically above him and supported a graceful canopy that looked like bleached fishnet. He shut his eyes, floating down to reality as the dream faded away into long-distant memory. His breathing steadied. His heartbeat slowed. Taking a deep breath, Brendan opened his eyes once more.

The first thing he saw was a telescope, its long barrel glinting in the hot sunlight and pointing out an open window through which bars of bright sunlight streamed. A mild breeze, heavy with the sweet fragrances of summer flowers and newly cut grass, stirred the gauzy curtains. As they wafted in and out, he saw trees, buildings, and in the hazy distance, marshes and glimpses of a silvery, mast-clogged river. An hourglass, a half-spent candle, and a fine model of a brigantine stood atop a bedside table, and from its lofty perch atop a carved mantel, a shelf clock spoke steadily, its rhythmic *tick, tock, tick* comforting and calming his jaded nerves. Just outside, a songbird trilled from a nearby tree branch, and he heard carriages passing on a street below. Shutting his eyes, Brendan sank back in a thick stack of fluffy pillows, let the breeze cool his brow, his cheeks, his damp and naked chest—

"Nightmare?"

—and bolted upright in the bed.

34

Just beyond his toes a young lad stood, his baggy trousers belted with a piece of frayed rope, his stockings caked with mud, and his shirt, probably borrowed from his father, hanging off him like a slack sail. A scruffy orange cat was tucked in the crook of his arm, and both were staring at him intently, the cat's eyes baleful and annoyed, the lad's the color and coolness of fresh celery. Dirt smudged the hollow beneath one pale cheek, more of it darkened his smoothly curved forehead, and above the questioning arch of fine dark brows, a floppy hat, also too big, covered his hair and cast most of his face in shadow.

The breeze bumped the door open and shut. Without taking that unnerving stare off him, the lad kicked it closed, let the latch fall into place, and casually tossed the cat to the bed, the movement of his arm stirring the thick, sultry air and sending a variety of scents wafting across the room. Horse sweat. Mud. And the harsher, cleaner one of lye soap and roses.

Roses?

"You could at least *answer* me," the boy complained, the high pitch of his voice that of a lad not yet into manhood, which, combined with his scanty height, told Brendan he couldn't be more than twelve, maybe thirteen at the most. "Pretty rude of you to just lie there gaping, don't you think? But then, if you *are* a Brit, 'twould explain why you're so darned snobby. Think you're above us provincials, huh?"

"I beg your pardon?" But Brendan, confused, was staring at the cat, now creeping pantherlike up his body with its yellow gaze fastened on his face and its paws pressing against his legs, his thighs, his bare stomach. Tensing, he groped for the sheet, yanked it up, and spilled the animal from the bed and onto the floor, where it belonged. With an indignant yowl, the cat leapt to the window seat and batted at the waving curtains instead.

"I asked you if you were having a nightmare. By the way, who's Eveleen? Your wife? Mistress?" The lad grinned slyly and cocked his head. *"Lover?"*

"What?"

"Eveleen. She your lover?"

"My *lover?!*"

"Aye, lover. You were hollering for her."

"My lov—Oh dear . . ." Swallowing hard, Brendan glanced about the room. It was a masculine chamber, with a chair rail running along its perimeter, and the woodwork beneath painted a deep, strong red the color of oxblood. The windows were deep and recessed, and framed with small, hinged panels rather like inside shutters. Now they were folded back, exposing window seats topped with embroidered cushions.

He had no idea where he was and no idea what had happened to him except that it had been something bad, something *very* bad. And as the horsey-smelling little stable hand came forward and idly picked up the brigantine model, it suddenly all came flooding back to him.

Crichton. *Annabel,* trying desperately to make the river. Cannon fire and smoke, and Newburyport, where he was to meet the shipbuilder to discuss—

The drafts.

He bolted upright, a thick, hot rush of terror draining the color from his face.

"The drafts!" he gasped.

The lad put the ship model down. "Huh?"

"The drafts!"

"Want me to close the window?"

"The win—? No, I don't want you to close the bloody window, I want to know where the drafts are!"

"Why, coming in through the window," the lad said, jerking his thumb toward the sunny panes. "Can't see how you're cold, though, it being summertime and all. . . ."

"*Drafts,* not drafts! *Ship's* drafts. Plans!"

The lad stared at him for a long moment; then his eyes gleamed, a sly smile curved his mouth, and little wrinkles appeared on either side of his impudent nose, fanning out like the whiskers of a cat. "Oh . . . *those* kind." Chuckling, he tipped his hat back with a grimy finger. "So Matt was right after all!"

"What?"

"No wonder Father's fit to be tied!"

As though punctuating his words, something broke somewhere with a horrible crash, and a chorus of shouting and yelling rose up from downstairs. But the lad seemed oblivious to the commotion, and wiping his grubby little hand on his trousers, held it out in greeting. "Fine job you did, tricking that British frigate onto the sunken piers last night. Whole town's talking about it. In fact, they've got its crew down in the jail now!" The hand was still there; confused, Brendan slowly reached out and took it. It was tiny, even for a lad's, the bones fragile and the skin as supple and smooth as a child's. "By the way, my name's Mira. Welcome to Newburyport, Cap'n!"

Brendan shook his head, trying to clear it. "I'm sorry . . . I didn't catch that. . . ."

Downstairs the shouting grew louder, angrier. Something else broke.

"Mira," the lad repeated, and then added proudly, "Y'know, after the star in the constellation Cetus?"

"Oh, *Mira* . . ."

It came out *Moyrrra,* with a pleasant, lilting roll on the *r*'s that most would've recognized as an Irish brogue; but either the lad didn't know his geography, disliked Irishmen, or found something in the way he said it that bothered him, for he stared, spread his feet in a defensive manner, and yanked his hat back down over his brow. "Aye, *Mira.* You got a problem with my name, *Brit?*"

The shouting was getting louder, closer. Brendan pressed his fingers to his temples. He had dim memories of yesterday—or was it this morning? last week?—of floating in the sea, of being fished out of it, lying on a sunny deck while a red-haired man bent over him. *Ashton.* Faith, he hoped he hadn't said or done anything stupid. His memory was terribly foggy where all that was concerned. . . . "No, I've no problem with it," he heard himself saying. "What I seem to be having a problem with is remembering the events of my life during the past several hours, or perhaps *days,* for all I know."

"Oh," the boy said, relaxing. "The way you said it, I thought you were picking on my name. You weren't, were you?"

"Weren't what?"

"Picking on my name."

"No, I was not picking on your name, though it *is* rather odd at that. . . ."

"Odd?! Ain't so odd a-tall! Why don't ye tell me *your* name and we'll see whose is odder?"

"Brendan," he said tiredly.

"Sounds Irish to me. You Irish, then?"

"Well, partly—"

"You a bloody king's officer?"

"What?"

"I said, you a king's officer? Father thinks you are. That's what all that damned hollering's about out there. Can't blame him, though. You talk like you're Irish but act as stuck-up as a damned Brit. And since Matt didn't say anything about the client being a Brit, I guess I was dead wrong and you aren't who we all thought you were."

"What?!"

"Aye, I was wrong, all right; you sure can't be the client! In fact, I'll wager you're just an imposter off that bleedin' frigate, trying to spy on us so you can go back to your countrymen and tell 'em all you know. Like how to get past those barriers in the river. And don't tell me you ain't a Brit, 'cause only a Brit would put on such stuffy airs."

"Stuffy!"

"Aye, stuffy. You Brits are all alike."

"I am *not* stuffy! *And stop calling me a Brit!*"

"Brit, Irishman, makes no difference. You sound like yer schoolin' was right out of Oxford."

"As a matter of fact—" Brendan bit back the rest of his retort, for his schooling *had* come from Oxford. He flung the sheets aside and tried in vain to untangle them from his legs. "Young man, I will tolerate no more of this nonsense! I'll have you know I am a privateer in the service of America, and have been for the better part of three years!"

"Right. And I ain't a shipbuilder's daughter!"

"That's for damned sure!"

"Ye wanned fight about it?!"

They stood glaring at each other while just beyond the door, the shouting and hollering intensified until the lad had to yell to be heard over it. "Look, I don't know who you are, nor just who the hell ye *think* you are—" the fine, paneled door began to pulse beneath the blows of a furious fist ''—but I'll thank ye to keep your smart mouth shut and your fancy airs to yourself! You're a guest here, and you'd damn well better remember it! And furthermore—''

''Mira?! Mira, you in there? So help me God, you open that door this instant!'' The door was bowing in and out now, the pounding so loud, it made Brendan's ears ring. The orange cat dove under the bed. The sea breeze retreated back through the open window, taking the curtains with it.

And the lad drew himself up to his full, scanty height and shouted, ''Go to hell, Matt! I'm having a conversation with this damned Brit you brought home, and I don't care to be interrupted!''

''You open that goddamned door!''

''I will not!''

''Open it NOW!''

''I said go to hell, Matt! Your arse can fry there till the cows come home as far as I'm concerned!''

''Yours is going to fry when I get this damned door open!''

Bang. Bang. *Bang*. The door couldn't take much more—and neither could Brendan. His damp breeches pasted to him like a second skin, he finally untangled himself from the sheets, swung his legs out of the bed, and clutching one of its tall, carved posts for support, rose above the bristling lad. ''I am *not*,'' he said archly, ''going to stand here and suffer the insults of a mere stable hand who stinks of horse dung and field mud! That's Captain Ashton out there, and I demand to see him now!''

Uncowed, the boy turned on him and stabbed a tiny finger into the middle of his chest. ''You'll see him in good time, Brit, and not a moment before! Ye think ye can give orders around her just 'cause you're laid up? You're a guest and nothing more, so remember it! Now sit down and cover yourself! I can see everything ye own through those breeches, and that ain't no way to appear before the lady of the house!''

''When the lady of this house arrives, I'll thank her to bring me the rest of my clothes so I can greet her with proper *British* courtesy!''

''Ye'll greet her with proper courtesy *now*, 'cause I *am*

the lady of the house, and I ain't going to stand here and suffer your crudity!''

"Like hell you are!'' he said, shoving the tiny hand away and moving toward the door.

"Like hell I *am!*''

And then, incredibly, the lad reached up and, in one angry, fluid motion, wiped the hat from his head and flung it to the floor, releasing a glorious mane of rich, glossy brown hair that tumbled down and down and down in an impossibly straight, impossibly thick fall all the way to that tiny, rope-cinched waist. Staggering back, Brendan grabbed the bedpost for support and sat down hard on the damp counterpane.

"Great God,'' he murmured, taken aback. *"Tá tú go hálainn. . . .''*

Yes, she *was* beautiful, but since he'd unconsciously reverted to his native tongue to say so, the strange words meant nothing to her. She stood glaring at him, her pixie face all but obscured by that wall of hair through which her impudent nose poked and eyes as green as the underside of a winter wave, and now, just as cold, glittered. Hooking a finger beneath it, she shoved it behind her ear and revealed the sweet curve of a pale, mud-stained cheek to him. Beneath the mud there were freckles and a spot of high color. Plainly, she was furious.

"Satisfied?! The next time ye speak to me, Brit, 'twill be with the respect I deserve!''

Numbly he reached down and drew the counterpane up over his lap, feeling liquid heat flood his face. She was right. The breeches revealed every curve and ridge he owned, and being wet . . . He swallowed, reddened, and looked at the ticking clock. "Will you please go away?''

"I will not! This is my father's house and I'm staying right here. And if you don't like it, *you* can leave!''

"Mira!'' The door bulged beneath angry blows, the latch rattled, the racket grew deafening. "So help me God, if you don't open that door *now,* I'm going—''

"To what?'' the girl hollered. "Sneak off without me again? You're a real louse, Matt, you know that? A real louse! You just wait! One of these days I'm going to best you at your own game, and we'll see who comes out laughing!''

"Damn you, Mira, I didn't sneak off, and if you'd been on the ship instead of with those damned horses, I would've waited!''

"You snuck off, Matt, admit it!''

"I did not! Now open the goddamned door!''

"I will not!''

"You will, too!''

Brendan shut his eyes. *Dear God.* He was trapped in here with a vicious female, a rabid cat, and no clothes. *No clothes.* Better to be stuck between the broadsides of two ships of the line than this. Females. After being at sea for most of his life, he had to admit they unnerved him. Intimidated him. Confused him. And this one, garbed in male clothing and screaming at the top of her lungs, had him totally aback.

Ashton was kicking the door now, viciously. A dark line split the fine paneling and left a gaping crack.

"Mira! *Open up!*''

Bang. Brendan winced. *Bang. BANG!*

"Go to HELL, Matt!''

Enough was enough. Someone had to intervene, and Brendan, sensing a desperate situation, intervened in the only way he knew how—with reckless humor. Stepping forward, he touched her arm and said politely, "Miss Mira, do you know that when you grin, the sides of your nose crinkle in a most endearing way?''

She'd been just filling up for another vocal blast when she stiffened, spun around, and impaled him with her green-eyed stare. *"What?!''*

How good it felt to have the upper hand again! But Brendan overdid it.

"And when you laugh, your eyes sparkle like dew on the morning grass. Like light through spring leaves, beneath the crest of a winter wave. 'Tis a most charming effect.''

Unaccustomed to such forwardness from a complete stranger—and a British one at that!—Mira also reacted in her customary manner.

She hauled back and slapped him.

Behind the door, Ashton's pounding ceased, and the silence hung heavily in the room.

They stared at each other. It was not a good beginning, and Brendan said as much as he dabbed his mouth with his knuckles and calmly inspected the back of his hand. Faith, she'd actually made his lip bleed! Grinning, he said, "Shall we start over again, Miss *Moyrrra?*" He arched a hopeful brow at her, and she stared at him for a long moment, obviously puzzled by his odd reaction. And then her own mouth twitched, and her cheeks took on a rosy blush as she looked away. Again, he'd taken her off guard.

Ashton chose that moment to crash through the door.

He charged into the room, red-faced and furious, spectacles fogged with steam and halfway down his nose. In his wake were three more cats, a bright flash that might've been a dog, and a glowering old man with white hair growing out of his ears, cheeks as red as Ashton's hair, and a voice that almost shook the paint right off the wainscoting.

"Tripes 'n guts, what the bloody tarnation's going on in here!"

Undaunted, the little hoyden put her hands on her hips and looked at him with a mutinous set to her fairylike chin. "Why, nothing, Father," she said sweetly.

The three cats—and yes, it *was* a dog—hit the bed as one. The orange one shot from beneath it, bounced off the windowsill, and landed amidst the tangle of flying fur with a high-pitched screech of its own, adding enough noise to the barking, howling, squalling melee to shatter glass. But it was nothing beneath the old man's cannon-roar. "Goddammit, Mira, get those creatures outta this room and outside NOW!"

She managed to snatch a cat from the tangle and get it beneath her arm. It went wild, clawing free and hurling itself back to the bed, where it disappeared in the spinning ball of fur and pure, earsplitting racket. Brendan shut his eyes and swayed on his feet. And through it all the girl, Ashton, and the white-haired old man battled it out with a ferocity that rivaled, then rose above, the bansheelike howling emanating from the bed.

"That's another damned cat, ain't it?!" the old man

roared. "How many times do I have to tell you NO MORE ANIMALS IN THIS HOUSE?!"

"It's just one little cat!"

"One little cat! One *more* cat! How many cussed cats do I have to put up with before they start stinkin' up the place? I want it outta here and I want it out *now!*"

"It's not an *'it,'* it's a *'he'*!"

"I don't care what it is, if it ain't outta here by the time I count to three, it's going out the gosh-danged window!" The old man ripped a watch from his pocket and held it out like an amulet blessed with the power of God. "One—"

"For Christ's sake, Mira, go put on some decent clothes! That's no way to dress in front of our guest!"

"Shut up and stay out of this, Matt. I'm sick of your advice!"

"Two!" the old man roared, brandishing the watch.

"Father!"

"Mira, I'm telling you, go put on—"

"THREE!"

Matthew slammed his fist against the wall, sending a fine Chippendale mirror tumbling to the floor in a crash of glass. "Dammit all, you two are an embarrassment to this town, to this house, and *to me!*"

The girl whirled on him with equal heat. "Shut up, Matt, and stop picking on me about my clothes! If they were such a big issue, you'd get our 'guest' something to wear so he doesn't have to stand there in a damned sheet!"

"Guest?" the old man roared. "He ain't no guest of mine! I'll have no snot-nosed Briton in this house, is that understood? DO YOU HEAR ME, MATT!"

"How many times do I have to tell you he *isn't a Brit!*"

"Don't listen to him, Father, he is too a Brit, and he walks like he's got a pole stuck up his—"

"MIRA!"

"Damn you, damn both of you!" Spectacles fogged with anger, Ashton tore off his hat and flung it so hard that a picture tumbled off the wall, smashed against the floor, and sent one of the cats streaking from the room, squalling at the top of his lungs. "I hope to *God* neither one of you ever has reason to prevail upon *British* hospitality, 'cause you'll find ours sorely lacking in comparison!''

"There, you just admitted yourself he's British!"

"That bloody well doesn't' mean he's fighting for them! And if you weren't such a brick-skulled old donkey, you'd know that, dammit!"

"Brick-skulled? I'll have no son of mine taking that tone of voice with *me!*"

"I'm not your son if you insist on treating your guest like a piece of baggage!"

"All Brits are baggage! And how many times do I have to tell you HE AIN'T MY GUEST!"

"Then he's *my* guest, and I'll not have him cast out because of your damned mulishness!"

"This is *my* house!"

"And as long as *my* ship is bringing money into it, I have as much damned say about who stays here as you!"

"Like hell you do! I *built* that bleeding ship for ye! Gimme any more lip and I'll—"

"Father!" the girl wailed. "Oh, Father, Ramsey's ear is bleeding!"

"MIRA!"

Brendan had had enough. With all the dignity he could muster, he turned on his bare heel, strode shakily from the room, and found himself in a glorious rectangular hall with several doors, behind which countless numbers of cats and dogs undoubtedly slept and fought and bred atop beautiful beds. The sheet dragged behind him like a bridal train, but he didn't stop, staring straight ahead as he strode purposefully across a Turkish carpet toward the wide staircase. His toes sank into the rug's plush depths, his hand found the carved banister and trembled on its sleek wood. Down the stairs he went. Past portraits of proud and forbidding Yankee sea captains. Around landings. Toward the square of light from the front door that spread itself across the carpet . . . Five more steps and he'd be there, through that door, and out of this crazy, nightmarish house.

Four more stairs now. Three. *Oh, legs, don't give out on me now. . . .* Two.

Above and behind him, a door slammed and voices exploded into the hall.

"Goddamn you, Matthew, I thought I raised you with sense! I thought I raised you with respect! *I thought you were a PATRIOT!*"

Brendan hit the last step and made for the door at a dead run.

"How *dare* you imply that—*Merrick!* Merrick, wait! Don't touch—"

The door. He grabbed the latch, yanked it toward him— and was slammed face-first against the wall, going down in a helplessly tangled heap of white fur, damp sheets, and terror.

"Luff!" the girl was shrieking. "Luff! No! Father, *do* something!"

"You do something; he's yer damned dog!"

"Luff, no! *NO!* Matt!"

Screams, yells, shouts, a dog's wet tongue—and then it was over. Shaking violently, Brendan got to his hands and knees. Ashton was holding the dog, looking sheepish and humiliated in the awkward silence, his red hair askew and his spectacles perched at a forty-five-degree angle to his nose. He stretched out a freckled hand and pulled Brendan to his feet, his eyes pleading for forgiveness before he turned to glare at the white-haired old gent behind him. Then he dug in his pocket, fished out a crumbling ball of dried-out pulp, and placed it in Brendan's hand.

"Here. Why don't *you* tell Father who you are." His voice was very quiet, *too* quiet, as though the effort to subdue his anger was costing him every bit of strength he had. "Better yet, tell him why you're here. It seems he's having a rather *hard* time believing me!"

This was worse than the nightmare. It was worse than being shot down on the decks of that long-ago frigate. It was worse then anything Brendan had ever imagined. But behind the bristling old man, the dog, and the troop of cats now filing down the stairs one by one, the girl stood. Grimy and dusty, covered with cat hair and smelling like horses, she was grinning at him in a way that could only be called . . . impish.

Something fluttered in his chest.

"Yes," she said sweetly, and put her fists on her hips. "Why don't you? We're all waiting."

That grin was infectious, perky, crinkling the sides of her nose in an endearing way that made the flutter in Brendan's chest become a downright palpation. It was a challenging grin, and Brendan, who'd been only five years old when Liam had dared him up the highest tree in Connemara and he'd paid for his courage with a fall and a broken wrist, had never been able to resist a challenge. He returned her grin, feeling his skin crack beneath the mask of dried sea salt that sheened his face.

"By all means," he said as the girl's blatant gaze slid over his bare torso and sheet-wrapped hips in an assessing way that pulled the heat to his cheeks and made him uncomfortably aware of how ridiculous he must look, standing here in a sheet and not much else. And now those green eyes had found his scarred chest, and she was staring at it with an intensity that only made him more uncomfortable. He bowed deeply, momentarily cutting it off from her view. "I am Captain Brendan Jay Merrick, master of the privateer *Annabel* and an expected guest of the shipbuilder Captain Ephraim Ashton of Newburyport." He opened his palm, where the drafts lay as crumbling bits of paper. "He was to have built a schooner for me."

The old man's face went dark. Observing it, the girl pushed her fist against her mouth as though to hold back laughter.

Brendan swallowed and said, "Am I correct in assuming, sir, that you're the man I came here to see?"

Please God, he thought, *don't let him be. Oh, please God, I'll do* anything . . . .

But providence isn't always kind, even to a half-Irishman. Something clouded the old man's face. His jaw tightened. He cleared his throat several times, passed a hand over his bushy white brows, and turned a brilliant, fiery shade of red. Slowly he reached up and pulled off his hat. "Aye, I'm Ephraim," he said gruffly, glaring at his son in a promise of just retribution. "And aye, we was expectin' ye. But hell, ain't nobody told us ye was English!"

"Irish," Matt corrected.

"Irish, English—why the hell didn't ye *tell* us, *Matthew?!*"

"Because I know how you two feel about Brits, that's why!"

"Please!" Brendan held up a hand before the fighting could start once more, unaware of the effect his helpless grin and unconscious charm were having on the heart of the impish little sprite. "You're both right. My father was Cornish, my mother Irish. But despite my upbringing, I can assure you my loyalties lie in the same place yours do. My first commission was penned in Washington's own hand, my sloop built in a Yankee's backyard. If she still floats, you'll find her papers in a locked chest beneath the window seat in her cabin. I invite you to inspect them for yourself to appreciate the validity of my claim."

Brendan's attempts at playing mediator did little good. Ephraim turned on Matt with the ferocity of an angry bear. "Why in tarnation didn't *you* tell me that?! Blood and wounds, ye think this is any way to treat a guest?! And one I've been expecting for clear over a month?! What the hell're ye trying to do, make me look like a bleedin' idiot?!"

Matt's glasses steamed up. "Damn you, I *tried* to tell you—"

"Don't gimme any of yer blithering excuses, you hear me? Tripes and guts, the two of ye are nothin' but a damned embarrassment to me, ye know that? A damned embarrassment! You with yer wenching and she with her damned cats!" He shoved a hand toward Brendan. "Merrick, I am *most* sorry. Ye have my heartfelt apologies. Here I thought I brought the boy up with manners as fine as my own, but I can see now I was mistaken!" He clapped his hat to his wide and barreled chest and gave Brendan a yellow-toothed grimace that tried to pass as a smile. Bowing, he came up slowly, indicating the grand hall and whatever lay beyond it with a velvet-clad arm. "My home is yers, Cap'n. Stay as long as ye like. A shame about those drafts, but we can work something out, eh? Here, let's find ye some decent clothes and put some good home cooking in yer gut. Ye look a little pale around the gills. Thin, too. I'll wager Abigail's got some leftovers saved from last night. If ye don't mind eating 'em cold, I'm sure you'll find 'em to yer liking. . . ."

Before he could protest, Ephraim was dragging him down the hall, hollering at the top of his lungs and making Brendan long for a kerchief to tie around his ears. He'd be fortunate to leave this house with his hearing intact, let alone his sanity. "Abigail?" The walls shook. "ABIGAIL? Find some of that stuff we had for sup last night and lay it out on the sideboard fer Cap'n Merrick! And some of Mira's pudding, too! And be quick about it, will ye?"

"God, Father, not the pudding!" Matt cried.

Impatiently waving his son off, Ephraim led Brendan to an elegant, wainscoted dining room hung with French paper, more portraits, and a chandelier that glittered like diamonds in the hot sunlight. A magnificent Willard clock dominated one corner of the room, and a shelf clock sat on the carved mantel. Someone in this house must have a fascination with timepieces, Brendan thought, for there was another one of equal size back in the entrance hall, one on the stairway landing, and of course, the one in his room; but he was too conscious of his half-nakedness to consider it further, a fact that he was painfully reminded of as he took a seat and looked down at a table that smelled of fresh beeswax and tossed his bare-chested reflection back at him like a mirror.

Stuffing his watch back in his pocket and still hollering for Abigail, Ephraim stormed out of the room. *Good God,* Brendan thought, his ears ringing. He slid the sheet from his hips, folded it carefully, and placed it on the empty chair beside him. He'd never felt so humiliated and embarrassed in his life. And now something soft was rubbing against his bare ankle, and he knew, without looking, that it was a cat.

And then he forgot his state of undress, his humiliation, and even the cat as a plate was shoved beneath his nose and a fork thrust between his loose fingers. There was his leg of mutton, stuffed with oysters and accompanied by thick wedges of cheese, sauce, and pickles—

And beside it, dwarfing it with enormity and ugliness, was a shapeless, lumpy mass of quivering yellow slime that looked like the remains of a dead jellyfish.

He dropped his fork.

"I hope you like Indian pudding!" Gulping, Brendan clutched his throat and looked up. A plump, apple-cheeked little woman bustled about, clucking like a mother hen and briskly arranging salt and pepper and a pitcher of cold milk. She smelled like flour and had bright, birdlike eyes that didn't miss a trick. "Our dear little Mira made it herself. She's quite a cook, isn't she? Here, help yourself," she said, *tsk-tsk*ing and plunking an elegant silver bowl down before him. "There's plenty more where that came from!"

That didn't surprise him. Slowly Brendan picked up his fork, stared down at his plate—and choked back a tide of nausea. The woman—Abigail?—was smiling at him, hands steepled beneath her chin, eyes glowing with pride.

Waiting.

"Go on!" she urged, excitedly.

There was no way out. Steeling himself, Brendan cut a piece of the mutton and slowly placed it in his mouth. It was cold, but it was good—and recognizable.

Mutton, all right.

"Isn't that good? Here, you eat up. You're awfully thin. We can't have our guests leaving the table with no meat on their bones, now, can we?!"

She hovered about, humming and clucking and *tsk-tsk*ing some more. Brendan took another bite of the mutton—a very *small* bite—chewing it as slowly as possible, prolonging the inevitable, and willing to make it last until Christmas if he had to despite the ravenous hunger it awakened in him. If only the woman would leave. He wished it with all his heart. He *prayed*. Anything, dear Lord, so that he wouldn't have to eat that . . . that *pudding*.

He was down to one last, pitiful bite of the meat when his prayers were answered from a most unlikely source—Ephraim. As the old man began bellowing from a thankfully distant corner of the house, Abigail, mobcap askew and petticoats flying, bustled out of the room with an "Oh dear," and a "Here we go again," and he was left—*thank God*—to himself.

He didn't waste a single precious minute.

Quickly scraping the slimy mass that didn't look like

any pudding *he'd* ever seen into a quivering ball, Brendan shot a quick glance at the door, grabbed his plate, and slid it beneath the table where the cat waited so expectantly.

Grateful purring. Soft fur brushing his wrist as it came running. And then the purring came to an abrupt end.

With a haughty sniff, the cat jerked its tail once, twice—and walked away.

Chapter 4

"Rise and shine, Merrick!"

Brendan groaned and opened his eyes, feeling as though he'd been dragged through the keyhole in the bedroom door. It was his second morning at the Ashton house, and the night had afforded him precious little rest. Every noise had kept him awake: the chirping of the crickets in the hot August night; an argument downstairs between Matthew and Ephraim; and later, when all was quiet at last—too quiet—the ticking of too many clocks. When he finally *had* fallen asleep, he'd been tormented by erotic dreams of Mira Ashton, awakening sometime around dawn in a bath of sweat with a painful, rock-hard arousal. *Faith!*

He dug his fists in his eyes and squinted up into the sunlight. Matt stood there, holding a tray and grinning. "Sleep well?"

"Like a babe," Brendan lied, throwing an arm over his eyes.

"Good. Abigail's got breakfast laid out on the sideboard downstairs, but I thought ye might be feeling a tad under the weather this morning." Matt set the tray on the bedside table. "Here's some coffee to wake you up, and a muffin."

"Thanks," Brendan said. He sat up, looked warily around the room, and breathed a sigh of relief when he saw that Miss Mira was nowhere in sight. She was the last person he wanted to see, after the still vivid dreams of last night. But there was only Matt, dressed in a pair of baggy trousers and a shirt whose sleeve needed mending.

The Yankee clasped his hands behind his back, put his eye to the telescope, and peered out the window toward the river. "Not much going on out there this morn," he commented, straightening up as Brendan stirred sugar into his coffee. He turned, and raked his hand through his hair. "Christ, Merrick. I feel so badly about those damned drafts. . . ."

Brendan shrugged. "Things could be worse," he said, grinning and sipping his coffee.

Matt picked up the ship model and ran a finger over the hull. "Worse? I doubt it. Your schooner would've been the finest vessel this town's ever turned out. But you can't build a ship without drafts. As a naval architect, I know you could probably redraw them, but it'll take months. . . ."

Brendan buttered the muffin, topped it with jam, and took a bite. "On the contrary."

"Huh?"

"I was very careful to keep notes on all my calculations and figures. To redo the drafts would be simply a matter of consulting those notes and finding the time to do it." Brendan grinned, wiped the crumbs from his lips, and picked up his coffee. "Which, given the fact I no longer have a sloop, is a luxury I can easily afford."

Matt's face brightened and he almost dropped the ship model in his eagerness. "Hell, if that's all it takes, then let's go get those notes right now! In fact, right after lunch I could take you down to the waterfront. . . ."

He trailed off, and a shadow passed over his face.

"Is something wrong?" Brendan asked, putting his coffee down.

Sighing, Matt took off his spectacles, wiped them with his shirttail, and stuffed the shirt haphazardly back into his trousers. "Oh, nothing's really *wrong*. . . ." His jaw tightened. "I just remembered I promised to take Lucy Preble out on *Proud Mistress* today. Damn it all. And here you must be going crazy, cooped up here with nothing to do—oh, damn. Damn, damn, damn!''

''Is Lucy your lady friend?'' Brendan asked.

''Aye, the current one,'' Matt said, almost disgustedly. He kicked at a rumple in the rug, ran a hand through his shock of red hair, and stared bleakly out the window. ''Ye know, Merrick, it really annoys me. When I was growing up, no one liked me. You know how children are, always have to have someone to pick on. Well, I had the red hair and glasses, so I was the one who got teased, laughed at, harassed. I got in more fights than you could shake a stick at, and it was that way right up until the war started and Father gave me *Proud Mistress.''* He stared dismally out the window, and picked at a hangnail. ''Christ, did things change then. All it takes is a bit of fame and fortune, and suddenly the same women who used to laugh at my red hair are fighting each other just for the chance to run their fingers through it. Ye know, Merrick, sometimes I think there's no bloody justice in this world.''

Brendan set his muffin down and gave Matt a sympathetic smile.

''It's not that I'm complaining. . . .'' Matt sighed and began to pace. ''It's just that—well, you know. I want to be appreciated for being myself, not for my money, my status as a *hero,* or anything else. It seems like I have a different woman every week. Everyone thinks it's a big joke, and maybe it is, but I'm sick of it. The only reason I let it go on is because I keep hoping I'll find one who's interested in me for myself. But no. It always comes down to the same old thing. My money. My success as a privateer. So I go on to the next one. And the next one . . .'' He looked up, his kind eyes full of despair. ''There *are* nice women out there, aren't there, Merrick? I mean, ones who aren't shallow and opportunistic?''

''Well—''

''I'd just like to meet someone *nice,* someone a man could take as a wife, settle down with, have a family. . . .''

''You mean someone who's like your sister?''

Matt's eyebrows shot clear above the rim of his spectacles.

"Oh dear, forgive me," Brendan said, hastily. "I didn't mean it like that. Faith, I mustn't be quite awake yet—"

"*Mira?* My *sister*, Mira?" Matt erupted in helpless laughter. "Jee-zus, Merrick, you must really be addled to even *picture* her in the role of wife and mother! I can't imagine her ever settling down—nor any man being able to put up with her long enough to give her a wedding ring, let alone a family!" Still chuckling, he peered at Brendan, his eyes beginning to gleam. "You're not entertaining any ideas of courting the brat, are ye?"

Brendan began to color, for the idea was not unappealing.

Matt stared at him for a long moment, his lips twitching and his eyes growing sly behind the thick lenses of his spectacles. Finally he grinned and picked up the empty tray. "Well, just be careful. My sister's not the most . . . *gentle* creature God ever made."

"I'll keep that in mind," Brendan said, grateful that Matt was kind enough not to pursue the issue further.

"Aye, you do that!" Matt warned, and shook a finger at him. He gazed out the window, and his grin faded. "Well, I'd better get going. Take your time over breakfast. Father's out for his morning walk, Mira's exercising her horse, and you'll have the house to yourself. There's ham on the sideboard downstairs, if the dog hasn't gotten it, and fresh cream in the kitchen, if Abigail hasn't given it to the cats." At the door, he paused and turned. "Oh, and by the way, since I'm going down to the waterfront, ye want me to get those notes of yours?"

"Could you?"

"Aye. They're in your sloop somewhere, I suppose?"

"In the locked chest in my cabin. My lieutenant, Liam Doherty, knows where they are."

"Good." Matt chewed his lip. "In fact, I heard your crew's staying down at Davenport's tavern. I'll stop by there on my way to meet Lucy, and fetch your lieutenant myself."

"Thanks," Brendan said, grinning. "You've a good heart, Matthew."

"Yeah, well . . ." Matt shrugged and adjusted his glasses. "Take care, Merrick. I'll see you at dinner." With that, he strode to the door with as much spirit as a person on his way to the gallows.

"Er, Matthew?"

Matt turned.

"Good luck."

"Thanks, Merrick." Matthew gave a short laugh. Then he opened the door and was gone.

Chapter 5

William Davenport had been a Newburyport man who'd seen General Wolfe die on the plains of Abraham, and it was something he never forgot. On his return to Newburyport, Davenport converted his home into a tavern, hung a sign out front on which was faithfully carved and painted a head and bust of the famous general, and swung open his door for business.

In the years since, Wolfe Tavern, at the corner of State Street and Threadneedle Alley, had become the most popular spot in town. The long, rectangular building hosted political, patriotic, and social gatherings, as well as travelers of all sorts. Here, men gathered to hear the latest news on the war, engage in spirited debates, or just amuse themselves with a game of cards. Back in '65, when the local Sons of Liberty had terrorized Newburyport, roaming the streets and making the lives of those in favor of the hated Stamp Act terrible, it had been in Wolfe Tavern that they'd met. Davenport had died back in '73, but the tavern had continued under the capable management of his sons Anthony and Moses, still offering stout drink and hearty food for weary traveler and townsman alike.

It would have been safe to assume that it was the stout drink and not the hearty food, although that was certainly being consumed with equal ardor, that had drawn *Anna-*

bel's company after they'd brought the battered sloop into port with the help of two Newburyport privateers. Now the mortally wounded *Annabel* lay in her bed of riverbank mud, while every man jack and officer of her crew—with the exception of her missing captain—sampled the fine food and drink for which the tavern was famous.

Miraculously, not a soul had been killed or injured during the short but scrappy engagement with Crichton's frigate. Oh, Dalby was complaining that his chest hurt when he breathed in—too much smoke had got into his lungs, he insisted—but aside from that, and a few scrapes and scratches here and there, *Annabel*'s crew had been lucky.

Dalby sat now with a mug of ale before him and a plate of beef and potatoes growing cold beneath his nose, his shipmates, no doubt the rowdiest bunch of tars to put into unsuspecting Newburyport all week, surrounding him. The tavern was clean enough, with well-swept, wide-boarded floors scuffed by the heels of a thousand boots and shoes, a huge fireplace, and wainscoting painted an unpretentious shade of ocher. The light from a tin chandelier, set with spitting candles, cut through the smoke.

His brow furrowing, Dalby scrutinized the other patrons. Men lounged at sturdy walnut tables drinking foamy mugs of beer and puffing on long clay pipes. Three tables away, a group of finely dressed gentlemen, either merchants or, more likely, shipowners, were engaged in a lively game of backgammon. A dog lay half-asleep at their feet, and a seaman, dressed in baggy trousers, torn shirt, and a threadbare vest, sat on a stool sipping an ale and conversing with a disreputable-looking man in buckskins and a fur hat.

None of *them* looked to be ill . . . and his own companions had never seemed to enjoy better health. He eyed them with increasing annoyance. Liam's hearty laughter was growing more so with every tankard of cherry rum he downed, and Dalby knew it would be only a matter of time before he picked up the fiddle propped against his chair leg and struck up a lively jig. Across from him sat John Keefe, his flowing silver hair and charcoal beard drawing disapproving scowls from some of the other patrons. McDermott had his nose in a book, Amos Reilly kept slamming his fist down on the table and shrieking with laughter every time Liam said what he'd like to do to the pretty maid who brought their ales, and George Saunders seemed about ready to actually do it.

Dalby's pinched mouth anchored itself in a frown. He stared down at his plate; it was the only one that had any food left on it, and his companions were all eyeing it like a pack of half-starved wolves. If the captain, God rest his soul, were here, he'd have finished it off. But the captain was gone. Dalby bit his lip and blinked back tears, wondering if life was worth living. The captain was gone, *Annabel* was a wreck, and his beef had a funny taste to it. Probably spoiled. As if to affirm that assumption, his stomach lurched and he had to swallow tightly to quell a quick flood of nausea.

A hearty whack across the back from Liam nearly brought the beef—and his stomach—back up out of his mouth. "God Almighty, Dalby, ye're spoilin' th' fun! First time int' port in three weeks an' ye're sittin' there lookin' like it's th' end o' th' world! Cheer up, would ye?''

"My stomach hurts."

"Yer stomach hurts? Then here, 'ave s'more ale, 'twill make it feel better!'' Liam dumped a flood of it into Dalby's half-empty mug. "What's this? Not drinkin', either? God Almighty, what's th' bloody matter with ye, laddie-o?''

Anyone in his right mind would know better than to ask Dalby what the matter was; it was something they'd all learned *not* to do. But Liam, in his cups, had grown careless.

"I told you, I have a stomachache. Probably from the beef. It's gone bad, I just know it has. And that ale tastes odd, too. Kind of brackish-tasting. How do I know where it's been? How do I know it wasn't in someone else's mug before mine? How do I know that person didn't have the smallpox, or a fever—''

"What's that, Dalb?'' Reilly screeched, his voice sounding like carriage wheels grating on stone. "Don't want your supper?''

"Heck, if you don't want it, slide it over here and I'll take it!'' Keefe cried.

Reilly leaped up, knocked Keefe's hand away as he reached for Dalby's plate, and grabbed it for himself. Keefe responded with a timely punch to Reilly's jaw. Reilly howled and drew his own arm back to return it, and Liam casually yanked the plate away before the dispute could get any worse. "Look at ye, fightin' like a pack o' curs o'er a bone." He curled his brawny arm around the plate to guard it and plunged his fork into a greasy, oozing slab of beef. Popping it into his mouth, he chewed loudly, washed it down with a dose of cherry rum, and stabbed another chunk. It tasted just fine to him. "And o'er a hunk o' meat that Dalby says 'as gone bad. F'r shame, lads! F'r shame!''

"Dalby'd say it's gone bad if they carved it off the pig right here in front of him!''

"Pig? You idiot, beef comes off a cow! The kind with udders!''

"Ye mean like the ones that serving wench has?''

"You keep your eyes off her, Reilly, you hear me? I saw her first!''

"The hell with ye, Keefe! I *spoke* for her first!''

Dalby lunged to his feet, so angry the cords in his neck began to vibrate. "How dare you all sit here and talk about food and drink and women when our poor captain is dead and drowned! How *dare* you!''

They all stared at him. Keefe with his thick, prematurely gray hair flowing down his back, and his tricorn on the floor beside him. Reilly in midcackle, his fist poised above the table and the left side of his jaw beginning to swell. Saunders with his attention divided between him and the serving wench, Fergus McDermott looking up from his book—a *Bible,* of all things—and marking his place with a callused finger, and Liam, mouth hanging open and a piece of greasy beefy clinging to his broad and stubbled chin.

"Now, Dalby." Liam plucked his napkin from the table, swiped at his jaw, then tossed the cloth back to his plate. "The cap'n's goin' t' be just fine. Ye don't see me worryin' now, do ye?''

"Just *fine?!*'' Dalby wailed, and made a sudden grab for his chest. He mustn't holler like that. It wasn't good for the heart. Taking several deep breaths to calm himself, he faced Liam angrily. "That's easy for you to say now, but you sure weren't so confident about things yesterday, if I remember right!" Tears shimmered in his eyes. "The captain's not just *fine,* and you know it! We all saw him get swept out to sea by the current!"

"Cap'n can swim," Saunders grunted, turning the rest of his attention on the serving wench.

"But it was cold last night!"

"It ain't cold, it's summertime."

"Aye, the seas are still warm."

"This is not the Indies!" Dalby wailed. "And what if a shark got him!"

"Ain't enough fat on the cap'n's bones. Shark'll spit him out."

"Not enough fat? Hah, not enough meat, either," Liam said, stabbing another chunk of beef. "Always told him t' eat more. Too damned thin f'r his own good. Course, if he 'ad some stoutness t' him, he wouldn't've tumbled off o' th' ship in th' first place. An if he 'ad some fat under his hide, he wouldn't 'ave t' worry 'bout stayin' afloat—"

"—or keeping warm, either," Keefe added, importantly.

Dalby sat down hard, clutching his stomach. The beef was bad; it had to be. His, anyhow. Maybe not anyone else's, but definitely his. Rubbing his belly, he stared at the others with an accusing eye. Oh, how could they sit here and joke about the captain like that? And Liam! Liam was the captain's best friend, and had been ever since Brendan's father, the distinguished old Admiral Merrick, had died and his widow had moved herself and her two children back to her beloved home in Connemara. . . .

"Ah, ye worry too much f'r yer own good, Dalby." Liam leaned back and crossed his massive arms behind his head, making his ladder-backed chair protest beneath his great, muscled bulk. "See what it's doin' t' yer stomach? Ye're makin' yerself sick o'er this. Cap'n's da was English, aye, but he's got the luck o' his Irish ma t' see t' him, and it's never failed him yet."

Dalby bristled. "The only Irish luck I see here is yours!

With the captain dead and gone, *you're* in command now. You tell me who's the lucky one!''

Fortunately for Dalby, Liam's temper was not easily ignited, for Liam was twice as big, thrice as strong—and half his age. He merely smiled, belched in happy contentment, and picked up his fiddle. ''An' would ye mind a-tellin' me just what i' 'tis I'm supposed t' command, Dalb?''

Dalby's mouth snapped shut. It would be a while before *Annabel* was seaworthy again—a long while. And the magnificent schooner that had been the captain's dream . . . her drafts had died with her creator. Dalby turned his face away to hide his tears.

Liam was an astute man, even with a quart of ale swimming in his belly. ''Here now, Dalb,'' he said, laying a big, square hand across the little sailmaker's bony arm. ''There's not a soul on earth who cares f'r th' cap'n more than I do. If I thought he was dead an' gone, d'ye think I'd be a-sittin' here drinkin' away his memory? God Almighty! Why, any minute now I'll bet ye my share o' th' next prize that door yonder'll swing open and our Brendan himself'll come strollin' in—''

As if on cue, the door *did* swing open and a tall figure stood silhouetted in the hot sunlight. ''Captain!'' Dalby cried, lunging to his feet. But it was not their gallant young commander who stood there but a stranger, with a freckle-dusted face that looked as if it would stand little, if any sunlight, and unruly red hair curling out from beneath a floppy felt hat. There was no doubt that he was a seaman; probably an officer if not a captain, judging by the way he carried himself and rocked back on his heels. His eyes, magnified by spectacles that gave him an almost scholarly appearance, swept the crowd, crinkling in a smile as they perused each of the serving wenches. Yet in true Yankee style, he had no pretenses; his jacket of pilot cloth had seen better days, and a strip of leather belted a pair of bell-bottomed trousers rolled up to display white hose and scuffed, buckled shoes. Forgetting his stomach, Dalby squinted through the smoky air and tried not to stare, for the man looked awfully familiar.

The newcomer took off his hat, raked a hand through

his wild red locks, and grinned broadly as the serving wench whom Keefe and Reilly had been arguing over for the better part of the morning flung herself into his arms with a squeal of glee. He caught her, kissed her full on the lips, and set her down, where she clung to his arm like a barnacle.

"The nerve of him! We've been sitting here for a bloody hour, and he comes in here, just like that, and draws her in like a fish on a line!"

Fergus looked up from his Bible. "Says a lot for your charms, Amos."

"Be damned to ye, Fergus!"

The serving wench, blushing hotly, then giggling under the Yankee's attention, nodded and pointed toward their table. They all watched as he strode purposefully toward them.

"Ahoy, there," Liam drawled, leaning back in his chair and setting his fiddle across his knees. " 'Ave a seat an' join us f'r a mug or two!"

Matthew Ashton perused this odd group, his eyes lingering on the grumpy little man whose gnarled hand was pressed to his gut as though ill. He wondered briefly what was wrong with him to make him so silent and surly when his mates were obviously well into their cups. "Much obliged," he said, accepting both the chair that the burly Irishman slid toward him and the ale Belinda set beneath his nose. At the door, Lizzie stood pouting and fuming, furious that Belinda had reached his table first. Figuring he'd let Lizzie bring his next ale, Matt dug in his pocket for a coin, pressed it into Belinda's palm, and closed her fingers around it before drawing her hand to his lips and kissing her work-roughened knuckles. "Now, off with you, Belinda, and fetch some more ale for these folks here." She twirled away, blushing furiously and cradling her hand to her generous bosom as though it had been blessed by God himself.

That settled, Matt blew the foam from his ale and looked at each of the strangers over the rim of his mug. They were all staring at him. "You the crew from the sloop *Annabel?*"

"Part o' it," the big Irishman said, extending a huge

hand. "I'm Liam Doherty, first lieutenant. This here's Dalby O'Hara. He's sick, so don't mind him. Oh, don't bother movin' away, 'tisn't contagious. Dalby's always got somethin' wrong with him, but it's all in his head. This here's John Keefe—"

"*Jack* Keefe, now!" Reilly shrieked gleefully. "Don't ye know that once a man's coin's all gone, he's just 'Jack' again like the rest of us?!"

Liam shrugged, his grin splitting his broad and beamy face. "*Jack* Keefe, an' this toothless cur by his side wi' th' purple jaw is Amos Reilly. Yonder's George Saunders, gunner, an' Fergus McDermott, able seaman, who'll need t' be askin' ye about th' churches in town as he's decided t' join one aft'r yesterday, right, Ferg? An' God only knows where th' rest o' the crew is, though some are at th' other tables, an' the rest, I'd wager, probably seekin' a warm bed with room f'r two." Dalby was elbowing him again. "Oh, an' our cap'n's at sea," he added, almost as an afterthought. "We expect him back any time."

"Oh?" Matt raised his red brows above the rim of his spectacles.

"He is *not* at sea!" Dalby cried. "He's dead! Dead and drowned!"

"That makes him at sea, don't it?" Reilly cackled, and slapped the table in insane laughter.

Matt eyed his companions curiously, thinking them a strange bunch indeed. "I, uh, take it he was a hard master," he said slowly.

Dalby lunged to his feet, stomachache forgotten. "He was the best master there ever was! Fair and just and honest! Brave and laughing and unafraid, right down to the end! And he knew everything there was to know about ships, *everything!* He could design one as well as he could sail one—"

"Aye, ye should've seen those drafts he drew up," Keefe admitted, shaking his silver-maned head as he broke an inch off his clay pipe.

Dalby was heading for an ulcer attack. "Those drafts! Those stupid drafts! If it weren't for them, he'd be safe and sound right now! But no, he had to find the best man in the colonies to build that ship for him. Said she'd need a good dose of Yankee know-how, else she just wouldn't do! And now look what's happened! If he'd just been content with *Annabel,* he'd be standing here right now—''

''Like hell he would, Dalb,'' Liam said, brushing bread crumbs from his shirt. ''He'd 'ave us out on some salty deck givin' th' Brits what for. He isn't one t' waste time ashore. Why, even when we made port, he'd stick aboard, workin' on those damned drafts, fantasizin' about this an' that, wonderin' if he should hang a tops'l above her mainmast or just let her go wi' th' one on her fore.''

''Oh?'' Matt watched them over the rim of his mug with sudden interest. ''And what did he finally decide?''

''T' put 'em on both.''

''Topgallants, too,'' Keefe added.

''An' studders outside o' that.''

''Good God.'' Matt almost dropped his mug. ''Wouldn't that make her a bit unsteady, hard to handle?''

Dalby puffed his chest out like a banty rooster. ''Our captain could sail a ship to the moon and back if he had to! If he wanted to string sails clear up to the stars, he could handle her!''

Liam put a restraining hand on Dalby's arm. ''She would've been deep-drafted enough t' take all th' sail th' cap'n asked o' her,'' he explained. ''Brendan's a wee bit reckless, sometimes even t' th' point o' seemin' empty-headed, but he's no fool. He knows his business right 'nough when it comes t' designin' ships.''

''*Knew* it!'' Dalby cried, perilously close to tears. ''Can't you get it through your head he's *dead?!*''

Seeing the telltale moisture in the little man's eyes, Matt decided he'd let the game go on long enough. Ordering another ale, this time from Lizzie so there'd be no fighting between her and Belinda, he leaned back, sipped slowly, and told them the reason he'd come here—and who'd sent him. By the time he'd finished, Liam was grinning down into his ale as though his captain's survival had come as no surprise, and Dalby was all but sobbing in relief.

Saunders shrugged. ''Told ye he could swim.''

''Praise the Lord,'' Fergus said, without looking up from his Bible.

"Think that serving maid's got any more beef and potatoes out in the kitchen?"

Yet Matt saw that they were all staring at him; Keefe, digging a finger against his front teeth to dislodge a string of meat; Saunders with a great gap where his own front teeth had been, and Reilly, with no teeth at all. "Well, what're we waiting for?" Matt picked up the salt-stained hat he'd been vowing to replace for the past eight months, knowing it would probably be another eight before he got around to it. "While we're sitting here drinking the place dry, the finest schooner this town—nay, this *colony!*—has ever seen waits to be built!"

"But the drafts are gone!"

"Gone—but not forgotten." Matt grinned, removed his spectacles, blew on them, and wiped them with a corner of his shirt. He put them back on, shoving them up the bridge of his narrow nose with a freckled finger. "Your captain tells me he kept detailed notes. Perhaps he can simply redraw those drafts."

"Aye, that he could, if he *had* all those notes and calculations. . . ."

Matt grinned in triumph. "Which are, I'm told, locked safely away in *Annabel*'s cabin!"

"Amen," Fergus said.

But the others had all gone silent, remembering that last terrible broadside that had smashed the stern and gutted the little ship. They'd be lucky to find part of the sea chest that Brendan had kept those notes in, let alone the notes themselves. But Matt guessed their thoughts. "And what was it you were saying about your captain's Irish luck, Mr. Doherty?"

They stared at him. And then, one by one, they grinned, and then they laughed, slapping one another across the backs and drinking toasts to that same Irish luck until finally Matt jumped to his feet and pulled the strapping lieutenant, complete with fiddle, with him toward the door. Outside, it was hot and muggy, and as a heavily guarded cart went past, the horses that drew it kicking up a cloud of dust, Matt never saw how Liam shuddered, paled, and blessed himself. In that cart were the officers of the British frigate that Captain Merrick had tricked onto the sunken piers last night, and the red-rimmed eyes of its commander sought Liam out and remained on him long after the cart was just a speck in the distance.

Had his vision not been hindered by the cloud of fresh dust filming his lenses, Matt might've shuddered, too, at the look of pure hate in the British commander's eyes.

Coughing and waving the dust aside with his floppy hat, he poked his head back inside the tavern, managing to catch the attention of the seamen—and the serving wenches—once more. "Gentlemen!" They looked up, their faces dim through the cloud of pipe smoke. "I forgot to tell you. If you'd like to visit your captain, please feel free to stop by our home on High Street tomorrow. It's the big white Georgian with green shutters, dormered windows on the second floor, and an anchor on the front lawn. Can't miss it."

"Why, thanks, Cap'n Ashton!"

"Any time after one o'clock's fine." He paused, biting his lip. "Uh, better make that one-fifteen, instead."

"One-fifteen."

"Aye, one-fifteen." He touched his fingers to his temple. "See you then!"

And with that, he clapped his hat atop his red hair, yanked the floppy old brim down to shield his face from the blazing sun, and together with Liam, sauntered off down the street,.

"Alive," Dalby breathed, eyeing Fergus's Bible with some reverence.

"Did any of us ever doubt it?"

"We have to go see him."

"Aye. But you heard Ashton. After one-fifteen."

Dalby stood up. "I'm not waiting for one-fifteen, I want to go now!"

"You heard him. *One-fifteen.* An odd time, if I do say so myself. Why not one o'clock? One-thirty? Or even two?"

Keefe belched. "Damned if I know. . . ."

But they were soon to find out. For one o'clock was when Ephraim Ashton left that fine Georgian home, climbed into his carriage, and drove himself through town to the Ashton Shipyards on the waterfront, where he would remain until precisely six o'clock and not a moment later.

One-ten was when his daughter went riding down High Street.

And one-fifteen was when Matt estimated that street to be safe for unwary passersby. . . .

Chapter 6

Unfortunately for Brendan, he was unaware of the Ashton schedule. He found the ham on the sideboard, as well as a hearty spread of codfish cakes, baked beans with molasses, and thick toast that he spread generously with Abigail's wild strawberry jam. By midmorn, however, he was bored, frustrated, and impatient enough to be roaming about the house, wondering why he was having such a hard time thinking of the schooner and the drafts he ought to be redrawing, and such an easy time thinking of Miss Mira Ashton. . . .

He stared out the window, restlessly drumming his long fingers upon the sill. Milky haze clung to thick, grassy fields that smelled sweetly of summer hay and wildflowers, and above gently swaying treetops, great, purple-stained clouds were stacked like shelves in a cornflower blue sky. His gaze followed the haphazard trail of a stone wall, choked with weeds and scraggly-looking wildflowers of every color. The fence led off into the woods, and the bent grasses along its border suggested that a horse had recently passed through. Miss Mira's, perhaps?

Perhaps.

The big house was empty. He'd toured it several times, counting no less than twelve clocks of various sizes, shapes, and colors, and no less than five cats—also in various sizes, shapes, and colors. He went to the library, hoping to escape both, where the ticking of two more clocks and the insistent purring of three more cats were enough to make him toss down the volume on shipbuilding he'd been thumbing through and make a hasty exit. In the kitchen (where there were neither clocks *nor* cats, thank God) he prowled restlessly about until Abigail, who was overseeing the fixing of supper, handed him a plate of hot buttered cornbread, watched him wolf it down, and told him to have some more of Mira's pudding if he was still hungry.

He fled the kitchen.

In the parlor he sipped a cup of coffee brought by a blushing servant girl, who then, blushing even harder, brought him his freshly washed clothes. As he stirred sweet cream and sugar into his beverage and heard the distant whicker of a horse, he thought again of Miss Mira Ashton and wondered where she was.

He shook his head. She was one puzzle he wasn't even going to *try* to figure out. Better to concern himself with the drafts, and the familiar challenges of a naval architect; challenges involving length, beam, speed, stability, and living and storing space; sail suits and mast heights, bow rake and stern design. Not cherry-lipped little hoydens with smart mouths and impish grins. But he couldn't help but think of one little hoyden in particular, and instead of envisioning his sleek and rakish schooner, he saw instead the lovely Miss Mira with her endearing cat-wrinkles fanning out from the sides of her nose when she grinned, her snapping green eyes, and her thick, flowing mane that tumbled all the way to her curving, delicious little hips. . . .

He drained his coffee cup and nearly scalded the back of his throat. *Faith, laddie, get to work!*

Maybe if he went upstairs, his room's nautical decor might stimulate him into redrawing the drafts. Yes, that was it. Clothing draped over his arm, he hauled himself up the grand staircase, passing portraits of Ashton ancestors on the wall, the giant grandfather clock on the first landing, and at the top, a brass-fitted chest. A fine Chinese bowl sat atop it, and there was a cat curled up inside. He turned away and headed for his room. Out of the corner of his eye he saw a streak of gray disappear behind his half-open door. Another cat. And another, padding silently up the stairs behind him. He pushed the door open. And there, *another*, curled up in a ball in the middle of his bed. It was not asleep, but staring haughtily at him over the top of its tail, as though annoyed that he dared interrupt its slumber. The tail twitched as Brendan let the door sigh shut behind him and strode across the room.

Shedding the frock coat that Matthew had lent him, he tossed his clothes across the bed, hoping they'd fall across the arrogant feline and further interrupt its sleep. He'd lost all intention of working on the drafts, for it was obvious he'd get no more work done here than he had downstairs. Besides, Ephraim had returned from his morning walk, and Brendan could hear slamming doors marking his progress through the downstairs part of the house. Sighing, he went to the window and swung the telescope toward him, bending at the waist so that he could peer through its long tube. Over the tops of the foreground trees he could see the cluster of shops and brick houses in Market Square, and a forest of masts stabbing skyward just beyond them. A cutter was just filling her sails and coasting out with the tide, the people on her decks scurrying to and fro like ants.

There was no sign of *Annabel*.

The shelf clock on the mantel ticked softly: 12:40. He could keep still no longer.

At 12:45 he coaxed his shaggy chestnut curls into a queue and tied them neatly with a piece of black ribbon at the nape. At 12:50 he got dressed, pulling on a crisp white shirt and stockings, an embroidered scarlet waistcoat, and dark blue breeches with fancy gold embroidery ringing the knee bands, and brass buttons running up the outer legs from knee to midthigh. Lastly, he donned his coat. Its shade mirrored that of the breeches, and its cuffs, edged in gold braid, shone grandly in the sunlight. Shoving his feet into brass-buckled shoes, he strode to the mirror and surveyed himself with a critical eye. British-born or not, he looked every inch the American privateer captain that he was. Matt had brought him a smart new tricorn edged in gold braid, and setting it jauntily atop his head, he grinned at himself in the mirror. Certainly he cut a far more dashing figure than he had when Miss Mira Ashton had first discovered him! Wet breeches and sheets were not conducive to gaining the respectful attention of fine ladies. But captains' uniforms most certainly were. . . .

He would endure the heat.

He was just straightening his stock when every time-piece in the house, led by the huge Willard case clock in the entrance hall downstairs, struck one o'clock. Down-stairs, the front door slammed. Neatly tucking the stock beneath his waistcoat, Brendan moved to the window in time to see Ephraim striding down the driveway, consult-ing his watch and growing so engrossed in resetting it that he almost plowed into the waiting groomsman and the horse that stood sweating beneath its harness in the sun. And then Ephraim drove away, still fighting with the watch and cursing loud enough to be clearly heard from two stories up as he nearly sent the horse into what Matt had proudly pointed out as the town's "Liberty Tree" before gaining control of both animal and carriage—and hope-fully, watch—and disappearing from sight.

At 1:05 Brendan decided he had better things to do than redraw drafts he already knew like the back of his hand—and hope for the appearance of a girl who was apt to turn up in anything from horsey-smelling breeches to a plain homespun gown made elegant by her very charm and poise. Faith, he'd come to Newburyport to have his ship built, not go a-courtin'! Why not have a look around town and see what there was to see? Anything was better than staying here and letting cats, clocks, and procrastination drive him mad.

Unseen eyes weighed heavily on him as he left the room and made his way back down the huge, angled staircase. Not just the Yankee sea captains staring from their por-traits, nor the dour gazes of their prim and proper wives, but cats. Hiding beneath the mahogany washstand in his room. Curled in the pewter bowl that sat atop it. Sitting on window seats in the parlor, draped along the fireplace mantel, and lying behind a model of Matthew's *Proud Mistress,* which held a special place between two candle-sticks on the gleaming surface of a fine pianoforte.

In the entrance hall he looked warily over his shoulder for the dog, and assuming it was probably off harassing one of the cats, opened the door and went out.

He stood for a moment in the hot, blistering sunlight, wondering why he felt like a prisoner escaping a gaol. The urge to peek over his shoulder was strong; his determination that he would not stoop to such foolishness was stronger. Taking a deep breath, he filled his lungs with the musky scent of late summer grasses, weeds, and wildflowers, his ears with the incessant chirps of the crickets that made the fields their home. Good thing Dalby wasn't here; he'd be complaining about a runny nose and itchy eyes. With a jaunty step and newly found purpose, Brendan paused to get his bearings, and without a backward glance, headed down the driveway and toward High Street beyond.

It was 1:15.

Beside the small paddock attached to the stables, Mira, who'd spent the morning exercising El Nath in the field that was Miss Mira Ashton's School of Fine Horsemanship, stood holding Rigel's reins and eyeing the empty saddle atop his back.

She wasn't one to believe in premonitions; if so, she might've heeded the little voice that warned her that riding Rigel for the first time today was *not* a good idea. The colt's dark eyes were rolling, he was dancing circles around her, and a nervous sweat had broken out beneath his girth, his saddle, and his thick and flowing mane.

Rigel was smarter than most dogs she'd known. No doubt he *knew* her intentions.

She glanced quickly up at the house, at the open windows of the upstairs east bedroom, where the chintz curtains that Mama had made so long ago—before the birth of a third child had claimed both her and the babe—were blowing in, blowing out. Was the handsome captain watching her? She imagined him leaning out the window, his elegant, long-fingered hands gripping the sill as he might a quarterdeck rail, that one fine brow that was set a little higher than the other raised as he smiled down at her and admired her flawless horsemanship. . . . Unexplainably, her heart gave a little flutter. But the window was empty, and her only spectator was Ramsay, formerly titled Rescue Effort Number Thirty-One—*was* it Ramsay?—no, 'twas Butterball, sitting in the shade of a rosebush and licking his tawny coat.

Some audience. But it was better than nothing.

Nevertheless, she glanced up at the empty window again and berated herself for letting her attention wander. Impressing that haughty Brit was not important. . . .

Was it?

No!

She turned away so she couldn't see the window. Above, clouds lolled in a silver-hazed sky, and barn swallows wheeled in and out of the stable's loft. "Now, Rigel," she said, trying to calm him. Touching his sweaty neck, she stroked the sleek muscles beneath and tried to force thoughts of the captain from her mind. "It's not going to be that bad. Do you think I'd let anything happen to you? Do you think I'd do this if I thought you were going to get hurt? Hell, do you think I'd do this if I thought *I* was going to get hurt?"

The colt stepped up his fidgeting, blowing hot breath through red-flaring nostrils and eyeing her warily. Mira glanced up at the window a final time. It was now or never. Taking a deep breath, she grabbed a fistful of reins and mane in her left hand, the cantle in her right—and vaulted lightly into the saddle.

She was on. On!

And almost off as Rigel exploded out from under her like a cannon flinging itself inboard.

"Whoa!" She fell half off his neck, losing her irons and clinging like a thistle by her knees as he bolted out of the paddock, tore blindly around the side of the house, and rocketed for the street. Powerful muscles rippled beneath her. His whipping mane stung her cheeks. Gripping the reins for dear life, she managed to get her seat under her and her feet back in the flying irons. "Rigel, whoa! Easy! *Whoa!*"

The side of house and the front door passed in a blur. Shod hooves thundered across the lawn, struck sparks off the cobblestoned drive, and hit the street. Desperately she drew on the reins. "Goddammit, Rigel, *easy!*" Houses flashed by in ribbons of white. Screaming passersby dove out of the way. An oncoming shay careened to the right, then to the left, and overturned against a tree. Rigel shied and found more speed. He had the bit in his teeth now, the wind in his mane, and there wasn't a damned thing she could do but sit back and enjoy the ride.

Too late, she saw the Jacksons' tricolored hound, sitting on his lawn with tongue lolling, waiting, as he did every afternoon at exactly 1:15, for the big stallion El Nath to come thundering down High Street in much the same manner his coltish son was doing now. Mira glimpsed him through the strands of Rigel's whipping mane, dug her knee into the colt's side to turn him—and saw the dog hurl himself across the lawn into their path.

"Damn you, Sniffer!"

Rigel never slowed, hurling himself sideways and across the street, flank and shoulder first. A woman screamed. Someone shouted. Mira saw a blue coat, a startled face, and then the colt's shoulder hit something hard and her seat went out from under her. She felt space where warm leather should've been . . . air whistling through her clothes—

She landed in a very undignified heap on a manicured front lawn, in plain and humiliating sight of everyone: Jonathan Jackson, clad in his banyan and a red velvet hat and hanging out of his second-story window; Nathaniel Tracy, rival shipbuilder and privateer, leaning from a carriage and touching his cocked hat to her in an amused salute; three women who'd been taking the air on the far side of the road, now standing in speechless horror as they watched Rigel's riderless flight back down High Street— and a man, lying crumpled in the road. Mira felt the blood draining from her face, and a hot flood of prickly horror wash through her veins.

The man was Captain Merrick.

As one, the three women picked up their skirts and rushed to his side. Tracy's carriage slowed, stopped, turned around in a cloud of dust. And coming up the street was a group of seamen who pointed, yelled, and broke into a dead run toward them. But Mira, forgetting her humiliation, saw only the captain, lying very still on the hard-packed dirt, and as the people surged forward, nothing but a wall of breeches, coattails, and skirts. "Let me through!" she cried, leaping to her feet and trying to shove them aside. "Please, let me through!" The circle grew tighter. *"Get out of the goddamned way!"*

Tracy, adjusting his powdered wig, was stepping down from his carriage. "You really ought to be more careful on those horses, Miss Mira. Racing down the street like that, 'tis a wonder you haven't hurt someone sooner."

"Hurt him?" A woman turned, biting her fingertips in wild-eyed horror. "I think she's killed him!"

"No!" Mira beat her palms against backs that wouldn't move, shoulders as hard as tree trunks. It was no use. With a cry, she ducked, darted between a seaman's bowed legs, and fell on her knees before the captain. He was as still as death, and just as white. "Captain!" She seized his limp hand, rubbing it, patting it, slapping it in frenzied terror. "Captain Merrick, oh God—"

Father was going to murder her.

"Captain, wake *up!*"

"You killed the poor fellow, Miss Ashton," Tracy said quietly, and took off his hat.

One of the women was screaming, another had conveniently swooned, and the third, gasping like a dying cod, clung to Tracy's arm, her wrist flung across her forehead. Sniffer raced to and fro, barking in mindless frenzy. And then the group of seamen thrust through the crowd, tossing people aside as though they didn't exist, their enraged roars—and the hideous wailings of the oldest, smallest one—bringing the clamor to din pitch. Tears rolling down her face, Mira fell forward, blocking out the screaming, the bellowing, the barking. She put her arms around the captain's elegant shoulders, a hand behind his head, and pulled him up against her chest, where she hugged him for all she was worth as though to hold the life in him.

He was warm and heavy and smelled faintly of seawater and shaving soap. His chestnut queue was silky beneath her fingers, the back of his head warm against her palm. And as she held him, pressing her lips to his forehead while the tears streamed down her cheeks and resoaked his fine blue coat, his arm moved and his hand came up to push blindly against her breast.

A shock wave tore through her at his touch, but she had no time to ponder it, nor savor the relief that she hadn't killed him after all. "Make way there, make way!" someone shouted, and then she was seized by a pair of brawny hands, yanked to her feet, and flung rudely aside, landing hard on her shoulder just beyond the throng of people.

One of the seamen—the big one with bare arms showing through slit sleeves—had done it. And now he was bent over the captain, slapping his cheeks hard enough to dislodge a tooth and yelling in an Irish brogue so thick, she could barely understand him.

"Brrrrendan, wake up, me laddie, wake up! F'r God's sake, wake up!"

Mira sprang to her feet. She was a child of the docks, of the sea—and of Ephraim Ashton. Screaming at the top of her lungs, she pounced on the big seaman's unsuspecting back like a hell-born sprite, fists beating against his beefy shoulders, and feet kicking at his stout legs. His ear was conveniently close. "Damn you for a bloody idiot! How dare you toss me aside like a piece of garbage, you big, stinking oaf! Now, get away from him, you heap of bilge rot, before I—"

The seaman was turning, an incredulous grin zigzagging across the lower half of his broad face, his bear paw of a hand already removing his tricorn. "God Almighty . . ." he said slowly. " 'Tis—"

"—a *woman*, Liam!" another shrieked, jumping up and down and grabbing the big one's arm. "By the blood of Christ, a woman!"

She glared at them through a wall of hair. "Damn right I am! You think because I'm in breeches and shirt, you can haul off and hit me? Try it again and I'll send your nose right through the back of your bleedin' skull. Wretch! Brute! Bastard! Now, let me through, you blithering barrel of sea slime, so I can tend to the captain!"

The one named Liam threw back his head and split the air with laughter. The toothless seaman was still hopping up and down and shrieking like a madman, the little one was holding his stomach and looking very ill, and the others were all bending over Captain Merrick. But the townspeople were staring at her; not in disbelief, for they were well used to her ways, but in a manner that bespoke all too well of their sympathy for poor Ephraim at having to take such a wild one in tow.

Ephraim. And as Mira stood glaring up at the big, burly Irishman, she heard hoofbeats—and saw her father's horse and shay coming back up High Street.

She stared, eyes widening in horror, the blood draining from her face. And then she panicked and ducked back through the forest of hanging coattails, stockinged legs, and buckled shoes.

Brendan was awake. Painfully so. He may have been stunned, but he'd never lost consciousness. Being run down, being slapped, being screamed at, *and being hugged*—he'd felt it all. He sat leaning heavily against Keefe's shoulder, his elbows on his knees, his aching head cradled in his hands, his shoulder on fire, and his ears ringing like a blacksmith's anvil. People were yelling, screaming, crying all around him. A dog was barking. Dalby—that *was* Dalby's voice, wasn't it?—was wailing at the top of his lungs, and someone else was shouting. Quite loudly, in fact. He would've recognized that voice anywhere. Ephraim. And with sudden, awful clarity, he recalled the face of the young laddie who'd run him down and knew it had been no laddie a'tall.

Miss Mira Ashton.

And she'd hugged him.

Not just hugged him. *Kissed him.*

He panicked. Fighting off Liam, Keefe, and a crowd of concerned people he'd never seen before in his life, he lunged to his feet. Above the screening buffer of their heads, Ephraim's bellowing was much louder.

"What are you doing out here dressed in those clothes? I told you I don't ever want to see you in public in anything but skirts and gloves *again!*"

"I can't help it, Rigel got away from me! And you can stop screaming, I can hear you just fine!"

"I'll scream all I want!"

"Then go right ahead! Scream a little louder and maybe they'll hear you clear over in Salisbury!"

"They'll hear me clear down to Boston if I ever again catch you outside of the back pasture wearin' *breeches!* What the hell kind of daughter have I raised?! Whaddye think the client would say if *he* saw you like this?!"

"Why the hell don't you ask him? He's sitting right there!"

But Brendan wasn't sitting anywhere. He was off at a brisk, limping walk that was just shy of being a dead run. Away from the crowd. Away from the commotion. Away from the *Ashtons*.

There were plenty of other shipbuilders in the world.

"Merrick!" Ephraim roared.

Brendan stepped up his pace, moving so fast that Liam had to break into a run to catch up.

"*Merrick!*" Ephraim's voice would've cut through a mile of fog. "Merrick, for God's sake, don't go!"

Liam's voice followed Ephraim's down the street. "Brendan, wait! Ye can't go off, just like that!"

"Watch me." He quickened his step just as Liam caught up to him.

"What about th' ship?"

"Someone else can build it. I'm through with this town!"

"But Ashton's th' best!" Liam cried, struggling to keep up with Brendan's long strides. "Ye said so yerself!"

Brendan turned and whirled to face his friend. "I'm through with Ashton, too. And his daughter, *and* her cats, *and* her dog, *and her pudding!*"

"Pudding?"

"Stow it, Liam!"

"But I thought ye *wanted* t' come t' Newburyport t' get th' schooner built! I thought ye were determined that this Ashton lad would do it! Besides, his daughter's not th' one buildin' the ship!" Seeing his captain's set, angry face— Brendan? *Angry?*—Liam tried a different tack, for Brendan was off again, faster then before. "What are ye, afraid o' her? A lassie? Ye sit there cool as frost on a pumpkin when th' ship's gettin' blown out from under us, yet ye run from a mere lassie, an' a wee one at that!"

"I am *not* running!"

"Oh? Then what d'ye call it, eh?" Liam edged around

in front of him, trotting backward to keep ahead. "I *dare* ye t' go back there an' confront her!"

"Forget it, Liam! Dare me all you bloody want, but this is one dare I will *not* take you up on! If I stay in this godforsaken town any longer, I'll end up buried here! Already I've nearly been poisoned with pudding, clawed by a cat, and now, run down by a horse! No, thank you! We sail on tonight's tide!"

Crossing his great, meaty arms over his chest, Liam stopped. He planted himself like a well-rooted oak and with an infuriating grin, drawled, "In what, pray tell?"

Brendan pushed him aside. "A damned rowboat, for all I care! *Find* something!"

Behind him the verbal battle between father and daughter had exploded into full-blown war. Liam set his jaw and pounded after his captain, cursing him for his sudden rashness. Brendan had put too much time into choosing the right man to build his dream ship; he couldn't just let him walk way from it all! But God Almighty, for someone who'd just spent a night on an open ocean and five minutes asleep on a bed of hard dirt, he was being surprisingly difficult. No, not surprisingly, he corrected himself. Brendan was a scrappy lad, and when he set his mind on something, there was no stopping him. Not his best friend's reasoning. Not the combined might of those crazy Ashtons. Not even dreams of the schooner—which would be a dead dream if he allowed him to leave Newburyport.

Down High Street they stormed, Liam stepping up his efforts to make his captain see reason, Brendan stepping up both his pace and his determination to ignore him. Past the giant Beacon Oak they went. Past the stately homes of seafarers, shipbuilders, and shipmasters. Past the windmill, Frog Pond, the powder house where they made saltpeter to aid the war effort, the long rope walk, and a flock of sheep that stared at them curiously. Down Fish Street, through Market Square, and to the riverfront. The others had caught up to them now, breathless with exhaustion. Dalby took up the rear, clutching his chest.

Everyone but Brendan came to an abrupt halt when they reached the harbor. Lying in the pungent muck of low tide was *Annabel*—or what was left of her. Without slowing his stride, Brendan sloshed through mud and marsh grass alike, hauled himself up and over her side by way of a severed line, and strode across her tilted decks as though she heeled in nothing more than a strong wind.

Peace. Solitude. And escape. He stormed down the companionway, found the door to his cabin, and slammed it behind him. Here, at least, there were no crew members, no cats—and no Ashtons.

Supper that night was a grim and silent affair. It was a delicious meal of wild goose roasted on the clockjack till it was juicy and golden-brown; peaches stuffed with mincemeat; golden cornbread, and sweet, creamy butter. Once again, Abigail had outdone herself—and once again, it was all for naught.

The client was absent.

Mira sat staring into her fish chowder while Ephraim glowered at her from the head of the table like King Henry VIII. Outside, a steady rain fell, pattering gloomily against the house and streaming down the many-paned windows. Only Matt, with one of his adoring females beside him, seemed to have any appetite. The chair the esteemed Captain Merrick should've occupied was empty.

It was most unfortunate, too, for Mira had made the chowder—as well as dessert.

"Heard Merrick's heading back to Portsmouth tomorrow," Ephraim muttered between mouthfuls of cornbread, to no one in particular. "Just like that. All my dreams, my ideas, right out the window. *Just like that.*"

Mira said nothing and stared down into her chowder, wondering why it was such an odd grayish color and not creamy and white as it was when Abigail made it. So much for trying to make amends.

Matt took pity on her. "Oh, lay off, would you?" he said offhandedly. "There'll be other clients." Turning to the pouting Miss Lucy Preble beside him, he smeared a pile of thick strawberry jam on a piece of cornbread before placing it on her plate. Matt, kind soul that he was, was treating her with sickening gallantry, Mira thought, but she knew it would only be a matter of time before Matt realized this woman was as selfish and unpleasant as the rest of them, and went on to try the next. As if to confirm her thoughts, Mira looked up and found the woman's haughty stare raking her with unconcealed disdain.

Mira straightened in her chair and smoothed the skirts of her homespun gown over her knees. What right did Her Bloody Highness have to look so damned lofty?! Did she think that just because she'd powdered her hair and piled it two feet above her head, garbed herself in fine silks and velvet, and was attached to the arm of Newburyport's most eligible bachelor, she could look down on someone else? Raising her chin, Mira shoved her hair behind her ear and returned the stare with a defiant one of her own. Miss Lucy Preble could be as lofty as she damn well pleased, but she'd never lifted one of those white fingers in the name of Liberty, never dirtied them making saltpeter down in the powder house, never pricked them sewing uniforms for the Continental army, nor, heaven forbid, used them to defend the bloodstained decks of a privateer!

But then, she'd never frightened off an important client, nor run a person down on a horse, and there was no way in hell she'd be caught dead in breeches. Tears of self-disgust burned behind Mira's eyes and she looked down at her cold, gray chowder to hide them. Someone as perfect as Miss Lucy Preble didn't *do* those things. Someone like Miss Preble didn't *bring* disgrace upon her family name.

"Oh, there'll be other clients, all right," Ephraim growled, glaring at his uncharacteristically silent daughter from beneath his bushy white brows. Just because she was all dolled up in her pretty gown and petticoats didn't change the fact that he'd raised a damned hoyden. "But none like Merrick."

"I thought you hated him. After all, he *was* an Englishman," Matt drawled with biting sarcasm.

"Irishman," Ephraim snapped, watching his son pour a glass of raspberry shrub for Miss Preble, who folded her hands primly in her lap and looked at the crystal chandelier as though thoroughly bored with the conversation. "Besides, it don't matter where he was born an' raised. He was privateerin' fer our side, and that's all that counts!" Ephraim stared at his precious Willard clock for a long moment, then slammed his spoon down so hard that flecks of chowder leapt from his bowl and spattered his white stock. "Cripes, did ye see those figures, those calculations? That man knew his stuff, let me tell ye! He ain't just a naval architect, he's a blasted engineer! That schooner he wanted me to build would've been the finest ship to ever slide down our ways. By God, Tracy, Greenleaf, Cross, and even *Hackett* would've all been drooling with envy, 'cause there ain't no way in hell any of 'em could've ever dreamed up something like that! Not even *Hancock* would've compared, and you know what the damned Brits said about her when Greenleaf and Cross turned her out back in seventy-seven! Finest and fastest frigate in the world! But she weren't nothin' compared to what that schooner would've been! And now—'' picking up his fork, he stabbed a peach and shoved it into his mouth ''—Merrick'll go and give his business to someone else. And someone else'll get the glory for building that ship, not me!''

Lucy appeared unfazed by Ephraim's tirade, but then, everyone in Newburyport was well used to his ways. Lucy, in fact, used Ephraim's nature to her advantage. She eyed Mira with cool disdain and said airily, "From what *I've* heard, that man will be Tracy."

"What?!" Ephraim's fork came down so hard, his plate cracked.

She shrugged her white shoulders and swayed slightly toward Matt, who was beginning to look disgusted with her snide behavior. "Oh, yes. Nathaniel tells Papa that Merrick's lieutenant came to him just this evening with a proposal."

"Of all the goddamned luck!" Ephraim's fist crashed down on the table, rattling china, upsetting the chowder bowls, and making crumbs of cornbread jump like fleas on a cat. "This is the first I've heard of this!"

"Oh, and I'm sure it won't be the last, Captain Ashton,'' Lucy said sweetly, heedless of Matt's annoyance with her as she glanced triumphantly at Mira from beneath her sooty lashes. "Why, it's all over town."

Mira shoved her hands between her clamped knees before she could give in to the urge to haul off and give Miss

Lucy Preble her due. *Act like a lady,* she told herself. *Just this once.* She smoothed her skirts—native *homespun* skirts, not that frippery Lucy was wearing!—and turned to face her father, determined, for once, to please him. Out of the corner of her eye she saw Lucy's smug smile. Ignoring it, she said dutifully, "I am sorry, Father."

"Sorry?! You think being sorry's gonna bring Merrick back?"

"I said, I'm sorry."

"Sorry! Well, ye sure weren't sorry after you ran him down in the street! Why didn't you think of saying 'sorry' then, huh? Cripes, maybe if you had, he'd be sitting there in that cussed chair and I'd have an agreement right here—" he raised his hand and shook an angry fist "—to built that schooner! But no! Thanks to you and yer damned shenanigans, Tracy's gonna do it! Why can't ye be a daughter I can be proud of?! Why can't you act like a lady for once instead of a damned brat—"

"I said I'm sorry!" she cried, fighting tears and desperately trying to avoid Lucy's eye.

"—and why can't you be like Matt?! Thank God I have one offspring I can be proud of!"

Matt choked on his cornbread, and Mira stood up so fast, her chair nearly went over backward. Tears blurred her vision and she had to bite down hard on her lower lip to keep from either losing her temper or crying in front of the other woman. "I—" She swallowed, gulping, "I—"

"Father, I suggest you take this discussion into the library," Matt said firmly.

Ephraim ignored him and fixed arctic eyes on his daughter. "As of tomorrow, you will start conducting yerself in a fitting manner." His tone was chilling, final, and one that Mira had never heard him use before. "I figger that since I can't handle ye, I'll let someone else give it a try. One year from now—" he shoved his plate aside and wagged a craggy finger in her face "—ye'll be a married woman. *One year.* You understand me, Mira?"

"M-married?!"

"That's right, married! And tomorrow ye can start looking for a victim. I don't give a damn who ye pick out, but pick out someone ye will." His words fell over her like an avalanche, cold, snowy, suffocating. Lucy was staring, speechless, and even Matt was openmouthed with horror. "Six months from now ye'll come to me and tell me who ye've selected. If ye haven't come up with anyone, I'm sellin' one of those cussed hosses. At eight months, ye'll report to me again. No name, and another one's goin'. And if, after ten months, ye still haven't found someone to put up with you, it'll be the last of em!"

"*Father!*"

"You heard me! If ye wanna keep those hosses, then find a husband, dammit!"

"Father, you *can't!*"

"I can and I will. And furthermore—" he tore his napkin from his throat and flung it to the table "—if I *ever* catch you sneakin' off in Matt's brig again, with or without his consent, I swear to God I'll pack ye off to someone of *my* choosing so damned fast, you won't know what hit ye!"

She stared at him, too shocked to cry, too shocked to speak, too shocked to do anything but reel away as though he'd struck her. Lucy hid a malicious smile, and dimly Mira saw her brother shove his plate aside and gain his feet, his spectacles fogging up and his face going crimson with fury.

"Blast you, that's unfair and you know it!"

"Sit down, Matthew."

"Like hell I will! You can't sell her horses like that!"

"I said sit down, dammit!"

"I'll sit when I've a mind to, but I *won't* sit and watch you dish out this sort of abuse and turn a blind eye to it! You think you can lord it over everyone in this house like a bloody dictator? You think you can make everyone's lives revolve around your wants and desires?"

"My wants and desires include running a business, and this is the third client this month I've lost because of yer sister's antics!"

"She said she's sorry; what the hell else to you want her to say?!"

"Goddammit, Matthew, don't you take that tone of voice with me!"

"I'll take any goddamned voice I feel like taking, you cantankerous old goat!"

"Cantankerous old goat?! Who you calling a cantankerous old goat. . . . ?"

On wooden feet, Mira pushed her chair in, turned away, and walked quietly across the room, her head high and diamonds of tears poised on her lashes. She saw Lucy reach out to calm Matt, but her brother merely tore away in disgust. Mira felt no triumph. Where her heart had been, there was nothing but a vast, empty hole. She waited for Father to apologize, to call her back, but he was too busy yelling at Matt to notice her.

As Mira left the room, her gaze fell upon the beautiful Delft punch bowl that commemorated the launching of the ship *Temper*. There would be no such memento to honor Captain Merrick's fine schooner.

The fine schooner that Tracy would build.

Putting her hand over her mouth to muffle her sobs, Mira fled up the stairs.

Chapter 7

The full moon frolicked in its night sky playground, riding high above Newburyport Harbor and playing chase with lofty clouds that scudded across the vast and purple heavens on their way toward the sea. Occasionally it showed its face, filling the sky with a pale incandescence; but mostly it hid behind silver-edged clouds and rained moonbeams down in perfect pyramids of mystical light. On this quiet night the river flowed like pale silk beneath it, and the shrouds and masts of anchored ships climbed skyward as though paying homage. Booms and yards were bathed in silver, sails glowed with its heavenly light, and a gentle wind whispered over all, stirring the

marsh grass and filling the night with the rhythmic creak
and ease of settling timbers and swaying rigging. The tang
of the sea lay thick and moist and heavy in the air, ripe
with salt and marshlands and the promise of fresher winds
on the morrow.

Just beyond the tide-swell, the little sloop *Annabel*
rested. The moon had found her, too, making pewter of
her battered decks, throwing shadows across her forecastle, softening the ragged edges of spars and torn planking,
and dragging ghostly fingers of light along the splintered
boom of her mainsail. To all appearances she was deserted, but if one was still up at this late hour and chanced
to look at her closely, he'd see the pale yellow glow of a
lantern in and beneath her shattered stern windows, glim-
mering and dancing upon the river's shimmering surface
as it rolled past on its way to the sea.

By the light of a tired candle, now spitting tallow and
sending up a finger of smoke to tickle the blackened deck
beams above his head, her master worked. But it was past
the candle's bedtime as well as his, and now it shivered,
faltered, flared once more, and started to die. Almost me-
chanically Brendan put his pencil down, rubbed his eyes,
and digging through his splintered sea chest until he found
another, lit the wick from the dying remains of the first and
stuck it in the lantern.

The temptation to seek his bed was almost overwhelming, but the drawing had to be finished first. Why he was
even taking the trouble to do so was beyond him. After
his foolishly rash behavior this afternoon, he'd have to
swallow his pride and go crawling back to Ephraim in the
morn, hoping to God he didn't get run down by a horse,
carriage, or pack of cats along the way. What an idiot he'd
been for letting his humiliation over the accident dictate
his behavior; he should've just got up, brushed away the
dust, and laughed the whole thing off. At any other time
he probably would have. But oh, with all those townspeople standing around gaping at him, and Miss Mira herself . . .

Miss Mira.

He bent his forehead into his hands and rubbed his
temples. How differently things might've turned out if

Crichton hadn't stumbled upon *Annabel* twelve leagues east of Cape Ann. Or if his arrival at Ashton's had been dignified, instead of one he didn't even remember. Fine way to make an impression on a man—and his daughter. *His daughter.* Groaning, Brendan went to the gaping stern and leaned his hot brow against the cool, misty sill of the shattered windows. Why should that impish little hoyden even matter? He was a seafarer, a privateer, with barely enough time for himself, let alone a lassie. And Mira Ashton . . . well, she sure didn't fit any definition of "lassie" he'd ever used. Lassies were supposed to be delicate, charming, wee confections who dressed in ribbons, lace, and gowns. They were supposed to ride sidesaddle and spend their time pursuing genteel things like sewing and reading and spinning. They were not supposed to wear trousers and coats that stank of horses, with cats draped like scarves around their necks. They were not supposed to curse like seasoned tars in a king's ship. And they were not supposed to ride wild stallions and run innocent people down in the street. . . .

Liam's words came back to taunt him. *What are ye, afraid o' her? Runnin' from a mere lassie, an' a wee one at that?*

Oh, he was running all right. After Julia's bitter betrayal, the last thing he needed was another entanglement with a bonnie lass—the last thing he wanted was some wee *cailleach* trying to keep him off the sea and away from the ships he loved. Julia, who'd found him washed up in Boston Harbor's rime of seaweed after Crichton's pistol ball had nearly done him in, hadn't been willing to share him with the sea, nor the ships he'd dreamed of designing for his newly adopted country after word reached him that His Majesty's Navy believed him dead and a traitor besides—thanks to testimony by Crichton and his officers that Brendan had been too sick, and later, too disgusted, to dispute. Why would Miss Mira Ashton be any different from his beloved Julia? No, better to guard his heart well, better to give his love to his ships—especially this one, a sweet and sultry beauty whose sharp lines and lithe sleekness already had his heart a-racing just by looking at her nearly finished drafts.

But despite his resolution to put her from his mind, Miss Mira Ashton was like a burr in his clothing. She bothered him, and had done so from the moment he'd found she was a lassie, and a maddeningly pretty one at that. She made him feel hot and cold. She made him think of stolen kisses and raging storms. And worst of all, she'd made him lose his temper and abandon his good sense. Since when had he been so quick to anger? Self-control was a trait that came naturally to him—but where Mira Ashton was concerned, it was one that didn't exist.

Faith. He thought of her strawberry-sweet lips against his brow, her hot, salty tears slipping into his mouth, her thick and silken hair tangling in his eyelashes. His manhood stirred, thrusting painfully against the taut fabric of his breeches, and suddenly the cabin was hot and stuffy and airless. Groaning, he leaned far out the window, breathing deeply of the night air as moisture beaded on his brow. But he could still remember her tears wetting his scalp and running through his hair, the delicious warmth of her breasts beneath his cheek, the scent of roses in her glossy hair, and fresh soap beneath her grubby clothes. . . .

She had a woman's warmth, a woman's heart.

She was a lassie, all right; no doubt about that.

In fact, she was the embodiment of all that a lassie was supposed to be—and all that a lassie was not.

He couldn't afford to feel again that wild yearning for a woman that would just leave him cold and shaken in the end. *That's what you're running from, isn't it?* And that's just how he'd end up if he stayed in that house another moment. Already he felt himself tightening with desire when he thought of her. Already he'd spent far too much time thinking of her when he ought to be working on the drafts. Already she was another Julia, stealing his heart and cleverly manipulating him into a position where he'd have to choose between her and his ship. . . . Well, this time it wouldn't happen. He wouldn't *give* his heart to any lady but one made of sails and wood and wind. They were safer, sweeter, and ever faithful.

But as he turned and wearily settled into his chair once more, he thought again of Liam's words and knew his longtime friend was right. He *was* afraid of her. Not in the physical sense, but in one that had to do with the heart; of feeling mortal and vulnerable, of being hurt again and betrayed, and of thinking too much about something that might steer him off course—a course that lay unfinished before him, beside a gold-laced tricorn, on a sheet of vellum . . . and in his heart.

The schooner.

He picked up his pencil once again, fatigue blurring the drawing's crisp lines. At least the task hadn't been as hard as he'd secretly feared it might be, and now he gazed at the drafts in relief and a sort of humble pride that brought a grin to his mouth and drew lines at the corners of his honey-colored eyes. A side view, a turned-turtle view, a fore and an aft view of the hull. The dimensions noted carefully in the corner of the paper; beam molded and beam extreme, depth in hold and craft. Particulars, of mast height and spar length, of cannon placement and rigging details. His grin widened. Old Ephraim had doubted his identity, eh? Well, *these* drafts would prove who he was far better than a dried-out ball of useless pulp!

He sobered. Maybe facing the blustery old shipbuilder tomorrow with his head held high wouldn't be so difficult after all, but face him he would, no matter how hard it was to swallow the pride that Liam insisted came from his stiff and proper "English side." Well, damn his English side! Always getting him into trouble and leaving it to his Irish side's luck to bail him out!

But could even his Irish side rescue him from Miss Mira Ashton?

Faith!

A rap on the door startled him and he jerked up, his gaze moving to the chipped sandglass. Two bells of the midwatch, though *Annabel*'s was now somewhere beneath the inky surface of the Merrimack River. In landsman's terms, one o'clock in the morning, almost twelve hours exactly since his fateful departure from Ashton's house—

The rap came again, desperate this time. "For heaven's sake, *foighne ort!*" he called, tossing his pencil aside and rubbing his tired eyes. He groaned. It was Dalby, no doubt, coming to complain about a fever, chest pains, indigestion, or whatever else he imagined he was dying from this time. Rising carefully to avoid hitting his head on the deck beams, Brendan made his way, stooping, across the steeply tilted deck and flung open the door. "Faith, Dalby, it's one o'clock in the morn . . ."

He trailed off. It wasn't Dalby O'Hara standing there with a hand held to his stomach, but Mira Ashton with a hand held to her delightfully lovely bosom. Obviously the way he'd jerked the door open had caught her by surprise—but it was nothing compared to the surprise *he* felt at seeing her standing there.

"D'ar m'anam," he murmured, so startled that he unconsciously reverted to Irish.

She gave him a queer look. "I-I'm sorry to disturb you, Captain Merrick. . . ."

"I'll bet you are." He forced a grin and tore his gaze from the creamy flesh and shadowed valley tantalizingly displayed above the lace of her décolletage. Nervous sweat broke out on his brow, his temple, and ran down the trail of his spine. "How the devil did you get by my watch?"

She fidgeted, picking at her sleeve as though her pretty homespun gown was not something she was accustomed to wearing. In all probability, it was not. "I . . . didn't. Your lieutenant stopped me as I boarded, but I told him my father was building a ship for you, so he let me through."

And then she brushed past him, barging into the cabin with almost as much force as the cannonball that had destroyed it. Seating herself in the one still-standing chair, she caught a handful of that thick, board-straight hair and began twisting it between her fingers and around her little fist, back and forth and up and around in a way that caught the light from the candle and did weird things to his heart and the temperature of his skin. His loins tightened and he swallowed hard, making himself look away. Already he was dead and damned for thinking how that glossy mane would feel in his own hands, how it would look spread in glorious disarray over a white pillow. . . .

Finally she flung it over her shoulder, sending a rose-scented breeze his way. A long moment went by while he struggled to gain control of himself, remembering the way she'd looked at his scarred chest with absolutely no maidenly modesty in that celery green gaze of hers, indeed, nothing but frank boldness that disturbed him as much now as it had when he'd introduced himself to her and her blustery sire in the Ashtons' front hall. "Miss Ashton." She glanced up, one green eye disappearing behind a drape of hair that conveniently tumbled down over her pixie face at that very moment. "I don't know if you're aware of the time or not—somehow, I should think that you *are,* given the fact that your household does not lack for timepieces—but don't you think it's rather late to be calling on a gentleman? And if, by some miracle of ignorance, you're *not* aware of the time, then certainly you're aware of the impropriety of visiting me in the dead of night, and all by yourself, at that. I would urge you to consider your reputation."

"My reputation?" That seemed to amuse her, but her smile was a fleeting one that went as quickly as it came. She stopped playing with her hair and caught both hands behind her back to keep them still, the motion tightening her bodice across her full breasts until Brendan, wiping his brow, had to look away once more. He poured himself a glass of water and gulped it down before finally trusting himself to look at her once again. Her lower lip was trembling. Her glossy mane swept down to cover her freckle-spattered face once again, thickening and swelling until nothing but her pert little nose and two green eyes peeped through. The fact that those eyes were now filling with moisture made short work of Brendan's hastily erected defenses.

She hugged me, he thought. *Good God, she hugged me. What would it be like to kiss her?* He gulped and reached for more water. *Really* kiss her?

He swung away before she could see the heat in his cheeks.

"I . . ." She took a deep breath and slowly let it out, the tantalizing whisper of fabric sliding up and down her creamy skin making his mouth go dry. "—I'm fully aware of the hour. But it was the only time I could sneak out. You see, Father has his nightcap at eleven-thirty, and goes to bed at eleven forty-five. He stays up and reads from the

New Testament until twelve-thirty. Right now he's up to Romans, Chapter Two, I believe. At exactly twelve thirty-three he puts out his candle—''

"Miss Ashton—''

And at twelve forty-five he falls asleep, which I know because I can hear him snoring—''

"Miss Ashton!''

"And at four-thirty he gets up to use the priv—''

"Miss Ashton, I really don't care! Now, *please!*''

She got up and swayed across the little cabin, her petticoat hem sweeping up dust and glass and wood splinters, her heels clicking on splintered oak, her finger trailing across his desk and leaving a wavery line through the damage dust left by Crichton's guns. He wished she didn't look as if she was about to cry, but she did. He wished he could take his eyes off her, but he couldn't. He wished she wasn't so sweet and pretty, but she was. He wished—oh, faith, he didn't know what he wished anymore. . . .

And then she spotted the drafts.

He lunged forward, too late. "Don't—''

But she had them in her hands, staring at them with her delicate little jaw hanging open and her thick hair tumbling down over one shoulder and brushing the vellum. Cringing, Brendan held his breath—but she didn't tear them up, didn't fling them out the window. She blinked. Once. Twice. And then she looked up, he looked down, and their eyes met somewhere in the middle.

Shock waves sizzled between them like lightning through storm clouds. Brendan's throat went dry, Mira's cheeks went pink, but she didn't turn away, merely staring at him for a long, searching moment while her eyes filled with that strange sort of awe that always came over those who saw the drafts and understood. That admiration never failed to make Brendan feel uncomfortable and self-conscious and red-facedly modest. Finally she looked back down at them, giving him an opportunity to study the dark spill of her absurdly thick hair, the spray of freckles across her cheeks, the cherry lushness of her softly parted lips, the swell of her bosom and the dark valley that cleaved it. And then she looked up once again—and caught him staring.

She was too stunned by the magnificence of the drafts to notice—thank God—his high color, the bead of sweat rolling down his temple. *"You* drew this?" she whispered. *"Designed* it?"

He glanced away, looking at his broken desk, the moonlit river outside, the glass-strewn floor—anywhere but into those translucent green eyes. He'd always found it difficult to accept praise without feeling self-conscious and embarrassed. Hearing it from this lovely little hoyden whose very presence had forced him to move behind his desk to hide the evidence of his arousal from her was about to become his undoing. He yanked his coat down over his loins, rushed to the table, and grabbed the pitcher, nearly knocking it over in his haste. "Would you care for a glass of water, Miss *Moyrrra?"*

She ignored his question. *"Did* you?" she insisted, gazing at his elegant artist's hands with their fine and graceful fingers. The nails were short and clean, the knuckles well shaped; auburn hair covered the back of those hands, thickening a bit at the wrists before disappearing beneath the frothy lace of his shirt sleeves. She stared until he hid had hands behind his back, hoping the act looked natural.

"You did, didn't you?"

He gave a little shrug, still looking away as his face suffused with color.

"Captain Merrick, I . . . I don't know what to say."

Neither did he. Shrugging once more, he picked up his water glass and went to the window, where he proceeded to pick shards of glass out of the broken sill with quick, nervous motions. "My sister was the better artist."

"Was?"

"Was." There was pain in his eyes, and his tone did not invite questioning. Obviously something had happened to his sister that he didn't want to discuss. Mira stared at him for a moment longer, while the lantern's glow burnished his rich chestnut hair and threw shadows beneath the high spheres and ridges of his cheekbones, along the cords of his neck, and between his elegant, Britishly rigid shoulders. He looked up and caught her staring. His handsome face went redder yet, and he began to fidget like a six-year-old at an all-day sermon.

"Do you always have such a hard time handling compliments, Captain Merrick?"

He turned and gave a fleeting grin. "Do you always have such a hard time stating your purpose in visiting gentlemen in the wee hours of the morn?"

"I don't usually visit gentlemen in the wee hours of the morn. But if I did, I should think my purpose would be quite clear."

He almost choked on his water. "Then what is your purpose now, Miss Mira?"

She gave one of her cat-smiles. "To try to get your business back from Tracy."

"Tracy?" He set the glass down and looked at her, puzzled. "Who's Tracy?"

"Patrick and Nathaniel Tracy? The shipbuilders?"

"Sorry, I don't know them."

"Well, *I* heard you're giving them your business!"

"Well, you heard wrong."

"Then you're going to place it with Father?"

"I didn't say that either," he said, although that was precisely his intent. He'd play her along for a wee bit and see what she was up to. As for this Tracy thing, it was no doubt a rumor fabricated by Liam and designed to come back and haunt him.

That haunt stood before him now, still clutching the drafts as though unable to let them go. "But you *have* to!"

"And why's that, Miss *Moyrrra?*"

"If you don't, Father's going to be furious!"

"So? It seems to me that he spends the better part of his life in that state. He should find it quite comfortable by now."

"But you don't understand!"

"Understand what?"

She stood there looking very small and helpless—Mira Ashton, *helpless?!*—with the dress clinging to her sweet curves, nipping a waist that needed no nipping and showing a full and lovely bosom that invited his stare, held it, and wouldn't let it go. After seeing her garbed in the loose shirt and trousers, the dress, which would've looked quite benign on anyone else, enhanced her fine figure almost blatantly.

He gulped his water and wondered if steam was rising from his pores.

She pushed the thick tumble of hair out of her eyes and hooked it behind one ear, where it promptly came loose and fell in her face once more. Brendan swallowed hard. It was all he could do not to reach out and smooth that rich mane back himself.

"Understand why I came here," she said softly, finally putting the drafts down. She looked him straight in the eye and said, "I came here to bargain with you."

He swallowed the wrong way and put his glass down, coughing. "Bargain?" Recovering, he raised an elegant russet brow. "And just what might a young lass like you have to *bargain* with?"

The instant the words were out of his mouth, he regretted them. *Faith and troth, Brendan, if she slaps you, you deserve it!* Again, he felt hot color suffusing his face. But incredulously, she merely looked at him in confusion. Either Miss Mira Ashton was more innocent than he'd believed, or his question had caught her off guard.

"Captain Merrick," she said slowly, meeting his eyes with a steadiness that unnerved him, "I didn't come here to trade barbs with you, to suffer your thinly veiled lust, nor to offer you charms that I'm . . . not willing to give. I came here merely to ask you a question."

Thinly veiled lust? Is that what she thought he harbored? Good God! he thought, willing his cheeks not to burn. Jauntily, to cover his embarrassment, he said, "Well then, get on with this question, lassie! I don't have all night."

She plucked at her sleeve again, and the frothy lace of her chemise just beneath. "You see, Father rises at exactly five forty-five—"

"Miss Ashton . . ."

"And since it's now fifteen minutes past one, and I don't have much time—"

"The *question,* Miss Ashton!"

"Yes, yes, of course, the question," she said hastily, and he saw her gaze dart back to the sheet of vellum on the table. But Mira was no longer thinking of the drafts. She was thinking of this handsome, witty man before her, and realizing the hour *was* quite late. Again, she took a deep breath, wishing she were anywhere but here in this tiny cabin with Captain Merrick so unnervingly close. The air felt hot; it was hard to breathe, hard to think. So much for trying to act calm and cool and . . . ladylike.

And now the captain was drumming those long, tapered fingers against the table, impatience—or damn him, amusement?!—beginning to dance in his eyes. They were light, honey-colored eyes that knew how to caress a woman without stripping her, to flatter her without insulting her. Those eyes were on her now; she felt her cheeks heating up and going pink, not out of maidenly embarrassment but in direct response to the assessing admiration and invitation in their laughing Irish depths. . . .

What would it be like to let him touch her? Hold her? Kiss—

"I'm waiting, Miss *Moyrrra.*"

Her head jerked up. He had a quirky mouth, always twitching in a ready grin, a smile as weightless as a kite on a windy day, and a boyishly cleft jaw that, coupled with his rich chestnut locks, gave him a devilish look that set her pulse to pounding. Taking a deep breath, Mira summoned her courage and blurted, "What would it take to get you to give your business back to my father?"

"What would it *take?*"

"Aye, *take.*"

He stared at her and she stared back, her skin growing damp beneath her gown, her heart racing, and moisture slicking her palms. His face was quite mobile; she could see his thoughts moving across it like wind over the ocean's surface. Disbelief, interest, and humor. Was there anything the man didn't find amusing?!

Picking up a quadrant from his desk, he said, "And why are you so desperate for my business, Miss Ashton?" There, that damned quirky grin again! The effect was immediate, and devastating. She'd been a blind idiot to think that Captain Merrick was *stuffy!* "Do mishaps such as those that have befallen me since I've made your family's acquaintance happen to *all* of your potential clients? Is that why you've come a-begging, lassie?'' The grin deep-ened. ''Business a bit slow lately?''

She colored, for his teasing speculation had found the truth. ''No. Well . . . some of them, I guess. But no one's been *really* hurt. Just little things . . .''

''Little things?''

''Aye. Like Caesar spilling the gravy in Mr. Whigham's lap—''

''Caesar? Mr. Whigham?''

''Caesar's a cat that I rescued. Rescue Effort Number Twenty-Nine, I think. Mr. Whigham was a client. Or, would've been, anyway, if Caesar hadn't jumped up on the supper table and spilled the gravy all down the front of his breeches.''

''Hmm. An interesting tale. And Caesar? What was his fate that he needed your, er, rescuing?''

''Caesar's a 'she.' She was ship's cat on Captain Green-leaf's brig when I found one of his gunners abusing her.''

''Am I correct in assuming that this gunner met with a fate that was far less, er, *pleasant* than, uh, Caesar's?''

Mira matched his grin, her face innocently impish. ''Oh, yes. I caught up to him that night and blackened his eye. Father was furious.''

''For blackening his eye?''

''No, for bringing the cat home. She was . . . preg-nant.''

''Oh.''

''And he was even angrier when she had her kittens.''

She looked very serious, and Brendan tugged at his mouth to hide his amusement. ''And why was that, Miss Ashton? Doesn't he like kittens?''

''Oh, he likes them, all right. He just doesn't like seeing them born on the dining room table. You see, we were entertaining a client that night. . . .''

''Who no doubt decided to take his business to this Tracy fellow instead?''

She shrugged. ''Something like that.''

''I see. Well, Miss Ashton, as you've come here without cat, dog, or horse, I assume that I'm safe for the time being. Therefore, your question, please? Or, rather, your bargain.''

She swallowed hard. The drafts lay atop the table, and she picked them up, her heartbeat quickening as she took in the schooner's rapine hull, the sharp rake of her masts, and her lean, predatory lines, once more. Matt hadn't been joking when he'd predicted this ship would see the Ashton yards out of their slump. He hadn't been talking through his hat when he predicted she'd be the pride of Newburyport. Hell, she'd not only be the pride of Newburyport, *she'd be the pride of Massachusetts*.

Wild despair filled her. She *had* to get Captain Merrick's business back, *had to!*

"Captain Merrick, I'm sure you realize that your schooner's design and, uh, differences from what is considered *standard* will make her quite costly to build." *If Father caught her at this, he'd be furious!* "According to these plans, you want her hull sheathed in copper. Where do you think we're going to find copper with a war going on? You want tops'ls and t'gallants, and *studding sails*, too. On a schooner? I've never seen the like! And you want hatches that face aft instead of forward, differences in rigging, and all sorts of unconventional modifications to deck features, let alone deviations from a standard hull shape—" she pointed toward the sleek bows "—like this forward-raked stern, for instance. These things cost money, you know!"

He was at the window again, sipping his water and staring off into the silvery, moonlit night. "Drier," he said simply.

"What?"

"Facing the hatches aft, instead of forward. 'Twill keep her much drier belowdecks. Never could see the sense of having them open toward the fore."

"Captain, with studding sails on her, I really don't think you'll have to worry about how *dry* she'll be. I guarantee that'll be the last thing you'll be thinking about when a gust of wind hits her and knocks her over!"

He turned then and smiled, patiently, the way he might've done with an uncomprehending child. "Miss Ashton," he said, coming forward and standing so close, she could feel the heat of his body and smell the pleasant aroma of his shaving soap. Gently he took the drafts from her suddenly limp hand, accidentally brushing her fingers; shivers coursed through her like heat lightning on a summer night. He was so tall, he blocked the lantern's glow, so handsome, she couldn't take her eyes off him. Her heart was jumping madly, her palms unexplainably moist, and now her mouth was going dry as she stared at his fine hand, its long fingers now tracing, no, *caressing,* the curve of the pencil-drawn hull. Gooseflesh rose on her arms as she thought of what those hands would feel like touching her, of how it would be to have him looking at *her* with such fond admiration as he did those drafts. She was actually breathing so loudly, she was afraid he might guess her thoughts. And then he spoke, his voice soft, mellifluous, and so close to her ear, she could feel it stirring the damp wisps of hair that curled against her temple. She squeezed her eyes shut and began to shake. "Kindly take a second look at the depth of her draft, Miss Mira. Do you honestly think she'll not handle a fine press of sail? A wet boat she may be, but a stable one."

"I don't question your designing abilities," she whispered, moving away from him in hopes of calming her racing heart.

"Oh? Then do you question my sailing ones?"

"Captain Merrick, are you going to listen to me or not?"

"Miss Ashton, are you going to offer me something I can use or not?"

"Fine!" Her chin came up and she stormed away, yanking out a chair and throwing herself into it with eyes flashing. Wryly he noticed that she didn't perch birdlike on the chair's edge as a lady would've done; but then, he knew enough about this wee sprite, this *bean sí,* to know that despite her clothes and this new polish to her speech, she still had the manners—and the temper—of a dockside brawler. He pitied the man who'd been abusing the cat. And as for playing the lady, perhaps if she had folded her hands in her lap, sat her sweet little rump on the edge of the chair, and kept her mouth shut, she might've carried it off. But no. She was leaning back, one arm thrown over the top rung, winding that thick hair around her wrist again; and it was only as she raised her leg as though intending to put her foot atop the table that she caught his eye and seemed to remember herself. Coughing discreetly to hide his amusement, Brendan watched her grin somewhat sheepishly and put that tiny foot back down on the deck where it belonged.

"I'll be honest with you, Captain Merrick. I *have* nothing to bargain with, really. Oh, I have cats, but you don't strike me as a man who's terribly fond of them, and besides, they don't like you either. I can offer you breeding rights to a fine Arabian stallion—" she ignored his shocked stare "—but I have the feeling you don't care for horses very much, and after today, I probably can't blame you. And I have half ownership of the brig *Proud Mistress*— but what good would she be to you? She's a fine ship, seakind and sturdy, but beside her, your schooner would look like . . . like a kestrel beside a turkey vulture."

"Kestrel," he said softly, his eyes thoughtful.

"Huh?"

"Oh, nothing. Do go on."

"So I guess what I'm trying to say is that you simply *have* to give your business to Father." She became desperate when he looked away in amusement. "Captain Merrick, please! I know you've had a . . . hard day, but you must understand how a shipbuilder like my father would sell his soul to build a vessel like your schooner! I'm prepared to beat any quotation that Tracy, Cross, Greenleaf, or even *Hackett* offers you! *Any!*

She didn't have that authority, but he didn't have to know that. Right now it was more important for him to see the light. She could make Father see it later.

"Any?"

"Yes! Oh, you could take those drafts to another, but he'll build you a ship and nothing more! But take them to Father and he'll make them *breathe!*"

"And what will you give me if I do so, Miss Ashton?"

"Give you?"

Brendan held the quadrant up to the lantern, squinting as though taking a measurement. "Aye, give me. I do believe you came here with a proposal? A *bargain,* as you called it."

"I just told you, I could lower the price!"

"Uh-huh," he said, acting unimpressed.

"Or we could better the delivery date, beat whatever Tracy or anyone else offers you. . . ."

The captain yawned, picked up the sandglass, and flipped it over.

"There *might* be some way to get that copper for you. I don't know how just yet, but I'm sure I could think of something. . . ."

Brendan sighed and tossed the quadrant to the desk. "I think it's past my bedtime," he said.

"But, Captain Merrick—"

"Miss Ashton, those offers are all well and good, but they're not enough to convince me that I should give my business to your father."

"Then what *would* convince you?"

He grinned, and she saw his admiring gaze drop to her bosom, slowly moving up her throat, lingering on her mouth, finally meeting her eyes. The roguish charm in that grin did funny things to her heart; the heat in his eyes made her blood turn. She hugged her arms to herself against the strange, prickly feelings and tried to still her involuntary trembling, but it did little good.

In fact, it did no good at all.

He came forward and brushed her cheek with the back of his hand.

She shivered violently.

"A kiss, from a pretty lass—" he grinned and moved closer, his fingers now trailing down her neck and leaving gooseflesh in their wake "—may be all the convincing I need, Miss *Moyrrra*. . . ."

Mira was no coward, and she rose to the challenge. Surely his business, and the schooner itself, were worth the price of a mere kiss. Feeling quite sure of herself, she boldly met his gaze. He didn't drive such a hard bargain after all.

"Well then, I . . . suppose that's fair."

"More than fair," he agreed, his fingers now burning a path over her collarbone.

"So . . ." It was getting hard to breathe, let alone speak. "So—am I supposed to kiss you, or you to kiss me?"

"Whatever you like, lassie," he murmured, his fingers now dipping into the valley between her breasts. "I'm sure you've done this enough times that you'd be quite comfortable either way."

He was dead wrong on *that* account, and had obviously drawn his assumption from the fact that she *had* come here at such an ungodly hour, that she was not intimidated by his proposal, and that she hadn't protested when he'd touched her. The truth was, she couldn't move, couldn't protest—and had never been kissed by a man before in her life.

He didn't have to know that, though. Besides, she'd seen Matt with his lady friends enough times to figure she was an expert on the subject of kissing. She'd just do as she'd seen them do to Matt. Feeling saucy and bolder still, Mira stepped forward, hiding her nervousness behind a sly smile and the very recklessness of her action. She reached out, touched the captain's shoulder, and let her fingers trail down his arm. He tensed, and his breathing quickened. His eyes went a shade darker, a degree warmer. Confident now, Mira slid her hands up his shoulders and pressed herself against his chest.

"So, Miss *Moyrrra,* I see you've decided to kiss *me,* eh?" The captain's eyes were hot, his breath warm and moist as he bent his head and let his lips graze her ear.

"Well, I . . . I . . ." Cripes, he was making it hard to think! ". . . do expect to be kissed *back,* of course."

"Believe me, lassie, you shall be. . . ."

She wound her arms around his neck, her head falling back as his mouth moved down her throat. Mira's heart slammed to a stop. Sensation faded from her limbs, and numbness swept in to take its place. Tingles drove up her spine. Her knees went weak, her arms began to slide, and dimly she felt him grasp her wrists and pull her back up. Her feet were moving, but she didn't know how. She felt his knee pressing against hers, forcing her backward, until her back came up against the bulkhead and she was pinned helplessly between the hard wood and his even harder chest.

He radiated heat like a furnace. She melted beneath it.

His head bent toward hers, and she sighed as his breath feathered over her face.

"Close your eyes, lass."

His thumbs rubbed lightly over her cheeks, pushing her hair aside. Her eyes fell shut and she trembled in anticipation. She felt the heat of his mouth before his lips actually touched hers. Then . . . contact.

The kiss was all that she'd known it would be, and more than she'd dreamed it *could* be. Mira wilted against him, shamelessly pressing herself against his body, pulling his head down to hers. She forgot to breathe. Her senses swam. His mouth ground against hers, the pressure forcing her lips apart. Wild colors burst behind her eyes, liquid heat singed her veins, and time and place slipped away. Her head was reeling. Spinning.

Air . . . Oh God, I need air. . . .

She whimpered as his tongue slipped out and touched hers, first tasting, questing, conquering, then plunging wickedly into her mouth. It was wet and warm against her own, teasing her, tempting her, and firing a response that brought a strange, hot dampness between the junction of her clamped legs. Mira moaned deep in her throat. The heat between her thighs intensified, becoming a burning sensation that made her drive her hips against him in a futile effort to relieve it.

He groaned, caught her hand, and guided it to the bulge in his breeches. It was hard, hot . . . and definitely worth a closer perusal. Mira pushed against his chest, tore her mouth from his, and came up gasping. She opened her eyes, and saw that he'd buried his face against her shoulder. His breathing was harsh, and his jaw clenched.

Her fingers still stroked his manhood through his breeches, and she thought it was growing harder. Curious, she looked down and her eyes widened. Her hand stilled.

"Don't stop, lassie."

"But . . . but what do you want me to *do* with it?"

His eyes shot open and he jumped back as though she'd burned him. They stared at each other; she, in puzzlement at his odd reaction and eager to explore this part of a man she'd never seen before, he in dawning, horrible realization that Miss Mira Ashton was no saucy temptress at all, but an innocent brat who didn't have the faintest idea just what she was about.

"What's wrong?" she asked, hurt.

It was a moment before he trusted himself to speak, and when he did, his voice came out husky and ragged. "You've never touched a man before, have you?"

"No . . . but what's that got to do with anything?"

"Oh, *faith.*" Mortified, he turned away.

She moved toward him. The kiss had left her with a strange, unsatisfied longing for something she didn't understand. Her lips were on fire. Her breasts were tingling and burning, her lungs aching for want of air. Even her fingertips felt hot and tingly where she'd stroked and touched that hard, manly organ. She closed her fist to contain the feeling in her fingertips, and pressed her hand against her bosom. Just touching that part of him made her feel all hot inside.

"Let's do that again," she said, eyeing the hard bulge beneath his breeches.

His harsh breathing echoed in the stillness of the cabin. He glanced at her swollen lips, her pale throat, the thrust of her breasts. Then he swung away, as though in pain. He began to fidget, to blush, and finally, clenched his jaw so tightly that a muscle jumped there, before he tilted his head back and squeezed his eyes shut. "I think you should go," he said, his voice oddly strained.

She could see him fighting to gain control of himself. He gripped the back of a chair, his knuckles whitening. The cords and muscles in his throat stood out in relief, and the look on his handsome face was tortured.

"But what about my offer?" she asked, confused.

"Faith, lassie, you're young enough that you've no idea just what it is you're offering—" he opened his eyes and stared desperately at the deck planking above"—and I'm old enough to know better than to take it. Now, go, before I change my mind and do something we'll both regret."

Mira reached out and touched his hand, feeling his fingers harden like steel beneath her own. "I can't see how we'd regret it."

"I said *go,* Miss *Moyrrra!*"

"I mean, *you* might regret it, but I won't," she coaxed,

still reeling from the heady, wild sensations that tingled through every nerve in her body. She moved closer to him, pulled him away from the chair, and pressing herself against his chest once more, tried to wind her arms around his neck.

Her hands never got past his shoulders. He grabbed her wrists, thrust her away, and spun toward the wall. Hurt and confused, she stared at his back. "For the love of God, *Moyrrra*, go! Faith, just *go!* I've already decided who shall build my schooner, and nothing you can say or do will change that!"

"Didn't the kiss *mean* anything?" If he'd slapped her across the face, he couldn't have hurt her more.

"Just . . . go."

Mira's volatile temper flared to life. "Dammit, what about our *bargain?* I gave you your kiss and it's still not good enough, huh?! What kind of a bleedin' bargain do you drive, anyhow, *Brit?!* I held up *my* end of it!" Embarrassed and humiliated, she picked up her skirts, holding them above the glass-strewn floor as she stormed toward the door. "If that's how you want it, then fine! Take yer drafts to Tracy or Hackett or Greenleaf and let them build the damned thing! See if I bloody well care!"

She nearly tore the door off the hinges.

"Miss Ashton?"

She whirled, her petticoats twining around her legs, her hair flying over her shoulder.

"I really don't think they could kiss as well as you."

The total ridiculousness of his statement—and the quirky grin on his face—melted her anger. For a moment she glared at him, trying to maintain it, but it was impossible. A sparkle had come into his eyes, and it was impossible to be mad at him when he was looking at her like that.

Especially when he was looking at her like that.

"Why did you *really* call me back, Captain?"

He rested his weight on one long, well-muscled leg and studied her, a grin tugging at the corners of his handsome mouth, his eyes beginning to glow with good humor. Again, she thought of boyish rascality and daring pranks, and she had a sudden vision of what Captain Merrick must've been like as a child. A real devil, no doubt, a real handful for his mama. She had no trouble imagining him at all. And she had no trouble imagining just what sort of man he could be when he wanted to be, either, despite his badinage and easy grin.

But what she could never have imagined was just what he was considering.

"Why, I have another proposal for you, Miss *Moyrrra*. A . . . *safer* one, I believe."

She arched a brow. "Oh?"

"There is one thing you haven't offered, but that I would take if you were to do so."

Feeling quite cocky now, Mira met his gaze. She shivered in anticipation. Then she went back to her chair, grinning like a smug cat and hardly daring to breathe. "Yes?" she said sweetly. "And what is it that you would like, *Captain?*"

"The colt."

Her smile froze.

"Excuse me?"

"The colt. That fine gray one that you were, uh, riding this afternoon? At—" he folded his arms and grinned— "—precisely one-twenty."

Ladylike polish vanished like silk beneath torch fire. Mira lunged to her feet. *"Rigel?"*

"Named," Brendan said, with a teasing grin, "after the sun in the constellation of Orion?"

"Are ye out of your bloody, goddamned MIND?!"

"Quite a nice display of horses you have in your paddock, Miss Ashton. I saw them from my window. And your brother tells me you're the finest horsewoman this side of the Atlantic. Although—" his grin widened, and a dimple appeared at his jaw "—from what I've seen this afternoon, I might tend to dispute that."

"What— How— *Oh, how dare you!*" Her tiny fist slammed down on the table, upsetting the quadrant, Brendan's lap desk, and the ink bottle, which spouted a thick glob of blackness that leapt up and raced madly across the tilted surface. Brendan grabbed the drafts and saved them just in time, but Mira didn't notice. She was too busy bellowing at the top of her lungs in a credible imitation of her blustery sire.

"I can't believe you'd even *ask* such a thing of me! You're out of your bloody, goddamned mind if you think I'd accept such a trade! I won't even *consider* it! I don't care who you claim to fight for, you're a typical Brit, ye know that?! Arrogant! Audacious! If you'd lived fifty years ago, you'd've been a bloody pirate! You don't even *need* a horse, you're supposed to be a privateer—"

He caught her wrists before she could do any more damage. "The colt would not be for me."

She stopped to catch her breath, uncomfortably aware of the strength of his grip and wishing she *had* killed him this afternoon!

" 'Twould be for my sister." He released her, as though the touch hadn't affected him in the least, and again she saw that quick flash of pain in his eyes when he spoke of his sibling. "You see, Eveleen will be celebrating her twentieth birthday next month, and I haven't the foggiest idea what to give her. Every year she grows harder and harder to please. But a horse . . . she's never had a horse before. Somewhat afraid of them, I think. But your wee gray colt would be just the thing. . . ."

"My *wee* gray colt is not a *thing,* and I can assure you he's more than an inexperienced rider can handle!"

"He seems to be more than *you* can handle, Miss Ashton. Are you saying you're inexperienced?"

"Stop taking airs with me! Rigel is out of the question!"

"Then so, too, is the schooner, I'm afraid." He drew himself up, towering over her by more than a foot. His hand closed on her elbow, scorching her skin even through the fabric of her sleeve as he guided her to the door. With a bow so . . . *British* it made her want to retch, he indicated the companionway beyond and came up grinning. "Good night, Miss Ashton. Or as we say in *Irish, oíche mhaith dhuit!* And do mind where you're going next time you take that wee gray colt down High Street."

"But—"

The door closed in her face, and she found herself staring at scarred planking and a musket ball nesting in the stout oak. She raised her hand to beat against it, then paused as she heard his footsteps moving back across the cabin.

Damn him! Arrogant British bucket of sea slime! She'd see him rot in hell before she gave him her *wee gray colt!*

Snarling a choice epithet at the battered door, Mira whirled and stormed up the companionway with no way of knowing, of course, that Brendan was laughing in helpless amusement as he heard her angry footsteps recede.

And he, of course, had no way of knowing she burst into tears the moment she reached the shattered decks.

It really wouldn't have mattered.

The Tracy Yards had never stood a chance.

It was a quiet night, made for thinking, reflecting, lamenting. The town slept, the fireflies winked, and inside the darkened gloom of the Ashton stables, the horses were all bedded down in their stalls. But in the big one nearest the door, Mira sat in the sweet and scratchy hay, her back wedged into the corner as she miserably watched the moon move into the frame of the tiny window and glow upon Rigel's pale and dappled coat. Above, the hayloft was a shadowed hole, and two stalls down, she heard El Nath get to his feet, slam a hoof against his door, and settle back down when he realized he wasn't going to get any attention, nor a heady gallop along Plum Island's silvered shores, this bright and magical night.

Tears of confusion and loss slid down Mira's cheek, glittering in the moonlight like cut glass. With a sob, she brushed them away with the back of her hand. Rigel lowered his head, nuzzling her, lipping at her fingers, and blowing warm breath over her knuckles. "Oh, Rigel . . ." She reached up and stroked his soft, velvety nose. "What has he *done* to me?! I hate him, yet he makes me feel things that I shouldn't feel. Things that I'd feel only if I *didn't* hate him! Oh, I'm so damned *confused!*" She sniffed and bit down hard on her lip. "And now he wants *you.* . . . I can't part with you, I just can't!"

How could they all be so cruel? If she didn't find a husband, Father would sell Rigel, and the others, too. If she accepted the captain's terms, she'd still lose her colt, and to some British hussy who couldn't even ride. . . .

Sniffling, she bent her cheek to her hunched shoulder to catch another tear. She'd been outmaneuvered. Not only by Father, but by a stranger with winsome eyes and a charming grin that hid the *real* devil beneath it. Damn him. Damn all of them!

And damn the way you make me feel! she thought, remembering again his warm hands, his hard body, his wicked, wonderful kiss that had pulled such painfully exquisite sensations up from the depths of her being and scattered them through her body, her blood, her bones themselves. *Damn you to hell and beyond, Captain Brendan Jay Merrick!*

Pawing the hay, Rigel folded his legs and carefully eased himself down beside her, stretching out his silvery neck and laying his head in her lap. Mira reached down and stroked his silky forelock, listening to the wind stirring the trees outside, the branches scraping against the roof overhead. Night sounds seemed especially loud tonight: the steady chirrup of crickets, the shrill rasp of an occasional locust, and somewhere off in the woods surrounding Miss Mira Ashton's School of Fine Horsemanship, the hoot of an owl.

Unbidden, she thought of the captain. Was he asleep now, his handsome body sprawled sensuously on his bunk, his chest warm and hard and—

"Damn you!" she cried aloud. She would not dwell on him, she *wouldn't!* A decision had to be made, and reliving all those sweetly delicious sensations his touch had evoked would only make it harder than it already was. She forced herself not to think of him. Instead, she concentrated on the problem itself, and her thoughts traveled, past the sleeping houses of High Street, beyond the cluster of shops in Market Square, and to the dark waters of the mighty Merrimack, where a battered sloop rested in the mud—and plans for a proud topsail schooner sat atop a moonlit table. Waiting. For the proper builder to bring them to life, to make them into the finest ship to ever taste the waters of the Merrimack, the vast Atlantic. She would be majestic, a work of art, a lean and lithe predator to do her new country proud . . . and she deserved better than Patrick and Nathaniel Tracy.

A stab of pain lanced Mira's heart and she swallowed a thick lump of tears that burned all the way down.

It's your own fault. Sooner or later, Father had been bound to lose his patience with her. In retrospect, she was surprised it had taken this long. Lately he'd been raging that her School of Fine Horsemanship couldn't boast a single student. And now, the schooner. The ship must've really meant a lot to him; so much so that he shamed his own daughter in front of Matt's latest conquest. So much so that he would sell her horses right out from under her unless she found a husband.

So much so that he'd gone to bed without winding a single clock.

And here he hadn't even *seen* the drafts yet, the ones the captain had been redrawing.

The captain . . .

She bent her forehead to her knees and hugged her legs. Father. He was a miserable old goat, but she loved him anyway. No doubt he already regretted his Ultimatum, but he had more damned pride than a bald eagle, and she knew he'd never revoke his decision. She thought of him now. Was he lying awake in his big carved bed, staring up at the ceiling and wishing he'd never had a daughter? Wishing that Merrick's drafts were safely in his keeping? Wishing that the Ashton Shipyards would turn out the schooner that, thanks to her, would never be?

But oh, she *would* be, if Mira wanted it. The schooner's fate rested in *her* hands . . . and so did Father's happiness.

The wee gray colt.

"I *can't!*" she wailed, lifting her face toward the dark hayloft above, her little hands clenched in Rigel's silky mane as though she could never let him go. "Oh, God help me, I can't!"

Sensing her distress, the colt edged closer, his eyes very large and dark in the gloom of the stall. No doubt he was wondering why she was upset, why her tears were streaking his dappled jaw, why she didn't scratch his velvety nose or pull a sweet carrot out of her pocket and offer it to him. Instead, she buried her face in the warmth of his horsey-smelling mane and let it absorb her tears. She cried because the captain had awakened her to something she craved but didn't understand. She cried because she would lose her beloved colt. She cried because she would never know either the captain's magical touch, or the thrill of riding her little gray colt again. Either way, she would lose.

But . . . it wasn't as though Rigel would be going to a complete stranger, was it? On the other hand, if Father had control of his fate, Rigel might end up with someone she didn't know or approve of, someone who might abuse him, who might not take good care of him. At least she *knew* Captain Merrick. . . .

But this sister of his was supposedly afraid of horses. Why, then, had the captain wanted to give her one, and one that was far from being a placid, gentle old beast? Rigel was not a horse for a beginner, and definitely not for someone who was *afraid* of them.

Of course, there was always the chance that the girl would be so terrified of him, she'd send him back. . . .

Plus, allowing this Eveleen to have the colt would guarantee her a link to her brother, the handsome captain. . . .

But she hated him!

Didn't she?

Just do it, Mira. You're being selfish. It's not such a sacrifice to make for your own father. . . .

But could she face this empty stall every day? And what of the plans she'd had for her *wee gray colt?* Of seeing him mature into the fiery stallion he would someday be? Of galloping him the length of Plum Island's barren beaches, the waves breaking at his thundering hooves and the spray flying up to wash her skirts, her bare legs beneath them. . . .

Such a small sacrifice to make for your own father . . .

She couldn't stop the tears now. They coursed down her face like rain on a windowpane, wetting Rigel's forelock until it grew sticky and damp beneath her cheek. Then she burst into full-blown sobs, burying her face in the colt's smoke-colored mane to muffle them, her heart feeling as if someone had wrenched it from her chest, kneaded it like bread dough, and stuffed it back between her ribs in pieces. . . .

"Oh, Rigel . . . Oh, God, Rigel . . ." she cried, the

warm and horsey scent of the colt's neck filling her nose and making her sob even harder.

And again her conscience, relentless, demanding: *You'll still have El Nath. You'll still have Shaula. There'll be other colts, fillies, even. . . .*

And then:

And maybe if Father gets the captain's business, you won't have to get married after all. . . .

She raised her head, and lifted her face to the dark rafters above her head. Tears ran from her tightly clenched eyes, down her throat, onto the neck of her wee gray colt. And then she took a deep and steadying breath, and let it out slowly.

Beyond the window, the moon was gone, the stall dark once more.

She had just made the hardest decision of her life.

Chapter 8

For reasons known only to himself, Captain Merrick returned to his rented house in Portsmouth immediately after signing paperwork with Ephraim Ashton.

Work began on the schooner without delay.

Her lines were lofted to Brendan's drafts in an empty room above Ephraim's office, her keel scarfed and laid on blocks a stone's throw from the Merrimack, not far from where *Annabel*, stripped of her guns, fittings, and furnishings, lay moldering in muck and marsh grass. Shipwrights, carpenters, planking gangs, and caulkers; sailors, strong-armed men, young boys, and old salts alike; they worked like hell to build her, fitting stem and stern posts, hewing sleek ribs from massive white oak, and finishing them with broad ax and adz. By first frost the cry of "Frame up!" was a daily one, and beneath the shrewd and wintry eye of Ephraim Ashton, all would drop what they were doing to heave and haul and hoist each horseshoe-shaped rib up, until a lean and lovely skeleton shaped itself beneath the matchless blue skies, and the tales of its unique beauty drew crowds from as far away as Boston to see it. Dubbers' adzes rang out in the crisp mornings before the birds were even up; planking gangs swarmed over her, managing to lay two, sometimes three, streaks of plank over her ribs per day, and it wasn't long before mallets were ringing against hawsing irons and driving oakum and cotton beneath her skin to make her watertight. Ports were cut along her sides in readiness for the sharp four- and six-pounders she would carry; bulwarks were strengthened, rails were fashioned, woodwork was sanded and varnished. Day by day she grew, proud and lovely and strong, until at last she was sealed with tar and kissed by the carpenter's planes in readiness for the paint that would protect her from the bite of salt water.

Her builder dressed her in black, painted a jaunty white stripe between her wales, and paid her bottom with a formidable mixture of tallow, brimstone, and resin. Her deck was varnished, her sleek and spartan stern counter left uncluttered by excessive scrollwork; that which was there was picked out in gold.

She was sleek, she was sultry—and she was the pride of Newburyport.

Her launching day dawned as a frosty, crisp-cold morning that promised frostier, crisper ones to come. It would be many weeks before her masts were in place, her rigging fitted, and she was ready for sea, but that special moment of launching—when the new hull touched water for the very first time—was always cause for a celebration. The people, gathering along the riverbanks, watched the sun rise up from the sea and haul itself up through creamy pink skies filled with dramatic puffballs of cottony clouds. The sweet fragrance of rotting leaves perfumed the air, and grass made a last stand of color before winter's brute desolation would wipe the slate of the earth clean. But everyone came, leaving pumpkins and squash dragging down the vines, apples to be harvested, pies cooling on windowsills, tasks left undone or put aside. Privateers re-

turned early from sea, their crews toasting the new ship
with grog and sweet cherry rum. Children were lifted atop
shoulders, adults craned their necks. Dockworkers and
deckhands, laborers, merchants, lawyers, and physi-
cians—all crowded into the Ashton Shipyards, pushing and
shoving against one another just for a glimpse of the lovely
ship that stood atop her ways looking down at them like a
princess at her coronation. People took boats out into the
harbor for a spot to see; others hung out of second-story
windows in a rapidly filling Market Square. Horses and
carriages lined the streets, ships of every size and style
clogged the harbor, apple cider ran like water, and hot
chocolate steamed the air.

And atop her blocks the schooner waited, her rails
draped with the flags of her new country, her slick black
hull glowing pink, then gold, in the strengthening sunlight. She heard the people's praise, felt their awe. She
endured their reverent hands upon her flanks. She was
confident, smug, self-assured, and utterly feminine.

And those who figured they knew better predicted she'd
sink before she even settled her sleek shoulders into the
water.

The sun rose higher, turning the morning skies to fire.
Standing atop an elevated platform, Reverend Edward
Bass, pastor of St. Paul's Church, spoke solemn words of
blessing and prayer over her. Beside him Ephraim Ashton,
whose business had quadrupled over the past two months,
stood gloating and swinging his watch, every so often elbowing his son in the ribs. The crowds milled and surged
and grew impatient. They hadn't come here to see their
pastor, nor their suddenly renowned shipbuilder, nor his
hotheaded son; they'd come to watch a launching—and see
for themselves the *real* mastermind behind that magnificent schooner, the blithe, handsome young Irishman (Englishman! some insisted) who would command her.

But Captain Brendan Jay Merrick, who'd spent the past
two months up in Portsmouth, kept to the back of the
platform, allowing the reverend to say his blessings,
Ephraim to do his bragging, and the schooner to speak for
herself.

Finally the pastor shut his Bible and stood back.

Ephraim cleared his throat, consulted his watch, cleared his throat once again. A final toast was made, a bottle of champagne cracked across the svelte black bow. The tension rose. A thousand spectators held their breaths, milling, murmuring, and waiting.

She's too sharp through the hull, some whispered.

Too singular in design . . .

They pressed closer—

She'll go right to the bottom, you just watch. . . .

And closer.

A cannon boomed out. And then her handsome young captain, impeccably dressed in a blue coat with red facings and gold buttons streaming down his chest, stepped forward to send her on her first journey to the sea. He looked at her long and hard, and some would later swear there was mist in his eyes—and then he waved his hand, stood back, and watched as the hammers rose and fell, rose and fell, smashing apart the blocks that bridled her and severing the harnesses that kept her from the sea.

The schooner stirred to life.

The crowd gasped. They held their breaths; and then they shoved forward with a roar.

"There she goes!"

She trembled, lurched, began to move. Then she gathered speed, whispering to herself as she slid down the ways, faster and faster and faster, slipping into the river with hardly a splash.

She dipped.

She righted herself.

She moved away, trembling a bit as she got the feel of the water.

But she did not sink.

She did not sink!

The crowd roared and went wild. The air rang with deafening cheers and music and the glorious thunder of exultant cannon. And at that very moment something small and hawklike darted out of the dawn with a keening cry, something on the predatory wings of a raptor, something that touched briefly upon the schooner's rail before wheeling, swooping, and skimming back out over the pink and gold waters of the river with a triumphant cry of praise.

A kestrel.
And so she was named.

Mira, sitting atop a prancing, fidgeting Rigel, didn't stay
to watch *Kestrel*'s glorious sea-wedding any longer than
she had to. Patriotically garbed in a red and white striped
gown that matched the flags along the schooner's rails, she
had felt her heart sink with every foot the ship traveled;
by the time it hit water, it was all she could do not to burst
into tears.

He was back, damn his British, Irish hide, after two
blessed months—and now he would claim not only the
schooner, but her wee gray colt as well.

Desperately avoiding both well-wishers and the captain's eyes, Mira sent Rigel through Market Square and
down the length of High Street at a speed that tore the
tears from her eyes and the ribbons from her hair. But it
wasn't until she thundered up the drive and into the stables, her nose red from cold and her earlobes frozen, that
she allowed them to fall.

They were leaky trickles as she tore off the saddle and
bridle and flung them aside, twin rivulets as she hauled
Rigel into his stall, genuine, heartbreaking sobs by the
time she took the brush to his silver-dappled coat with a
vigor that nearly knocked him on his side. Around and
around she scrubbed, loosening dirt and sweat and horse
hair that clouded the cold air, made her sneeze, and settled
all over her pretty striped gown. She didn't care. Rigel
didn't care. He swayed, angled his neck, and grimaced in
sheer enjoyment as she dug the heel of her hand into the
brush and scrubbed even harder.

Her tears came faster. They burned her nose, plugged
it up, and glistened on her cheeks, running over and under
her jaw, down her neck, and beneath her bodice. With the
back of her hand she angrily swiped them away, but they
kept coming, faster and faster, again and again, no matter
how many times she swiped—

''Hello?''

Her hand froze atop Rigel's withers, the brush with it.

''Hello? Anyone in there?''

The captain. She choked back a last angry sob, swatted

the tears away, and shouted, "Leave me the hell alone, blast you!"

"That you, Miss *Moyrrra?*"

"I said get the hell out of here, you slimy bucket of bilge water!"

That felt better. Immensely better. But it didn't stop the tears from returning, harder than ever, as she attacked Rigel's coat with an ardor that nearly tore the hair from his dappled hide.

And it didn't stop the captain from entering the barn.

The patch of sunlight that streamed through the open doorway was suddenly blotted out. Straw rustled behind her. Rigel craned his neck around, pricking his ears forward. Hating herself for the tears she was powerless to stop, Mira clenched her jaw, her hand moving faster and faster as she hauled the curry brush across Rigel's dappled flank. She could sense the captain's nearness, could feel him looming over her. Her blood began to tingle in response, in memory, and she hated herself for it. Without looking up, she hollered, "Did ye hear me, you stinking pile of gull's dung? I said go away!"

And then his hand closed over hers, warm and strong and gentle, sending shock waves up her arm and stilling the frantic movements of the brush—

Her other arm swung up, and she cracked him across the face.

"Are ye bloody deaf? Are ye stinking blind? Damn it all, *I want to be left alone!*"

She tore free of him and covered her face with her hands. Rigel's horsey scent clung to her fingers, making her cry even harder. "Go away, would you? . . . Oh, just go *away*. . . ." But he didn't go away. He moved closer, his fingers dry and warm against her cold, wet ones as he gently tried to pry her hands from her face, and failing, let his palms slide down her wrists, her lower arms, finally grasping her by the shoulders and drawing her stiffly up against his smartly buttoned coat. His stock folded beneath her cheek; beneath it, his chest was a slab of rock. She caught the clean scents of wool and seawind, felt buttons pressing against her lips, her brow, her cheek.

She hated his guts—the English ones, the Irish ones,

and even the American ones, if he had any. But he was solid and warm and comforting, and she clung to him like a child, her face buried against his chest while he stared down at her with a helpless expression robbing his handsome face of its usual good humor.

Brendan was totally undone. Holding her stiffly, he was not quite sure what to do with her, and remembered hearing from someone—probably Liam—that the best way to comfort a weepy lass is just hold her until she stops. Part of him wished she'd stop soon, for his throat was constricting in a way that was making it quite hard to breathe, his loins tightening in a way that was making it quite hard to think.

Another part of him wished she'd cry forever.

At least she hadn't hit him again! His jaw was already beginning to throb. Faith, she could deliver a bloody deuce of a wallop, but one would never guess it to look at her, so small and fragile did she seem. He should've remembered from his past encounters with her that she was anything *but* fragile, and not let himself be deceived just because she'd tried to do her hair all up and garbed herself in a pretty little gown. He'd been in brawls where toughened seamen had hit him less hard! Yet she was such a wee mite, she barely came up to the middle of his chest, and if he bent his head, he could just feel her silky hair tickling the bottom of his jaw. The desire to rest his chin there was strong; his fear of what it might lead to was stronger. He'd had all he could do to restrain himself from this brazen little innocent that moonlit night in his cabin— he did not wish to be tested like that again. So instead he just stood there, holding her awkwardly and forcing himself not to think of how good she smelled, of warmth and horses and spring roses, nor of how good she'd feel, all curves and softness, if he could have her as a lad should have a lassie. . . .

Faith. He swallowed hard, torn between wanting to flee and wanting to stay and explore those curves, that softness, right here in the sweet straw of the barn where there was absolutely no one to watch them but the wee gray colt. The intensity and direction of his thoughts appalled him; the downward movements of his hands shocked him.

She was an innocent lass, and this business had to stop! Grasping her wrists, he pried, pushed, and gently set her away.

Confused, she stared up at him, her eyes huge and defenseless in her pale and freckled face. Tears glistened like dew on her cheeks, and one fat one trembled on her lower lip. Brendan couldn't help himself. He reached up and, with his knuckle, tenderly caught the tear as it fell.

And while he knew very well why she was crying—after all, she probably thought he'd come to take her horse—he asked, gently, "Tears, Miss *Moyrrra?* Might I ask why?"

"You may not!" Recovering quickly, she realized how close she stood to him, how close she'd *been* standing to him, and remembering how he'd rejected her before, jumped back as though he had the pox. "It's none of your bloody business!"

Her sudden reaction took him by surprise, but he hid it well. Nodding thoughtfully, he turned away, buttons flashing in the sunlight, hands clasped above his pleated coattails, chestnut queue lying between his perfectly straight, perfectly *British* shoulders. Like many of the other privateer captains, he wore a blue uniform with red facings, fashioned after those of the American Continental navy— but he wore his with the dash and aplomb of a king's officer. Despite herself, Mira found herself staring . . . and thinking he looked quite handsome in it. Quite handsome indeed.

But Brendan, turning, saw only her flashing eyes, her angry stance, her tightly clenched little fists. Faith, what the deuce had compelled him to take her in his arms like that?! Leaning against a stall door, he poked at the straw with his toe and wondered if such a prickly lass could be humored. "But I should think it *is* my business," he said logically. "After all, 'twas at the launching of my ship that you looked so distressed. I might wonder why."

"I have my own troubles, all right? If I wanted to share 'em with you, I would!"

His gaze flickered over the colt, standing hock-deep in straw and watching them curiously. "And might they concern our . . . er, *bargain?*"

"I said I don't want to talk about them!"

"Yes, I heard you. You may think me stupid—er, what was it you called me? A bucket of gull's droppings?" He grinned. "But I can assure you I'm not deaf. Besides, gull's droppings smell quite foully. I don't smell, do I?"

"*What?*"

"Buckets of bilge water can be quite malodorous, too, I might add. Though I admit it's been a while since I've actually bent down and stuck my nose in one. Actually, I prefer to wash with soap and clean water, like most people do. That's why I'm puzzled."

"Puzzled?" She stared at him. "Puzzled about *what?*"

"Why you seem to think I smell, of course."

"I never said you smelled!"

"But don't gull droppings? And bilge water?"

"Oh, for heaven's sake!" She was about to turn and storm away from him when she saw that one corner of his mouth was twitching, and laughter danced in his gold-flecked eyes.

"You're teasing me, Captain Merrick, and I don't like it one bit!"

"Am I?"

"You are!" She didn't add that the reason she didn't like it was that it made it just a little bit harder to hate his slimy pile of English guts!

"Faith and troth, why would I do that?"

"Because you're . . . you're trying to make me feel better!"

"I am?" He cocked his head, eyes bright and deceptively innocent beneath the shadow of his tricorn. "And why would I do *that?*"

"Blast it all, I don't know!"

"Hmm. Neither do I. Therefore, I suppose that's not what I'm trying to do, is it?"

"Then what *are* you trying to do?"

He looked at her blankly. "Why, I don't know."

"You and your damned Irish blarney! You're toying with me! You're making me look and feel like a bleeding fool! You came all the way over here just so you could do that, didn't you? Just so you could—"

"Good God, Miss Ashton, that's not the reason I came over here at all. Oh, no. I would never do that. Not to a lady. I mean, make you feel like a fool. And if you *do* feel like a fool, then I'm profusely and sincerely sorry—''

"Captain Merrick, would you please *STOP!*"

Again he flashed that damned Irishman's grin that was so at odds with his proper English bearing. "Only," he said jauntily, "if you will stop addressing me like that. I really prefer to be called *Brendán*. Or Brendan, if you like. 'Tis me name, ye know," he said, piling on his brogue, "given t' me by me ma aft'r th' patron saint o' sailors."

"As long as there's this . . . this *friction* between us, I'll call you Captain Merrick!"

"Friction? Faith, is there friction between us?"

She was going to kill him. Damn and thunder, she would, she would, she *would!* Slamming her fist against the stall door, she swore like a sailor and shouted, "Then why the hell *did* you come here?"

He was looking at her hand, not grinning quite so hard now. "Ouch," he said simply, raising a brow and reaching for her wrist. Mira jerked away, jamming the hand into the pocket of her skirt to hide it—and keep herself from striking him with it.

"Well?"

"Well what?"

"Why *did* you come here, *Brendan?*"

"Ah, yes. Why did I come here?" he mused, bending his head down into his hand and pinching the bridge of his nose, as though trying awfully hard to remember. And then he looked up, grinning, his eyes sparkling with mischief. "To get a ship built. Your father builds the finest ones this side—"

"*Not* Newburyport, *here!* To this barn!"

"Why, to make another deal with you, of course."

Instantly suspicious, Mira forgot her throbbing hand. "What, don't you like your damned schooner?" she snapped, wishing he didn't look so damned handsome.

"Oh, I like her very much. In fact, I couldn't be more pleased with her. I've given your father some, uh, enticement to get her masts stepped and rigging strung in half the time he'd originally planned."

"You must be a terribly rich man, Captain."

"Brendan."

"Brendan." She glared at him. "Are you, then?"

"Am I what?"

"Rich, dammit!"

"Oh no, not really. Not anymore. I gave the bulk of my savings to your father so he could build the ship. Of course, 'twas a pity he couldn't get the copper hull sheathing I'd wanted, but I suppose if I'd had to pay for that, I could never have afforded her."

"She's prettier without it," Mira affirmed, and then wondered why she was even *trying* to make this . . . this rotted pile of sea kelp feel better! Rotted pile of sea kelp? Oh God, *don't say it,* she thought. She'd never picked up a rotted pile of sea kelp and held it to her nose, but she'd bet her right arm that it if she did, it would smell. . . .

"You think so?" he asked, earnestly, his eyes smiling in appreciation as he gazed at her. "That she's prettier the way she is?"

"Don't you? *You're* the naval architect."

Still caressing her with his gentle, laughing gaze, he plucked a halter from a nail and swung it by one of its metal rings. "Naval architect? How flattering. I always fancied myself a sea captain."

"You're nothing like any sea captain I've ever known."

He looked a little hurt. "And why is that?"

"You're too . . . *polished.* Too blithe. Besides, whoever heard of a sea captain who doesn't swear, spit, or drink—"

"How would you know I don't drink?"

"I saw you take *water* that night in *Annabel*'s cabin!"

"Oh."

"And you don't spit or swear, either," she reminded him, trying not to think of the way his assessing, admiring gaze was making her feel.

"Spitting's a nasty habit, and I do, too, swear."

"Not very well."

"That's true. You're far better at it."

"Damn right I am!"

He quirked a brow. And then he grinned, and laughed. She flushed hotly, feeling her stomach go to pudding and her insides get all squishy. Furious at her body's reaction and itching to slap that grin way, she spat, "So what are you, some devout religious fanatic or something? Is that why you don't drink?"

"Oh, no, that's not the reason a'tall. Although I do hold a shipboard service every Sunday for those who wish to partake of it."

"Then what *is* the reason?"

"Why, to worship, of course."

"That you don't drink!"

"Oh, that." He was staring at her again.

"Yes, that!"

"Must I give you one?"

"I would like one!"

"Do you care?"

"Not really!"

"Then why must you know?"

"Because I . . ." Her mouth snapped shut and she turned away, fingernails biting into her palms and leaving red crescents in the damp skin as she willed herself not to hit him. "You're right," she ground out through clenched teeth. "I don't need to know. It's none of my business, is it?"

"No, it's not, but if it really matters to you—"

"It doesn't really matter to me, all right?"

"Are you sure?"

"Yes, I'm sure!"

"But I'll tell you anyway."

"Dammit, Captain Merrick, I said I *don't care!*"

"But you did a moment ago. Either you were lying then or you're lying now. Do you care or do you not?"

"Aaargh!" Flinging her hair out of her face, she railed, "I don't care! I don't care! I DON'T CARE!"

"I think you really do. Otherwise you wouldn't have asked. People ask questions because they wish to know the answers. People answer questions because they've been asked them. A very logical system, really. So therefore, I think that I should answer your question, simply because you asked it, and must really want an answer despite the fact your pride prevents you from admitting it. Actually, the reason—"

"Damn you, you're the most irritating, vexing, exasperating—"

"—I don't drink is because spirits don't agree with me."

She came up short, choking on tears and anger, her face as red as the stripes of her gown. "Don't agree with you? Hah, I'm not surprised! I'm sure there are many things in this world that don't agree with you! Let's just hope for your sake, *Captain,* that your bleedin' schooner isn't one of 'em!"

"And why do you say that?"

"With all that sail you intend to pile on her, one gust of wind'll knock her flat on her side!"

"Well then, I guess we'd just better hope I'm as good a captain as you suspect I'm not, and thank the good Lord that I don't drink, eh?"

She scrunched up one side of her face. *"What?"*

"I said, I guess we'd just better hope—"

"Never mind, Captain, I heard you the first time!"

"Brendan."

"BRENDAN!"

Gripping the brush, she turned to Rigel once more, her heavy hair swinging against her rump, her eyes glittering with temper. The man was a lunatic! As empty-headed as a chickenless egg! As nonsensical and idiotic as—

"Why are you scrubbing so hard?"

"I am *not* scrubbing!"

"Seems to me that you are."

"I am not!"

"Don't you think it hurts, to be scrubbing like that?"

"I told you, *I am not scrubbing, and besides, he likes it!"*

"He does?"

"Yes, and any fool who knows a damned thing about horses would know that!"

"Funny, I never considered myself a fool, though of horses I am quite ignorant."

"Don't you know *anything* about them, *Captain?"*

"Not much."

"Obviously. If you did, you wouldn't be standing there within easy reach of his hooves!"

He stepped back. "Oh. Do you think he'll kick me?"

"If he doesn't, I sure as hell will! Now, would you *please* go away and leave me alone?"

"In a bit."

"Why not now?!"

"Well, for one thing, you're crying again. If you weren't, you see, I would go. But 'twould be most ungallant of me to leave a lassie in tears, wouldn't it?" Angrily she spun away to hide them, hearing his lilting, musical voice from behind her. "Would you like me to hold you again until they stop?"

"*No!*"

He reached into his pocket. "Would you like my handkerchief, then?"

"Just go *away,* would you?!"

"You're crying."

"I am NOT CRYING!"

"Do you sniffle because of the hay, then? 'Twould be a shame if so, you loving these horses and all. Why, I should think it a real inconvenience to you. I wonder if you might be better off using a different sort of bedding material—"

Mira swung around and slammed her fist against the stall door. "GO AWAY! Just go away, go away, *GO AWAY!*"

"Oh, I would, but I'm supposed to be meeting your father at precisely one o'clock." He drew out his watch, its once fine casing dented by a musket ball. "I have twelve thirty-five. I'm sorry. Twelve thirty-six—"

Mira leaned her forehead against the stall door, took a deep breath, and as Matt had taught her to do to control her temper, forced herself to count to ten. Then she counted to twelve just to be sure. But the method had never worked for Matt, and it didn't work for her. Furthermore, it did absolutely nothing to cool the caldron her blood had become, nor to still the wild pounding of her heart. Mira glared at him out of the corner of her eye. "Fine. As it is now exactly twelve thirty-six, I suppose I have to put up with you for the next twenty-five minutes?"

"Twenty-four."

"And you think I can get anything done with you standing there bothering me? You said you had a reason for coming here, Capt—"

"Brendan."

"Brendan!—and since you have only twenty-four minutes in which to state it, then you'd better get started!"

"Twenty-three, now."

She raised the brush as though to hit him with it, and he laughed, ducked, and shielded his face with his hand. "By faith, have mercy, lass! Must you always be so *brutal?*"

"Only when I'm provoked!"

"Am I provoking you?"

Her temper exploded. *"You have gone past provoking me!"* She flung the brush, and he deflected it off his elbow with a howl of pain. "There! Next time it'll be a more potent weapon, believe me!"

Rubbing his elbow, he said, "You mean you have some?"

"Some what?"

"Why, more potent weapons, of course . . ."

"That's *IT!* I can't TAKE this anymore!" With a strangled sound of frustration, she tried to storm past him before he drove her beyond insanity and into killing him. But he caught her as she passed, easily holding her as she tried to jerk away. Beneath that handsome coat he must be all sinew and gristle, as wiry and hard as nails. She stopped struggling, and he let her go.

"I'm sorry, Miss Ashton. I was just trying to make you feel better."

"No one can make me feel better, least of all you!"

"No, you're wrong. I think I'm the only one who can ease your torment."

"You're the one who caused it all in the first place! And I don't want to hear any more of your stupid bargains, all right?!"

"You'll like this one."

"Like hell I will!"

"But you don't even know what I'm offering—"

"I don't want to know, do you hear me?" She stamped her foot in rage. "I *don't want to know!*"

"All right." He shrugged, grinned, and touching his hat to her, turned to leave.

"Wait!"

He stopped in the patch of sunlight just inside the doorway. The sun deepened the blue of his coat and picked out golden highlights in the rich russet tones of his hair, queued and tied with a black ribbon between his elegant shoulders. He was all British polish and Irish charm combined—and she didn't have to see his face to know that he was grinning. He turned then, slowly, and proved her right. Something caught in her chest. "Yes, Miss Ashton?"

Her gaze darted away. "I *do* want to know." She took a deep breath, brushed away a tear, and set her jaw. "And I promise not to get mad."

Even Rigel craned his neck around at *that* statement.

"Oh, you won't get mad." He looked down at his feet, glanced up, and shrugged. "I came here to give you your horse back."

"To give me my . . . horse back?"

"Yes." He kicked idly at the straw, avoiding her stare.

"Why? Why would you do that?"

"Oh, I don't know. . . ." He looked up and grinned helplessly.

"Don't you like him?"

"Very much."

"Don't you like the schooner?"

"Oh yes, she's a fine little lass. All that I'd hoped she'd be, and more."

"But you don't like me. So why would you do something nice for me if both the schooner and the colt suit your fancy?"

He looked up then, *blushing,* of all things, and there was such a helpless look in his eyes and on his handsome face that Mira was completely undone. "I never said I didn't like you."

"But you don't, do you?"

He reddened further. "Miss Ashton, do you want to keep your horse or not?"

"What about the schooner?"

"I'm paying handsomely for her. You've no reason to fear that I'll not return from Portsmouth to claim her when she's ready for sea."

"But I don't understand!"

"I'm not asking you to. I'm merely asking if you'd like

to keep your horse. Forget about our bargain of last summer. I was not acting very chivalrous, I'm afraid. 'Twas a bad time you caught me at.''

She looked away, guiltily. Oh, it *had* been a bad time for him, and she remembered it well—*too* well, as it had been all her fault. No, he certainly hadn't had good reason to be himself last year! But could he really be offering her her beloved colt back? Mira's heart leaped at the thought.

''Besides,'' he was saying, ''I've done some thinking. My sister is not a good rider. You see, she's . . . lost the use of one hand.'' Pain flickered briefly in his eyes. ''I would be somewhat afraid to put her on such a fiery animal as this one. . . .''

Rigel merely flicked an ear. ''Yes, he is that,'' Mira agreed, solemnly.

''So I guess it might be best if we just annulled our agreement. You keep your horse, I'll take my schooner, and that'll be that.''

''What about your sister?''

''Oh, I'll find some pleasant old nag who won't give her any trouble.''

Mira bit her lip. It was a tempting offer, and she'd be a fool not to accept it, nay, *grab* it, without further ado. She could keep Rigel, he would get *Kestrel,* and everyone would be happy!

Everyone, that is, but his sister.

She swallowed hard, suddenly feeling very small. If someone promised *her* a fine and lovely colt, how would she feel to have it suddenly taken away? Visions of a female version of Brendan flitted through her mind, of a thin little girl with a big grin and laughing eyes, a grin that would fade and eyes that would turn sad when a fat old nag was given to her instead of the sleek and lovely steed she'd been promised.

Slowly she said, ''Does your sister already know about him? Rigel, that is?''

''She does,'' he said quietly, not wishing to influence her decision.

''When . . . did you tell her?''

''On the morning of her twentieth birthday, last year.''

"And did she seem quite eager?"

He shrugged, looking ill at ease. "She did."

"And she might feel sort of cheated if you brought home a nag after promising her Rigel, huh?"

He didn't answer.

Mira turned to look at her horse, seeing his dappled gray coat through misty eyes. She'd made an agreement, fair and square. She was an Ashton, and Ashtons didn't renege on their agreements. Besides, Brendan had said the poor girl had lost the use of her hand. The least that she, Mira, could do was give her Rigel. It would tear her heart out to do it, but she would send Rigel to the girl. Oh, God help her, she would.

"You're very kind," she said, forcing the words out and agonizing over every one, "but I told you you could have the colt, and I mean to uphold my part of our bargain. A deal's a deal. You can take him back with you when you go back to Portsmouth."

Brendan saw her eyes filling up again and felt helpless and horrible. "You're too proud, Miss Ashton."

"Perhaps."

"I want to give the horse back to you."

"I want you to stop asking me to take him."

"I don't want you to start crying again."

"I want you to stop *thinking* I'm crying."

"But you are. . . ." He stepped forward, drew his handkerchief, and very gently, dabbed at the moisture beginning to leak from the corners of her eyes. The very tenderness of his touch made her throat burn, and the tears flow in earnest. She closed her eyes, her lashes spiky and wet against her cheeks, and felt something huge and choking well up in her chest. "Won't you keep him?" she heard him say, his musical voice stirring the soft hair at her brow. "He belongs with you, and you with him. I realized that as you rode away this morn. No one else could look as pretty on his back as you do . . . not even my little sister."

She bit down hard on her lip to still its trembling, desperately clenching her fists to keep from crying.

"So please take him . . . *Moyrrra.*"

"I can't!" Her eyes flew open. He was standing very

close, his handsome face just inches from her own. "God help me, I can't! I *promised!* I wish to God I didn't, but I *did*, Captain—"

"Brendan," he said softly, his thumbs sliding beneath her jaw and tilting her head up to his.

"Brendan . . ." She squeezed her eyes shut, this time not resisting him as he drew her up against his chest and held her close to his heart. She melted against him, no longer caring about the tears that slid cruelly down her cheeks, betraying her. She felt only his knuckles grazing her throat like the brush of a butterfly's wings . . . his thumbs sliding along her jaw, gently raising it . . . his warm breath against her face, the barest tightening of his fingers beneath her chin, and then his lips, gentle and tender, warm and firm and sweet and wonderful. . . .

Her body's response was no different than it had been two months before. Her legs buckled and she would've fallen if not for the arm he'd locked behind her back. She pushed against him, forcefully at first, then gently, then not at all. Her fingers fanned across the shiny buttons running down his taut, hard chest; they brushed across his red facings, through his crisp white stock, and finally clenched his lapels with an intensity that left her knuckles pale. Her senses swam. Her tears stopped. And from that point on, nothing mattered.

His tongue swirled around the soft insides of her lips, slipped between her teeth, and touched her own, robbing her of breath, of resistance, of sanity and reason and thoughts of anything but him and him alone. Shock waves drove through her and she clung to him, meeting his kiss with a hungry response that frightened her with its very magnitude. Moisture gathered in her palms, liquid heat burned through her veins. Anger melted and desire rose, and Mira knew only his hands dragging through her hair, his palm sliding down the curve of her back and caressing her bottom. She molded herself to him, feeling every hard muscle, every rock-slabbed rib, every button of his coat pressing through her gown and against her body—and his arousal, pressing intimately against her belly. Her legs trembled and her knees turned to water. She felt faint; she felt dizzy; she felt heat burning in her womanly nether regions, and then, that hot dampness between her thighs that shocked, bewildered, excited her.

With slow, languorous tenderness he ended the kiss, leaving her numbed lips cold and empty. Dazed, she stared up at him, flushing and gasping and trying in vain to draw air into her lungs. And the she found her voice.

"Holy sh . . ." her voice trailed away.

They stared at each other, shaken by the depth of feeling that still crackled between them and threatened to meld them together once again. Mira's green eyes were wide and stunned, her soft lips ripe with color; Brendan's heart was fibrillating so wildly, he feared it would shake itself into a stop.

He drove an unsteady hand through his tousled curls. God help him.

He had to get away from her. Back in his cabin that night, when she's so innocently and brazenly offered herself in trade for a ship, he'd known it would come to this. He'd known, too, that he was powerless against her allure; but that hadn't stopped him from taking her in his arms and kissing her. *Faith*. He could feel it happening all over again just as it had with Julia; that heady, reckless desire that burned through him like a fever, that overwhelming urge to know her and nothing but her, to say the hell with the schooner, the war, and anything else that wasn't Miss Mira Ashton. Fear snaked through him, cold and ugly and real, fear of having to choose once again between the things he loved, fear of losing one of them if the choice was wrong. He looked down at Mira's glossy head, her wee, shaking shoulders, and knew that there'd *be* no choices if he succumbed to this wild urge to make her his own, for she was a siren, a sylph, a nymph. Once she had him in her power, he'd be undone.

Look what she was doing to him already.

But he couldn't leave her crying, her tears seeping through his clothes and baptizing the old scar that Crichton has left on his chest in pain and sorrow. A sharpness fanned out there, like the piercing pain of that long-ago pistol shot, making him feel sick. What a wretch he'd been for bargaining for her colt in the first place, a bargain he'd made in a moment of fun and, yes, anger. Now there was no way he could annul it without stealing her pride as well as her happiness from her.

" 'Pon my soul,'' he said gently, laying his cheek atop her silky hair and willing himself not to think about how fast his heart was pounding, how good she felt in his arms. "We've certainly gotten ourselves in a fine pickle, haven't we?''

She sobbed harder at the utter absurdity of his statement.

"Miss Mira—'' He took her arms and forced himself to gently set her back, away from him. "If I had an idea, would you listen to it?''

She couldn't trust herself to speak. Not only was his touch affecting her breathing, her throat was so flooded, her heart and senses so overwhelmed, that she could only nod mutely.

"I was just thinking. You have a school for horsemanship, do you not?''

She nodded again, and lifted a shoulder to catch a tear.

"How would you feel if I sent my sister down here, to you?'' His eyes brightened and unconsciously he gripped her proud little shoulders tighter, warming to the idea and hoping, for her sake, that she would, too. "Why, you could teach her how to ride right here, on the colt himself—what was his name? Rigel? She'd be learning from a fine teacher, and I wouldn't have to spend my time worrying about her welfare when I'm supposed to be worrying about that of my ship and crew. . . .''

She was staring at him, a dazed look in her eyes, not saying a word. One diamondlike tear was poised on the spiky fringe of her lower lashes. He couldn't know she was still reeling from his kiss, eager to try it once again and see where those sweetly agonizing sensations radiating out from her womanly regions would lead. . . .

His fingers dug into her arms. "You could teach her to ride right and proper, and how to care for the horse as you would wish for him to be cared! You could teach her how to work around them, how to understand them, how to keep from getting hurt—oh, Miss *Moyrrra*, I think this might work out quite nicely!''

"I suppose it could. . . .'' she heard herself saying, his

words finally penetrating the foggy cloud her mind had seemed to become. She gazed at him, seeing him in a new light; suddenly his handsome face was even handsomer, his eyes even warmer. She bit her lip, then ran her tongue across it, tasting him once again and shivering despite the heat that burned through her blood, swirled in her thighs, drove through her sleeves where his elegant hands rested. *Oh, Captain,* she thought, hugging her arms to herself and clamping her legs together to contain those weird, wonderful sensations he'd awakened. *Why is it that every time you touch me, my body reacts like this?*

She saw by the warm glow in his cider-colored eyes that she'd affected him, too. "Well?" His voice sounded strangely hoarse.

She pulled away from him, her skin all hot and prickly despite the chill of the morning, her legs weak and boneless. Damn him. Damn him for what he was doing to her! *And bless him for what he had done.* Swallowing hard, she said, "I . . . I suppose it would be a g-grand idea. Your sister could stay with us. I'd love to have a friend, and besides, we do have so many extra rooms. . . ." Not only that, she added to herself, having his sister in the house might keep the handsome captain around, and Mira was determined to get to know him better. But then a sudden, horrible thought jolted her back to reality. "Do you think, though, that she could get used to Father?"

He hadn't thought of that, but yes, he assured her, he supposed she could.

"And the cats?"

He nodded, his eyes gleaming as he gazed at her graceful throat, her tumbledown hair, her pixie, heart-shaped face. It was an Irishman's gaze, full of bold charm and heady recklessness—a recklessness that went as quickly as it came beneath the ruling hand of his English side.

But then he made the mistake of looking into her eyes.

She was gazing at him, intently, her lips lusciously swollen and redder than strawberries, her hair swirling around her freckle-splattered cheeks. Then she smiled, an impish, tart little grin that wrinkled the sides of her nose and made him realize, in that one, quick moment, that he was not merely thinking of her happiness and his sister's health by suggesting that Eveleen—and Rigel—stay in Newburyport.

Oh no, not at all.

He was thinking it would be a wonderful excuse to leave Portsmouth and make *this* town his home port. To come back to it. Again and again and again.

Faith. What the devil was he *doing?!''*

She was waiting.

His Irish side returned and sent his English one fleeing.

''So be it, then!'' he said gleefully, and would've sealed the agreement with another kiss—but at that moment they both heard the squeak of a carriage, the hoofbeats of a horse, and a blustery, arrogant voice shouting at an unearthly volume for a groom to come tend to the animal.

Their precious moments were up. It was exactly one o'clock.

Ephraim was home.

Chapter 9

''**G**et your bloody hands off me, you stinking rebel louts!''

The epaulets had long since been ripped from his blocky shoulders; his white waistcoat, breeches, and stockings were now gray with filth; and his once fine uniform was torn in a dozen places. But the pride and arrogance with which Captain Richard Crichton had worn that uniform were intact—even after three months of confinement in this hellhole of a prison ship anchored in Boston Harbor.

That the British counterparts of this prison ship were supposed to be even worse mattered not to Crichton. He'd been mocked and taunted by his American jailers, fed putrid pork and water so foul that he'd had to strain it through his teeth just to get it down, and moldy biscuit crawling with weevils. But that was nothing compared to the humiliation they'd made him suffer, and in front of his own officers and men, too. They'd torn the buttons from his coat that proclaimed his seniority as a captain; they'd ripped the epaulets from his shoulders, the buckles from his shoes; they'd even taken his fine gold-laced hat and paraded up and down the ship, laughing at his rage and damning the king and all who served him.

Bloody bastards.

And it was all the fault of Brendan Jay Merrick.

Today was the day that Crichton was being exchanged for American prisoners of war, but he wasn't one to let bygones be bygones. Oh, he'd get even with Merrick. He'd go back to Sir Geoffrey, get command of another ship, and make Merrick *pay* for the poor treatment and humiliation he'd suffered at the hands of the Americans. . . .

Angrily he flung off his jailor's hands as they herded him abovedecks, still vowing to get revenge.

And Captain Richard Crichton always made good his vows.

If Britannia thought she already had enough troubles with her rebellious colonies—1778 had marked the official French entry into the conflict—she was soon to find that those troubles had only just begun. Forced by the French involvement into what some called a world war, Britain was hard-pressed to protect her coasts from a possible invasion by her old enemy, keep up her strength in the West Indies, where both she and France held possessions, and subdue the unsubduable Americans with a fleet that was already spread far too thin to be perfectly effective.

While the few ships that made up the American Continental navy surpassed those turned out in British yards in both quality and design, they were poorly officered, and the caliber of most of their commanders fell short of the ships themselves. Such was not the case, however, with the American privateers. Like clouds of hornets, they swarmed out of their nests—Salem, Beverly, Newburyport and Portsmouth, hiding in coves and inlets, hunting in "wolf packs," and preying upon British shipping whenever the opportunity arose. They stole supplies and munitions destined for British troops and rerouted them to Washington's forces. They armed everything from whaleboats to fishing schooners to fine frigates. They harried and harassed England, created panic around her coasts, and drove insurance on her merchant ships out of control.

Their names were anathema to British shipping and Admiralty alike: the plucky John Paul Jones in his *Ranger* out of Portsmouth, New Hampshire; Silas Talbot, sailing from Providence, Rhode Island; Hardy in the *General Hancock;* Haraden in the *General Pickering;* Nathaniel Tracy and Matthew Ashton from Newburyport. They were men with grit and guts and valor, and their tough little ships were their equal in every way.

And now, swinging proudly at her cable in the icechoked waters of the Merrimack was a sharp new schooner, with topsails and topgallants furled on gleaming yards, black hull reflecting on the rippling river, masts reaching forever up into a sky that blazed with winter sun.

Kestrel.

She was ready for sea at last. On the day her windlass was fitted and the last of her rigging strung, a jubilant Ephraim Ashton sent the word to her commander, via the Portsmouth Flying Stage Coach. And exactly one week later, Captain Brendan Jay Merrick, vacating the house he'd rented in Portsmouth, arrived in Newburyport by that same coach, trunk snugged under his arm, ditty bag slung over his shoulder, laughter in his eyes, and a jaunty smile lighting his handsome face.

Mira, who'd waited for Ephraim to leave for the shipyards before riding out to the snowy, frozen field that was Miss Mira Ashton's School of Fine Horsemanship, would've been hard-pressed to know whether it was Father's order that she meet the stage, or her own admitted eagerness to see Brendan again—and his expression when he laid eyes on the schooner—that sent her barreling down the frozen High Street at a speed that surpassed dangerous when the word came that the captain was back. Her intentions were good, they really were. She wasn't thinking of her woolen coat, the stockings that clung to her slender calves, nor the trousers that were so baggy, they resembled a skirt in themselves. She didn't consider how annoyed Father would be when it got back to him that she was not only riding astride, but charging through town dressed in Matt's clothes again. She could placate him later.

And it was not her fault, of course, that she never did get to meet the Coach as it came over the ferry. As Rigel thundered down High Street, lopped off the corner of Fish Street, and charged toward the waterfront at breakneck speed, traveling so fast that the wind ripped tears from her eyes and froze them to her wind-whipped cheeks, she saw the ferry just coming across the river, the six horses that drew the stage tossing their heads and whinnying in equine welcome.

And that wasn't all she saw.

Merchant ships and privateers tied up at the wharves, their bowsprits stabbing far out over weathered dock planking that was patchy with ice.

A boy crouched in their long shadows, hunched down on his heels cleaning fish and tossing the scraps into the half-frozen river.

And an emaciated gray wharf cat prowling around him, rubbing against his bent legs and begging for a handout.

All this Mira took in at approximately thirty-five miles per hour, through the lash of Rigel's mane and the haze of her own mounting excitement. And it was the boy's misfortune that he chose that exact moment to tire of the cat's pestering and, rising, kicked viciously out at the hapless creature and sent it sprawling across the wharf.

Poor sixteen-year-old Billy Jacobs never knew what hit him. One moment he was cleaning fish and thinking about one of the wenches who worked at Wolfe Tavern; the next he was flung onto the back and set upon by a fury straight from hell.

Dockyard brawling had never been Mira's forte, but she could certainly hold her own when she had to. In her wrath Mira was heedless of the fact that Billy outweighed her by a good fifty pounds. What mattered was that *he* outweighed the cat by a hundred forty!

"Kick a defenseless animal, will you!? Abuse something smaller than you?!" Screaming at the top of her lungs, she pummeled his nose, his lips, his cheek, with merciless fists. "How *dare* you, you worthless pile of puke! Slinking skin of a maggot! I'll teach you never to do it again!'' She smashed him a good one to the side of his eye, landed another to the bottom of his chin. "You think you're the only critter God put on this earth?!'' His nose crumpled under her fist and sprayed blood. "I ever see you hurting an innocent animal again and so help me God I'll kill you, you heaping pile of moose manure!''

So caught up was she in giving Billy his just rewards that she never saw the gang of shipyard and dockworkers, seamen, fishermen—and passengers from the Stage—who all dropped what they were doing and came racing head-long down the wharf to see the fight. But she heard them cheering her on, those from the Ashton yards yelling at the top of their lungs and jumping up and down in wild excitement. "Go, Mira! Go, Mira! Whip 'im good! Bloody his nose s'more! C'mon, Mira! *KILL 'IM!*''

Billy, howling in pain, was now giving as good as he got, slamming his fist into the side of her chin so hard that he nearly dislocated her head from her neck. She swung viciously back and blackened his eye. Again, and she cut her frozen knuckles on his tooth. They were blind punches, for she saw nothing through her tangled hair, heard nothing but the roar of the crowd cheering her on, felt nothing but a haze of red anger and his cowardly tears diluting the blood that ran from her knuckles. And she was barely aware of her own voice, although she was yelling at a volume that would've done Ephraim proud. "And further-more, if I *ever* again hear that you've been mistreating your horse—''

"Stop,'' he sobbed, "oh please, for the love of God, stop—''

"—I'll make you wish you were never born!''

"Stop!" He was screaming now, terrified. "Mercy! *Mercy!*''

"Cowardly scum!'' she raged, slamming him hard. "Do you think that cat could ask for mercy? Or your horse? Damn you for the sniveling rat you are! Only *cowards* mistreat helpless animals!''

And as she drew back for another blow, her wrist was seized in a hard and unyielding grip.

Blinded by fury, she sprang to her feet, already swinging at the idiot who dared pull her off a fight she'd clearly been winning. She saw a blur of cloth and lace as his arm flashed up, catching her fist against his open hand before it could connect with his face. She opened her mouth to fire a stream of choice curses at him—

It was Brendan.

He stood holding her by both wrists, looking shocked but not surprised. Behind him the crowd sent up a clamor of protest, some muttering, some yelling, but all quite vocal about their dismay that he'd put an end to their entertainment. He ignored them, looking polished and handsome in an elegant green frock coat trimmed in gold brocade, too polished and handsome to be troubling himself with a one-sided dockyard fight. But his expression was an interesting mix of amusement and admiration as he stared down into what he could see of her flushed and furious face, for most of it—save for that impish nose he remembered so well and those glittering green eyes—was all but hidden behind her thick and tangled wall of glossy brown hair. She drew herself up, wiped a heavy fall of it out of her face—and not knowing what else to do, grinned sheepishly.

"Hello, Brendan."

"What was that you were saying," he said slowly, with a meaningful glance at the sobbing Billy, "about picking on poor defenseless creatures, Miss *Moyrrra?*"

Oh, *wounds,* she thought, beginning to feel quite awkward. She'd done it again, hadn't she? The awkwardness progressed into downright embarrassment at being caught in such an unladylike pursuit as fighting. But damn it all, Billy had deserved it! So what if Brendan disapproved?! What did his opinion matter, anyhow?!

It mattered quite a bit, otherwise she wouldn't feel so awkward and uncomfortable, nor would his mere touch make her remember the kisses that had burned themselves into her memory. She cursed, inwardly. No doubt he thought of her as some little street urchin, with her hair a wall of darkness she couldn't even see through, and her clothes—her *brother's* clothes—ripe with horse-scent. Nearby, Billy, his face in his hands, was sobbing, and she could hear the loud grumbles and complaints of the crowd.

She tossed her head, and her hair flung itself out of her eyes and over one shoulder and she could see again. A hundred people were staring at her, those who knew her laughing and jostling one another in the ribs, those who didn't staring in shocked horror when it became apparent that the scrappy little lad who'd been beating up another twice his size was no scrappy little lad at all. There were a few women, who didn't look quite so amused or admiring as the men. Especially the fat one in the pink silk gown and thick cape who stood gaping at her just behind Brendan.

Mira's wrists were still held in his viselike grip, and she tried to jerk free so that she might reclaim her dignity. "Defenseless?" She attempted a smile and wished she could melt into the ice-clogged cracks between the wharf planking. "Billy is *not* defenseless. He carries a knife in his belt, and if he'd tried to use it on me, it wouldn't have been the first time. And would you please—" she renewed her struggles to free herself "—let got of my wrists? Really, Brendan, I don't consider *you* defenseless. I won't hit you, if that's what you're afraid of."

He laughed and let her go, his expression instantly sobering when Billy, with a strangled sob, lunged to his feet and hurled himself at Mira. Brendan grabbed him before any more damage could be done. "Here now," he said disapprovingly. "We'll have none of that. She won the fight fair and square, m'lad. Go on home now before you two end up bloody well killing each other."

"I'll not be bested by a mere woman!"

Mira whirled, her thick hair flashing about her face. "You *were* bested, Billy, and if you lay one finger on me, so help me God I'll send you spinning on your arse so hard, you won't be able to get up in the morning!" She hunched her shoulders and tapped her chin, her angry breaths coming out in frosty puffs. "Come on, try it! Hit *me*, not a poor little cat! C'mon, I dare you, you frigging pile of cow sh—"

"I said, *enough!*" Brendan yanked the two apart, his voice sterner than she'd ever heard it. "And that goes for both of you. Young man, take your fish bucket and go. Miss Mira, please tend to your horse. He seems to be eating the adornments in that woman's hat, and I daresay she's likely to swoon—''

The crowd exploded in laughter, and when Mira saw whose hat—and whose hair—Rigel was chomping on, she did, too. ''Rigel!'' She placed two frozen fingers into her mouth and whistled, and the colt lifted his elegant head from Miss Lucy Preble's perfectly outlandish hair arrangement, a few silk daisies caught helplessly in his mouth, and his head swinging toward his mistress with guilty obedience. Chewing loudly, he stepped away from his victim—who chose that moment to do exactly what Brendan had predicted she would do—and started toward Mira, his shod hooves booming hollowly upon the wharf as he broke into a trot.

The crowd roared, and even Brendan's russet brows lifted in high amusement. But the sulky girl in pink who stood behind him did not smile. In fact, she didn't look amused at all.

''Really, Brendan. Can we please go now?'' she sniffed.

Mira, catching Rigel's bridle, felt the grin freeze upon her mouth. The fat girl had a possessive hand on Brendan's sleeve now, and she was looking at both Mira and Rigel with a mixture of dislike, disdain, and unfriendliness she made no attempt to hide. She had pale golden hair that was powdered into even more paleness, twenty pounds of jewelry hanging around what little neck she had, and a very full, pouting mouth that was firmly anchored on both beams. And that wasn't all she had. Two double chins sunk into a band of flesh that circled her throat like a collar. Short little legs and inflated wrists, also draped with jewelry. Doughy white skin and gloved, pudgy hands, one peeping beneath yards of lace, the other tucked into the pocket of her voluminous skirts, as though she was trying to hide it.

Despite Brendan's leanness, there were enough similarities between the two—the same caramel-colored eyes, the same nose, *cripes,* even the same way one brow was set slightly higher than the other—that there was no doubt in Mira's mind just who this girl was. Except his sibling's eyes held hostility where Brendan's held amusement, her nose was haughty while Brendan's was not, and while the set of Brendan's brow lent him an air of Irish good humor, on his sister it spoke only of disdain.

Drawing Rigel close, Mira looked from one to the other and said baldly, ''Oh, don't mind Miss Preble. She's just mad 'cause my brother dumped her last month. But she really shouldn't be, 'cause he's since dumped the girl he dumped *her* for, and I have a running bet with Father that he'll dump the present one before the month is out. Besides, anyone could see by the way she was looking at Brendan that the swoon was a calculated attempt to get his attention. There's nothing wrong with her, believe me.''

Brendan made a strangled sound.

'' 'Bout time Matt put a new coat of paint on *Mistress*'s figurehead, seeing's how he's made it a tradition to make it resemble his lover every time he decides to find himself a new one.'' She jerked her head toward where the brig stood anchored in the harbor. ''Right now, that figurehead has so many layers of paint on it, I figure it'd take ten workers wielding a hundred chisels a year to dig it all off!''

Her attempts at humor—though truthful—brought a sparkle to Brendan's eye, but only further contempt to his companion's.

''Brendan . . .'' The girl whined and tugged at his sleeve.

''Fan go fóill, Eveleen. Just a moment . . .''

He was looking at Mira, his eyes mellifluous, his smile warm, his hair—that curious color that wasn't quite brown, wasn't quite red, as though it had tried hard to reflect his Irish blood, but failing, had settled for that rich and lustrous shade in between—curling devilishly about his handsome face.

''But Brendan, I'm *hungry.*''

He pushed his tricorn back, watching as the crowd, uninterested now, begin to disperse. ''I said, just a moment, Eveleen. I think introductions here are in order.''

''Introductions? You mean you're *acquainted* with this . . . this creature?''

Mira's hands tightened possessively on Rigel's reins, and she drew herself up to her full height of exactly five feet. ''Are you calling my horse a *creature?*''

The girl gave her a long, haughty look, the sort a queen might've given a fishwife. There was no warmth in her eyes, just plain, open hostility. "No, I am not. I was referring to you."

"Oh, dear." Brendan caught Mira as she lunged forward. "Please, ladies, we'll have none of this."

Mira struggled in his grip. "She just insulted me!"

"Brendan, can we *please* get going? You promised to take me to this Wolfe Tavern for a piece of apple pie. . . ."

"I'll give you the goddamned knife to cut it with!" Mira yelled.

"It's been two hours since I've eaten, and I'm positively famished. . . ."

"Eveleen, just a moment, please! Oh, dear. Oh, dear me. Oh, *shit*. Eveleen, this is Miss Mi—"

"Brendan, you always think of yourself and not me. How would *you* like to be starving and hungry? But no, you're so eager to go see this stupid ship of yours that you're ignorant of my needs. Can we please go? That animal smells most horribly, my feet hurt from standing here for so long, I'm freezing, and as I've told you two times already, I'm *hungry*."

"Smells?!" Mira raged. "He does not smell!"

"I think she was referring to you again," Billy got in.

"You shut your damned mouth, Billy, or I'll shut it for you!"

"You just try it!"

"Oh, I plan to, so help me God!"

"Brendan, I told you, I'm *hungry*. . . ."

"Eveleen, *wait*. Young man, I said go home! Mira, settle down, would you?! Faith and troth, this is ridiculous!" He grabbed Mira's scrawny arm and yanked her away from Billy, hauling Eveleen forward by the elbow at the same time. Mira was a spitting cat, Eveleen an unruffled queen. "Let's start over again. Mira, this is my sister, Eveleen. Eveleen, this young lass is Miss Mira Ashton. She's the one whose family you'll be staying with, and who'll be teaching you how to ride."

Eveleen's pale eyebrow, so like her brother's in shape and set, lifted at Brendan's reference to Mira's gender. Her haughty gaze took in the boyish garb, the unbound hair,

the clenched and bloody fists. Airily she said, "Let's just
hope, then, that the rest of her family conduct themselves
in a more . . . *genteel* way. And also that they've invited
us for supper tonight. I would really love some apple
pie. . . . Brendan, do you think her servants may have
made some for dessert tonight?"

"*I* made dessert for tonight!" Mira bellowed.

Brendan paled at that remark and turned his attention
toward the vessels in the river instead, seeking *her* out.

"Did you? Well, I daresay I hope you washed yourself
before making it. I happen to be very particular about my
food, you know."

"I would never have guessed!"

"And what do you mean by that, Miss Ashton?"

"Get a mirror and maybe you'll see!"

"Brendan? Oh, Brendan? Stop looking at those dumb
ships, would you? This . . . this *person* has just insulted
me, and I don't appreciate it at all. Brendan?"

"Lovely," he said absently.

"She is *not* lovely," Eveleen sniffed. "Her hair is too
straight and it's hanging in her face. Her frame is picked
so clean, it looks like the crows have been at it, and she's
wearing *masculine* clothes. Foul-smelling masculine
clothes, I might add. I can't believe you'd suffer the thought
of her teaching me how to ride. . . ."

"Suffer?!" Mira railed. "You tell me *who's* doing the
damned suffering!"

"Brendan . . . Brendan, can we *please* go now?"

But he was ignoring them both, staring past the brigs,
sloops, and ketches and out toward the middle of the river,
where *Kestrel*, at anchor, stood proudly atop her shadow
and rocked impatiently with the pull of the river as it
merged with the incoming tide. "Lovely . . ." he repeated, his eyes soft and dreamy. *"Thar cinn. Go hálainn.*
All, and more than I hoped for . . . My God, she'll
fly. . . ."

His comment was overheard by a grizzled old seaman
who stood biting a hangnail nearby. "Aye, she'll fly, all
right—if she don't overset herself with the first puff
o'wind."

"Brendan, please . . . What's more important, that stupid ship or me?"

"Huh?"

"Brendan, I've had it with your fascination with that stupid ship. I'm beginning to think you care for *it* more than you do me. And here I am, forced to stand here and suffer this creature's insults, the cold, and a growling stomach, when you could be taking me to this Wolfe Tavern and buying me a piece of apple pie and a glass of buttermilk to wash it down with, but no, all you want to do is stand here and go all sap-eyed over some stupid hunk of wood and cloth!"

Reluctantly he tore his gaze from *Kestrel*, who beckoned to him with the sweet seduction of a woman who is more than sure of herself. He was aching to go aboard her, to explore every fitting of her deck and every inch of her hold. He wanted nothing more than to take her helm and feel her leaping through wind and wave, to just *be* with her. But Brendan considered himself a patient man; he'd developed a fair share of it where Eveleen was concerned, following that horrible day on *Dismal*'s decks when Crichton had drawn his pistol, shot him in the chest—and left his sister with a hand that would be crippled for life. It saddened him that she didn't share his excitement over the schooner, but he alone knew why she was the way she was. Drawing and painting had been her love—but Crichton had robbed her of that precious gift.

"Now, Eveleen." Stepping forward, he slipped his palm beneath Rigel's warm and heavy mane and gently stroked the animal's crested neck. He felt Mira's gaze upon him and didn't trust himself to look at her for fear she'd see the desire burning in his eyes. Rigel, however, had no inhibitions. In happy affection, the colt promptly knocked his head against Brendan's chest and rubbed up and down, leaving little gray hairs all over his impeccable frock coat and tearing one of the enameled buttons off. "I can understand your not caring about *Kestrel*, but don't you like the horse?" He grinned hopefully. "This is the one that's to be your birthday present, isn't it, Miss Mira?"

Mira nodded reluctantly, realizing, in dawning horror

just what this *bargain*—and her offer to let Eveleen stay with her family—was going to mean.

"Oh, he'll do, I suppose. . . . A little small, but sort of pretty, I guess. Brendan, the pie? You *promised*. . . ."

"He's an Arabian," Mira said tightly.

"A what?"

"An Arabian! They're supposed to be small! I can see you don't know a darned thing about horses!"

"I didn't know what an Arabian was either," Brendan confessed, but Mira took it as defense of his whining sister and felt a stab of indignation. She opened her mouth to retort, then closed it with a snap that was almost audible. Thank God *she* had such a wonderful sibling in Matt. She didn't envy Brendan one bit for having to put with this spoiled bitch! And then she realized that Brendan, once he took *Kestrel* out to sea, wouldn't have to put up with this spoiled bitch any longer.

She would.

"What difference does it make *what* he is? I really don't care. I never wanted a horse anyhow, Brendan. They smell. They bite. And this one has his tail up. Oh heavens, if he makes a pile, I'm going to swoon. . . ."

"He's an Arabian!" Mira yelled.

"Does that mean his droppings don't smell, then?" Brendan asked innocently.

"It means he has a shorter back than other horses! It means his tail is set naturally higher as a result! It means that I'm not going to stand here and listen to some ill-tempered bitch who cares more about apple pie than her brother's happiness, and a horse that's the result of centuries of planned and careful breeding!" Tearing free of Brendan's grip, Mira scooped up the cat, faced Eveleen, and hollered, "And furthermore, if he *does* leave a pile, I hope it's smack-dab in the middle of your fine and blasted shoe!"

She vaulted atop Rigel's back and, with Rescue Effort Number Thirty-Seven tucked safely beneath her arm, tore off down the wharf, Rigel's shod hooves booming against the planking and sending up clods of snow as he hit the street.

Dammit to hell and back! She wasn't going to sit around

town and put up with that bitch! When *Kestrel* sailed, she'd be on her!

Chapter 10

"**F**ather won't allow it," Matt predicted, shaking his head. He took off his spectacles and swiped at them with a corner of his shirt. "It's one thing to sneak aboard *Proud Mistress,* but he'll not hear of you going aboard *Kestrel.*"

Mira leaned against the doorframe and stared in disgust at the mess that was Matt's bedroom. Clothes were thrown here, books there, and the bed was unmade. "You're absolutely right, he *won't* hear of it . . . *right,* Matt?"

"Is that a threat?"

"Of course." She flashed him her sauciest grin.

"You won't get away with it."

"Oh? You just watch. *Kestrel* makes her maiden voyage tomorrow, and I intend to be on her."

Matt crossed his arms and shot her a sly glance. "And just why are you so eager to be aboard that schooner, Mira?"

She glared at him. "For the hell of it."

"Right." He grinned at her. "*I* think you've got your eye on its captain."

"Maybe I do."

"I pity the poor man."

"Yeah? Well, I pity all those women you keep courting and dumping."

Matt scowled. Steam appeared in the bottom of his lenses, and his lips thinned out in a straight line. "Look, Mira, I told you how I *really* feel about those women—"

"Well, don't get mad at me, 'cause *you're* the one who keeps putting up with 'em! You're too *nice,* you know that? Too bloody *gallant!* You told me you're looking for a *good* girl, but you sure as hell are looking in the wrong place to find the kind of woman you're after! Yet you keep on buying 'em things, treating 'em like gold. . . . When're you ever gonna realize they're all the same, nothing but a pack of bitchy hussies who only want your money and the prestige of having been your latest lover? No, I don't pity them, not one bit! I pity *you* for suffering such nonsense!''

"Yeah, well, maybe I'm lonely, all right?"

"So you settle for something you don't want?"

"Wouldn't you?"

"Hell, no! I go for *exactly* what I want, and you know it." She tossed her hair over her shoulder and willed herself to calm down. Matt didn't need to be reminded of his weakness for love and affection.

"So what *do* you want, then?" he asked.

"Captain Merrick."

"Cripes, Mira!"

"He'd do quite nicely for Father's Ultimatum, don't you think? But first I have to learn more about the man. You know I've always vowed that when—I mean, *if*—I ever marry, it'd have to be to a sea captain. Well, Captain Merrick may do, but first he has to pass my Test. That's why I have to go aboard his schooner—to make sure he's a competent sailor. We know he can *design* a ship, but he has to prove to me that he can sail, and most importantly, *command* one, as well."

"Jeez, Mira . . ."

But she was already pacing the room, scheming, as usual. "The only way for me to find that out is to go aboard *Kestrel* and see the captain in action. And as for Father, he'll never know, 'cause he'll have his eyes peeled looking for me to go aboard *Proud Mistress,* just like I've always done!"

"And I suppose you think Captain Merrick's going to allow it, no questions asked?"

"Of course not, you dolt. And if he did, he'd fail part one of the Test. No captain in his right mind—except *you,* of course—" she laughed and made a face at his infuriated expression "—is going to allow a woman aboard his ship, especially as a gunner. But getting away with it will be half the fun. In fact, I'll have just as much fun pulling the wool over *Captain Merrick's* eyes as I will over Father's!''

Matt grinned, getting caught up in the idea. His eyes began to gleam. "I assume you have a disguise all figured out?"

"Of course."

"And I suppose this is your way of paying Father back for making that Ultimatum in the first place?"

"Uh-huh."

"Well, I wish you luck, but you'll never get away with it. Father'll catch you at it, guaranteed."

"Wanna bet?"

"Aye, I'll bet! What do you want if you win?"

She looked around the room. "Let's see. . . ." Her gaze fell upon the musket on the wall. "How 'bout that fine Brown Bess?"

"Cripes, Mira, that's my favorite gun!"

"Chicken."

Matt's lips tightened. "All right, fine. If you get away with this and win the bet, you can have the gun. But if Father catches you and *I* win, then I get—"

"—A black eye."

"What?!"

She smirked at his blank look. "Let's face it, Matt, the only way he's gonna find out is if *you* tell him."

"Forget it! I can't win either way!"

"Oh? You've been bellyaching for ages about me sneaking aboard *Proud Mistress* and getting in your hair. Well, now that Father's wise to me, there's no way that can continue. So you've *already* won. . . . You'll be rid of me, and I'll be Captain Merrick's problem instead."

"I think you already are."

"What do you mean by that?"

"Ain't it obvious? The man's in love with you."

"Well, half of Newburyport's in love with you," Mira flung back. "When're you going to bring home this *good* girl you keep promising to find, huh, Matthew?!"

"Look, just lay off and stay the hell out of my love life, would you?"

"Then stay the hell out of mine."

"You don't have one."

"But I will."

They stood glaring at each other, neither willing to give any ground. But then they thought of Mira's scheme, and the outrageous implications of it. Mira's lips began to twitch, and Matt threw back his head in laughter. They were all in for some rough sailing ahead. Mira. Ephraim. And especially the unsuspecting Captain Merrick.

Many hours later, when darkness was old, supper had been eaten, and Mira's apple pie fed to the dog, Eveleen stood in the room that would be hers during her stay in Newburyport. The shutters were closed against the night; thick gingham curtains with a stenciled pineapple design were further protection against the cold drafts. Wind rattled the windows in their casements, and she could hear snow whispering against the frosty panes.

Shivering, she dug her toes into the thick hooked rug that covered the wide-boarded floor. Her trunk lay half-unpacked at the foot of an elegant Hepplewhite four-poster, and a candle, safe within a hurricane globe, cast a soft and flickering glow over the pillows heaped against the carved headboard. A linsey-woolsey counterpane topped the bed, and a thick cotton patchwork quilt was folded neatly at the foot. But despite the bed's inviting look, Eveleen was not ready to retire for the night.

She felt bad about being so hateful to Mira Ashton, but she just couldn't help herself. Now, pale and naked, she stood before a big cheval mirror, looking at herself as Mira had so cruelly suggested. The candle's soft glow would've made artwork of Mira's slim curves, but it was not as kind to Eveleen. It pulled shadows from beneath her heavy cheeks, darkened the puffy hollows that framed her eyes, and cast thick and heavy shadows beneath her equally thick and heavy breasts. She glared at her reflection, hating it, wanting to spit on the mirror, and thus, herself.

Downstairs, she heard hearty male laughter coming from the study, where Brendan and old Captain Ashton and his handsome son with the wild red hair had gone. Their good spirits brought a sour taste to her mouth, but she was too mired in self-hatred to recognize it as jealousy. If only she had something to laugh about. She couldn't remember a time she'd been happy since the day Richard Crichton had nearly killed her beloved brother and taken away the one thing she'd ever been good at.

Good at? She'd been gifted. . . . But Eveleen would never paint again. And now she held her right hand behind her back so she wouldn't have to see it reflected in the mirror, for it was even more hideous to look at than her thick rolls of fat.

Her heart ached, making her stomach feel hungry and empty. Now she wished she'd grabbed one—or better yet, two—of those chewy molasses cookies left over from supper. They'd certainly make her feel better, as only food could. Not even Brendan, whom she loved more than anyone or anything else in the world, could fill up that emptiness the same way one of those cookies would. Poor Brendan. He tried so hard to please her . . . renting that fine house in Portsmouth, buying her all kinds of jewels with his privateering profits that she really didn't want, and now this good-for-nothing horse. She curled her lip in despair. What on earth was she supposed to *do* with a horse? She'd never ridden one before in her life, and with only one functional hand, how could she? Obviously Brendan believed this Mira Ashton capable of working miracles.

Mira Ashton. Funny, she thought, how we expect miracles from those we're head over heels in love with, as though they're infallible, incapable of failure, *perfect*. And the way her brother had been staring at Mira all during that fine supper, barely commenting on the delicious mushroom pasty with its golden, latticed crust, the spit-roasted partridge, the peaches stuffed with spicy mincemeat, even the hot brick-oven bread with the thick slabs of butter and cheese . . . why, he'd even *blushed* when Mira had happened to look up and catch him staring! No, there was no doubt in Eveleen's mind that Brendan was utterly and totally taken with this . . . girl—a girl who went from young boy to fine lady with the same ease with which she vaulted on and off that gray colt's back.

Maybe Mira *could* work miracles. Maybe she *could* teach her how to ride . . . but Eveleen doubted it. For one thing, Mira had not demonstrated a great reserve of patience. And more important, Eveleen had absolutely no desire to learn. And certainly not from the likes of *that* creature. Besides, she was a cripple. Even if Brendan couldn't face that fact, she could.

And there was her body, still reflected in all its fat glory, reminding her just how big and awkward it really was. Grimacing, Eveleen poked the flesh circling her waist; or rather, what used to be her waist. Like soft bread dough, it sprang slowly back when she removed her finger. Fat. It hung from her upper arms, rippled like ocean swells beneath fishy white skin, stole the space that used to be between her thighs. It stuck out in front of her by a good foot, catching all the bread crumbs and sauce and pieces of pie and cookies that weren't lucky enough to make it into her mouth. It was thick, it was ugly, and in the soft glow of the candle, it had never looked worse.

Men never looked at her anymore, except with pity. Now they simply acknowledged her presence with a polite nod, a tolerant greeting, and that was it before going on to more interesting matters, such as fine, *slender* women whose bodies were worth looking at. Not her. She didn't count as a woman. She didn't count as anything.

If only she could still draw and paint . . .

They sure looked at Mira Ashton, though. Every single one of them back on that wharf had been utterly taken with her, and it wouldn't have mattered if she'd been wearing a dirty sack and a bag over her head, they *still* would've looked at her because Mira Ashton was bold, she was beautiful—and she was *thin.*

Eveleen poked at a wrist that was once as gracefully elegant as her brother's. Now she couldn't even see the bones that defined it, although she could feel them if she pressed her fingers hard enough into the flesh. This she did with cruel hatred, hard enough to bring tears to her eyes. Her wrist and hand weren't at all like Mira Ashton's, which seemed equally suited to pummel a boy's face or bake what had turned out to be a positively *dreadful* pie. And speaking of food, Mira Ashton hadn't made a glutton of herself, as *she* had. Mira hadn't had three helpings of pasty and roasted partridge, two-thirds of the stuffed peaches, four pieces of bread, and enough milk to feed a hungry calf. She hadn't drowned herself in a quart of syllabub buried under a froth of whipped egg white and sweet, thick cream. And she hadn't hidden the little pastries the housekeeper had brought out following the failure of the pie in her napkin, stuffed them in her pocket, and sneaked them upstairs in case she got hungry between suppertime and breakfast.

But she, Eveleen, had.

No, Mira had picked at this, picked at that, and spent most of the evening staring at Brendan when *he* wasn't staring at her. Oh, if she could only be like her. Hottempered without being vindictive. Soft and impish and slender. As equally at home in the blue woolen gown and demure mobcap she'd worn to supper as she was sitting astride a galloping horse in a man's breeches. Oh, Mira Ashton could have any man she wanted. She didn't even have to try. Mira was pretty. Mira had both hands. And Mira was *thin*.

Eveleen's days of having men hovering about her, her dreams of marriage to a fine and handsome prince, were long gone. Now there were only two males in this entire world who cared that she existed: her beloved brother and that gray dockyard cat, whose gender she'd discovered after finding it curled up on her clean white coverlet and tossing it to the floor.

The cat. It had been quite a violent scene when Mr. Ashton discovered it during supper. Or rather, it had discovered him. The cat had shown the bad sense to come into the dining room while they were *eating*, of all things, rubbing itself against the old sea captain's bowed legs and setting off a yelling match between the shipbuilder and his equally vocal daughter that had made the blood drain from Eveleen's face in terror for her life. From the nature of the argument—and that was a *mild* word for the shouting that had nearly left her deaf—the gray cat wasn't the first stray that Mira had brought home, and Eveleen felt a twinge of shame for secretly gloating when Ephraim had exploded with wrath against his daughter. That gloating, however, had turned quickly to grudging admiration when Mira had leaped to her feet and hollered back at her father at the top of her lungs until her handsome brother, Matthew, who had let the yelling go on for several minutes, finally chilled the hot tempers by his tactful and timely mention of a rigging detail of Brendan's dumb schooner.

And Brendan? He'd taken it all in with that patient, quirky grin of his, obviously accustomed to this family's strange ways and unwilling to let them spoil his own appetite—an appetite that had been quite hearty until he'd come to Mira's apple pie. . . .

Despite herself, Eveleen grinned, then, just as quickly, frowned. Mira Ashton could do anything; she was perfect. She could probably bake a good pie, too, if it suited her to do so. But tonight? Obviously she'd left out the sugar and replaced it with vinegar in a deliberate attempt to be nasty to her, Eveleen, because she was fat. Yes, that was it. But why, then, had Brendan scrunched up his face and grabbed for his napkin? And why had Ephraim and Matthew passed over the pie, as though they'd *known* better than to try it, and gone for the cookies instead? Had they known that Mira had deliberately sabotaged it?

Ephraim, maybe, but she couldn't believe that Matthew would be a party to such. *Matthew.* Eveleen's eyes went dreamy. Oh, he didn't look like a sea captain at all, with that flaming red hair and boyish freckles, those spectacles that kept sliding down his nose and giving him more of a scholarly appearance than a militaristic one. But appearances are deceiving. She had no trouble visualizing him commanding the deck of his ship, no trouble envisioning him plucking her poor, half-dead brother from the ocean and restoring him to life. Matthew was gentle and attentive and kind; to the Ashtons' staff, to Miss Mira, even to *her,* Eveleen, as though he really *cared* about making her stay at his home comfortable. And he had a charming Yankee twang to his speech, a penchant for setting his easily ignited sister off, and wonderful brown eyes that were made all the more wonderful and brown behind the magnification of his spectacles . . .

Eveleen caught sight of herself in the mirror once more . . . and her dreams of handsome princes fizzled out. She pinched the roll of fat around her middle and stared hatefully at her reflection, then turned away from the mirror, biting the inside of her lip to keep from crying. The candle had burned low and was beginning to flicker. Cold drafts chilled her ankles, raised gooseflesh on her arms. Eveleen eyed the bed, its fluted and carved posts supporting a lacy canopy, and its thick patchwork quilt (no doubt made by Mira; she could do *anything*) just waiting to be snuggled under. It was a feminine bed, a delicate creation. It was a bed made for a *woman*, not a fat and ugly slob like her.

But if she retired now, breakfast would come that much sooner. Shivering, she crossed the cold room to the fire-place, filled the bed warmer with hot coals, and passed it quickly between the crisp sheets to warm them. Unthinkingly, she reached for the coverlet with her right hand—and saw that horrible thing that was attached to her wrist, that ugly, crippled, scarred, and useless thing she kept hidden from the rest of the world.

Half of her thumb was gone . . . and where her fore and middle fingers had been, there were only—stumps.

Chins quivering, tears streaming quietly down her broad cheeks, heavy breasts trembling with the effort it took to contain the pent-up sobs so no one else would hear them, Eveleen dug her nightgown out of her chest and yanked it hatefully over her head. Already it was too tight beneath her arms, and the material cut into the soft flesh. Angrily she started to slam the lid of the chest down, but as she did, her gaze fell upon a gift that Brendan had given her for her eighteenth birthday.

It was a box of pencils and a pad of paper, now yellow with age, peeking out from under the folded clothing.

She stared for a long time. The sobs caught in her throat, and tremulously she reached out and touched the paper with the stub of her forefinger. How hopeful Brendan had been when he'd given her that gift, how encouraging he'd been when he'd urged her to *try* to draw, even if it meant using her left hand, instead.

But she'd never had the courage.

Unbidden, Eveleen thought of Mira Ashton, who could do anything. Mira had the full use of both hands . . . but if *she* were a cripple, would she allow it to ruin her life?

No. Mira Ashton would've *made* herself draw.

It was no wonder that Brendan was attracted to her. Mira was strong, resourceful, brave. Perhaps she, Eveleen could be brave, too. Maybe if she tried to help herself, the handsome Captain Ashton might pay her a bit of attention. If Brendan admired the trait in Mira, wouldn't Matthew admire it in her? And if she could turn out a drawing as fine as the ones she'd been capable of before she lost the use of her hand, surely Matthew would notice . . . and perhaps even admire her for it.

She may be fat, but inside, she was a gifted artist . . . if only she had the means of tapping that gift.

For the first time since Crichton's shot had taken off her fingers, Eveleen wanted to *try*.

The paper lay there, seeming to stare up at her. Eveleen stared back. She started to withdraw her hand and then, biting her lip, reached out a final time and awkwardly grasped the pad. It had been nearly four years since she'd touched a sketchpad, and just having one in her hand bolstered her courage.

Shaking now, she placed the sketchpad on the nearby desk and reached out to pick up a pencil.

And dropped it.

A tear rolled from her eye, and angrily Eveleen brushed it away. She would not give up. She *wouldn't!*

The fire crackled. The pencil lay on the floor. Eveleen choked back another sob, picked it up, and this time managed to hold it between the crook of her half thumb and the stub of her forefinger. It felt stiff . . . familiar . . . terrifying.

Could she do it? *Oh, please God . . .*

Shaking madly now, she bit down on her lower lip in concentration and slowly, fearfully, touched the pencil to the paper. A line appeared, shaky, uneven, faint—

So intent was she, that she never heard Mira's soft knocking.

Her brow furrowed in concentration, became beaded with sweat. Her breathing quickened and she moved her hand, letting her arm do the work, hoping against hope that she could do it, oh please, God, just do it—

The pencil fell from her grasp and rolled away.

It was too much. Angrily Eveleen hurled the sketchpad across the room, crying bitterly as it slammed against the wall and tumbled to the floor. She never saw it lying there, its pages in forlorn disarray. She never saw Mira, who'd come to try to make amends after their initial meeting, standing silently in the doorway with tears of sympathy rolling down her own cheeks. Throwing herself down on the bed, Eveleen pressed her face into the pillow to muffle her sobs and wished with all her heart she were dead.

Eveleen wasn't the only Merrick who had trouble sleeping that night. Three hours later Brendan lay awake in his own bed, watching moonlight glinting off the brass telescope at the window and listening to the ticking of all sixteen—it *was* up to sixteen now; he'd actually counted—clocks that Ephraim had set in strategic places throughout the house. He listened to that ticking, that tocking, while his engineer's mind calculated how many ticks there were in every hour, if one assumed the clocks—all sixteen of them, that is—ticked every second. Take sixty, multiply it by sixty again, then by sixteen—

Faith, no wonder he couldn't sleep.

He looked again at the telescope and considered getting up. It had snowed a bit, earlier; now dark clouds were filing out to sea and leaving stars, glittering like chips of blue ice, in their place. His eyes were well adjusted to the darkness, but moonlight would illuminate the distant river well enough that he should be able to see *Kestrel* waiting down there in the harbor. . . .

Shivering, he got up and went to the window. The great constellation of Orion the Hunter had just crawled out of his eastern bed over the Atlantic; now, brandishing his shield to the starry zenith, he lay on his side over the dark wedge of land that was Plum Island.

Ah, Orion . . . In the crystalline night, the Hunter's stars had never seemed brighter: the fiery Betelgeuse, glowing red at his right shoulder; Bellatrix at his left; Saiph and the bluish Rigel at his feet.

Rigel. Brendan grinned to himself. He'd spent the better part of the afternoon arguing with Mira over that wee gray colt before finally convincing her to keep the horse for herself. The steed was too much for Eveleen, and it was obvious his sister was terrified of him—but Mira had been determined to uphold her part of the bargain. They'd finally arrived at a compromise. Eveleen would take Rigel's dam, Shaula, who was, Mira had assured him, of a more dulcet temperament than either Rigel or the black stallion, El Nath. Brendan hoped she was right. That black devil-horse was, at the moment, making one hell of a racket down in his stall, slamming his hooves against the door and shrilling in anger.

He wondered if there was a clock in the stable. 'Twould explain the steed's bad temper.

He sighed, then shivering, crawled back into bed and pulled the covers up to his chin. He was freezing, despite the crackling flames in the big fireplace, the sheet-wrapped brick snugged up against his toes, the coverlet, the wool blankets, and the three thick heavy quilts he was lying beneath. An average person would be suffocating right about now. But Brendan's long legs, long arms, and long fingers weren't average. It took time for the blood to reach those far-distant points from his heart; no wonder it was cold by the time it got there.

Maybe that's why he couldn't sleep.

Tick, tock, tick, tock . . .

"Faith."

"M-r-r-r-r-r-r-rrrrreow?"

"Oh, go away!"

"M-R-R-R-R-EEEE-O-O-O-O-OOOOW!"

Faith, what a screech! Cursing, he grabbed the animal and shoved it beneath the covers before it could wake up the whole bloody household, where it promptly flattened itself against his leg and set up a purring loud enough to drown out even the shelf clock that ruled the mantel.

At least its fur was warm.

But as he lay there thinking of tomorrow and counting off the moments—*tick, tock, tick, tock*—till morning, when he would be rowed out to his new command to take *her* on her first cruise, he knew why he couldn't sleep.

It wasn't because of the clocks, though they certainly didn't help any.

It wasn't because he was cold, though he certainly was.

And it wasn't because of *Kestrel,* waiting for him down in the moonlit river, although his heart began to pound every time he thought of her.

It was because of Miss Mira Ashton.

She was in the next room over from him. Separated from him by naught but a plastered wall. Carefully, so as not to crush the cat, he turned over in bed and stared at the moonlit curtains and the night shadows playing across the floor. *Just a plastered wall.*

If only she were a moon-maiden. She'd float right through that wall and come to him. Shutting his eyes, he imagined her standing in the silver light coming through the window, her thick, unbound hair all but dwarfing her curvy body, her nightgown swirling about her bare feet and surrounding her trim ankles in a gossamer cloud of fairy white.

He groaned, feeling himself growing hard.

The image sharpened. . . . That nightgown would be sheer and ethereal and diaphanous, like the moonlight floating through the curtains. That dark, silken mane of hers would be streaming down her back, tangled with sleep and scented with roses, sweet hay, and the warmth of slumber. Her lips would be soft and parted and inviting. . . . Her hands would slip up his torso, his chest, then down his hips and—

He flung himself on his stomach and buried his face in the pillow.

And then a sudden thought occurred to him.

You see, Father goes to bed at 11:45. . . . At exactly 12:33 he puts out his candle, and at 12:45 he falls asleep. . . .

Brendan sat up.

Tick, tock, tick, tock . . .

It was well after one o'clock.

He perched on the edge of the bed for a long moment, shivering in the drafts, his toes and the soles of his feet going numb where they touched the chilly, wide-boarded floor. Being cold, however, did nothing to relieve the burning ache in his loins. Finally he crossed the room once again and, after a brief struggle with the frozen sill, threw open the window. A blast of clean, frigid air drove against his face. Outside, the moon, so bright it hurt his eyes to look at it, threw shadows across the snow-dusted lawn and gleamed upon clusters of dead leaves, still clinging stubbornly to skeletal branches and shaking and rustling in the gusty, wintry wind.

Teeth chattering, he leaned out, looking off across the frosty rooftops toward the harbor. A few lights glowed from one of the buildings in Market Square, and in the distance he could just make out the last fading sounds of merriment coming from the direction of Wolfe Tavern. Otherwise the night was quiet, the air clear and cold and crisp. Overhead, clouds glowed with blinding silver light, drifting beneath the stars and leaving them twinkling in a vast and lonely sky.

Stars. They were distant in contrast to the sharp edges of the clouds, yet burned so brightly, he felt he could reach out and touch them.

Mira . . . as in the constellation Cetus . . .

Distant, yet close. Like Mira in the next room.

Ah, Faith.

Caution and good sense took a backseat to Irish recklessness. He'd been aching for her since they'd met, damn it. He would just go to her room, ease the door open, and look at her, sleeping. Just look—and nothing more. There was no harm in that. . . .

Shivering with cold and anticipation, he padded across the room and carefully opened his door. In the great hall, shadows danced against darkened portraits, and clocks echoed loudly in the stillness. Outside, wind rattled a windowpane and drove around the eaves, and from behind one of the closed doors came the loud, heavy sounds of Ephraim's snoring. Brendan swallowed, feeling like a thief in the night. Then he moved on, stifling a nervous gasp as something twined around his legs and fur brushed against his bare ankles, nearly tripping him. Slowly he reached for Mira's door.

It was unlocked.

He paused, hesitating.

Don't do it, Brendan, warned his English side.

Open the door, laddie, and be done with it! urged his Irish one.

He opened the door.

Blessed silence. There were no clocks in this room. Automatically his gaze went to the graceful Hepplewhite four-poster, its high canopy and pale muslin hangings glowing silver in the moonlight. But the bed was empty, the pile of pillows heaped against the dark headboard haphazardly askew. And then he saw her, curled up on the window seat and looking out into the night as he had done. Her arms were wrapped around her knees, her tiny feet tucked beneath her so that only her bare toes peeped out from beneath the edge of the quilt she'd wrapped herself in. On a lowboy, a candle glowed from a hurricane lamp, reflecting her face in the windowpanes; its soft, orange glow made her eyes look dark and luminous, her hair warm and burnished, her skin soft and golden.

He caught his breath and she stiffened, seeing his reflection in the glass.

"Captain Merrick?"

He was caught. Helplessly and horribly caught. "I'm sorry . . . I was looking for—for Eveleen's room, and must've chosen the wrong door—"

She turned then, her long, dark hair falling around her shoulders, her eyes soft. "There's no need to apologize, Captain. In fact, I'm glad you're here. I . . . would've sought you out if you hadn't come to me."

Brendan was glad it was dark enough in the room that she didn't see his shocked expression and the rush of color that flooded his face. His hand tightened on the doorknob and he turned to go.

"Wait."

He paused, not daring to turn around. His hand began to sweat on the doorknob.

Behind him came the creak of the floorboards as she padded softy toward him. He swallowed hard, his heart beginning to pound. If she touched him, he would be totally undone. He could feel her, just behind him. He could smell her, that alluring mix of roses and soap and femininity. *Faith,* he had to get out of here—

Her hand fell upon his arm just as he would've bolted. "Brendan?"

He stiffened, breathing hard.

"Brendan, I want to talk to you about . . . about your sister."

He breathed a sigh of relief, for he'd been terrified she

was going to ask him to kiss her again. He was already
falling in love with her. He needed no encouragement to
fall even harder. Slowly he turned, and tried not to think
of the sweet pressure of her little hand on his arm.

"What happened to her, Brendan?"

He'd known she would ask—and he'd had every intention of explaining the reasons for the anger and bitterness
that lay behind Eveleen's actions. But Mira's nearness was
making mud of his thoughts. He bit down hard on his lip
and backed up against the door, trying to put some distance between himself and this endearing little imp who
was now showing him a sweet side he never knew existed.
Hurriedly he said, "I'm sorry she behaved so badly toward you. Perhaps having her stay here isn't such a good
idea after all—"

Mira tightened her grip on his arm, holding him. "No.
I *want* her to stay."

He stared down at her, then shut his eyes in an attempt
to block out the sight of her breasts, clearly outlined beneath the sheerness of her nightgown. Her hand was gliding up his arm, down . . . up, down. . . . *Oh, faith, lassie,*
he thought, desperately. *Don't do this to me. . . .*

"She's hurting, Brendan," he heard her say. "I didn't
realize it this afternoon, so I merely reacted to her anger.
But I shouldn't have. Your sister's miserable, isn't she?"

A shadow came over his face and he looked away.

"Brendan, what happened to her to *make* her so unhappy?" she persisted. Then she thought of Eveleen hurling the sketchbook against the wall and sobbing in
frustration. "It's her hand, isn't it?"

"I'd rather not talk about it."

"But you must. Eveleen needs a friend, Brendan. I'll
bet she doesn't have any, does she? I'll bet you're the only
person in the world who cares about her, aren't you?"

He set his jaw.

"Dammit, Brendan, I'm trying to *help!* For Christ's
sake, trust me, would you?!"

He looked down at her, standing so close to him, her
breasts pushing against him, her hands moving up his
shoulders. Her arms went around his neck. Her eyes were
soft and pleading, the set of her chin determined. He

reached up, grasped her arms, decided he liked having them around his neck after all, and tilting his head back, rested it against the doorframe.

Finally he sighed and raked a hand through his hair. She was right, of course . . . but still, he found it hard to talk about it, even now—especially with Mira so close to him. "It happened almost four years ago," he said quietly. Shuddering, he stared at the candle flickering atop the lowboy. "I was the newly promoted flag captain in a British fleet. We were aboard a frigate in Boston Harbor. There was a commotion . . . an, uh. . . accident. Someone fired a pistol, and the ball caught Eveleen in the hand." He paused, wondering if he should elaborate, then decided that nothing would come of spreading more bitterness. The silence stretched on. "She . . . lost most of her thumb and a good part of two fingers."

"My God, Brendan."

He was silent for a long time. His eyes were distant, sad. "My sister was a gifted artist," he said. "Our mother used to say she was born with a paintbrush in her hand. In fact, Eveleen was doing our portraits before she was five years old, those of the London nobility by the time she was fifteen. What a sensation she was. . . . They used to pay handsomely just for the chance to sit for her." He gave a little smile, remembering. "She used to joke that someday she would study with the masters and that her work would hang in the museums alongside theirs. But Crichton's shot changed all that."

"Crichton?" Mira frowned. "Who's he, the one who accidentally shot her?"

"It doesn't matter who he is. What's done is done."

Mira stared up at him. His hair was tousled, curling darkly against his neck. Pain darkened his eyes, robbing them of the Irish good humor she'd come to know and love. So maybe Eveleen hadn't always been like this. Perhaps, with a little understanding, the girl Eveleen had once been could come back.

"Now I understand why she's so bitter," she said slowly, pushing her fingers into the soft hair at Brendan's nape and getting as close to him as she could. His eyes grew wary, but he did not move away. Cripes, but his body was hard! "And because I do, I can try to help her, and make a friend out of her. Father's been bellyaching lately that I don't have any students for my school. I think Eveleen will be my first one."

"She'll insist she can't ride," Brendan said quickly, beginning to fidget.

"I'll insist she *can.*" Again Mira thought of Eveleen's pain and frustration when she'd come upon her earlier, desperately trying to draw—and failing. "Maybe she can't paint, but she needs to know she can do something, something she'll really have to strive for. And once she does it, she'll get the self-confidence she needs—

"Mira?"

"And once she has self-confidence, then, and only then, can she be happy again—"

"Moyrrra?" His voice sounded strangled.

"Aye?"

"Please don't press your hips against me like that."

"Why not, does it hurt?"

"Faith, it doesn't hurt—just stop!"

Mira grinned, putting aside the challenge of Eveleen Merrick and suddenly thinking of Father's Ultimatum. A delightfully wicked thought ocurred to her. "I will, if you kiss me," she declared saucily, pressing herself against him even harder. Panic shone in his eyes and he tried to back away from her. She tightened her arms around his neck and held on. He pulled, and her bare feet began to slide upon the floor.

"Brendan, if I get a sliver in my foot, I'm going to haul off and bloody your nose."

"Faith, lassie, if you'd just let go of my neck—"

She giggled and buried her face against his chest, letting her lips play with the soft, wiry hair that grew there. He was breathing hard, and it had nothing to do with his efforts to detach her arms from his neck.

"Let go."

"No."

Her knee, silken and smooth beneath the gauzy fabric of her nightgown, began to slide up and down his thigh, rubbing him like a cat. He took a last step back and came up against the wall. She had him pinned now. His heartbeat thundered in his ears. Her fingers loosened, trailed a path down his neck. His throat. Into the hollows above his collarbone, down the cleft of his chest, over and around the scar that Crichton's pistol shot had left so long ago.

"Faith, lassie, what're you *doing?!*"

"Seducing you, of course."

"That's not how you go about seducing a man!"

"Well then, how *do* you?"

"I don't know, I've never tried it!"

"Jesus, Brendan, has anyone ever told you that you come out with the damnedest things?"

"And you, *Moyrrra,* has anyone ever told *you* that you're far too bold for your own good?"

She grinned. "Many times."

He looked down at her, obviously trying to be aggravated—but she could see his defenses crumbling like a poorly built fort. One corner of his mouth was twitching, and his eyes were beginning to sparkle, drawing her into their laughing depths, then buoying her up like bubbles in a glass of champagne. Her nipples tightened in response, and her stomach gave a little quiver, as though she'd swallowed a dozen fluttery moths; now that strange, tingling feeling worked itself up into her head to leave her flushed and slightly giddy and more than a little breathless.

"Do you want to sit on the window seat with me, Brendan?" Unconsciously her tongue slipped out to wet her lips, and she saw his eyes darken. "We can . . . watch stars."

He stared at her. "Faith, how is it that one moment we're talking about my sister, and the next you've got me so aching and befuddled, I can't think straight. . . ."

Her laughter cut him off. Grasping his wrists, Mira dragged him toward the window, anticipation making her giddy and reckless, for he wasn't protesting at all. Starlight bathed their skin in silver, then candlelight gilded it with gold. Shivers coursed up Mira's spine, radiated into her limbs, pushed the gooseflesh up on her skin, and made her tremble with delight. What would it be like to try and seduce him, to explore these mad sensations that burned through her blood? "I've been wanting to do this to you ever since you first kissed me," she breathed, pushing him down atop the cushions. Her hands moved over his chest, pinning him down. Her fingers traced a ridge of sinewy muscle, and his breathing came a little faster, a little harsher. "I know you're scared of me, but I won't hurt you, I promise—"

"Faith, *Moyrrra*, I'm not scared of you."

She straddled him, sitting on his belly and leaning toward his neck, feeling bolder now, getting braver. "*Moyrrra*," she repeated, her warm breath feathering against his skin. "I love how you say my name." Her hair fell around her face as she kissed his chin, his neck, his throat. "It sends goose bumps up my back."

"There's no other way to say your name . . . *stóirín.*"

His arms had come up to close around her back now, and she sank down atop him, feeling the heat of his sinewy body burning right through their nightclothes. She wanted to kiss him, to touch him, to rub her breasts against the hard curve of his chest and ease their stinging ache. Moisture dampened her thighs, and the strange, hot tinglings began to throb there, spreading up, spreading out, finally centering in her heart and lungs until it was an effort just to breathe. She buried her face against his neck, the stubble there harsh against her cheeks, the spicy scent of his bath soap intensifying with the heat and moisture of her breath—

But what had he just called her? Raising her head, Mira clawed her hair out of her eyes so she could see. "Stor—?"

"*Stóirín*," he repeated, catching a handful of her dark tresses in his fist as it fell down over one eye. " 'Tis Irish for darling. Little treasure."

"Oh." Her eyes were impish. "Do you think I'm a little treasure, Brendan?"

He rubbed her hair between his thumb and forefinger, then pushed it to his lips. His eyes gleamed, sparkled with mirth and spirit. "Oh, you're a treasure, all right. What surprises me is that no one has stolen you yet."

"No one would dare." She bent her head once more, kissing his neck and murmuring against his hot skin. "You see, Father is . . . uh, rather intimidating. And Matt is very protective. Those that get past Matt are frightened off by Father. And those that Father approves of are sent packing by Matt—sometimes with his musket.'' She lifted her head and gave him one of her cat-smiles. "Of course, I really don't need Father and Matt to discourage . . . unwanted attention. Sometimes I think men are more afraid of me than they are Matt and Father combined, though I certainly don't know why.''

He said nothing, clenching his teeth in sweet agony, for he was growing painfully hard.

"Anyhow, the reality is that I've never had a sweetheart, and all the men I know are just friends.''

Her lips were moving down his throat now, nibbling here, nibbling there, driving heat out of every pore in his body.

"Beware, lassie, of men who call themselves 'friends,' '' he ground out, his voice ragged and his breathing hard. "They're usually the most dangerous of sorts.''

"And what are you, Brendan? Are you a . . . friend?''

"A friend?'' Her hand was moving lower. And lower. He tensed, groaned, set his teeth. "Faith . . . Oh God, I can't take this. . . .''

"Take what, Brendan? Am I hurting you? I don't want you to be afraid of me. Here, I'll sit back on my haunches and give you some air—ooh! Cripes, what's—''

He caught her hand and leaped to his feet, the feel of her little rump branded into his aching manhood. "I've got to go—''

"You *are* afraid of me, aren't you?''

"Afraid of *you?* A wee lassie?'' He laughed nervously and tore himself away as she tried to wrap her arms around him. He felt suffocated and out of control. His loins were throbbing, his heart about to explode out of his ribs, his skin covered with perspiration. "Of course I'm not afraid of you, at least not in the way that you think—''

"So you *are* afraid of me, just a little bit—''

"No! I mean yes—'' Images of Julia flashed through his mind, and panicking, he clawed free of her arms once more. "I think, lassie, 'twas a mistake to come here—''

"Mistake—''

"Shh, you'll wake your da!''

"I ain't gonna wake my *da!* Besides, you can't leave; we . . . we have to look at stars!"

"You look at stars from your room, I'll look at them from mine, and tomorrow we'll compare notes over breakfast!"

"But—where are you going?!"

"Back to my room. We'll both be safer that way!"

"Safer from what?!" She stood there in a shaft of moonlight, a mystical maiden wielding a power she didn't even know she had. He stared, his gaze fastened to her curvy body in delicious silhouette beneath the gossamer veil of her nightgown, her hair tumbling over her eyes, flowing around her shoulders, fanning out and around her back in dark contrast to her skin, and in perfect harmony to the dark triangle of hair he could see just beneath her nightgown—

His throat constricted and he dove for the door.

"Brendan, what's the *matter?!*"

He was gone, and she was left standing on the cold floor, confused and more than a little angry. She stared through the open doorway, her blood throbbing, her heart pounding, her body needful of something she didn't understand. Damn him! What the hell was wrong with him? What had driven him away from her, made him take flight when both of them had felt that strange, magical attraction that had brought him here in the first place?

Cursing, she picked up Rescue Effort Number One—a fat, lazy old tom whose eyes were foggy with age—and snuffing the candle, crawled back into bed. Her lips felt swollen, and her blood was still tingling. She pressed her fingers to her lips, and her eyes narrowed in determination. Whatever the handsome Captain Merrick was running from, she'd find out what it was. He couldn't run forever. Sooner or later, he'd kiss her again. He'd *have* to.

Smiling now, she gazed out into the starry night. Orion filled her window, glittering and twinkling against a backdrop of black velvet. She looked at it for a long time. Then she turned onto her back, hugged a pillow to her aching breasts, and with Number One nestled beneath her arm, fell asleep.

In the next room, Captain Brendan Jay Merrick threw

open every window, kicked the thick covers away, and put a pillow over his face so he *wouldn't* have to look at those stars. It was a long time before he found sleep that night, and when he did, it was filled with dreams of maidens who came to him on the silvered beams of moonlight.

Chapter 11

Luckily for Mira's schemes, a strong easterly wind kept *Kestrel* bottled up in harbor the next day. She watched from her window as Brendan, Father, and Matt drove down to the waterfront to inspect the ship—then wasted no time in deciding to set to work on Eveleen Merrick.

If she wanted to sneak aboard *Kestrel* tomorrow—without Brendan's or Father's knowledge—she had to win Eveleen's friendship, and subsequently her promise to keep her presence aboard the schooner a secret. That was, of course, a lot to ask—but Mira had a very attractive bargaining tool in mind.

Matthew.

She'd have to be blind not to realize that Eveleen was totally taken with her brother.

She laughed to herself, picked up Rescue Effort Number One, and buried her cheek against his soft fur. Of course, winning Eveleen's friendship had other advantages, too. Mira had been truthful in wanting to help the girl get over her bitterness and get on with life, but she also realized something else—that Eveleen could be quite valuable when it came to securing the interest—and attentions—of her brother, the captain.

Mira stood by the window for a long time, scheming. The only sticking point concerned keeping Eveleen occupied while she was out on *Kestrel*. The girl would be left back in the house with just Father, the staff, and sometimes Matt. There was always Abigail, of course, who could take her under her wing when Mira wasn't there—but Mira was looking for something that would start Eveleen on the path to liking herself, something that would build her confidence, something that would help turn her into a woman they all could live with.

Especially Matt.

Mira gave a devious little laugh as the answer came to her. The horses . . . Eveleen was terrified of them. But if she taught her the basics, such as feeding and grooming, and Eveleen practiced working around the horses while she was gone, then she'd be well on her way to gaining self-confidence, just by getting over that terror.

Of course, that would mean starting as soon as possible—for *Kestrel* would make her maiden voyage tomorrow.

That point settled, Mira dressed in a linen shirt and Matt's trousers, and drew on a heavy wool coat. The sun was already well above the horizon. Picking up her riding crop, she left her room and made her way down the hall, stopping briefly at Brendan's closed door. Memories of last night assailed her, and she laid her hand against the door, reliving those memories, flushing hot and cold, and again vowing that Brendan could only run from her for so long. And if she liked what she saw when she went aboard *Kestrel* tomorrow and saw him in action, then the handsome captain wouldn't have a chance. . . .

Buoyed by purpose and determination, she set out for Eveleen's room, marching down the hall like a militant general and slapping her crop against her thigh. She steeled herself for a fight and shoved the door to Eveleen's room open.

"Eveleen?"

The girl was still in her nightgown, sitting up in bed with a tray balanced on her legs. On it were several muffins, the remains of several more, and a huge glass of milk. She looked up, saw Mira, and instantly her features took on a sour look.

Mira paid her no heed. She'd expected such a reaction. "Get into your old clothes, and make it snappy," she ordered, knowing that she was going to have to use force and not pamper the girl. "It's already late and we've work to do if you expect to be riding that mare anytime soon."

Eveleen glared at her from the bed and said haughtily, "I don't *have* any old clothes."

"Fine, then. You can wear what you had on yesterday. That pink dress, *without* the jewelry."

"But—"

"First, you're going to learn how to feed and water your horse. Then you're going to learn all about how to groom and take care of her. That includes mucking out stalls and picking manure out of her hooves—"

"Picking *manure!*" Eveleen gasped, going white with horror.

"Aye, picking manure. Now, hurry up."

"But I can't wear my pink dress!"

"Then don't. But find something, 'cause I'm not waiting all day."

Eveleen glared harder at her.

Mira grinned.

"Why are you doing this to me?" Eveleen snarled.

" 'Cause your brother asked me to."

"You're in love with him, aren't you?"

"What's it to you?"

"Nothing," Eveleen said smugly, her smile growing malicious.

"Well, it oughtta be," Mira snapped, unwilling to back down, "because I happen to know that *you* have your eye on *my* brother, too." She smiled as Eveleen paled. "So there."

Eveleen's eyes were full of hatred. She said nothing, merely sliding her maimed hand beneath the covers.

"Don't worry, I've no intention of saying anything to Matthew," Mira said. "In fact, I would love nothing more than to see him and you get together. I think you would be wonderful for Matt." Mira was rewarded by the sudden show of friendliness in Eveleen's eyes. "But that won't happen unless you take charge of your life and rise above the circumstances that have made you so miserable. You can be happy, Eveleen, with a little work. That's what I'm here for. To make you work." She grinned as Eveleen's shy smile turned to shock. Mira began to walk the room, thoughtfully slapping the crop against her palm. "To that end, I have a bargain for you." She turned and crossed her arms. "You help me net *your* brother, and I'll help you net mine."

"*What?*"

Mira shrugged. "Your brother's a real test of my patience. He's terrified of me, though God only knows why! But Father's making me get married, you see, and I've decided that Brendan's the one who'll be my husband . . . provided, of course, he passes the Test."

"*Test?!*"

"Aye. I have to see him in action aboard the schooner . . . and *that* is where I need your help."

Eveleen stared at her as if she'd lost her mind. Then Mira began to walk the room again, slapping her crop against her palm once more as she outlined her scheme to go aboard *Kestrel,* and stressing the need for secrecy and cooperation on Eveleen's part. When she'd finished, a flicker of distrust and suspicion shone in the girl's eyes. "So, what is in this for *me?*" she said.

"Why, Matthew, of course."

"I fail to see how."

"You leave matters up to me, and I promise you my brother'll be yours before summer's end." Mira crossed her arms and gave Eveleen a level look. "But that requires doing everything and anything that I ask of you, no matter how unpleasant that may be."

It was a challenge, and Eveleen knew it.

Mira watched her distrust fade to wary hesitation, her suspicion to the barest glimmer of hope. Eveleen looked at her, glanced away, and picked up a muffin.

Mira stepped forward and took it away. "You can have your breakfast later," she said, ignoring Eveleen's suddenly mutinous look. "In this house, we take care of the horses first."

"*You* take care of them. I can't hold a bucket or a brush, anyhow."

"You can, too."

"I cannot. My hand's useless. I'm a cripple."

"You only need one hand to hold a bucket or a brush, or, for that matter, a halter or the reins."

"I said, *I'm a cripple!*" Eveleen shouted.

Mira sat down on the bed. She reached out, took the tray, and set it on the table behind her, out of Eveleen's reach. Tears glittered in the girl's eyes, bitter tears that she tried to hide by turning away. Gently Mira reached out and touched her arm.

"Eveleen . . . you don't have to hide your hand from me."

"It's hideous."

"It is not."

"How do you know? You've never seen it!"

"I have, too," Mira said, softly. "Last night."

Anger, hatred, and betrayal glittered in Eveleen's eyes. "You're a bitch," she whispered, trying not to cry.

"I'll tell you something, Eveleen." Unflinchingly Mira met the other woman's accusing stare. "You know how I said I'm doing this for Brendan?"

Eveleen set her jaw, and tears of hatred stood poised on the tip of her lashes,.

"Well, I lied." Mira stood up. "I'm doing it for you."

With that, she strode from the room. She felt Eveleen's gaze boring into her back. She heard her quick sniffle and the catch of her breath. *Don't disappoint me, Eveleen . . .* she thought. *Show me what you're made of.*

She'd reached the door when Eveleen's tremulous voice stopped her. "Mira?"

She paused, and turned.

Eveleen looked down, biting her lip. "Do you think you might have some . . . old clothes for me to borrow?" Then she glanced up, and offered a wary smile.

"Well now, I believe I just might." Mira nodded, and grinning, slapped her crop a final time against her hand. "Come with me, and let's see what we can find."

Chapter 12

~~~~~ ᗞᗞ ᕚᕚ ~~~~~

The following morning, Newburyport awoke to a pink and pewter horizon hiding beneath gray clouds that promised bad weather. By the time Brendan had shaved, dressed, and bolted down a plate of fried hasty pudding smothered in molasses, it was snowing hard.

Pulling his tricorn down over his brow, he now stood outside in the falling snow, waiting for Ephraim and glancing up at Mira's darkened window. She had not appeared at the breakfast table, nor had she come down to see him off, and her absence made him feel strangely empty inside, hollow-hearted and sad. Doubtlessly she was not only bewildered by his flighty behavior of the other night, but downright angry. But faith, didn't she realize what she was *doing* to him? How close she'd driven him to succumbing to the sweet temptations of her delightful little body? What was he to do, stay there and make love to her in her father's own house?!

Great white flakes of snow tingled upon his cheeks, caked on his eyelashes, melted in clean, cold rivulets that ran down his face and drove the achy tiredness from his still foggy brain. He tore his gaze from that empty window and dug his boot into the fresh snow. Maybe it was good he was going away for a few days. Maybe it was best that he put some distance between himself and the feisty little hoyden—

"Ye ready there, boy?" Ephraim came out of the barn, leading a fractious, prancing El Nath, who didn't look at all happy about being hitched to the smart red sleigh.

Brendan shot a last glance to that darkened window, eyed the unruly black stallion with no small degree of trepidation, and with a fleeting, nervous grin, climbed up

171

into the sleigh beside the old shipbuilder. Fumes of rum hit him the face. "As ready as I'll ever be."

"Well then, let's be off. It's already—" Ephraim tore his mitten off with his teeth, yanked out a watch, and studied it with a scrunched-up scowl "—half past six, and the crowds'll be gatherin' down at the wharf to watch. We don't wanna be late, eh? Cripes, they'd never let me forget it down at Davenport's!" He cracked the air over El Nath's head with a whip. "Gee-dup there, ye ornery ole nag!"

The sleigh's runners whispered through fresh snow as they swept down the driveway and into the street. Plumes of steam rose from El Nath's flared nostrils, snow crusted his flying black mane, and the red and white ribbons on his harness streamed back in the wind. Powerful muscles churned in his hindquarters, and his tail was an inky banner of glory. Brendan felt a thrill go through him. *Today was the day!* And down at the waterfront, *Kestrel* was waiting. He sat a little straighter on the cold, hard seat and drew his coat around his fine new uniform, fidgeting with excitement.

"Hee, hee, hee, would ye look at the old devil!" Ephraim, his cheeks red with cold, flashed him a yellowish grin. "Acting just like he knows the day's a special one, eh, Merrick?"

But Brendan wasn't looking at the stallion. As they passed darkened houses sleeping beneath snowy roofs, the people, already out of their warm beds and stoking up dying fires, came running out on their doorsteps to wave and shout and cheer, some still holding candles and clad in their nightgowns and banyans. He swallowed hard, dreading the reception that no doubt awaited him at the waterfront.

He was not disappointed. The people were there, all right, bundled up in thick woolen coats and colorful scarves, milling about and obviously waiting for him. At sight of the sleigh, they gave a wild, roaring cheer and rushed forward, hauling him out of it, clapping him on the back, and toasting him with mugs of hot buttered rum and steaming black coffee. A group of young lads, their noses red with cold, struck up "Free America" on fife and drum, a cannon banged out from somewhere nearby, and then he looked up and saw *her*.

The crowd's roar dimmed. The music faded away. He heard nothing but the ice floes, glowing gray in the morning light, that drove up against the shore and creaked and groaned like a square rigger in a gale. Felt nothing but the snow melting on his cheeks. And saw nothing but *her*.

She stood out in the river, proud, lovely, and impatient, shifting her weight from beam to beam as though she had no use for the land and was quite eager to be free of it. The current was so strong, it made a little wake against her bow, and high up, almost lost in the clouds, pennants fluttered from her masthead with joyous abandon. Her deck was crowded with seaman, officers, and the rifle-toting backwoodsmen who would serve as her marines. Someone must've seen him standing there, for there was suddenly a flurry of activity as his crew prepared to receive him.

He was dimly aware of Matthew detaching himself from the arm of a young woman nearby, and barely felt him hauling him through the parting crowd and down to the wharf, where *Kestrel*'s boat waited. A crew of smartly dressed seamen, handpicked by Liam himself, rowed him out to her, their oars rising and falling in perfect unison through the ice-clogged water. Their discipline would've done a king's ship proud. They passed beneath the sharp-eyed little hawk that was the schooner's figurehead—and then the boat was alongside.

Jamming his tricorn firmly down, Brendan tilted his head back and gazed up through the falling snow. His eyes grew moist and a strange lump filled the back of his throat. It was all the same, poignant and familiar, stirring and bittersweet. The barked orders . . . the bosun's whistles . . . the marines, presenting arms and snapping to attention, the seamen lined up behind them in perfect rows in readiness to receive him. It was the same special, glorious salute of a ship welcoming her commander—and it brought back memories of other days, other ships, and of the first time the mighty *Dauntless* had welcomed him as Sir Geoffrey Lloyd's flag captain—

He shook his head, willing the memories away. And then a fife pierced the air, and drums, too, and to the rousing notes of "Yankee Doodle," Brendan hauled himself up *Kestrel*'s sleek sides and stepped onto her deck. He was dimly aware of the raised swords and shrilling pipes, the officers who saluted him smartly, the crew lining the rails and clinging to tarry shrouds, the little lad who stood with a possessive hand upon an old fourpounder, head thrown back, eyes bright with life, and leading the rest of them in a lusty, full-throated version of "Yankee Doodle" that carried from stem to stern:

"A Band of Brothers let us be, while Adams guides the na-tion, and still our dear bought Freedom guard, in ev'ry situa-tion!"

He grinned.

"Yankee Doodle, guard your coast! Yankee Doodle Dan-dy! Fear not then or threat or boast, Yankee Doodle Dan-dy!"

Saluting smartly and pretending not to notice his captain's misty eyes, Liam stepped forward. "Welcome aboard, sir!"

Brendan returned the salute, doffed his hat to what would've been the quarterdeck if the schooner had one, and surveyed his command.

Forward, her long bowsprit angled up toward the gray sky. Guns, lashed down and waiting, sat upon brilliant red trucks dappled with snow. Lines lay neatly coiled upon tidy decks, and sails were furled upon booms and yards. The scents of fresh paint and tar, sweet hemp and varnish, filled the air, mixing with that of clean, newly fallen snow and the heady, wild hint of winter seas.

Liam was trying his best to contain his great, beamy grin. "Well?"

"Go hálainn. . . ." Brendan said simply, for there was nothing else *to* say. He glanced skyward, blinking, as the snow sifted down out of the heavens and melted upon his cheeks. She was lovely, all right. Tall, raked-back masts, their pennants obscured by snow and mist, traced gently spiraling circles against the heavy clouds. Shrouds were black crosshatches against the pale sky. Snow capped her guns and swivels, pinrails and deck planking, rigging, spars, and booms like frosting on a cake. A fine westerly

sang through the rigging, and the tide was going out. He couldn't have asked for a finer day to put to sea.

And *Kestrel* was ready. Brendan felt her restlessness beneath his booted feet, the tension thrumming through her stays, her shrouds, even the tiller bar, as he strode aft and gripped it for the first time. Snow melted beneath his palm and his fingers grew numb, but he kept his hand there until the wood grew warm and wet. It felt as if he were touching the schooner's very heart—and he cherished the moment for a long time before he finally loosened the tiller and mainsheet and turned to face his waiting crew.

Out of the corner of his eye he could see the people of Newburyport clogging the wharfs, the decks of other ships, the little boats bobbing among the ice floes that hovered near shore. Somewhere out there was Mira Ashton. She hadn't been at breakfast, but he *knew* she was here, could almost feel those impish green eyes upon him. He swallowed hard and turned his face into the stinging wind to cool his suddenly hot brow. Mira Ashton, who thought he could sketch—but not sail a ship. She would be watching with a very critical eye indeed. . . .

With a sudden grin, he turned to Zachary Wilbur. The boatswain's protruding potbelly was dusted with snow, his bowed legs spread as though the ship was already plunging through fifteen-foot seas. "Well, laddies, what're we waiting for? Haul in that anchor, Mr. Wilbur, and let's be about our business!"

The crew sent up a rousing cheer that rippled from bow to stern and back again on a thunderous wave of sound.

"Get the boat in and signal our pilot, Mr. Wilbur. We'll head out on jib and rudder alone." Brendan couldn't control his excited grin. "And be lively about it, Zach! We have an audience today!"

"Aye, sir!"

The boatswain swung himself forward, his gruff voice cracking the brittle air, "Let's get this lady under way, you worthless pack of saw-toothed old bangabouts! Lively now, so we can show them folks back yonder how it's done!"

The mainsail boom lay alongside the tiller and rested atop the stern rail, its triced sail as white as the snow that fell atop it. A tingle raced up Brendan's spine. Soon *Kestrel* would thrill to the power of that great sail; soon the wind would shove against its hardened belly, and spray would slash his cheeks as the schooner drove through the stormy gray Atlantic. He shivered, not with cold but excitement, finally shoving his hands behind his back and gripping them hard to still their mad trembling. That excitement rose as he watched the crew hoist the boat in, the water streaming from its little hull. At the capstan, Liam's fiddle jumped to the tune of an Irish jig, then a lively chanty that brought fifty raucous voices rising over the squeal of winches. Lines were hauled, and forward, the jib shook itself free and impatiently waved the snow aside.

Kestrel began to drift downriver.

"Anchor's hove short, sir!"

With a final heave on the capstan, the anchor came swinging up from the river's black depths in a cloud of silt and mud.

"Anchor's aweigh!"

Her jib-boom leading the way, *Kestrel* swung with the current until she faced the wide-open mouth of the Merrimack.

Beyond, the sea waited. Expecting them.

And behind, the crowds lined the shore, waiting to see if she would overset herself.

Kestrel was moving now, a study in soundless grace. Wharves and frozen marshlands fell behind them. Water slid along her sides. Just ahead, the pilot vessel that would guide her through the treacherous channels and out to sea fell into place. As they passed the battery at Plum Island, big field pieces roared out a thirteen-gun salute to Newburyport's newest, and finest, warrior. Brendan gave a barely perceptible nod and *Kestrel*'s guns spoke for the first time, returning the salute and the faith of the town that had built her.

"A beauty, sir, a real beauty!" At the helm John Keefe beamed with excitement, his eyes sweeping the panorama of shrouds and masts and rising canvas with a sort of awed reverence. "She'll do ye proud, sir! She'll do her *country* proud! And judging by the merry look in your eye, I can tell you're in love with her already! Ha ha, Cap'n, we'll show them Brits the stuff we're made of! We'll give 'em what-for! We'll show 'em *we mean business!*''

Brendan grinned and pointed through the shrouds. ''See that little boat full of spectators off the starboard bow? Hit it, Mr. Keefe, and you won't think I'm quite so merry!''

''Aye, Aye, Cap'n.''

The wind began to pick up as they neared the river's mouth. They'd left the wharves and crowds and marshlands behind, and now sand dunes, patchy with snow and tufts of dead beach grass, slipped past on either beam. It was so quiet that even the hiss of snow falling on deck and whispering through the rigging sounded loud. A gust of wind caught the jib, cracking it like thunder in the stillness. Keefe eased the tiller bar and the schooner answered, swinging slightly to larboard in her escort's wake.

Brendan gripped his hands behind his back. Soon now, they'd be in open ocean and he could put her though her paces.

And as they passed the northern tip of Plum Island, the wind drove hard against them, *Kestrel* rose up on her heel in eagerness, and every man aboard caught his breath. There it was, the gray and stormy Atlantic, spread out before them in all its winter splendor.

The pilot boat fell back, her guns rumbling in salute.

''Hands to the sheets and trim for beam reach on the larboard tack! Hoist foresail and main! Smartly, Mr. Wilbur!''

They were a bit slow, but they'd get the feel of her soon enough. They all would. Brendan went to the after rail and gripped the cold, snowy wood, watching necklaces of foam writhing in their wake, the pewter seas rolling past. In his fingertips he felt the vibrations of wind strumming through shrouds, of mast hoops crawling skyward as the mainsail rose with its boom, higher and higher until snow blurred the gaff's outline and the proud pennants that snapped above it. ''Sheet home!'' he called, and *Kestrel* leaned hard into the sea and driving spray, showing her heels to the land she would soon leave far behind.

And she did not overset herself.

The crew gave a mighty cheer, the huzzahs ringing up to the very clouds themselves. The rum would flow like water tonight. They had the finest ship to ever hail from Newburyport, the luckiest captain this side of Ireland, and an ocean full of British shipping just waiting for them. One by one and in pairs, in groups, they went below to warm up, to sing, and to drink toasts to their future success. All of them except a skeletal crew and one gunner from Newburyport, a tiny mite in an oversize hat, a tarpaulin coat, and a seaman's braid that hung like a rope, halfway to his trouser-clad rump. Standing beside the cannon he'd dubbed *Freedom* and already claimed as his own, the little gunner watched his captain reclaim the helm, seeing the squared shoulders, the queued and snow-encrusted chestnut hair, the smart tricorn, dark coattails, and crimson waistcoat through a wall of driving snow-flakes.

Already the footprints of his crewmates were filling with snow, but there would be time to join them later. Time to swap stories with friends from Newburyport, to make new ones among the Irishmen who had yet to find out he wasn't quite the *lad* he appeared. But for the moment, Mira, dressed in her disguise, was content to watch that lone figure at the helm as Salisbury, Plum Island, and the land itself fell beneath the sea and *Kestrel* drove toward a horizon buried in spray, snow, and, it was hoped, glory.

Brendan . . . a captain alone with his ship for the first time. It was a private moment, and she had no right to intrude.

Shivering, she dragged her numbed feet across the snowy, plunging deck and made her way toward *Kestrel*'s unconventional aft-facing hatch. But just before she dropped below the coaming, she turned for a final look at him.

He was still standing there.

And though the distance that separated them was blurred by falling snow, she could see that he was grinning.

After spending the night arguing with *Kestrel*'s officers—Lieutenant Liam Doherty, in particular—before finally convincing them that her gender had nothing to do with her abilities as a gunner, it was no wonder that Mira slept right through breakfast, which was really just as well; she'd never been overly fond of cold oatmeal anyhow.

They'd finally agreed to let her stay, if only for their own amusement at having a "wee mite" aboard whose identity would remain a delightful secret from their captain. Of course, the emphatic testimony of her abilities from the Newburyporters aboard the schooner who'd sailed with her before on her brother's privateer helped sway things in her favor; after all, the legendary success of *Proud Mistress* was not only due to the command of Captain Matthew Ashton, but to the skills of his little sister at her favorite gun.

Brendan was not the only one who was unaware that Miss Mira Ashton was aboard a ship; Ephraim, thumbing to the Marine News Section of the *Essex Gazette* at exactly seven o'clock that morning, was also unaware of it—although when he hadn't seen hide nor hair of his daughter by ten o'clock, he had no delusions as to her whereabouts, and neither did his neighbors, who heard his roaring all the way down to the Beacon Oak and beyond.

Ephraim may have thought she'd sailed with Matt, who'd put to sea an hour after Brendan had, but at ten o'clock aboard *Kestrel*—or rather, four bells of the forenoon watch, in ship's time—Mira was sound asleep in a hammock snugged up against the curve of the inner hull. Suddenly cries came drifting down from above.

"On deck!"

She opened an eye and groggily pulled her wool blanket up to her chin. It took her a moment to remember where she was; then, upon realizing she was on *his* ship and he was somewhere nearby, a slow, happy warmth spread through her and she smiled like a kitten with a full belly. Topside, she could hear wind moaning around the masts, footsteps pounding above her head. She placed a hand against the hull's thick wooden curve. It was cold to the touch but dry, and on the other side she could feel the sea surging past. The hammock swung with the motion of the ship, and in the gloom around her she saw one or two others, still abed, raise their heads.

Brendan's musical voice, faint through wind and distance, drifted down. "Report, Mr. Reilly!"

Mira propped herself on an elbow, balancing herself with natural ease against the hammock's unsteadiness.

"Sail fine off the sta'b'd bows, Cap'n!" A gust of wind hit the schooner, and the rest of the lookout's words were lost.

Shivering, Mira bounced out of the hammock, buttoned her long coat up to her chin, stuffed her braid down beneath her collar, and hastily grabbing her hat and yanking on her boots, went on deck. The wind hit her like an arctic blast, driving snow and salt spray into her eyes. *Kestrel*'s bow rose and fell, rose and fell, smashing down on long gray swells and sending great sheets of foam hissing past. It was still snowing out, but wind had swept the rails and hatches clean. Mira blinked and peered aloft. A man clung to the shrouds, a glass to his eye and his coattails flapping in the wind. She looked again. It was Brendan.

"Looks like the luck of that fool Irishman's with us," said Abadiah Bobbs, a stout, thick-jowled Newburyporter with a mole the size of a musket ball just below the left corner of his mouth. He shook his head and gave her a wry grin. "Out of port not half a day and he's already found us a prize." Bracing his feet against the roll of the deck, he squinted and pointed off through the snowy mist. "See there? Fine-lookin' brig, eh? Surprised her, we did. She'll not get out of her hidey-hole now."

Tucking her chin into her coat, Mira peered off to starboard. The world was white, and she couldn't see a thing.

"There, Mira." Abadiah pointed again, and this time she saw the fuzzy outline of a ship, barely visible through the swirling snow. Her sails were down, her head was to the wind, and she wallowed heavily in the gray, foamy seas.

Abadiah rubbed his mole and jerked his head toward an ice-encrusted four-pounder, lashed tightly several feet away. "Better station yourself by *Freedom,* missie. These bloody Irishmen'll have their eyes on ye, to be sure."

Not only the Irish*men,* she thought wryly, but the half-Irishman, too. *The Captain from Connacht,* as his men called him. Now he was climbing down the stiff shrouds, his boots steady on the icy ropes, his sword belted to his waist. He'd still been topside when she'd sought her ham-

mock last night, yet he didn't look—or act—tired at all.
His eyes were full of mirth, his russet brow was frozen in
place—literally—, snow frosted his long lashes, and his lean
cheeks were healthy with cold. Mira thought he had never
looked more handsome. Landing lightly on the deck, he
straightened his coat, thumped his tricorn against his knees
to knock the snow off, and made his way toward them.

She quickly yanked her hat down and looked down at
her toes.

"You're right about that brig, Mr. Bobbs," Brendan
said, stamping his feet to get his blood moving and rubbing his hands together. "I believe her to be the *Caper*.
Fourteen guns, and launched three years ago in Gloucester." He shot a curious glance at the small, bundled-up
figure standing beside the Newburyporter. It was the same
wee lad whose lusty voice had led the singing yesterday,
though now he seemed shy and quiet. Brendan frowned.
There was something terribly familiar about him, but he
couldn't quite put his finger on just what it was. "Pardon
me," he said, bending and peering closer. As though terrified of him—and at that age, most of them *were* of their
commanding officer—the lad drew his face in between hat,
lapels, and scarf, reminding him of a turtle going into its
shell. "I don't remember signing you up, Mr. . . ."

"Uh, Starr."

Liam, casting the lashing from a nearby gun, saw Mira's
predicament immediately. Grabbing the steaming mug of
black coffee that Dalby was just bringing to his captain,
he all but shoved it into Brendan's hands. "A shy one, he
is! Ye don't rememb'r him 'cause I signed him up meself,
right, bucko?"

Mira nodded, still staring at her toes.

"Well, take off your hat so I can have a look at you,"
Brendan said, grinning.

"Can't," Mira mumbled.

"Scared o' ye, he is!" Laim explained, placing a massive hand between her little shoulders and shoving her
gently toward the hatch. "Ye know how the wee mites are
wi' their commandin' offic'rs, Brendan!'

Brendan was persistent. "There's no need to be afraid
of me, Mr. Starr. I ask only your trust, not your life!"

"Can't take off m' hat, sir."

"Faith, why not?"

She thought quickly, wildly. "Because . . . because my skin can't take the sun, sir. Can't take the . . . light. I'll break out in little bumps all over if I take it off."

"But it's *snowing* out, Mr. Starr!" Brendan wrapped his hands around the hot mug and stared at her curiously.

"Don't matter." She pointed skyward. "Sun's still up there."

Liam made a big show of clearing his throat. "Uh, Brendan," he said, curving his big, brawny arm around his captain's shoulders and drawing him away, "Mr. Starr's one o' those albino people, he is. He cannot take *any* light."

Brendan stared at her for a moment longer. But the answer must've suited him, for he nodded, shot a final glance at her, and then seemed to dismiss her with no further thought. Over his massive shoulder Liam winked, and Mira caught the conspiring grins of her crew mates. She clapped a hand over her mouth to still her laughter.

Beside her, Bobbs tugged at his mole to hide his own smile and eyed his new captain speculatively. "You sure about that brig, sir? *Caper*'s American . . ."

"So she is. And that brig yonder flies the Union Jack above her true colors, Mr. Bobbs. Here, have another look." Brendan handed the seaman his glass and sipped his coffee, totally unconcerned. "She's *Caper*, all right—and an Englishman's prize."

Abadiah took the glass, wiped the snow from the lens with his elbow, and raised it to his eye. "What d'ye intend to do with her?"

Brendan downed the rest of his coffee. "Why, make her *our* prize and send her back into port under her true colors, of course."

Lowering the glass, Bobbs stared as though his ears had failed him. "Sir?"

Brendan shrugged and gave an innocent grin, his honey-colored eyes sparkling with mischief. "Well, America has few enough ships without Britain helping herself to them. Greed, Mr. Bobbs! 'Twill never do anyone any good, remember that."

"But, sir, *Caper* mounts fourteen guns—which means that whoever captured her must mount a hell of a lot more. They ain't gonna be too agreeable about letting a fancy schooner with a mere ten guns and a handful of swivels take her back. . . ."

But Brendan was already striding aft, humming something Irish-sounding and looking about as worried as a fox checking out a henhouse. "Mr. Wilbur!" he called, over one elegant shoulder. "We'll ease the fore and main and prepare to tack!"

"Aye, sir!"

Seconds later, the commands came from aft, were repeated forward, and carried out with brisk efficiency.

"Ease the foresail!"

"Let fly!"

Mira stared, her jaw hanging open in amazement. Then she turned to Liam. Her voice was a fierce whisper. "Is he *always* like that?"

"Like what, lassie?"

"So . . . cool! So blithe, so totally unconcerned!"

For answer, Liam merely gave a broad grin. Miss Mira Ashton would find out about her captain's *other* idiosyncrasies soon enough! Chuckling to himself, he took station near the smart row of starboard four-pounders and waited.

"Stand by on the forward guns!"

Mira grabbed a priming iron and ran forward. Her breath came hard and fast, and the cold air dragged tears from her eyes. Swiping them away, she drew herself up and waited impatiently as Abadiah and several other Newburyporters cast off *Freedom*'s lashings. She was uncomfortably aware of Brendan's curious stare upon her. "Hurry up!" she urged. Grunting and cursing, the men hauled the gun inboard for loading. Powder monkeys scurried up from belowdeck, religiously carrying powder and shot.

They were getting closer. And closer.

Without taking his eyes off their quarry, Brendan yelled, "Mr. Doherty! Choose your best gun captain and have him demonstrate to us how fine his eyesight is! If he can take out that brig's mizzen, I'll give him *my* share of the prize money!"

Someone nudged her shoulder, and Mira looked up into

Liam's twinkling blue eyes. He held a linstock, a forked rod used for holding the match to the cannon's touchhole; now he shoved it into her numb hand and jerked his head toward the big gun beside her. "Here's y'r chance, lassie! Don't waste it!"

She nodded eagerly and laid her hand upon *Freedom*'s ice-cold breech, her fingers quickly brushing the snow away from the Scripture words so faithfully—and appropriately—inscribed there: *It is more blessed to give than to receive.*

That was for damned sure!

Leaning far out of the gunport, Abadiah sponged out the gun, ramming a cartridge down its bore, and followed it with bar shot and wadding.

"Lively, now!" Brendan yelled, obviously testing her.

Mira shoved a priming rod down *Freedom*'s touchhole to pierce the flannel powder cartridge. Her hands were shaking in nervous excitement, and she was sweating beneath Matt's heavy coat.

"Easy," Abadiah said, touching her shoulder. "Ye can do it."

She nodded and passed a wrist over her brow. Forward, Brendan strode to the shrouds and raised his speaking trumpet, his feet braced against the roll of the ship, his chestnut hair caught in a piece of black ribbon and hanging between his handsome shoulders. "Ahoy! What ship are you and what are your true colors?!"

Tension mounted. The crew exchanged glances. Beside her, Abadiah tugged nervously on his mole. Mira pictured what *Kestrel* must look like to the brig's crew, sweeping out of the gray mists like a ghost.

The answer floated eerily back through the snow. *"Caper*'s the ship, and her colors are the king's own!"

"Well, haul them down, my friend, or I shall do so for you!"

The brig, *Caper,* came alive. A shot banged out in reply, skipping through the waves and hissing into the sea a quarter mile away. Canvas tumbled from the brig's yards, someone cut her anchor cable, and she leaned hard over, showing her belly as she fell away with the wind.

"Very well, then!" Brendan raised his trumpet once

more, grinning. So they wanted to play, did they? He
glanced at the little mite standing at the gun dubbed *Freedom*, and felt his jaunty good spirits fade to trepidation.
If having the lad there was Liam's idea of a joke . . .

"Ease the main a wee bit, Mr. Wilbur! And Mr. Starr!
You may run out now!"

Behind him came a protesting squeal as the big gun was
moved up to its gunport. The little gunner, his face tight
with concentration, flung his braid over his shoulder and
crouched down beside *Freedom*'s ugly snout.

"Point your gun!"

Handspikes, crowbarlike instruments used to heave and
lever a gun into position, lifted *Freedom*'s mouth. Her heart
pounding, Mira gripped her linstock, wiped the snow from
her eyes, and sighted along the barrel. The iron was cold
against her cheek. With the sea heaving *Kestrel* up and
down and her target a dim shape in the snow, it was going
to be hard to hit *Caper*'s hull, let alone her mizzen! "Maximum elevation, Mr. Starr!"

She felt every eye upon her. Brendan, resplendently
handsome, clinging to the shrouds and watching her intently. Liam, his arms folded confidently across his mighty
chest. Dalby, his teeth clamped down on a clawlike hand.
And the crew, elbowing one another in the ribs and making bets on whether she could do it or not.

The Irish ones, that was. The Newburyporters knew
better than to waste their money.

Catching Bobbs's eye, Mira sighted one last time along
Freedom's snowy breech, stepped back to avoid the re-
coil—and lowered her match to the vent. With a mighty
roar the gun flung itself inboard, nearly ripping ringbolts
from bulwarks and coughing a cloud of flame and smoke
from its angry mouth. The crew rushed to the rail, and a
great, awed sigh rose up from their midst.

"Holy Mutherr o' God."

It was Liam, white-faced and shocked, and staring at
her with a strange, frozen grin on his beamy features.
Behind him, Mira saw the brig's mizzen toppling into the
sea, dragging a tangle of spars, rigging, and sail with it.
There was no need to load up again. That one shot had

destroyed the nerve of the brig's crew. Already the Union Jack was slinking down the mast in defeat.

Liam's throat worked as he tried to find words. Beyond him Brendan was staring at her, his mouth hanging open and his speaking trumpet dangling uselessly from his wrist. The crew, turning from the rail as one, had gone mute. At last Liam shook his head. "Tha' 'twas mighty fine shootin', er, Mr. Starr."

"Thank you," she mumbled.

Brendan was still staring at her.

Kestrel, however, was not impressed, taking her skills for granted and as though they were her due. She came up on the defeated brig, confident and assured, and fretting rather impatiently while her captain sent a prize crew across to man it. The brig was disabled, but she could still be sailed. And then both victor and vanquished swung their noses through wind and snow, sails shivering and filling once more.

They were just clearing the point of the cove when the lioness came after her cub:

HMS *Viper*, a frigate with thirty-two guns and a new captain at the helm, Richard Crichton, hell-bent on revenge.

Chapter 13

It had been two days since the confrontation between *Kestrel* and HMS *Viper*, a confrontation that had been disastrous as far as the Royal Navy—and especially Captain Richard Crichton—were concerned.

"Not good, Richard." Sir Geoffrey Lloyd cleared his throat and turned another page of his frigate captain's report. "I daresay, not good at all."

The great cabin of the seventy-four-gun ship of the line

Dauntless was drafty and cold, but Captain Richard Crichton, R.N., was sweating beneath his shirt and fine blue coat. Aside from his pale, milk-colored eyes, his physical attributes were quite unremarkable; his height, his build, even his face, which might've been lost to its own fairness if not for the naturally red-rimmed eyes and lusterless hair that didn't seem to grow from his head, but rather, to lie atop it like sparse and lifeless thatch. Currently that hair was yanked bank in a severe queue between his blocky, epauletted shoulders, and only his fingers, not resting atop his sword hilt but caressing it as they might a lover, gave any indication of his agitation. His face was a carefully schooled study of acceptance, for he knew better than to respond to Sir Geoffrey's remark. Instead, he drew himself up a little straighter and stared over the admiral's sloped shoulder, his eyes cold, his mouth harder than marble and his heart burning with hatred for a certain American privateer. . . .

Sir Geoffrey turned another page, and a trickle of sweat raced down Crichton's back.

Brendan Jay Merrick. The very name brought a rancid taste to Crichton's mouth, and his hand tightened on the sword hilt. After the exchange between British and American prisoners that had returned him to Sir Geoffrey's fleet, Sir Geoffrey had given him a less than enthusiastic welcome when he'd come aboard *Dauntless* last autumn—and had been skeptical about giving him command of another ship. But *Viper*'s ex-captain had died in action, and the frigate had needed a new one. Otherwise, Crichton would've had to wait months to get another command.

And now Merrick had made him look like a fool once more.

A muscle jumped in Crichton's jaw. He should've made *sure* the bastard was dead four years ago—

"I say, Richard, this is balderdash, all of it." The admiral was still bent over the reports, his brows cinched as he tried to read Crichton's words. The bloody bugger should've retired long ago, Crichton thought. Maybe he'd do them all a favor and keel over dead one of these days. But of course, that'd put the fleet's command under Sir Geoffrey's flag captain, the haughty Hiram Ellsworth—a

pompous prig who, when not placing snuff up his lofty
nose, spoke an occasional snide comment *through* it.

Crichton far preferred Sir Geoffrey.

The admiral sighed and turned another page. Crichton
sweated some more and hoped the dampness wasn't showing through his fine blue coat. Across the table, the flag
captain, Ellsworth, shot him a lofty, condescending grin
and reached for his snuff. Crichton ignored him. He'd
spent hours rewriting that report, trying to spare himself
as much humiliation as possible. It was taking the old goat
just as long to read it. Crichton bit the inside of his lip
and maintained his stiff poise. Dread tightened his gut.
The report was not exactly . . . heartening.

Finally Sir Geoffrey pushed the papers aside with a tired
motion, leaned his brow into his hand, and pivoted it in
his palm to gaze up at his frigate captain. "What I cannot
understand, Richard, is how the *devil* a thirty-two-gun
frigate such as *Viper* could be outmaneuvered, outfought,
and then *robbed* of her own company! I daresay, this is a
disgrace!"

"Preposterous!" Ellsworth exclaimed.

Crichton's fingers tightened on the sword hilt. "I told
you, sir—it was *Merrick.*"

That, of course, explained everything. Sir Geoffrey dug
the heels of his hands into his eyes, rubbed them tiredly,
and stared bleakly down at the report, now pinned beneath
his elbows. "Are you *sure*, Richard?"

"Positive, sir."

"I'd thought him dead. I suppose I should've known
better."

"We *all* should've known better, sir."

"A fine young man, a credit to the navy that made him.
And a disgrace to the country he's turned against. I daresay I'm glad to hear he's hale and healthy, but damme,
Richard, he *is* a thorn in our side. God rot it, I'm growing
too old for this."

"Yes, sir."

"What?!"

"That is, yes, sir, he *is* a thorn in our side."

Sir Geoffrey turned away to stare bleakly out the salt-
caked stern windows. A faint smile of remembrance

curved his stern mouth. *Brendan Jay Merrick.* His former flag captain had been a laughing young rake with a mirthful grin and the cleverness of a fox. As a lieutenant, he'd been commendable; as a captain, he'd been the best. God only knew what he would have made of himself had some mutinous seaman not marked him down four years ago on *Dismal*'s decks, for 'twas men like Merrick who made the British navy proud. Men like Merrick who became public heroes.

And men like Merrick who made the most dastardly foes. . . .

Sighing, Sir Geoffrey picked up a brass protractor and absently toyed with it. Merrick's Irish luck, it seemed, was stronger than ever. Any man who could survive a gunshot wound to the chest could certainly survive being swept out to sea on a piece of driftwood, which was what Crichton's *last* report had revealed. But intelligence, especially when it concerned events in the colonies, could not always be relied upon. No, he wasn't surprised to hear that Merrick was alive. He wasn't surprised to find that the young rake had turned up again when they least expected him.

And he wasn't surprised to hear about this schooner.

She was a dangerous thing in herself, by the sound of it. But in the hands of Captain Brendan Merrick . . .

His smile faded abruptly. He didn't need this; he really didn't. Yanking the reports toward him, he squinted and tried once again to decipher Crichton's crabby script, finally shoving the papers away with a sound of disgust and annoyance. "A pox on the written word, Richard! My eyes are killing me. Tell me *exactly* what happened."

"Of course, sir." Crichton straightened his shoulders and gave him a pale, flat stare that revealed no emotion whatsoever. "I had taken *Caper,* an American brig of fourteen guns, and put a prize crew aboard her under the command of Lieutenant Sanderson." His voice was calm, as though he were discussing politics over tea. "It had been snowing off and on throughout the day, and by nightfall the wind was blowing quite a gale. Near dusk, I brought *Viper* into open sea to wait it out. Sanderson sought shelter in a cove. Shortly after dawn I heard gunfire, and went to investigate."

"And?"

"Twas then that I found the schooner."

The vice admiral leaned back in his chair. "Ah yes . . . the schooner."

A muscle twitched in Crichton's iron-hard jaw. "She was the most singular ship I've ever seen. Tall, raked-back masts, a low profile, very little freeboard . . . quite similar to those clippers coming out of Baltimore, I'd say. She already had my prize brig, *Caper,* under her wing and was making off with her when I happened upon them. I went after her, of course, given the fact that she alone was obviously worth far more than *Caper* and all her cargo."

"And it was at this point that the brig parted company with the schooner?"

"Yes, sir."

Ellsworth placed a bit of snuff in each nostril with the precision of a marksman. *"I* would've went after the brig, it being a prize and all. I say, Crichton, d'you know what became of it?"

"Presumably, it was sent back to an American port," Crichton said tersely.

"Gentlemen," Sir Geoffrey warned, noting the mottled flush creeping above Crichton's neatly tied stock. There was no love lost between these two. "Please continue, Richard."

Crichton moved this thumb rapidly over his sword hilt. "Sir, this is really most humiliating."

"I realize that, Richard. It is humiliating to you, to me, to the entire British navy. But the problem must be dealt with in a fitting manner. And Merrick, if *not* dealt with, shall become quite a problem indeed, I'm afraid."

Crichton drew in his breath. It was all there, right in the report, yet still, the old buzzard wanted him to relate it all over again—and in front of Ellsworth, too. Crichton clenched his back teeth together, hard. Hell would freeze over before he'd give either Sir Geoffrey *or* the pompous Ellsworth the satisfaction of seeing him react in anything but a professional way. No matter how poor his luck had been, no matter how political the system was that placed men like Merrick, whose father had been an admiral himself, and Ellsworth, whose father was an earl, in coveted positions, there was always a chance for promotion. Except this time, Merrick might've destroyed his chances for good.

Again, that bitter taste in his mouth, that twist of hatred in his gut. Sir Geoffrey was waiting, his bleary old eyes keen and piercing. Another trickle of sweat raced between Crichton's shoulders, but he managed to keep the uneasiness out of his voice. "So then I crowded on as much canvas as *Viper* could stand, which, given the strong wind, sir, was not as much as I would've liked, and gave chase to the schooner. I thought her most sloppily handled—the rebels had too much sail on her, and it seemed as though she'd overset herself at any moment. At the same time, I found it odd that despite all that cloth, she wasn't making much headway." His milky eyes grew hard, their translucency emphasized by the pink-tinged lids. "I know now, of course, that it was all a trick. They'd simply rigged a sea anchor to make it *look* as though she was faltering."

"Sounds like Merrick, all right," Ellsworth sniffed.

Crichton shot him a poisonous glance.

Sir Geoffrey tossed the protractor to his desk. "Go on, Richard."

"After a turn of the glass, I realized the schooner was no longer faltering, that she was indeed a fast sailer and quite skillfully handled. She'd adopted the ploy to lead me away from the brig, of course. I fired upon her, hoping to cripple her, but barely managed to clip her wings, so swift was her flight once she'd cut loose the sea anchor."

Sir Geoffrey gazed down at the report to hide his expression. *Ah, Merrick,* he thought, *even now, you don't disappoint me. . . .* He looked up and found Crichton's gaze upon him, those strange, milky eyes as barren as the Arctic and just as cold. Sir Geoffrey's smile faded abruptly. "Given what you told me about the schooner, I don't find it surprising that she led you a merry chase, Richard. But I think you're avoiding the real issue—the engagement."

Crichton's fingers tightened on the sword hilt until his knuckles went white. "The schooner was most elusive, sir. And let me remind you it *was* snowing hard. The wind was a westerly, yet she headed almost into the teeth of it. 'Twas most remarkable—"

"The *engagement*, Richard?"

"Er, yes, the engagement." Crichton faltered, and went on. "I chased her into a cove, sir, where she holed up, turned on her heel, and presented her broadside to me. The channel into the cove was too shallow for a vessel of *Viper*'s draft, so I went in as far as I dared. Had it been deeper, I could've brought all of my guns to bear, and that would've been the end of it; as it was, I could only use my bow chasers, while the schooner, safely in the cove, could give me her full starboard battery. This, of course, she did." Crichton willed himself to stay calm, knowing that the story was leading up to the most humiliating part of all. "We stood this abuse for an hour, sir, during which time I lost my fore topmast and received considerable damage to both bowsprit and hull. We couldn't get in to get her, and she damn well wasn't about to come out."

"So you retreated?"

"I er, *left,* sir. I don't wish to think of it as a retreat."

Ellsworth made a snorting sound.

Crichton's eyes flashed.

Sir Geoffrey rustled the loose pages of the report. "So it was then that you decided to go in search of the brig instead. Is that correct, Richard?"

"Yes, sir."

"And shortly thereafter you found the schooner trailing you and were forced to engage her once again?"

"Had she not had the element of surprise, sir, I vow that the outcome would've been different!"

"I thought you said Merrick was commanding her," Ellsworth said loftily.

"Please mind your tongue, Hiram." Sir Geoffrey warned. "You'd not have fared any better, I daresay."

Ellsworth snorted and reached for his snuff.

Sir Geoffrey kneaded his aching brow. "So it was during the following engagement that you lost your main topmast, your rudder, and subsequently, your steering. Merrick must have a jolly good gunner aboard to accomplish all that with a vessel whose armament was far inferior to yours." He looked up and met Crichton's flat and unblinking stare. "At least I can commend you for not striking your colors, Richard. In a sea fight, of course, anything can happen. I shan't blame you for your conduct, despite the fact that Merrick had less than half the guns your *Viper* did.''

"And they were very well used, I might add. And if that damned schooner hadn't slipped up like a ghost behind us and crippled us with her first shot, I *vow* she would've been my prize and I'd've had Merrick dancing a jig from his own bloody foremast!''

A heavy silence ensued. Outside, the sea gurgled beneath the rudder, and cries drifted down from above as the first lieutenant gave the order to tack. Sir Geoffrey stared thoughtfully out the huge windows, his eyes distant and maybe even a little sad. Then, remembering himself, he picked up a page of Crichton's report. "So it was at this point that you anchored *Viper* to make your repairs." He set the paper down and shook his head. "This is where I grow confused, Richard. What *I* can't fathom is how the devil *forty-five* men could just disappear!''

"They didn't just *disappear,* sir. They were stolen from me! The bloody bastard did it that night, when *Viper* was quiet and most of the watch asleep—''

Sir Geoffrey nodded and motioned for him to continue.

"Midshipman Everett had the watch. Being only twelve years old himself, he didn't see anything amiss about two boys in a fishing dory trying to sell him part of their day's catch. He let them aboard, the idiot. Apparently, while he was speaking to one of them, the other managed to slip this, er, *note* to one of the seamen. And that's all it took. By dawn, forty-five men, including a good master's mate, were gone."

Sir Geoffrey gave him a sharp look.

"Oh, have no fear, sir. The little midshipman has been, er, *dealt* with.''

Sir Geoffrey looked away, his jaw tight with anger. He had no delusions about Crichton's manner of "dealing" with people—but as an admiral, and above such things, it was not his place to interfere with the way Crichton ran his ship. That was Ellsworth's duty, and he would speak with the flag captain about it later; let Ellsworth stress his desire for *temperance* to Crichton, who was not apt to be very temperate at all.

"This note, Richard. Do you still have it?"

"Yes, sir."

"I should like to see it, please."

Crichton dug in his pocket and handed it over, watching glumly as the admiral, farsighted with advancing age, held the paper at arm's length so that he could read it.

"Pray, what does it say, sir?" Ellsworth moved closer, trying to look down his nose without lowering his head.

"I shall read it to you, Hiram. And then, perhaps, it will give you a sense of our Captain Merrick's character." Sir Geoffrey's eyesight may have been failing, but the writing was so bold, so sure of itself, that he had no trouble at all reading that elegant, artistic script.

He held the paper out in front of him and cleared his throat. *"Gentlemen,"* he quoted, *"in due respect and understanding of your unhappy situation under the rule of one of the King's most brutal masters—"* Sir Geoffrey paused to glance sideways at Crichton*"—I invite you to join the crew of the new privateering schooner* Kestrel, *whose acquaintance you made earlier and whose presence can be found a cable's length to windward of your current anchorage. Those of you who wish to cast off the yoke of the tyrant King, and become the glorious defenders of Liberty instead, shall be treated and honoured as free citizens of American and shall partake of all prize monies secured by said Schooner. Signed—"* Sir Geoffrey lowered the paper *"—Captain Brendan Jay Merrick, formerly R.N."*

There was a long moment of silence. Ellsworth smirked and coughed delicately into his hand, Crichton's pale eyes hardened to ice, and Sir Geoffrey tossed the note aside with a defeated motion. Obviously Merrick had used Crichton's reputation for cruelty to his advantage; it must've been an easy matter indeed for him to steal seamen from HMS *Viper*. Hauling himself wearily to his feet, the admiral poured three glasses of Madeira from a crystal decanter. "Gentlemen," he said, staring down into the ruby depths, "normally I would not be so concerned about subduing one little privateer. But given the fact that Captain Merrick is her commanding officer—and no doubt her designer, too—I cannot, in all conscience, allow the matter to rest here. Situations such as these, Richard, are most humiliating to our navy as well as upsetting to our people's morale." He gave a heavy sigh. "And where Merrick is concerned, I'm afraid they are also likely to happen again."

Silence. Ellsworth sniffed and reached for his handkerchief.

Sir Geoffrey stared out the windows. A few flakes of snow swirled into view, pirouetting and dancing in the wind. Beneath him, the deck tilted as *Dauntless* leaned heavily over on the opposite tack. He looked at Crichton, standing there with his milky eyes expressionless and unblinking, his hand resting atop his sword hilt. The task he was about to give Crichton was a damn near impossible one. But Crichton *was* one of his captains, and though Sir Geoffrey had never cared for him, it was only fair that he be allowed the chance to redeem himself.

"Describe Merrick's vessel to me if you please, Richard. You say she was a topsail schooner?"

"Not *just* a topsail schooner. She stacked topsails and topgallants above both fore and main, and looked like she could've rigged studders, too, if her captain desired to fly them. She had a long, slooplike bowsprit strung with at least two jibs, a hull so slick, it hardly rippled the water, and a deck design that, from a distance, barely made a profile. 'Twas obvious she was not built as a fisherman, a blockade runner, nor even a smuggler, sir." He looked hard at Sir Geoffrey. "She was designed as a *predator.*"

A predator. Sir Geoffrey nodded slowly, considering Crichton's words and staring off into the heaving gray sea beyond *Dauntless*'s windows. Crichton had been correct in forsaking the brig for the schooner. Admiralty would go to great lengths for the chance to study such a singular vessel. Why, if he could only get his hands on it, he could leave the sea and retire to his home in Kent once and for all, with a fire in the hearth to warm his tired old bones and a sleeping hound at his feet. . . .

"Intelligence tells me that a much-heralded schooner was recently built by Captain Ephraim Ashton of *Newburyport,*" he said, stressing the town's name and watching Crichton closely. But that translucent gaze never wavered. "From all accounts, she was quite unlike anything either this, er . . . *country* or ours has ever seen. A forward-swept stem, narrow beam, extremely raked masts, and a hull so sharp that most predicted she'd sink the moment she touched water. Obviously she did not, but if Merrick designed her—and I am quite confident that he did—it doesn't surprise me in the least. He was the best, you know. A man ahead of his time.''

Ellsworth reached for his snuff. Crichton's eyes remained unblinking.

Sir Geoffrey set his glass down. ''In any case, 'tis my belief that Merrick collaborated with the senior Captain Ashton to build the schooner for him. You've heard of Ashton, have you not, gentlemen?''

''I've heard of his son,'' Ellsworth said loftily.

''Yes, who *hasn't?*'' Sir Geoffrey muttered. ''An unruly hellion if ever there was one. But young Matthew is not so different from his sire. Ephraim made his fortune in the rum-smuggling trade some years ago before turning his talents to shipbuilding, where I understand he has been moderately successful.'' He took a deep breath. ''That is, *extremely* successful, since word got around about this schooner. And Matthew, of course, has become quite infamous as a privateer, and something of a town hero.''

''He's something of a pain in the arse, if you ask me.''

''He's *nothing* compared to what Merrick will be if something is not done about him!'' Sir Geoffrey's voice was hard. Already his cozy Kent home seemed more and more distant, a wistful dream if ever there was one. He sighed and continued on. ''In any case, both Ashtons are active in town politics, having served on the Committee of Safety, which was, as you well know, instrumental in stirring up sentiments against Britain. In fact, Matthew was only fifteen when those damned radicals, the Sons of Liberty, popped up in Newburyport back in sixty-five, but my sources tell me that he was one of the hotheaded young firebrands who roamed the streets wielding clubs, protesting the Stamp Act, challenging the opinions of passersby on it—God help them if they'd been in favor—and hanging and burning effigies of the local stamp distributor from some damned thing they called the Liberty Tree.''

Ellsworth sniffed, "I say, 'twill be a nasty affair indeed if Merrick and the young Ashton have gotten together."

Crossing the cabin, Sir Geoffrey leaned tiredly against the bulkhead and watched storm clouds filling toward the horizon. His bones ached, a good indicator that it would snow again soon. "My sentiments exactly, Hiram." He sighed heavily and ran his finger along the rim of his glass. "Especially since there's a convoy of merchantmen sailing from London as we speak, expected to put in to New York within the fortnight. Captain Merrick no doubt will have heard of it, as will have every other damned privateer worth his salt." He drew himself up, seeing his dream of his Kent home resting upon Crichton's blocky shoulders. "Which is why I think it prudent to stop Merrick before he can do too much damage.

"There are two things I want you to do, Richard. Or shall I say, given the fact that Captain Merrick's involved, *try* to do."

Crichton drew himself up.

"First, I want you to bring me Matthew Ashton. *Alive*. The Americans will trade most handsomely to have him back, I should think, and there are some things I might learn from him about Newburyport and the inaccessibility of that damned river."

There was a long pause. "And secondly, sir?"

The sluice of water against the hull and rudder was the only sound.

"Secondly, Richard—" the admiral regarded him over the top of his wineglass, and his bleary old eyes were suddenly sharp *"—I want that schooner."*

Ellsworth lifted his haughty brows.

"Afloat, intact, and *before* Merrick can use her to inflict any more damage upon our vessels, our shipping, and the morale of our men. If she is truly as magnificent as you—and eyewitness accounts—have described her to be, she's worth far more to our navy than a hundred ships. Let *our* architects dissect her, piece by piece. Let them study her as a biologist would a butterfly. Perhaps they will learn something from her."

Crichton's eyes were paler than ever, but a smile touched his hard mouth.

"So be it, gentleman." Sir Geoffrey sent Ellsworth from the cabin and stared hard at Crichton. "Here's your chance, Richard. To redeem your name, your honor, and my faith in you. Bring me Matthew Ashton, and Admiralty shall remain ignorant of your misfortunes of last night. But bring me Merrick and his schooner, and I can promise you flag rank by the end of the year."

"F-flag rank, sir?"

"Yes, Richard. *Flag* rank. I know it's what you've been waiting for." He grinned, and guided the younger man toward the door. "Now go, and do not dally. I'm an old man, with little patience and limited time. You have a fortnight to make good your efforts. Don't waste it."

Crichton smiled, an evil drawing back of hard lips that sent an involuntary shiver up Sir Geoffrey's arthritic old spine. "Thank you, sir. I shall not disappoint you." He touched his hat and strode from the cabin. Moments later, the shrill of pipes drifted down from above as he left the flagship and climbed down into the boat that would return him to *Viper*.

Sir Geoffrey stood at the windows for a long time. He thought of his home in Kent once again. He thought of Merrick and Ashton, and what Crichton was likely to do to them if he *did* succeed in capturing them.

And then he thought of the little midshipman Everett.

Sir Geoffrey was loyal to Britain, first, foremost, and last.

At least *Viper*'s abused people would be safe for a while longer.

Chapter 14

F ive o'clock and darkness.

Brendan was whistling as he trudged through Newburyport's cold and snowy streets, his hands shoved deep in his pockets, his tricorn pulled low, his chin tucked into his stock, and his coattails dragging in the drifts behind him. Anticipation sang in his blood, for in one of those pockets was a dinner invitation from Ephraim. Whether that invitation reflected genuine hospitality on the old sea captain's part, or an interest in hearing about the eight prizes *Kestrel* had dragged in from the sea and whose British crews were even now being marched to the Newburyport jail, Brendan didn't know. Those prizes certainly had something to do with the wild reception he'd received several hours earlier, when *Kestrel* had brought them all into the river and lined them up, one by one, alongside Ephraim's wharf!

He grinned wryly to himself, remembering *that* particular horror . . . the parade of nearly a hundred boats, full of wildly cheering Newburyporters, that had met *Kestrel* at the river's mouth to escort her into harbor; the adoring young lassies swooning at his feet once he'd arrived there; the seamen of every age and description pleading, nay, *begging* to sign aboard the lucky *Kestrel*. . . . Faith, how did Matthew, who'd returned from *his* cruise a few hours before, tolerate such abuse? 'Twas a wonder he'd managed to escape with his life!

But as he'd grinned and laughed and pretended to enjoy it, clawing his way through cheering throngs who'd been fighting one another to get his autograph, his attention, and probably the clothes off his back, someone had thrust a paper into his hand and he'd found himself with a personal invitation to supper from Ephraim Ashton himself. The invitation suited him just fine. After a cold, tossing bunk, oatmeal in the morning, and lobscouse with hard-tack at night, even thoughts of Miss Ashton's pudding were almost welcome.

Almost.

More so were thoughts of Miss Mira Ashton herself.

He grinned at the thought and stepped up his pace, forgoing the packed sleigh tracks in favor of the deep drifts bordering the road instead. Snow yawed into his boot tops and numbed his cold toes, but he forced his legs to work hard, pumping up his heart and generating plenty of warmth. He turned onto High Street. Big, handsome homes rose out of the snow, their many-paned windows glowing with candlelight. Woodsmoke lay heavily upon the brittle air, mixing with the tangy scent of the sea and fresh, clean wind. He heard revelry and laughter coming from one home, the faint tinkle of a harpsichord from another.

He kept walking, a little faster now. Snow draped the Beacon Oak's massive branches, swirled out of the black sky, and whispered against his cold cheeks. From somewhere off in the night he heard sleigh bells and the distant whicker of a horse.

Mira Ashton, out for a drive with her "wee gray colt?"

He grinned, and floundering in a drift, moved a bit closer to the relative safety of the road's edge. Just in case.

By the time he spotted the anchor, shapeless under a foot of snow, that marked Ephraim's grand mansion, Brendan's breeches were damp, his wool stockings soaked, and his coattails caked with snow. But the sight of the elegant Georgian was enough to make him forget his discomfort. The chimney sent up a tuft of smoke that appeared silver against the black, low-hanging sky. Snow lay like frosting on the roof, and giant icicles spanned the distance between eaves and ground, sparkling and twinkling like diamonds in the candlelight that shone from every window. It was a breathtaking sight, for the house appeared to rise straight up from a bed of light.

And inside that house was Mira Ashton.

Brendan's heart began to race, and he trembled with

nervous excitement. *She* was the only one he hoped to impress with *Kestrel*'s good fortune on her maiden cruise; the devil take the rest of the town!

He hit a seemingly bottomless drift, sank all the way to his hip, and laughing with boyish exuberance, scooped up a handful of snow and tossed it playfully at a darting shadow. He missed, of course. Faith, even if he'd been *trying* to hit the cat, he would've missed. He'd never be as good a marksman as Mr. Starr!

Still chuckling, he watched as the animal fled, bounding through the snow until it reached the front steps, where it reared up on its hind legs and scratched pitifully at the door. It stopped in midclaw to twist its head around and stare at him, tail twitching and ears pasted angrily to its skull.

Haughty creatures, cats! Perhaps a snow-shower would bring this one down to its proper station in life. Grinning, Brendan bent, scooped up another snowball, and aiming for a harmless spot on the door several feet above the cat's head, drew back his arm and fired his missile hard.

The door opened, and the snowball caught Matthew Ashton full in the face. His spectacles went flying.

"Son of a *bitch!*" Yelling in Ephraim-like rage, Matt clawed the snow from his eyes, dropped to his knees, and swept his palms over the frozen steps in a desperate search for his spectacles. His fiery hair stood out from his head like a conflagration, and behind him the door yawned wide. The cat darted into the house. "Miserable young scamps! Good-for-nothing brats! Show yourselves, damn you, or so help me God, I'll give you a licking you'll never forget!"

"A *lickin'?*" Brendan folded his arms, threw back his head, and let his laughter split the night. His Irish brogue might be a bit mellowed by years in the British Royal Navy, but when he wanted to, he could still pile it on thicker than rocks on a Connemara hillside. "Faith, I'd like t' see ye try 't! Blind as a bloody bat y' are withou' 'tyer specs, Ashton!"

"Why, you blasted bugger! That you, Merrick?!"

Brendan's peal of mirth was confirmation enough. "Nay,

'tis Saint Nick, come t' bring ye a present f'r Christmas! 'Ave ye been a good laddie, *Maitiú?*''

"For what I've done or for what I'm about to do?!"

"Why, f'r wha' 'tye've done, o' course! Wha' t'ye intend t' do is naught but th' Lord's business, an' not Saint Nick's. Therefore, ye'd best make yer peace with 'im before ye do anythin' rash, laddie-o!''

"Oh, I'll do something rash, all right!" Matt found his spectacles, hastily wiped them clean with his shirttail, and shoved them up the bridge of his nose. His eyes gleamed as he scooped up a handful of snow and molded it into a hard white ball the size of round shot. "And speaking of peace, you'd better make *yours,* Irishman, 'cause it's the last damned prayer ye'll ever pray!''

Brendan laughed, for Matt, eyeing him with a promise of retribution from behind speckled lenses, looked quite ridiculous. Behind him the door swung wide and revealed the house's brilliantly lit interior, but Matt, standing in the cold in nothing but his vest, his shoes, and a shirt that was half-in, half-out of his breeches, didn't give a hoot about wasted heat from either the house or himself. The fun of a good snowball fight was paramount. He drew back his arm and slammed the ball into a tree three feet beyond Brendan's ear, cursing loudly when he saw he'd missed his target. "Rumor has it that *Kestrel* tangled with a frigate mounting three times her guns, left her chewing her own bow wake, and made port with some seven prizes. That right, Irishman?''

"Oh no, tha' 'tisn't right a'tall!''

"Damned rumors, never can believe 'em!''

" 'Twas eight prizes, laddie!''

"Eight prizes!" Matt scooped up another handful of snow.

"Aye, eight prizes. A lad's got t' make a livin', y' know!'' The snowball came singing out of the darkness. Brendan dodged it, clenching his teeth as cold powder sifted down his neck, and came up with one of his own. He hurled it hard. With an Indian-like war whoop, Matt dove into the bushes beside the front door. The snowball missed him by a mile, exploding against the side of the house with a slapping *thunk.*

A head poked up above the scruff of the bushes. "Bah, I don't know how you managed to take one prize, let alone eight! Why, you couldn't hit the broadside of a barn, let alone a ship!"

"Y'r absolutely right, *Maitiú*, I couldn't! But I've a fine wee gunner who c'n take out a ship's mizzen on th' first shot!" A snowball exploded out of the bushes and burst against the tree behind him. "Faith, Yankee, ye talk about *my* aim?!"

"I'm just warming up!"

"Like bloody hell y' are; y'r aim's no bett'r than mine!"

Matt's shadowy form darted out into the open, and a snowball whined harmlessly past Brendan's ear. His fingers were numb and throbbing, but he managed to scoop up more snow and shape it into a good ball. He flung it hard, cringing as it headed toward one of Ephraim's windows, relaxing as it thwacked harmlessly against the sill. Matt's next came singing out of the darkness, passing his ear with a silent *whoosh* and trailing powder like the tail of a comet.

Laughing, Brendan cupped his hands around his mouth. "Methinks ye'd bett'r wipe off y'r specs, Ashton!"

"And *methinks* you're the one who needs 'em, not me!"

Brendan bent, grabbed more snow, and straightened up. "Then kindly lend me y'rs so that—"

Thwack! He staggered backward, the impact flinging him into a two-foot drift. He landed in an undignified sprawl on his backside. Stunned, he looked down, gasping like a fish out of water and cringing at the pain of sucking in great lungfuls of brittle air. Part of a snowball caked his lapels and chest. The rest of it was already sliding down the front of his coat. He shut his eyes for a moment, dizzy beneath the reawakened agony of his old injury.

Matt's howls of glee split the night and he slapped his thigh, the impact sounding like rifle shots in the frigid stillness. Coughing, Brendan pressed a hand to his chest and looked up. The front door was still open, but it was no longer empty.

Miss Mira Ashton stood there.

And she was making another snowball.

He lunged to his feet, hands outspread and raised in

surrender. "Mercy, lass! *Quarter!* What're you trying to do, kill me?!"

She smiled sweetly, already drawing her arm back. In that demure gown, with her hair caught up beneath a lacy white mobcap, a cameo at her throat, and her lovely, curvy body backlit by the chandelier, she looked too beautiful, too delicate, to do any damage.

He couldn't have been more wrong. And as he gingerly brushed the snow from his chest and wondered if she'd cracked a rib, she proved it.

The snowball hit him like a charge of grape, exploding against his collarbone and sending a cold spray of powder into his eyes, his nose, and down his neck. She brought him down once more, to his knees this time, and as he gasped for breath, he heard her laughter pealing like bells in the crystal night air. Her brother's last snowball, casually thrown, sent his tricorn flying. "Serves you right, Merrick," he complained good-naturedly. "Coming into port with eight prizes your first time out. What're ye trying to do, show me up? Hell, I have a reputation to uphold, you know!"

Brendan forced a grin, his shoulder throbbing and the old gunshot wound a familiar, dull ache in his chest. He ran a finger inside his stock to dig the snow out and retrieved his tricorn. Knocking the snow from it, he set it atop his head, grimacing as a fresh sifting of cold powder found its way beneath his queue and slithered down his nape. "A reputation?"

"Hmph! He has a reputation, all right!" Mira stood in the doorway, an ethereal snow princess in a sea green gown shot through with silver. But unlike Eveleen, who'd appeared behind her, there was nothing regal about her; her knuckles rested saucily on her hips, her lips were twitching, and the sides of her nose were crinkled with laughter. That helplessly thick hair, shining and freshly washed, was gathered atop her head, a few dark strands of it tipping her white shoulders and falling over her milk-smooth brow. Brendan's chest went tight. He stopped breathing and stared at her, transfixed. It was hard to believe that this was the same girl who'd run him down in the street, swore like a sailor, and went about town in her brother's clothes when the urge struck her. He shook his head to clear it, no longer feeling the snow trickling down his throat, his neck.

And faith, she sure had one hell of an arm!

"Aye, a reputation with the ladies!" she called saucily. "He's afraid that if you replace him as the local hero, they'll all flock to you instead!" Seeming oblivious to the cold, she gathered up more snow, this time eyeing Matt, who had the good sense to back away. "Isn't that *right*, dear Matthew?"

"Absolutely," he said, gauging the distance between himself and the doorway and wondering if he could make it in time before she brought him down with that deadly missile.

Mira rounded out the snowball, her calculated, planned manner reminding Brendan of the way Mr. Starr had tested each ball before ramming it into his gun. Her eyes were sparkling, her cheeks were cherry red with cold, and behind her he could still see Eveleen, watching Matt with wistful eyes. "Did you see *Mistress*'s figurehead as you came into port, Captain?" Mira said.

Brendan eyed that deadly snowball, wondering if it was intended for him or her brother. "Her figurehead? Er, no."

"You really should go and take a look at it. Matt's painted it again, to resemble his latest *lady friend*. Currently it has red hair and green eyes, right, Matt?"

"Blue eyes, damn you."

"Oh. Sorry, I haven't been as *close* to Miss Greenleaf as you've been, dear brother! So how should *I* know, hmmm?" *Pat, pat.* The snowball looked cold, hard—and deadly.

"So help me, Mira, you throw that snowball and I'll—"

She never gave him the chance to finish. Laughing, she drew back and threw it hard, clapping her hands as it caught him dead center in the chest with an exaggerated thump. Shaking with mirth, she fell against the doorway as Matt let out an enraged howl and violated the crisp, white night with a string of curses so loud that across the street, a window shot open and a stockinged head poked out.

"What the tarnal hell's goin' on out there?!"

Laughter greeted his angry query. The man slammed the window down with a sharp crack. *"What the tarnal hell's goin' on out there?!"* Mira mimicked in a singsong voice. She looked at Brendan across the snowy lawn, he looked at her, and she saw something in his eyes, hungry and wanting, as they'd been when he'd first seen *Kestrel*. Her laughter trailed off. She smiled her cat-smile. And Brendan, stuffing his painful thawing hands into his pockets, watched the snow swirling around her lovely face and swallowed hard.

Suddenly the night didn't seem so cold.

Matt charged onto the steps and grabbed her before she could fashion another snowball. Rubbing his elbow, he hauled her past Eveleen and over the threshold. *"You're going inside,"* he muttered, "before you end up killing one of us! Christ, Father'll have both our hides if you end up taking poor Merrick's head off with one of your damned snowballs!" He turned, wiping his wet hand on his breeches before extending it in greeting. "Come on in, Merrick! 'Gads, 'tis good to have you back!"

Brendan returned the greeting and together they entered the hall, red-cheeked, dripping, stomping snow from their feet and breathing hard. Inside, it felt steamy and hot after being out in the cold. A brilliant array of candles sputtered and hissed from a chandelier overhead, filling the air with the scent of tallow. As Brendan stood blinking, his eyes unaccustomed to the sudden brightness, a servant took his dripping coat, hat, and sword, and Eveleen thrust a mug of mulled cider into his raw hands. He was barely aware of the attention. His gaze was on Mira, just disappearing into the dining room with a tiger-striped tomcat yowling in her wake.

His chest ached, but it had nothing to do with the snowball. His neck was cold, his stock wet and itchy against his skin, and like the first time he'd arrived at this fine home, his breeches were soaked—but he was heedless of these discomforts. And then he heard the sounds of dishes clinking against one another, the pop of a cork, Ephraim's cursing. He saw the cat come bolting out of the dining room with Luff hot on its heels. He smelled hot turkey, fresh gingerbread, cinnamon, and baking apples—and fleetingly wondered if Mira had done any of the cooking.

He suddenly realized that he didn't give a damn if she had or hadn't.

Grinning wolfishly, he followed her into the great dining room.

There was hot turkey and squash baked in maple syrup. Corn pudding, codfish cakes, and skillet cranberries, frosty with sugar. Chestnut flummery with sweet sauce, Abigail's chewy molasses cookies, gingerbread and eggnog and whipped syllabub. Hot buttered rum and plates of glazed almonds, raisins, cheese. As usual, Abigail had put on a feast, this time using *Kestrel*'s success as an excuse to engage in her favorite pastime—cooking up a storm for her very appreciative menfolk.

Unlike Eveleen, Mira didn't do the meal much credit. She was too aware of the man who sat beside her. *Brendan.* His arm was near enough to lean against, his long thigh was heating up the space next to hers, and he was so close, she could smell his clean, masculine scent: spicy shaving soap, wet wool and damp cotton, fresh air and melted snow. He grinned a lot, complimented Abigail on the meal, caused the housekeeper to blush, and talked with his hands. His laughter was pure as the sea wind and as Irish as that whiskey Liam had nearly poisoned her with last night. He seemed very unaware of the fact she sat beside him, never turning her way, never talking to her, and being very, very careful not to let his arm or thigh accidentally brush hers. But his skittish attitude didn't deter her. Every time she looked at him, she saw him again as he'd been on *Kestrel*'s decks, laughing and gallant and quite full of himself as he'd put the little ship through her paces. . . .

"You're in love with him," Matt had taunted, grinning devilishly as she'd restlessly paced the house just hours before, eagerly peering out the windows and glancing at Ephraim's clock.

"Am not."

"Are, too." He'd tweaked her nose, and she'd kicked him in the shin. "I know the signs."

"I ain't in love with him. The man's a blasted lunatic. Any captain who stands on his deck and draws pictures of the enemy's ship during battle's gotta have rocks in his head!"

"Our Captain from Connacht hasn't rocks in his head, dear sister, and you know it. But I *do* think he's got something in his heart for you. . . ."

"You're full of crap, ye know that, Matt?! Full of crap!"

To which Matt had responded with hearty laughter and a careless wave of his freckled hand.

Heck, she hoped Matt was right and Brendan *did* feel something for her. Yet why was he taking pains to avoid her? She glanced at him out of the corner of her eye and picked at her food, too tense, too flustered, and far too excited to eat. Her stomach felt as though someone had tied a double reef in it. Her lips were dry and she had to keep wetting them; during one of these times Brendan happened to glance at her, and his honey-colored eyes had darkened perceptibly, making her lips go drier and her stomach even more jumpy.

And of course, there was the very real danger that he'd find out just *where* she'd been these past several days. . . .

Following *Kestrel*'s triumphant return to port, she'd darted through the throngs, scooted home, and managed to get halfway up the stairs before she was set upon by Ephraim, who'd spent a good ten minutes bawling at the very top of his lungs before remembering the Ultimatum.

"I told ye I don't want you out on that damned ship of Matt's! I told ye I want ye to start actin' like a proper female! And here ye are, defyin' me again! What'll Merrick think when he finds out! He don't know, does he?! Tripes 'n guts, that's all I need is fer *him* t' find out! You 'n' yer unladylike behavior's gonna be the bleedin' death of me!"

Of course, it wouldn't be long before he *did* know, Mira had flippantly predicted, for not only had the household staff heard every word—but so had every neighbor within a half-mile radius.

Ephraim had been undaunted. "Ye have exactly two months and ten days to gimme the name of yer future husband, Mira!" He'd torn his watch from his pocket, brandishing it in her face like a crucifix. *"Two months and ten days,* before that colt goes! Don't think I don't already have a buyer fer him! Patrick Tracy's just hankerin' to have him, and have him he shall!''

"Over my dead body!" she'd screeched back, and fled upstairs.

It was a good thing that Father didn't know what ship she'd *really* been out on! Mira thought as she picked at her food. And thank God that Shaula, at least, was safely beyond his reach and under Eveleen's ownership. Of course, Father remained unaware of *that* fact, too, which was just as well. But there was still the dilemma of Rigel. And El Nath. *Two months and ten days* . . .

"Shit," she said.

"Excuse me?" Ephraim looked up, scowling.

"Uh, *sit!*" she said to Rescue Effort Number Thirty-Seven, who was rubbing his whiskers against her leg and waiting for a handout. The cat stared at her uncomprehendingly and let out a long, plaintive howl that echoed around the room.

Ephraim grunted and stabbed a piece of turkey. Beside her, she saw Brendan's lips twitching. His long, pale lashes swept down over mirthful eyes. "So, *Moyrrra,* how did the riding lessons go, eh?"

She almost swore again. *What* riding lessons? She'd been aboard *Kestrel!*

Surprisingly, it was Eveleen who came to her rescue. "They've been going very well, Brendan."

Mira closed her eyes and let out a sigh of relief. Thank God the girl had not betrayed her.

Eveleen, however, had no intention of giving away Mira's secret—for not only would it spoil things for Mira, it would spoil them for Brendan, too.

Before she'd come to Newburyport, Eveleen had been prepared to hate the woman whom Brendan hadn't stopped talking about. The last time her brother had fallen in love, his heart had been broken, and Eveleen had no wish to see it happen again. But Mira Ashton was nothing like that other girl, Julia, who'd not only abhorred the things that Brendan loved—the sea and ships—but would never have defied her father to sneak aboard a ship just for the chance to be close to him.

There was something very special between Brendan and Mira—and Eveleen, despite her own dismal chances for happiness with Matthew, had no wish to destroy Brendan's chances for it with Mira. She felt Mira's grateful gaze upon her, and went back to her meal.

As for Mira, she was grateful not only for the fact that Eveleen had kept her silence, but that in her absence, she had actually ventured into the stables. The stable hand had confided that he'd caught Eveleen grooming Shaula and fearfully leading her around the paddock.

Mira grinned to herself. Hopefully Eveleen's progress would continue, and she'd take a real interest in the horses, therefore taking her mind off her maimed hand and her own delusion that she was a "cripple." But that was going to take some time—and a lot of work. Mira looked up and, at that moment, caught Eveleen staring at Matt from above a pile of gravy-soaked turkey some six inches high, averting her eyes only when Matt, who was launching into some plan to attack a convoy of merchant ships on its way to New York, swung his bespectacled face away from Brendan long enough to choke down a spoonful of Mira's own fish chowder before going at it once more. Before the main dessert was even served—a rich bread pudding dripping maple syrup and brandy and topped with clouds of cream, which Brendan didn't touch and Eveleen began to devour like a starving child—Mira was determined that she would see the two of them together if it was the last thing she did.

Matt wasn't helping the matter any, either. Mira cursed him beneath her breath. As usual, he tended toward exaggeration—sometimes wildly so—when he had an attentive audience. Brendan, who was familiar with the tavern boasts of fellow sea captains, merely raised a brow and reached for a piece of fruit, the little smile playing about his mouth indicating he believed only half of what Matt was saying. Eveleen was another story altogether. She listened with rapt attention, finally abandoning even her dessert and staring at Matt in fascination.

Mira frowned. Perhaps it was time to get Eveleen's attention on something other than food and her brother. Very aware of Brendan's leg, which had drifted slightly toward hers, she dabbed her lips with her napkin and said brightly, "So, Eveleen. Are you looking forward to your riding lesson tomorrow?"

Eveleen's head jerked up, as though she hadn't heard Mira's question. "Excuse me?"

"Your riding lesson," Mira chirped, flushing a bit when she felt Brendan's gaze upon her. "Ten o'clock, *remember?*"

Eveleen gave her a sour look. "Oh . . . yes. I'd forgotten." But she remembered her half-finished dessert, and attacked it with renewed vigor. "I *do* hope it's after breakfast. I get positively faint if I exert myself before eating. . . ."

"Breakfast's at precisely eight o'clock," Ephraim announced, as though it wasn't already a well-known fact.

"So there, you see?" Mira said cheerfully. "You'll be full, but not *too* full to ride—"

"Of course . . . More pudding, please, Captain Ashton?"

Matt, still going on about the convoy, passed it without even glancing at her.

And so the evening went, with Eveleen staring at Matt, and he ignoring her, and Mira staring at Brendan, and he ignoring her, until Mira boldly reached beneath the tablecloth and placed her hand on Brendan's thigh just as pretty as you please, at which point he shot out of his chair and knocked over the fine bottle of Madeira that Ephraim had just brought out. A red stain raced across the white linen, and Brendan colored with mortification.

"Nervous there, boy?" Ephraim asked, bushy white brows drawn close in a frown.

"Er, no . . . Just—"

"Don't fret, Merrick, happens to the best of us. Sometimes the fear and reya-ly-zay-shun of how close ye come t' gittin' yer head blown off in a sea battle don't hit till yer safely back on land." He glanced at his prized Willard clock and cleared his throat importantly. "I think it's about time we go retire fer a swig or two, eh, boys? We don't want to talk about killin' and blood and guts in front of the womenfolk. Let's go to the library and do it there."

He cackled at his own joke and dragged Matthew up from his chair.

Somewhat reluctantly, Brendan got to his feet. He glanced ruefully at the ruined tablecloth and felt his face flame. His thigh seemed to throb where she'd touched it. Pins and needles danced up his leg. And he was tired, dead tired. If only he could get away, get back to *Kestrel* without offending the old man. They could all discuss this convoy tomorrow—aboard *Kestrel*. But Ephraim was already headed down the hall, bellowing for a bottle of brandy and more of Abigail's cookies. Brendan stood up, feeling Mira's green-eyed stare on his back, and resigned himself to joining the old sea captain. He'd stay just long enough to be polite, and then he'd leave. Get himself *out* of this house before Miss Mira's charms did him in.

Yet despite himself, he happened to glance at her as he pushed his chair in. She was still sitting there, chewing her lip until it was delightfully red and swollen, her little hand stroking that gray dockyard cat, and her eyes glinting with a secretiveness that belied her apparent demureness. He wondered what mischief she was plotting now. And then she happened to glance up, and their eyes met. A current of electricity sizzled between them, one that had been crackling and sparking all night. Brendan's chest tightened and his heart fluttered and jumped, the way it often did when he'd had too much coffee in the morning.

With a rigid elegance that did his English side proud, he nodded stiffly and followed his host into the library.

Mira, her eyes dreamy, watched him go. A little smile lifted the corner of her mouth, and she sat gazing at the closed door long after the servants arrived and began to clear the table.

Brendan.

Her Captain from Connacht.

Matt was right, she *was* in love with him.

Two months and ten days.

Mira stuck her finger in her mouth and thoughtfully bit off a hangnail. Brendan had passed the Test with flying colors, proving himself *more* than competent as a seaman—*and* a commander.

She could live with Father's Ultimatum, she thought, grinning slyly. She'd just found her victim.

Chapter 15

Long after the men had retired to the library, Mira still sat at the table thinking about Eveleen's hopeless infatuation with Matt, and considering the best way to set Step One of *The Plan* into motion.

Brendan. He was quite a clever fox where the British were concerned, and he'd already proved he could be just as elusive with *her*.

Deep in thought, Mira had all but forgotten that she wasn't alone at the table. Eveleen was still there, eating up the last of the hasty pudding and maintaining a sulky silence. So quiet was she that Mira jumped when the girl heaved herself out of her chair and ambled off toward the stairs, her step heavy and her eyes, so like Brendan's but lacking their carefree mirth, downcast and miserable. Mira's heart went out to her. As usual, Eveleen had been wearing a pink silk gown, which did nothing whatsoever to flatter a figure that needed all the flattering it could get. Perhaps tomorrow—after her riding lesson, of course— she'd haul the girl down to Patrick Tracy's store in Market Square and coerce her into finding a more attractive—and patriotic—fabric to sew a gown out of. Of course, as one who spent half her time in her brother's shirt and trousers, she probably wasn't justified in making suggestions, but she *did* know that pink silk was the last thing that Eveleen Merrick ought to be wearing.

That resolution made, Mira returned to her scheming.

There was a new twist to it, though, a complication she'd been totally unprepared for, and one that was *definitely* not supposed to be part of the Plan.

She was in love with Brendan.

And she couldn't deny it. What had started out as a mere response to the Ultimatum had grown into far more. She should never have sneaked aboard *Kestrel* and seen the schooner's dashing captain in action. Captain Brendan Jay Merrick had passed the Test, all right. Mira thought of his mirthful eyes, his laughing mouth, his elegant hands, and wanted to see herself reflected in those eyes, to be kissed by that mouth, to be touched, held, caressed, by those hands. . . .

His every action told her that he was attracted to her, too. The knowledge brought a singing thrill to her heart and a warm glow to her skin. She gazed at the library door, idly playing with a lock of hair that had tumbled loose from her coif and winding it absently around her finger. She may be innocent where men were concerned, but given a roving brother, a seaman's upbringing, and a town full of male friends in whose eyes she could do no wrong, she was far less so than most women of her age and marital status. She recognized a lusty man when she saw one, no matter how hard he tried to hide it! And he *had* been hiding it—or trying to—all along, she now realized. Tonight, however, there was no way that Brendan could've concealed the hunger in his eyes every time he'd happened, albeit accidentally, to glance her way. Glance? Ha, it seemed that he'd barely taken his eyes off her all evening!

Maybe she ought to stop wearing Matt's clothes altogether and go around dressed in pretty gowns more often!

And, maybe, she thought with a puzzled frown, it wouldn't hurt to learn how to cook, either.

Thoughtfully chewing the inside of her lip, she plucked a limp chunk of fish out of her chowder and tossed it to the floor, where no less than twelve prowling felines fell upon it like there was no tomorrow.

Mira paid them no heed. She was still thinking of Brendan.

The library was close enough that she could hear the musical lilt of his voice and his decidedly Irish laughter, if she sat very still and strained her ears. Oh, to be in that room right now, smelling the old books and leather, the

beeswax and fine cherry rum that Father would be serving . . . She could picture the flames crackling in the
hearth, and Brendan sprawled carelessly in one of the big,
overstuffed wing chairs, the firelight gleaming off the gold
buttons of his waistcoat, finding the depths of his sienna
eyes, bringing out the honey-colored highlights of his rich
chestnut hair. . . .

The chowder went cold. The fire in the hearth began to
die, taking its light with it. The candles burned low, and
shadows danced along the wainscoted walls. Father's great
Willard clock banged out the hour, and the library door
blasted open and crashed against the wall.

"Nonsense, Merrick! East room's all made up fer
ye. Fire's already laid in the hearth, bed's all turned
down, and there's a brick heatin' in the flames to warm
yer toes. Ain't no need fer ye to go back to that damned
ship; she'll be there a-waitin' fer ye in the mornin'!"

"Thank you for the invitation, but honestly, sir, I'd feel
far more comfortable back on the schooner," Brendan
protested, remembering the *last* sleepless night he'd spent
in this house. Cat, clocks—and Mira Ashton.

"You young captains and yer blasted ships! Ye think I
don't remember how it is? I told ye, she'll be there in the
mornin'! Now don't be a-snubbin' my hos-pit-ality, boy!"

Muttering, he stormed into the dining room, grabbed a
plate off the table, and seeing his daughter still sitting
there, gave her a conspiring wink. "Any more lip outta
this young Adonis here and I'll sic Luff after him. Tripes,
where the hell is that blasted dog, anyhow? Luff?
LUFF?!" He gave a piercing whistle that almost shattered
the window glass and rapped his fork against the plate
hard enough to crack it. "Luff? Here, boy! He-e-e-e-e-re,
boy!"

A suspicious thump sounded against the ceiling, and it
occurred to Brendan that a brick was not the only thing
that had been warming his bed.

"C'mon, Luff! Here, boy! Daddy's got some goodies
fer ye!"

An avalanche of sound thundered down the stairs, claws
skittered madly on hardwood floors, and the setter came
skidding into the dining room on his haunches. Cackling

with glee, Ephraim set the plate on the floor after a wary glance to ensure Abigail's absence, and watched as the dog bolted the leftovers.

Luff did not touch Mira's pie.

"Abby'll have a damned fit if she sees him eatin' off the plates. Ye don't mind, do ye, Merrick? They git washed real good. Oh, Matt! Come back here, boy, I almost fergot! Annie Pillsbury dropped by while ye were out this morn, a-wonderin' if yer gonna take her to the Christmas ball tomorrow night at the Daltons' house."

Matt, his cheeks flushed with drink and his red hair rumpled, stared at him, uncomprehending. He pushed his spectacles up with a freckled finger. "Annie?"

"Aye, Annie! Ye know, that pretty little blonde—"

Matt made a dismissing motion with his hand and continued down the hall.

"You git back here! I'm askin' ye a question, dammit! Are ye takin' her or aren't ye?"

Matt was almost to the stairway. "I'm taking Leah Rutherford."

"That where ye were today when Annie came a-callin'? With Leah?"

"None of your damned business!"

"Is, too, my business! Ye were with Leah, weren't ye. *Weren't ye?*"

Matt whirled, his freckles fading into pre-temper redness, and thin crescents of fog nestling in the bottom of his lenses. "As a matter of fact, I was *not* with Leah, nor Annie! I was with Penny Morrill, all right? Now, shear off! Who I see, who I don't see, who I bed, who I don't bed, and who I take to the goddamned Christmas ball is none of your stinking affair!"

"Penny Morrill?!"

"Aye, Penny Morrill!"

"You mean to tell me ye have the likes of Annie Pillsbury and Leah Rutherford a-yappin' at yer heels and ye prefer some blowsy tart who ain't nothing but a she-bitch in heat?!"

Matt went crimson and slammed his fist into the wall. "Goddammit, just stay out of my life, you cantankerous old goat!"

"Cantankerous old goat?! "Who you callin' a cantankerous old goat?! Why, I'll have no cussed son of mine takin' that tone of voice with me, you hear me? I raised ye to show respect, and I'm damned sick and tired of not gittin' it! And furthermore—"

Seeing Brendan standing there in helpless confusion, Mira grabbed his arm, nearly tearing it off in the process, and hauled him down the hall at a speed that would've done Rigel proud. Behind them, the argument exploded, permeating the walls, sending cats streaming out of the room in every direction, and bringing candlelight to the windows of the previously darkened house across the street. Reaching the relative safety of the kitchen, they skidded to a stop, clutching their sides with laughter.

When he could speak, Brendan gasped, "You display an amazing ability to extricate yourself from these, er, situations, Miss *Moyrrra!*"

"It comes from many years of practice, Captain!"

Laughter stilled, and he found himself looking down at her, his smile growing winsome as he studied her mischievous eyes, the impish tilt of her nose, the creamy perfection of her skin. It was a striking foil to her dark hair, carelessly upswept and now coming loose from its pins after their headlong flight. How simple it would be to plunge his fingers through that thick mane and free the rest of it. He swallowed, suddenly feeling all tight inside.

"Are you all right, Brendan?"

"All right?"

"Well, your face is rather flushed . . . and you're breathing hard. . . . I didn't hurt you with that snowball, did I?"

He'd totally forgotten about the snowball.

Any more of her innocent flirting and he'd be lost. "No. I must go back to the schooner."

"You aren't going to stay here tonight?"

"I can't."

"Why not?"

"Because . . . well—" He flushed, glanced away, and said hastily, "Because you're a bonny lass, *Moyrrra,* that's why."

Moyrrra. She loved how his tongue seemed to roll over

the *r*s, his lilting voice rising up and down like the notes on a musical scale. He looked down at her, a lost expression in his eyes that was totally at odds with the actions of *Kestrel*'s blithe and gallant commander. She shivered and crossed her arms over her chest, grasping her elbows and having the weird premonition that he was going to kiss her.

And wishing with all her heart that he would.

"What does my being . . . *bonny* have to do with anything?"

He was so concerned with escaping before he did something he'd later regret that he failed to notice the glint in her eyes.

"It has everything to do with it! Now, please, I must go. *Now.*"

She touched his arm. "Brendan, I think you're running from me."

He flashed a desperate grin. "I'm not running, I'm *fleeing.*"

"Why? And from what?"

"From . . . from . . . faith, I don't know!"

His coat had been drying beside the great hearth that ruled the kitchen; now he tore it from its peg, shoved his arms into the sleeves, and yanked his shirt cuffs down with quick, jerky motions. It was the same coat he'd worn into battle on *Kestrel,* and in it, he looked perfectly dashing, perfectly handsome, and every inch the gallant young privateer that he was. Mira watched him with hungry eyes. His wool stockings and breeches defined the hard musculature of his legs, the lean, masculine beauty of his thighs. His neckcloth was loose, his sleeve lace spilling over his fine hands. He snatched up his sword and buckled it on, his hands moving quickly. She'd seen him wield that sword on *Kestrel*'s decks with a dancer's grace, a fencer's expertise, yet still, those hands—sensitive, fine, and skillful—belonged to an artist.

She wondered what they'd feel like against her skin, and shivered again.

And if she didn't stop him now, she might never know. He was running away *again!* Acting like a damned fish out of water, like so many sea officers who spent too much time aboard ships and not enough in sleazy dockside taverns. Where was that Irish lightheartedness? That weightless grin? That blithe, carefree spirit? Hell, if she wanted him to kiss her, she'd have to initiate it herself!

She planted herself between him and the door, crossed her arms, and announced, "So, Brendan, are you going to kiss me or not?"

His hand, just reaching for his tricorn, froze. That one higher-than-the-other brow shot clear up to his hairline. The muscles in his throat jumped and he stared at her, speechless. Mira was hard-pressed to conceal her grin. After Matt's philandering ways, Brendan's reaction was almost comical.

She put her hands on her hips. "Well, *are* you?"

He looked very flustered. "Am I what?"

"Going to kiss me." Saucily she tilted her chin and gazed up at him with mischievous eyes. "I loved it when you kissed me the last times. I promise I'll like it even more now."

He opened his mouth, shut it, colored, looked at the wall, looked at her, and began to fidget. "Well, to be truthful, I *was* considering it, but given the fact that your arsenal ranges from wild horses to brutal snowballs, I think it might be a folly, and therefore—"

"Captain Merrick, *please,* none of your blarney!"

"Brendan," he reminded her, slamming his hat down on his head and diving toward the door.

She caught his arm. "If you think you're going back to that damned ship without giving me a kiss, you *will* be sorry!"

He stared down at the little hand on his sleeve, that little hand he could've shaken off so easily, that little hand whose strength had the means to keep him rooted in the kitchen merely by the power its owner held over his heart, his desire, his very will. He gave a fleeting—desperate—grin, his arm as tense and hard as steel beneath that little hand. How could he resist her impish charm? How could he resist *her?* It was usless.

He let out his breath and stared hopelessly down at her. Her eyes were bright, the sides of her little nose wrinkling. And she was waiting. *Knowing* that she'd won.

He grinned—the rakehell grin of an Irishman—and Mira felt as though someone were pouring sweet, hot syrup over her heart and dribbling it right down into the nether regions of her stomach. His eyes sparkled with mirth. Softly he said, "I suppose if you don't do me any bodily damage, I might beg a kiss from you before I leave. . . ."

"There's no need to beg, Brendan." She smiled up at him, and touched his arm. "You see, before you, I'd never been kissed before. Not *really* kissed. And I've decided that I like being kissed by you very, very much, and therefore want to be kissed again. You don't mind, do you?' My breath's clean and I know how to kiss back. As for what should follow, I'm uneducated, but I know you can teach me. Honestly, Brendan, don't look so shocked. You're on your way to becoming the town's newest hero, and I want first claim on you."

He flushed, as humble as ever. "But . . . faith, you used to hate my guts!"

"*Used to.*" And to herself: *Before I saw you in action on your ship. Before you convinced me of your loyalty to America. Before I saw the man you* really *are beneath all that badinage* . . . She dragged her finger up his arm and smiled up into his eyes. "Now I find I like you very much." She glanced coyly down at the floor and poked at it with her toe. "Maybe a little bit *too* much."

He was paling beneath his seaman's tan.

"Of course, if you don't *really* want to kiss me, I'll understand. Maybe you already have a girl in some far-off port. Maybe you have one here. Maybe you don't like *me*. After all, what encounters you've had with me have been far from, uh, *pleasant.*"

"Oh no, Miss Mira. Even the most painful ones have been pleasant."

He said it with such sincerity that she almost burst out laughing. But he was no longer trying to escape. He stepped closer, so close that she could see the little sunbursts of tawny light amidst the darker, sienna-colored irises of his eyes; the russet tips of his lashes; the golden swirls that last summer's sun had painted into the rich chestnut tone of his hair. Again she caught the scent of shaving soap and wet wool, fresh air and melted snow.

And the sea. Always the sea. He looked down at her, impossibly tall, impossibly handsome—and reached up to cradle her jaw with his warm, sensitive hands.

She felt herself melting like a blizzard in July.

"Are you sure, *Moyrrra?*"

She closed her eyes and nodded.

"You're not afraid then, lassie?"

She stared up at him in a daze. "Afraid? Sh-should I be?"

"I don't know. My, er, capacity for self-control goes only so far."

She gulped and said with more bravery then she felt, "Would you care to demonstrate *how* far?"

"Excuse me?"

She reached out, shakily touching his lean cheek and letting her fingers slide all the way down his neck, where she ran her forefinger around the inside of his stock.

Eyes widening, he caught her hand. "Faith, lassie, d'you think I can practice restraint if you keep that up?!"

"Who said we have to practice restraint?"

"You've no idea what you're saying!"

"I do, too." She managed a bold grin that belied the dizzying rush of sweet, wonderful excitement that was slamming through every blood vessel in her body. "Now, stop being such a scaredy-cat and kiss me!"

Her demand ended on a note of laughter, and Brendan's defenses fell. So did his English side with all its attempts at chivalry and gentlemanly restraint.

He raised a brow. "You want to be kissed, then, eh?"

She looked demurely up at him, nodded like a little girl, and clasped her hands in front of her.

"All right, then. You shall be."

He was damning himself even as he reached out, slid his palms over the crisp fabric of her sleeves, and slowly drew her forward until mere inches separated them, and then not even that.

Gooseflesh rose on her arms. His hands burned through her sleeves, his breath fanned her brow and stirred a wisp of loose hair. She closed her eyes and trembled violently. That honey-hot feeling was seeping downward, following the lead of his hands as they moved over her arms, the inside of her elbows, her wrists, and finally the tips of her fingers, which he lifted to his mouth and kissed, one by one, until she thought she would die with the butterfly sensations his gentle nipping evoked.

His eyes held hers, his mellifluous voice making her tremble. "Just say the word, *Moyrrra,* and I'll stop. . . ."

A Spanish Inquisition wouldn't have brought a sound out of her.

His tongue was touching and tasting each fingertip, sending rockets of sensation shooting up her arm, and she knew she couldn't have stopped him if her life depended on it.

And it was getting awfully hard to stand up. . . .

He dragged his hands up her arms, smoothing the gooseflesh away and leaving fire in its place. His thumbs touched her collarbone, dipping into the hollows above it, stroking the sleek flatness just below it, then moving back up again to find the pulse that thumped madly at the base of her throat. She stared up at him, mesmerized and shaking. There was no stopping now, no going back. But she did not want to stop. She did not want to go back. *Ever.* She wanted to be kissed . . . and more.

So much more.

He slid his hands behind her nape, his thumbs stroking the sides of her jaw, the graceful arch of her cheekbones. His palms were rough in the seaman's way, his fingers painting the shape of her face with the gentle skill of a sable brush. He cupped the back of her head and gently tipped her jaw up, lifting her face to his like a flower to the morning sun. It was gentle imprisonment. Her legs shook so badly, she feared she would fall. He stroked the dewy softness of her cheeks, clearing away loose, damp strands of hair with his thumbs; and then he bent his head down toward hers.

Her arms rose and wound around his neck. His queue brushed her knuckles, the little hairs at his nape as soft as down against her palms. She pulled him down toward her, thrust herself up on tiptoe—and met his lips.

As before, the shock was instantaneous, like a spark set to powder, shaking and rocking her to her very core. Sensation slammed through her; dizziness and heat, honey and syrup, all whirling through her blood and congealing in a hot, gripping mass of nerve endings somewhere beneath her belly button and between the junction of her thighs. She clamped her legs together, the strange but wonderful ache intensifying as she pressed herself against him and felt his manhood, stabbing hard against her own feminine softness. The honey-hot sensation went up in liquid heat. His lips ground against hers, sweet and demanding, hungry and hot, forcing her head back against his hands, driving her body up against the wall. He sank his fingers into her hair, freeing the last of the pins and sending her glorious tresses tumbling down her back. Strength left her body and she clung to his neck by her arms alone. Where her knees had been, there was only water.

The world was swimming by the time he tore his mouth from hers. Dazed and shaken, Mira reached up and placed a trembling hand to her lips. They were still there. Throbbing, tingling, singing. She stared up at him, her eyes huge in her suddenly pale face.

"Now," he said softly, "I think you realize what I was trying to warn you about."

She could not speak. She could not think. And she could not trust her legs to support her weight. His arm was a steel brace against the small of her back, and she leaned against it heavily, gratefully, knowing that without it, she would've crumpled to the floor like a rag doll.

She closed her eyes, feeling his knuckles brush softly against her cheek.

"Are you happy now, *Moyrrra?*"

Opening her eyes, she nodded, swallowed, and ran her tongue over her lower lip. It felt swollen, and tasted of him. "Brendan?"

"Yes?"

"Have you . . . kissed many women?"

He laughed. "Enough."

"Do you ever kiss the same one twice?"

"On occasion."

"Wh-what occasion?"

"If she's pretty enough. If I happen to like her. If I think her da won't come after me with a loaded musket."

"Am I . . . pretty enough?"

"Aye, *mo stóirín,* you're a right bonny lass."

"And . . . and do you like me?"

"Aye." He hesitated, then added, "More than I should."

"And does my father—my *da*—make you nervous?"

"Nervous?"

"Aye." She swallowed, and kicked at an imaginary spot on the floor. "He's scared off plenty of other would-be suitors. . . ."

"Your da doesn't scare me, *Moyrrra.*"

"Are you sure?"

He laughed, a rich, melodious sound that brought the heat back to her insides. "I'm positive, lass!"

"Then, Brendan?"

He stared down at her, thoroughly enchanted.

"Kiss me again!"

"Good God."

And with that, he pulled her against him once more.

Chapter 16

He was insistent upon returning to his ship for the night.

She was insistent upon keeping him at her father's.

And so they argued, until Ephraim caught them at it and threw his considerable voice volume to Mira's side, and Brendan, outnumbered, outshouted, but certainly not outwitted, finally said that she could drive him down to the waterfront to pick up his things. Although he'd agreed that he would return to the Ashton house, it was his secret intention to bid her good-bye and spend the night safely aboard *Kestrel.*

In the stable it was cold and dark. He felt Mira's lips against his once more, as she reached up and put her arms around his neck. She pressed herself against him for a long moment, and he laid his cheek atop her rosy-smelling hair and hugged her tightly. Then she slipped away, laughing, and he heard a horse whickering softly as a stall door opened. He stood there in the chill gloom, his heartbeat filling his ears, his breath sounding hoarse in the darkness, his breeches feeling very, very tight across his manhood. He leaned back against a stall door, groaning inwardly.

Outside, snow fell on bushes and frozen branches with a soft hiss. Above, a mouse scurried in the hayloft, sending a few wisps of straw down atop Brendan's nose. He sneezed and flicked them away with a cold-numbed finger. His nose was even colder, and he cupped his hand over it and blew into his palm to warm it. He wished the rest of him was as cold as his nose. Faith, he was burning up down there. . . .

Wind drove snowflakes through the open doorway and dusted the threshold in a blanket of white. Gratefully Brendan turned his face toward the cold. Mira was coming out of the stall now, leading Rigel. "Ready?"

He saw the colt as a ghostly gray form in the darkness, heard his hooves whispering through straw, then ringing on stone. Mira's fingers brushed against his as she thrust the lead shank into his hand; then she closed his fingers around it, holding them there for a long moment as though trying to warm them. Something tightened in his chest. He shoved his other hand deep into his pocket and thanked God for the darkness that hid his desire from her. She was harnessing the colt now, performing the task with a businesslike purpose. Watching her, he wondered if she could see in the dark like one of her cats, so well did she know every buckle, strap, and fastening.

But despite her brisk efficiency, Mira was anything but calm inside. At least the simple act of harnessing her horse was familiar, and steadying. Her heart was still thumping up a storm—both in remembrance of Brendan's kisses and in anticipation of further ones. Damp heat still pulsed between her thighs, and her lips felt bruised, ravaged—and wonderful. She slipped the bridle over Rigel's head, pried open his jaws with her thumbs, and briefly warming the cold bit in her hand, gently eased it into his mouth. He stood chomping it for a moment, his breath white in the gloom, tossing his head and sending his silver-sheened mane flowing over her hands like heavy silk. Outside, snow hissed gently against the roof, the eaves, the window, and a gust of wind drew creaks from the eaves.

Thank God for the darkness that concealed her trembling hands. He'd probably tease the hell out of her if he saw them. Turning, she backed the colt into the traces of the sleigh, guiding him with soft words of encouragement and a hand on his warm chest.

Brendan's lilting voice disturbed the gloom. "You don't have to do this, you know. I walked over here, I can certainly walk back."

Determined to hide her nervousness, she tossed a bundle of quilts and furs into the sleigh with a saucy motion. "Are you playing scaredy-cat again?"

"No . . . but I think you are."

"I am not!"

He spread his hands in a gesture of truce, for there was an edge to her voice, tenseness in her stance. "All right, all right. Faith, you're just like your *fathurrr!*"

She laughed skittishly at the exaggerated way he rolled his tongue over the word, and led the colt out of the barn and into the wintry night. After the comparative warmth of the stable, the cold struck like an Arctic blast, pasting her nostrils shut and making her eyelids ache. Snow swirled out of the black sky and stung her cheeks, and her nose began to run, her teeth to chatter. But she was determined; the cold be damned! Not for anything in the world would she trade this time with Brendan!

Her skin grew hot in anticipation as he hauled the big door shut, tugged his tricorn down low, and briskly rubbing his hands together to restore their warmth, came toward her. Rigel was already fretting, tossing his head and stamping his foot in eagerness to be off. With typical English gallantry, Brendan handed her up into the sleigh, took a seat beside her, and shook out the heavy quilts and furs, tucking them around her shoulders and spreading them over her lap with infinite gentleness. She shuddered as he joined her beneath them, his hard thigh pressing against hers and burning the skin through layers of petticoats, skirts, and cloak. The shuddering was soon a violent trembling. With unsteady hands, she sent Rigel down the drive and into the snowy night, the runners of the sleigh whispering silently through the drifts.

"Warm enough?"

She nodded, eyes straight ahead, face very pale against her hood and that absurdly thick wall of dark, snow-flecked hair that concealed most of her face. She looked scared. Fragile. And, bundled up in wool and fur and quilts, like a little girl. His heart swelled and he gripped his hands together in his lap. She thought to merely drive him down to the wharf so he could go out to *Kestrel,* pack a ditty bag, and return to the Ashton house, did she? Well, Ephraim could rant and rave and stew in his own juices as far as he was concerned. His daughter was no little girl. There was no way he'd spend another night in that house, where Mira's innocent charms could further test his restraint. No, he would stay aboard *Kestrel,* Mira would stay in her own safe bed, and they'd all be better off for it.

Faith, maybe he'd even get some sleep—but he doubted it.

As it was, he wondered how the devil he was going to make it as far as the wharfs. Her warm little body was pressed against his, building a fire in his heart, his blood, his loins. Swallowing hard, he turned away, forcing himself to watch the houses filing swiftly past, most of them dark and silent at this late hour. Tree branches bowed beneath snow, and in places the road was indistinguishable. Rigel snorted and pranced. Clumps of snow flew from his hooves, and his tail, streaming in the wind, lashed Brendan's cheeks.

Mira slapped the reins against the colt's back and sent him into a swifter trot. The night was cold enough to freeze the devil's breath, but beneath her woolen cloak and the heavy draping of quilts, her skin was moist and hot, feverish, even. This was *Brendan* beside her, his rock-hard thigh pressed immediately against hers, his elegant shoulder swaying against her with every movement of the sleigh. His nearness dried her throat and sent heat gushing through her blood. She looked at her hands, gripping the reins, and wondered that the snow that drove against them didn't go up in steam. She scooted over on the seat, moving a little closer to him, reveling in his warmth, his strength, his presence. Would he kiss her again? Oh, *would* he?

Don't get your hopes up, she thought. *You don't know if he feels the same about you.*

But *he* was the one who'd kissed her until her knees had given out.

He was the one who'd reached for her a second time.

And *he* was the one who'd just covered her hand with his, melting the snow there until it ran down in the cracks between her tightly clenched fingers. She transferred the reins to her left hand, and allowed him to pull her right one beneath the sheltering warmth of the thick pelts and quilts. Her breating grew ragged as he rubbed the inside of her palm with his thumb. Clamping her legs together against the strange feelings in her lower regions, she slapped the reins once more against Rigel's back.

Oh, Brendan, my gallant captain, my Captain from Connacht . . . I think I love you. . . . I know *I love you. . . .*

Love. A few kisses, a handsome face, and some daring deeds in a fast sailing ship, and she was hopelessly smitten. Yet he was everything a woman might dream about, and more. Dashing and witty and full of fun. Humble, clever, and best of all, a sea captain. Hadn't she always vowed that if and when she married, it would be to a sea captain? But a *British* one? She frowned. No, he was Irish. . . .

Who cared, as long as he fought for America! But she couldn't help wondering *why* he'd switched loyalties; the one time she'd asked him about it, he'd deflected her question with his usual laughter and said something about mermaids liking Yankees better. And Liam would only say that Brendan had distinguished himself in the Royal Navy before some *unpleasant business,* as he'd put it, had swung him over to the American side instead. . . .

She'd find out. Maybe not tonight, maybe not tomorrow. But sooner or later, she'd find out.

They passed the Beacon Oak, the Liberty Tree, sleeping houses, and white, empty fields that rolled away into darkened woods. At Fish Street, she slowed Rigel so they could make the corner. The Dalton house swept by on the right, smoke pouring from both chimneys, and one upstairs window still glowing with light. Almost across the street, the Tracys' big brick mansion stood like a leviathan; both Dalton and Tracy had entertained General Benedict Arnold when he'd brought his troops through en route to the Quebec wilderness back in '75, the expedition to involve Canada in the patriot cause ending in disaster. Now even those memories seemed distant as the snow whispered against her face and the sea wind blew in off the frozen river, colder, wetter, and harsher now as they neared the ocean.

She slowed Rigel to a walk when they reached the waterfront. The Ashton Shipyards were quiet and dark. Snow covered the roofs of the little blacksmith shop, the mast house, even the long ropewalk. Giant masts of spruce and cedar lay locked in the frozen mast pond, and the air was sweet with the scent of cold sawdust. A ship's skeleton, dark against the night sky, was taking shape on the ways, and a big three-master was snugged up to the wharf, its bowsprit looming high above their heads. Crates lay stacked neatly on the wharf, buried beneath snow and awaiting loading on the morrow. In the darkness, the wharf creaked with the push-pull of the river against the incoming tide, and giant ice floes groaned in agony as the current shoved them up against the frozen shore. But out in the harbor the current ran strong, the water cold and black.

And out in the harbor, *Kestrel* rode silently at anchor.

Mira drew back on the reins. The moment had come far too soon, and not once had Brendan taken any liberties with her that propriety dictated he shouldn't—and her hopes dictated he should. She felt strangely cheated, deprived, empty.

"Well, here we are!" she chirped, trying to mask her dismay. "I'll wait while you go pack a ditty bag."

He didn't move, and she sensed that he was struggling with something inner and deep.

"Brendan?"

"You'll do nothing of the sort." He looked down at her, seizing her hands, one warm from his touch, the other ice-cold from the bite of the elements. "You'll go back to your da's house, Mira, and you'll go alone."

It was the commanding tone of a captain, the tone that gives orders and expects them to be obeyed.

"Alone—?"

"*Alone.*"

"But, Brendan . . . you heard Father—everything's all ready for you!"

"Mira, I can't. Please understand."

"I don't understand anything!" Coldness swept against her thigh as he stood, then leaped down from the carriage with easy grace. She stared at him, unconsciously spreading her palm over the seat where he'd been and cherishing the warmth that lingered there beneath the heavy fur.

"Brendan!"

He was walking away from her!

"*Brendan!*"

He paused only long enough to touch his hat before striding determinedly toward the wharf. And she knew then that *he* was afraid, that he was putting as much distance between them as possible, probably trying to escape what must be the same temptations he'd spoken of back at the house. Agape, she watched him walk away from her. Toward the river, toward his little boat, and toward the schooner, waiting silently, triumphantly, out in the river for her captain.

Was *Kestrel*'s call more powerful than her own?!

Jealousy, insane and ridiculous, swept through her. Agony and hurt, and then indignation. Desert her for a *ship*, would he?! She jumped down from the sleigh, scooped up a handful of snow, and with all her strength, sent it slamming through the brittle air. It caught him between those elegant British shoulders with a dull thud.

"Ouch!"

"Where are you going?"

"To get my boat. And then out to my ship, and *then* to bed for the night!"

"You can't do that!" She raised her voice. "Father'll be furious!"

He stopped, his form hazy through the falling snow. "No. I think his *daughter* will be furious. Now, get back in that sleigh and take yourself home."

"I'm not going alone!"

"Well, you're not going with me, either. Good night, lassie."

"Brendan!"

He turned, expecting another snowball to come slamming into his back at any moment. She was still standing there, bewildered, hurt, and lost. *Faith.* Didn't she understand? Didn't she realize the inner turmoil she was causing him? He didn't *trust* himself around her! Ten minutes pressed against her in that damned sleigh and the agony in his loins was unbearable! Ten *more* minutes and he'd find himself acting upon it!

But she'd sure managed to get his attention, hadn't she? And now that she had, she used it to her best advantage. "Fraidy-cat," she called softly through the falling snow.

"Temptress."

"Chicken."

"Waif."

"I'm going with you, Brendan."

"Oh no you're not."

"Oh yes I am!"

She turned and unhitched the horse from the sleigh, her feet spread, her shoulders thrown back, and her movements sure and committed. She removed the bridle and tossed it into the sleigh, and before he realized what she was up to and could dive forward to stop her, she slapped the flat of her hand against Rigel's backside and sent him galloping away in a cloud of snow, leaving the sleigh standing there, immobile in the drifts.

Her laughter rang out in the night.

"You little fool!" he cried, horrified.

"Guess you have no choice now but to take me out to the ship, do you, Brendan?" She smiled coyly, folded her arms, and leaned back against the sleigh. He wanted to strangle her. "Unless you want me to walk home *alone.* Or perhaps you'd like to escort me, hmm?"

He gritted his teeth. "I don't know how your da puts up with you."

"He doesn't. That's why he issued the Ultimatum."

"The *what?*"

"The Ultimatum. You see, if I don't find a husband by September fifteenth—at exactly twelve o'clock—he's going to find one *for* me. In the meantime, he's selling one of my horses every three months until I can come up with a suitable candidate for him.''

"So you've singled me out as your victim, eh?''

"Oh, no. The thought *never* even entered my mind!'' She shrugged to lend credence to her fib. "You see, I have absolutely no intention of getting married to *anyone*. You said yourself that you don't know how Father can put up with me—if he can't, how could anyone else? Certainly not you. You're quite safe, Brendan.'' She smiled, the sides of her nose crinkling endearingly. "So take me out to your ship.''

"If I do that, neither one of us'll be safe.''

"If you do that, neither one of us'll be cold.''

"If I do that, both of us'll be sorry.''

"If you *don't* do that, I'm going to take your head off with this snowball!

They stood there in the falling snow, freezing in the sharp wind, and neither willing to give an inch. Finally Mira tossed her head. She dropped the snowball and clasped her arms about her. "All right. So I'll stand here and f-f-freeze to death.''

"Why are you doing this to me?''

"I'm testing your qualities as a gentleman.''

"You're testing my *restraint* as a gentleman!''

"Maybe we'll both be lucky and it'll soon break.''

He made a frustrated sound and clenched his fists at his sides. "You're impossible, d'you know that?!''

"No. Just very good at getting what I want. It comes from long years of practice, Brendan. Sorry.''

"And what *do* you want, *Moyrrra?*''

She touched her cold lips. "For you to kiss me again. And then for you to take me out to *Kestrel* for the grand tour you've never given me. As her builder's daughter, I deserve one, don't I? Besides, you *promised.* . . .'' He began to fidget, and she knew he was wavering. And then she played her ace. "She's awfully pretty sitting out there in the snow, isn't she, Brendan.''

She hid a secret smile as his expression softened at mention of his beloved ship. It was easy to find the holes in Brendan's defenses. *"Faith,"* he began.

"And then I want you to walk home with me, sleep in the room next to mine, and have breakfast with us. Just like Father asked you to."

"He didn't ask, he ordered."

"Orders are meant to be followed."

"I follow no one's orders but my own, and half of the time not even them. I owe your da nothing!"

"But you owe *me*. After all, *I'm* the one who'll be standing here freezing to death if you don't—"

"Damn you, Mira Ashton!"

"And damn you, Captain Merrick! You take one step toward that ship without me and I'll lay you so low with this here snowball, you won't get up for a week!"

Their eyes met, spunky challenge in hers, frustration in his that was helpless against her impish charm. As he'd said, he didn't always follow orders, even his own. Impulse and desire won out over control and wisdom. There'd be time for regrets later.

He jammed his hat down over his brow. Then he strode back to her as purposefully as he'd left her, yanking her into his arms and stilling her triumphant laughter. Wet hair clung to her freckled cheeks. Snow melted on her face, running between their lips as his mouth slammed down on hers, relentless, driving, almost punishing. She tasted of fresh air and melted snow, smelled of roses, sweet hay, and the promise of springtime. He dragged her hood off, plunged his hands into her thick, warm hair, and held her face to his, kissing her hard. And still the snow fell, frosting their shoulders, her hair, his hat.

Out in the river, *Kestrel* watched, and waited.

He tore away, breathing hard, before falling back against the sleigh and throwing a hand over his eyes.

She ran a tongue over her lips, licking off snow and savoring the taste of him. There was an unspoken invitation in her eyes, a challenge.

And Brendan had never been able to resist a challenge.

Nor, when one threw herself at him, a wee bonny lass.

Faith, why was she *doing* this to him? So innocent, and yet, so totally, utterly *woman*—

She shuffled forward through the snow and laid her hands on his arms. Catlike, she rubbed herself against his chest, causing white-hot flame to explode in his loins. "Show me your ship, Brendan. . . . I'll even help you row out to her. . . ."

"Mira—"

"Brendan, you *promised*. . . ."

"D'anam don diabhal!" he swore, taking her hand and hauling her toward the boat. *Faith. Faith and damnation. Faith and hell and damnation. . . .*

She had to run to keep up with him. Mira stared up at his proud back, the elegant span of his handsome shoulders, the grim, desperate set of his jaw—

And smiled.

Chapter 17

*K*estrel lay like a nesting hawk, her sides as black as the river. Her gunwales were lost beneath a mantle of snow, her sharply raked masts spiraled with the tide, and her blocks and rigging creaked and knocked. The sounds were loud in the frozen stillness of the night, and louder still as Brendan rowed their boat closer and closer.

"Lovely, isn't she?"

His voice broke into her thoughts. Again Mira felt that quick stab of jealousy. "Aye," she agreed, trying to keep the dismay out of her voice. "Quite lovely indeed."

"You ought to see her under full sail. She'd take your breath away."

I have seen her under full sail, Mira thought. *Plunging through trough and crest alike, wreathed in the smoke of her own guns, and skimming a snowy sea with fore and main set wing and wing.* Instead she said, "I'll bet she's gorgeous."

"More than gorgeous. Sometime I'll take you out for a short cruise. You don't get seasick, do you?"

"Once in a while," she lied.

"Well, we'll go out on a calm day. Maybe I'll even let you take the helm for a bit."

He looked quite pleased with himself, as though taking the tiller of a fine and dancing ship would be a new experience for her. *If he only knew.* She'd taken *Proud Mistress*'s more times than she could remember; in battle, in calm, in stormy seas and in gentle ones. She'd brought prizes into harbor, guiding them through the tricky bars, sunken piers, shifting winds, and dangerous currents at the Merrimack's mouth. She'd learned to sail before she could walk, tie knots before she could talk, and had been in and out of boats her entire life.

But what Brendan didn't know wouldn't hurt him. Especially if it might later be used to her own advantage . . .

"That would be nice," she agreed. "Maybe in the springtime when the seas are calmer."

As they passed beneath the schooner's figurehead, Brendan gazed up at the little hawk, snow capping his shoulders like twin epaulets and frosting his brows, his eyelashes, the bridge of his nose. Wind tugged at his queue, dark beneath his snow-covered tricorn, and molded a stray piece of hair against his lean cheek. Mira thought of him in command of this fine ship, calm, carefree, and dashing, and again felt that hot, dizzying sweep of admiration for him. *Newburyport's newest hero,* they called him. *The Captain from Connacht,* the Irishmen aboard *Kestrel* called him. Oh, now she understood what love was all about; the world could crumble to dust and it wouldn't matter one bit as long as she was with *him.*

Fighting the pull of the tide, Brendan maneuvered the boat close to the schooner and secured it to her chains. Mira could've easily made the climb up *Kestrel*'s icy sides with no assistance, but she dared not reveal her seagoing skills. Besides, it was much more fun to tuck her hand in Brendan's and allow him to help her.

Up the side they went, Brendan carrying the quilts and furs, still warm with their body heat, over his arm. The schooner's decks were bare, her hatches, ringbolts, and guns looking weird and unreal beneath the thick blanket of snow. There were no footprints. *Kestrel* was deserted.

They stood there for a moment, neither saying a word as the wet wind blew snow into their hair and faces. A tense expectancy built between them. ''Well, you wanted to see her, and so you shall,'' Brendan said blithely, but Mira caught the nervous edge to his voice. ''Watch your step. I wouldn't want you to trip and fall over anything.''

Just to be sure she didn't—or so he told himself—he took her hand, trying to warm it, although his own fingers were nearly frostbitten. They shuffled through six inches of snow, heading aft and leaving dark trails across the deck. Beneath their feet, *Kestrel* rocked easily; above their heads, shrouds whined and blocks banged, as though the schooner were begging her captain to take her back to sea. Mira watched him lay a fond hand atop her gunwale and gently brush the snow aside, heard him murmur something beneath his breath; and then he cleared the snow from the hatch, tugged it open, and led her down into the cold, dark depths of the ship.

Onshore, he'd been reluctant to have anything to do with her. Now, the decision made to bring her aboard, he was determined, almost purposeful. Again Mira marveled at the way a ship could change a man, and felt a twinge of resentment.

Around her, *Kestrel* seemed to laugh softly to herself.

It was drier belowdeck without the wind, but the cold hung about them like a block of ice, still and heavy and silent. Their footsteps echoed on varnished planking. Their breathing sounded unnaturally loud. And surrounding them Mira felt *Kestrel*'s own presence; watching her, assessing her, sizing her up as a rival for the attentions of her captain. It was an unnerving feeling, one that a landsman would never have recognized. But Mira was no landsman. She was well aware of the special affection that ships and captains had for each other—and knew that if she wanted to win this handsome sea officer from his lady love, she'd have her work cut out for her.

Kestrel would not make an easy rival. Sweet and demure in one moment, sexy and sleek the next, a predator, a courtesan, a lady all in one. Mira smiled wryly in the darkness, her hand still folded in Brendan's as he pushed open his cabin door. *I can be sweet and demure, too,* she thought, silently transmitting her thoughts to the listening bulkheads, the gently rocking deck, the creaking masts that sounded unnaturally loud down here in the still quiet. *And I will fight you for him as long as I live!*

I met him first, the schooner seemed to whisper, *and I will no more give him up than you will. . . .*

"We shall see," Mira said aloud.

"What?"

"Oh, nothing," she said hastily as Brendan turned, his face pale in the darkness. Around her, the bulkheads seemed to shake with frivolous laughter.

She wondered if she was coming unhinged.

She waited silently, shivering, as Brendan rooted in the darkness for a flint. Moments later, a lantern's soft glow filled the little cabin. It was the first time that Mira had been in *Kestrel*'s cabin since Brendan had taken up residence here, and she was pleased, very pleased, with what he had done.

The cabin was clean, tidy, and functional. A table, carefully rubbed down with oil, was snugged up against the bulkhead. A mahogany lap desk, an inkwell, a goose quill, a set of brass navigational instruments, and the schooner's leather-bound log were neatly arranged atop it. A braided rug covered the deck planking, and a pile of wood was carefully stacked beside a tiny wood stove. A sword hung on the bulkhead, and the neatly made bed was spread with a thick blue and white checkered quilt whose workmanship looked suspiciously like Abigail's—and probably was, given the housekeeper's fondness for "Captain Brendan." Above the bed, a small cabinet was built into the bulkhead, and beneath it were several drawers, all neatly closed with no clothing hanging out of them, as was the case in Matt's cabin aboard *Proud Mistress*. And unlike that other cabin, there was no liquor cabinet, no decanter of brandy on the table, no assortment of glasses scattered about in various stages of emptiness—nothing but a porcelain bowl and pitcher that probably contained water, no doubt frozen solid by now.

"You've done a fine decorating job," she said earnestly.

"Think so?"

"I do."

The silence hung between them, thick and heavy and awkward. He was fidgeting again. She watched him for a moment, cursing his shyness, loving it. Finally she looked at the wood stove and said, "I think you should light a fire."

"A fire? Why?"

"Well, it *is* cold. It would take the chill out."

He stared at her, frustrated, confused, and defenseless.

"Good heavens, Brendan. You did say you're going to sleep here tonight, didn't you? You might as well make yourself comfortable." She picked up a piece of firewood and tossed it to him. "Here. What are you waiting for?"

He looked trapped. "Er, don't you want a tour of the ship?"

She groaned silently. "Later. Just light the fire, Brendan. It's unbearably cold in here."

He deliberated, knowing that she was cornering him into something, not sure that he wanted to be cornered, and wishing he'd never let her manipulate him into this in the first place. *Let* her? He could've stopped it at any time. He could've walked back to the waterfront without her having to drive him. He could've left her at the waterfront. He *should've* left her at the waterfront.

And he didn't *have* to light the fire.

But he did.

She smiled an impish, triumphant grin that hid her own nervousness, for she knew as well as he did that once it was burning, he couldn't leave the ship to escort her back home. He would be staying aboard *Kestrel* tonight.

And so, she vowed to herself with sudden recklessness, would she.

Now he was squatting down on his heels and tossing kindling to the crackling flames, the scent of burning wood mingling with that of tallow, melted snow, oil, and new varnish. His hands were spread toward the heat; snow melted from his boots and puddled beneath them. One by one he pulled them off, thrust his toes toward the fire, and shut his eyes. From behind the little glass door the flames glowed against his face, making him look like a sun god. Adonis, Father had called him.

She stood there, drinking in the sight of him. Wanting

him but not very sure how to go about getting him. She was bold, but terrified. So she stood there wondering what to do as she let her gaze rove over the long, pale lashes fanning those sculpted cheekbones, the sensitive hands with their fine, tapered fingers, that boyishly tousled and windblown hair, now coming free of its queue and curling damply over his brow, his ears, his collar. It was hair that looked as though the sun had taken a brush and painted it with sunlight before yielding it to his capable hands. It was hair that was damp and curling at the ends, hair that she wanted to loosen from the black ribbon at his nape and run her fingers through. . . . Hair that—

She noticed then that he was shivering, too.

"You should've told me you were so cold, Brendan!"

"I'm not c-cold." He looked up with a helpless grin, his teeth chattering. "I'm *freezing.*"

She looked at his breeches and stockings, dark around the calves with dampness and clinging to him like a second skin. His nose was red, his cheeks flushed, and a trickle of melted snow ran down his temple.

Wickedly she had a sudden desire to hold him in her arms and catch that crystal drop on her tongue.

The snow was melting on him, but the ice that lay between them had a long way to go before it was thawed. And suddenly Mira knew what she had to do. They were here, alone, in this cozy little cabin with a warm fire, a safe harbor, and the snow swirling just outside the frosty cabin windows. She had manipulated him into bringing her here, and she would have to make the first move. She sensed his desire for her; she didn't have to sense hers for him, for it surged and pounded through her blood like a fever left unchecked. And it would stay unchecked if she allowed him to hide there beside the fire and pretend she wasn't even here.

It was obvious that whatever cursed gentlemanly instincts he possessed would not invite her to sit with him. That in mind, she took a deep breath, picked up one of the furs, and tossed it down before the wood stove. He stiffened and a muscle tensed in his jaw. Kicking off her boots, Mira removed her cloak, tossed it over a chair, and stretched out beside him.

He edged away, warily.

"Brendan, you could at least *share* the fire. I'm cold, too, you know."

She was anything but. He glanced at her, flashing that desperate smile once again, as though the effort pained him. Still he didn't invite her to join him, but she sensed, with a woman's intuitiveness, that he wanted her to more than anything. And so she sidled closer to him. So close that she could feel the rock hardness of his thigh burning against her own through layers of thick, quilted petticoats. So close that she could feel the quick rise and fall of his chest as he drew breath. So close that their body heat mingled.

She ached to touch him, to hold him, to have more of him than the kisses they'd shared earlier. . . .

His sleeve was wet against her arm. "Take your coat off," she said.

"I'd rather not."

"Dammit, Brendan, for being Newburyport's newest hero, you're more jittery than a schoolboy with his first girl!"

He actually blushed.

"Now, take your coat off. It's soaked. No wonder you're freezing!"

He swallowed and looked away, still shivering. The silence, punctuated by the snapping hiss of burning wood, waited, as though *Kestrel* herself were testing her. That challenge did it. Without further deliberation Mira reached out, found the buttons of his lapel, and one by one, undid them. He endured her feathery touch, his shoulders stiff as she drew off the heavy coat and tossed it over the chair back to dry. His crimson waistcoat followed. Still he didn't move, only staring into the fire with his jaw set and his knuckles showing white with the effort it took to contain himself. Mira picked up a thick fur pelt and draped it over his shoulders, letting her fingers linger there to trace the rise of his collarbones.

He tensed, but made no move to stop her. Then he shut his eyes as she sat before him, his face mere inches from her own. Another drop of water trickled down his temple, glittering with firelight. Gathering her courage, Mira pressed her lips there, and put her tongue against his skin.

He groaned, his eyes opened, and her heart melted beneath that mellifluous stare.

"Why are you doing this, *Moyrrra?*" he said, in an agonized whisper.

"Doing what?"

"Driving me insane. I can't take much more of this and still behave like a gentleman."

"I do wish you'd *stop* behaving like a gentleman. I'm beginning to find it quite boring."

"Faith." He shut his eyes once more.

"The world is full of gentlemen and rakes. You've already proven to me that you can be a gentleman. Prove to me now that you can be a rake."

His eyes shot open. "A rake!"

"Well, you *are* an Irishman, aren't you?"

"Only half!"

"Well, then start acting like one. I want you to kiss me again."

"No, *Moyrrra.*"

"Yes, Brendan."

" 'Tisn't safe, lass!"

"What, do I have some sort of disease or something?"

"You know very well what I mean!"

She slid her hand between the closure of his shirt and touched his chest. The muscle there was tough and hard and sinewy, just as she'd known it would be. He groaned, knowing he could never win this fight, and hating himself for not wanting to. And now she was unbuttoning his stock, sliding it off his neck and tossing it to the floor. Her fingers whispered over his throat, his chest, the little white circle left by Crichton's shot. He shivered violently.

"Moyrrra, lassie, you must stop this. . . ."

"I will not, Brendan."

"But—"

She laid a finger over his lips. "And I don't think you want me to, do you?" She inched closer, pressing the length of her body against him, driving him crazy with her nearness. *Kestrel* didn't ease the situation any, her slight rocking motion throwing them together.

She was terrified that he'd push her away, but he did not. And while Brendan certainly considered it, indeed, wished he had the will to do it, the sweet feel of her supple, curving body against his, the scent of her freshly washed hair beneath his cheek, the bold but nervous exploration of her fingers, did him in. He reached up and recklessly drew her into his arms instead, feeling her melt against him.

"No, I don't want you to stop, lassie." His voice was muffled against her neck, his breath hot. "But faith, *Moyrrra,* you make me mad with wanting you. I can't help myself. . . ."

She shut her eyes, shivering. "I don't *want* you to help yourself, Brendan."

"And I—" he nuzzled the sensitive skin behind her ear, his lips warm against the curve of her throat, her damp hair "—don't want to either. . . ."

Slowly, languorously, he eased her down to the thick furs. She shut her eyes, feeling her bones go to butter as he swept her throat with hot kisses. *At last,* she thought, and the heat surged against her face, her neck, her bosom, leaving her to wonder if it was generated by his hands, the stove, or maybe both, for they had ceased to be separate entities and now were just one hot, hungry flame. His lips nuzzled aside the damp fabric of her gown, and then her chemise. His hands pushed her skirts up, burned twin paths up her legs. Something was tingling in her nipples, burning in her breasts and between her thighs. Something hot and hungry and aching to be filled. She tilted her head back and clenched her back teeth together as his lips found the soft valley between her breasts. His breath was hot and moist there, his hands gentle as they cupped the creamy globes on either side and pressed them against his cheeks. His fingers burned over the dusky aureoles, coaxing them into stiff peaks, pushing the fabric of her chemise aside. He looked up, and she saw the golden starbursts of light in his honey-colored eyes. The love mirrored in their depths. Then he bent his head, his rich chestnut locks tumbling over his brow, and his tongue swirling around one rosy, aching nipple with a lazy, teasing motion that made the breath explode from her lungs.

And then he drew it into his mouth.

She gasped and dug her elbows into the floor.

"Oh . . . oh, Brendan—"

Soft suckling noises. Exquisite sensation. Her blood pounded through her head, her heels dug into the floor, her hands fisted at her sides, then opened to claw at his back. A moan escaped her and she shut her eyes in blissful agony, pushing against his head and burying her fingers in his soft, loosely curling locks. The ache in her thighs was peaking, making her squirm beneath him. He raised his head only long enough to drag his mouth to the other breast, flicking his tongue over the tight bud until it was as sweetly engorged as its twin. He drew it into his mouth, in and out and in and out, licking, suckling, tasting, nipping. Moisture broke out on her brow, wetness between her thighs. She arched upward, pulling his head down and raking her hands through his hair while she pressed herself against him in mad delight.

He was relentless.

She moaned beneath her breath as he moved his head back to the other nipple once again, taking it fully into his mouth and swirling his tongue around it, gently nipping, sweetly pulling, while his hand moved down her silken curves, her sleek sides, and into the soft triangle of damp curls between her thighs. His palms were rough, his fingers gentle, as he drove his hands beneath her heavy skirts and stroked her. His finger gently parted her swollen folds, found her moist and ready, then penetrated her. She cried out with the sheer, sweet agony of it, her fingers digging into his taut back, his neck, the damp hair at the base of his skull. Her own moisture pulsed against his knuckles, and she arched wildly against his palm.

"Damn you, Mira Ashton . . . *d'anam don diabhal, grá mo chroí. . . .*"

It was the furthest thing from damnation for either of them—yet it was all that, and more. He unbuttoned his breeches and peeled them off while she gazed up at him with eyes glazed with desire. There was nothing shy about him now, nothing at all. He drove an arm beneath her back and dragged her up, his lips, then his hands, already at work on the buttons of her gown. It sagged from her white shoulders, its buttons tangling in her thick hair. Petticoats lay white against his dark hand. His palm slid the length of her inner thigh, moving up toward her waistband. Gentle fingers drew the petticoats off, tossing them aside where they fell in a snowy froth of muslin and lace.

There was nothing against her skin now but the thick, satiny pelt beneath her damp back, the fire's heat—and him. She reached up, pulling him down atop her and seeking his mouth. His hardness stabbed against her belly, tickled the moist recesses of her womanhood, made her burn there and ache with longing.

"Brendan—oh *God*—"

"Easy, *Moyrrra* . . ."

"But, Brendan—"

"D'you want me to stop, lassie?"

She opened her eyes and managed to gasp, "You stop, and I'll send you back to sea with a black eye and a broken nose to go with it . . ."

He might've laughed, she wasn't sure, for all she felt was the flutter of his breath against her neck, stirring the hair there, tickling the skin. " 'Twill hurt, though, *mo stóirín*. . . ."

"I don't give a damn."

"But only for a wee moment . . ."

"For God's sake Brendan, just *do* it! Nothing could hurt as much as what you're putting me through right now. . . ."

"I shall do my best to be gentle with you, *Moyrrra*." His hands cradled her face, his lips covered her fluttering lashes, her dewy cheeks. She felt pressure between her thighs, felt their slick, subtle protest as he gently eased himself down, down—and into her.

Sliding.

Wet heat.

She moaned, sobbed, and drove herself recklessly upward.

Pain exploded in fiery bursts and she thrust herself higher, into it, into him, because *he* had caused it and it was his gift to her. And then the pain faded and a sweet languor washed in to replace it, surging over her like a rising tide, leaving her helpless, leaving her powerless to do anything but merely drift upon it, with it, in it. And then she realized that he was causing that tide, he *was* the tide, his powerful, hard thrusts rocking her body, rocking her soul, building that sweet languor into a fiery agony between her thighs, a burning conflagration that hurt more than the initial pain—

"Brendan—"

He silenced her with his mouth, his hot breath fanning her cheeks, his hands moving down her sides once more to lift her up to him. The fur pelt slid beneath her damp shoulders, her spine, back and forth, back and forth. He drove her down into it, his movements faster and faster, building that searing, ripping ache to a crescendo—

"Brendan!"

He exploded into her, his hot seed filling her entirely, pulsing against the walls of her very being and sending her soul leaping out over a cliff and spinning into space. She cried out, drove herself against him, and clung there, convulsing, her wet hair pinned between their chests, his mouth, her lips. She held on long after the spasms passed, unwilling to let him go, unwilling to end this euphoric, blissful miracle that they'd shared.

At last, reality returned. She saw the flame-glow dancing against his bare shoulder, his richly colored hair, her fingers where they stroked his back. She felt its warm, drugging heat against her skin. Her arm felt as if it were attached to *Kestrel*'s anchor, but she managed to reach out, grope along the floor, and find one of the quilts. She dragged it toward her and, still clasping him to her, draped it over his shoulders, cuddling him, nuzzling him, loving him.

"Faith," he mumbled, into the damp, hot curve of her neck.

She merely smiled and tightened her arms around his shoulders. And when her heart resumed its normal pace and she could speak at last, she teased, "Still cold, Brendan?"

He raised his head and looked down at her, and the magnitude of love in his honey-colored eyes sent her heart into a crazy, fibrillating spiral. One hand came up to touch her face, one finger to smooth the little cat-wrinkles at the side of her nose.

"No," he said softly. He lowered his head and kissed her, so gently, so tenderly, she felt herself melting like spun sugar.

"You know how I said you're a bonny lass, *Moyrrra?*"

"Uh-huh . . ."

"I think what I really meant to say was that I'm . . . I'm in love with you."

. . . *in love with you.*

She shut her eyes and drew a deep, shaky breath.

. . . *in love with you . . . love with you . . . love with you . . .*

For once in her life, Mira was speechless. And so she just sat there with him, worshiping him with her hands, her eyes, her heart. If she didn't know him better, she would've thought he'd had too much to drink, so different was he from the skittish man she'd dragged out of the house. His voice sounded sleepy and heavy, its Irish cadences more pronounced than usual. His breath stirred the hair that cloyed and clumped in the curve of her neck. He nuzzled her, kissed her, murmured strange Gaelic words that she didn't understand and didn't need to understand to know what he was saying.

Time passed. The fire flickered and popped and spread its warm glow over them like a blanket. Outside, the wind howled. They lay silently together, neither speaking, both content just to hold and be held. His lips whispered against her throat, kissing her softly. His hands threaded through her hair. And when he became too heavy, he sensed it and reluctantly moved away, settling on his back on the thick fur pelts beside her.

Mira looked down at him. He had one arm flung out to his side, the other over his face. Planting a kiss in the inside of his elbow, she raised herself up, snuggled up to him, and with her thick, glossy mane spilling over his torso and onto the floor, laid her cheek against his bare chest, moving her hand over its softly furred expanse and warming that odd, cold scar above his heart with the palm of her hand. For a long moment she gazed at that little circle of ridged flesh, then she placed her lips against it, kissing it and silently telling him it was nothing to be ashamed of, nothing to hide. Her arms went around his neck and clasped him to her, and she sensed the pain of his unspoken memories, the hurt that still lingered there.

Around them, *Kestrel* creaked in silent witness.

"We should go now, *Moyrrra.*"

She raised her head, placing her hand over the scar to hold the warmth in, the love. "We don't have to."

"No, but you do."

"No, I don't. I can stay here all night and no one will be the wiser."

"Your da—"

"Doesn't rise until five forty-five."

"Matthew—"

"Is probably warming Alice Little's bed."

He sat up, his tall body bent while he tiredly rubbed his eyes with his knuckles. Her gaze traveled hungrily over him. "But think of what they'll say when Rigel returns to the stable without the sleigh. . . ."

"And his bridle." She pulled him toward her, her heart going soft as he leaned heavily against her and turned his cheek in toward her chest. His eyes were closed and he looked lik a sleepy angel, his skin golden, his damp hair tousled, his hand lying trustingly against her belly. She brought the quilt up and covered him with it.

"Without his bridle . . . ?"

She stroked his hair, loving its crisp softness between her fingers, the glorious highlights of red and gold that the firelight coaxed out of the rich chestnut color. "Yes. You see, when he returns to the barn without it, they'll know I intentionally set him free."

A long moment went by before he answered, as though he was having trouble collecting his thoughts. She untied his queue and combed his hair with her fingers, feeling all warm and happy inside that he was finally trusting her. His brow sank into her beasts, his head grew heavy, and she knew she was putting him to sleep.

"But they'll worry. . . ."

"No they won't." He was warm against her, his muscles relaxing, his breathing deepening. His hand stopped stroking her belly and began to slide, his elbow coming to rest heavily against her thigh. Reaching down, she picked up that lax hand and softly kissed those artist's fingers, one by one, before pressing his warm palm to her cheek and holding it there for a long time. He gave her a sleepy, loving grin; then his head drooped and she cradled it to her chest, bending her cheek to his brow, his hair, while *Kestrel* gently rocked them both.

"Sleep, my love," Mira whispered, closing her eyes in bliss and wrapping her arms around him. "Sleep, my captain, my gallant, handsome lover. . . ."

"Yes, sleep, my captain!" Kestrel echoed.

In her arms Brendan lay heavy and still, his arm jerking once before slumber finally claimed him. Mira raised her head, suddenly feeling very alone.

Around her, *Kestrel* laughed softly.

Chapter 18

Brendan awoke very late the next morning, to the sound of water gurgling past the rudder and the feel of a hard floor beneath his back. He opened his eyes, momentarily disoriented. Above, the river's reflection danced on the deckhead beams; at least the sun was shining today. But a chill permeated the room, his bones even, for the little wood stove had long since gone out. He shivered, and pulled the heavy quilt up over his bare shoulders.

Faith, what was he doing on the floor?!

And then he remembered. *Mira.*

Good God. He sat up with a start, his body stiff and sore but filled with a languid satisfaction that could only have come from a night of lovemaking. *Faith.* Where was she? Had he actually fallen asleep in her arms?

He must have. Why else would he be on the floor?!

He grabbed his shirt, hopped into his breeches and boots, swept up his tricorn, and slammed from the cabin.

Topside, the deck was white with snow, catching the sun's glare and reflecting it back with such blinding brightness, it hurt to look at it, let alone the river, where huge ice floes were no more immune to the bright rays than *Kestrel*'s decks. He stood there, blinking, listening to the trickle of running water as snow melted on shrouds and sheets, furled canvas and spars alike. Giant clumps of it slid down the masts, dropped from the lofty yards, left depressions in the pristine whiteness at his feet. There, a faint set of footprints led to the rail and stopped. They were hours old.

Then he noticed that one of *Kestrel*'s boats was gone.

Mira.

Raw terror struck him. What if she'd slipped and fallen into the ice-choked river? She would've been swept out to sea with no one the wiser!

Ten minutes later, Newburyport's newest hero was racing headlong down High Street, coattails flapping behind him, legs pumping madly, and the demons of hell on his tail. From a tavern window Liam, wiping the frost from the panes with the heel of his big hand, looked out, saw his captain's flying form, and threw back his head in hearty laughter.

"You dare to laugh! I'm sitting here, coming down with something horrible this time—oh, Liam, it's *smallpox,* I just know it is!—and you have the gall to sit there and laugh!" Dalby, sitting miserably on his bed, had his hand clamped to its usual place over his gut. His face was wretched. "Come feel my forehead, Liam! I *know* I've caught something, and this time I just know it's something *bad*—"

Liam turned from the window. "I think, ol' Dalby me friend, that our cap'n's caught somethin' far more deadly than th' smallpox!"

Dalby went white, his own imagined illness forgotten. "Oh, Liam . . ."

But the lieutenant was clutching his sides, his helpless laughter ringing out against the low-beamed ceiling in great peals of booming sound. "Aye, he's caught somethin', all right!'Tis called *love,* Dalby! An' unless I miss me guess, th' one who got him infected is none oth'r than th' Ashton lassie herself!''

"Good heavens, Captain Brendan! Whatever on earth is *wrong?*''

Abigail stood in her kitchen with her hands plunged wrist-deep in a bowl of bread dough, flour dusting her apron, and her cheeks as red as apples from the heat of the fire. Surrounding her was a collection of black iron stew pots, caldrons, and frying pans, some hanging on nails from the walls, some hanging from cranes above the fire.

Brendan yanked off his tricorn and clapped it to his chest. He was breathing hard, sweating as if it were mid-July, and his face, unshaven, was the color of Matt's hair. "Mira! My God, where is she?!''

Never had Abigail seen the normally blithe, laughing "Captain Brendan" in such a wild-eyed panic. "Calm down, young man! Miss Mira's just fine. Why, she's off in the back pasture, giving your sister a riding lesson.''

Brendan reeled back against the cupboard, flinging his arm over his eyes. "Thank God.''

She eyed him curiously. "Captain?''

"Thank God, thank God, thank *God.* ''

"Yes, I'm sure He heard you the first time. You all right, young man?''

He let his arm fall to his side, tipped his head back, and sucked in great lungfuls of air before letting them out in bursts of hysterical laughter.

"Sit down, Captain, before you collapse. How 'bout a slice of hot buttered toast? You have your breakfast yet?''

He sank into a chair, wiping his brow with the back of his sleeve and shaking his head. But she was already cutting a chunk of hot, freshly baked bread from the loaf cooling on the little drop-leaf table, putting it in a wire-framed toaster beside the hearth, and humming to herself as she placed jam, butter, and a knife before him. His mouth was watering by the time she added a slab of cheese, a steaming cup of black coffee, and a piece of ham the size of a dinner plate.

"That's it, eat up, young man!" she chirped happily. "We'll get some meat on those bones of yours in no time!" But Brendan was wolfing the food down as fast as she could set it before him, oblivious to both her fond smile and the admiration in her bird-bright eyes. Abigail loved to cook; she loved to see a vigorous young man enjoying her fare even more. She refreshed his coffee, set a bowl of fried hasty pudding and maple syrup before him, and watching him approvingly, went back to kneading the bread.

"I'll wager you didn't know you're the talk of the town this morning, did you, young man?"

He almost choked on the hasty pudding. Was it already common knowledge that he and Mira had been out last night, alone and unescorted? Good God, did everyone know she'd spent the better part of it aboard *Kestrel?!*

Abigail's bright eyes didn't miss a thing. "You're far too humble for your own good!" she scolded, noting his high color and clucking like a mother hen. "Look at you, blushing like that! Why, everyone's talking about how you stole the crew right off that frigate. And all those prizes you brought in! Why, they just *love* to hear of such audacity, you know! Britain needs that haughty nose of hers tweaked, and fellows like you—"

"More butter, please?"

"—are the ones to do it! Imagine, *eight* prizes . . ." She put her hands on her hips and shook her head in admiration. "And on that schooner's maiden voyage, too! Matt hasn't stopped talking about it." She flipped the dough over and punched it down, missing his expression of relief. "And of course, Ephraim was just beside himself with glee. Can't wait to get down to Davenport's Tavern and do his share of bragging about you. He's like that, whenever one of his ships does well for herself." She dumped the dough onto a floured board and grabbed a rolling pin. "In fact, he tells me that the man who captained this ship you, uh, *robbed* was none other than a man named Crichton."

He wiped the crumbs from his mouth with a large linen napkin and reached for more hasty pudding.

Abigail peered at him slyly. "This Crichton fellow

wouldn't happen to be the same one you tricked at the river's mouth last year, would it?''

"Could be," he said, with a mirthful, crooked grin.

Abigail wagged a flour-caked finger at him, her bright eyes shining. "I knew it! And I'll bet he didn't take kindly to your recruiting his men!"

"Don't know." Brendan scraped the last of the crumbs off his plate. "I didn't stop and ask him."

She managed to stop staring at him long enough to look down at his empty plate. "Gracious, Captain, you still hungry after all that?!"

He had the grace to look sheepish. It was amazing, she thought, how much he could eat and still maintain that lean, sinewy form of his! Heavens, if she were thirty years younger . . .

"So how's Miss Mira this morning?" Brendan asked suddenly.

"Miss Mira?"

He nodded in boyish eagerness.

Abigail grinned, and her eyes grew brighter than ever. *So,* she thought, *the handsome young captain is taken with our little Mira, huh?* She turned away to hide her pleasure, and decided against teasing him about it. "Why she's as chipper as a spring robin. If she keeps up like this, who knows? Maybe she and that sister of yours might actually get along!"

"Get along?"

"Oh, they've been caterwauling all morning. I've never heard the like."

Brendan put down his fork. "What are they, er, *caterwauling* about?"

"Heavens, you name it." Abigail rolled out the dough in smooth, precise movements. "The cat your sister found in her bed this morning. The ownership of that foolish colt. The blackberry tart Eveleen had for breakfast—"

"Blackberry tart?"

"Most of the time they get along quite well . . . but Mira, you see, has a short fuse. It doesn't take much to set her off."

That's for sure, Brendan thought, with a wry grin.

"Anyhow," Abigail continued, sighing, "Mira figured

your sister might like a blackberry tart with some fresh cream for breakfast this morning. Found her in the kitchen here before the sun was even up! Did it all by herself, too. Rolled out the dough and everything. Unfortunately, though, Miss Eveleen thought Mira deliberately left the sugar out.''

"Did she?"

"Leave the sugar out? Oh, probably, but I'm sure she didn't mean to. Mira can be a real handful, but there's not a vindictive bone in her body. And she doesn't like being accused of something she didn't do. . . . Young man, *now* where are you going?!''

Brendan slapped his tricorn onto his head, pausing long enough to lean down and kiss her matronly, flour-scented cheek. She blushed like a schoolgirl. "Seems to me I hear some, er . . . *caterwauling* going on right now. Think it warrants some . . . investigation?''

"It most certainly does!'' She saw the eagerness in his laughing eyes, and knew that he was just itching to get out there and see his little sweetheart. "You just mind yourself, though, and stay out of the line of fire! Them two aren't likely to show mercy to anyone unlucky enough to get between them!''

He dove out the back door, landing knee-deep in snowdrifts and almost falling on his face. The sound of angry shouting drew him around the back of the house where a majestic black stallion was trying his best to reach a demure little mare in a neighboring paddock, through a stand of oak and maple and pine, and into a big field ringed by a fence, atop which sat no fewer than three cats in various stages of repose. One of them was eating something. He shut out the crunching sounds and tried not to imagine what it was—or had been.

And then he looked toward the center of the field.

There was Mira, sitting astride that wee gray colt, her back toward him, her impossibly thick, straight hair caught in a red ribbon and hanging all the way to Rigel's frosty back. She looked very small and very angry, her shoulders stiff and her crop thwacking repeatedly against her thigh in vexation. As he watched, she stood in her stirrups, her little rump shockingly revealed by a pair of trousers that fit her like a glove. Dropping her reins, she cupped her hands around her mouth and began hollering in a voice that would've had no trouble at all carrying the length of *Kestrel*'s decks in a raging gale.

"I said, head *up!* Knees *in!* Heels *down!* And for God's sake, make her move! You ain't gonna learn a damned thing just letting her stand there like that!"

And there was Eveleen, glaring down at her instructor from her lofty perch atop the elegant white mare. She was splendidly garbed in a pink—*faith, he wished she'd stop wearing that color*—riding habit that did nothing to flatter her body. Her golden hair was stuffed beneath a little hat, one hand clenching the reins and the other carefully hidden beneath the closure of her jacket. Although she was trying her best to look regal, Brendan knew her well enough to know she was terrified.

Mira was pitiless, unwilling to let Eveleen back down no matter how scared she was. "For one thing," she said, no, *shouted,* "the horse ain't going to move if you just sit there like a bump on a log! For another thing, she is not *bucking,* she's merely swishing her tail! You are *not* going to fall off by merely making her walk around the field, and if you do, there's enough snow on the ground, you damn well won't hurt yourself! *Now, make her do it!* I am *not* asking you to take that fence yonder, I am merely asking you to press your knees gently to her sides and make her *walk!*"

Beneath the yards of voluminous pink skirts, it was impossible to tell if Eveleen moved her knee or not. Spellbound, his heart aching for his sister, and his desire for her instructor beginning to swell painfully against his breeches, Brendan watched. He tried not to think of his arousal, a condition that was worsening every time she stood up in those stirrups and presented that little rump. Instead, he forced his mind to focus on the drama before him. *Please,* he thought, *have patience with her, Mira.*

"Well?"

Eveleen raised her fleshy chin. "I did. She doesn't like me. She's not going to do it and I want to get off. Now. My legs hurt and my back's starting to ache—"

"You can dismount *after* you make her walk around that

field in one—full—circle!'' The crop began to slap rhyth-
mically against Mira's trim thigh. Brendan swallowed
tightly and drew his coat over the front of his breeches.

Leaving the reins looped loosely atop Rigel's dappled
withers, Mira folded her arms at her chest. ''Now try it
again.''

''I can't.''

''Do it, Eveleen.''

''You're just making me do it because you know I'm
afraid! Because I'm *fat*—''

''I'm making you do it because this mare is *yours,* and
you are going to learn how to care for, handle, and *ride*
her! That means getting your hands dirty, taking a few
falls, and shoveling manure! Now, press your knees to her
sides, darn it, and try it again! She's not going to respect
you if you don't make her do it!''

Eveleen's face was white beneath her hat brim. Her hand
clenched the reins as though they were a lifeline. They
came up a single inch, her body made a slight jerking
motion, and the fabric below her knee rippled slightly. But
Shaula, grinning if horses actually could, simply batted an
ear, craned her elegant neck around to stare at Eveleen's
foot, and lowered her head to sniff at the snow. Eveleen
shrieked and dropped the reins. Shaula's head shot up,
Eveleen screamed in bloody terror, and vaulted to the
ground with a speed and agility that Brendan wouldn't
have believed her capable of had he not seen it with his
own eyes. Mira raised her face to the sky as though seeking help from above.

Admittedly, Brendan couldn't blame her.

''You hate me!'' Eveleen sobbed, wailing at the top of
her lungs. ''You've hated me since the moment you first
saw me, and I did nothing at all to deserve it! You hate
me because you don't want me to have this horse! You
hate me because I have jewels and you don't! You hate me
because I have my brother's love and you don't! *You hate
me because I'm fat*—''

''Get back on the horse. Or I'll have your brother pick
you up and *put* you on her, as he's been standing there
watching you for the past ten minutes!''

Eveleen froze, her mouth a perfect O. Instantly her tears

stopped, her face regained its composure, and she adopted that whining voice that so grated on Brendan's nerves. "Brendan! Oh, thank *God,* I just *knew* you'd come. She's trying to make me ride this smelly, horrible creature! She knows it's going to buck and rear and end up killing me! Oh, Brendan, *do* make her stop! I don't *want* to ride!"

He bit his lip, glancing from his sister to Mira's strained face. She'd stopped slapping her crop against her thigh, but her fingers were still drumming agitatedly against Rigel's thick mane. She looked angry and fiery and beautiful, her eyes flashing and a determined set to her dainty jaw. He thought of her thighs against the saddle, and remembered them against his own. *Faith,* he thought, and plunged his hands into his coat pockets, anchoring the coat over his breeches to keep his arousal well hidden.

Arching his neck, Rigel stamped and snorted, his nostrils flaring red. Brendan stepped forward and, sliding his fingers beneath the colt's heavy mane, briefly gripped Mira's cold hand. She closed her eyes, and some of the tension left her face. Looking up at his sister, he said gently, "Now, Eveleen. Miss Mira's a very accomplished horsewoman and she's just trying to help you. In fact, I'll bet she's taught many young ladies how to ride, haven't you, *Moyrrra?*"

"Er . . . yes."

"Young *thin* ladies," Eveleen sobbed, "not like me."

Mira ignited. "Well, if you'd stop eating so damned much, you wouldn't have that problem!"

"You continue with your apple pies and blackberry tarts and I won't!"

"And what the hell is wrong with my apple pies and blackberry tarts?"

"Try using sugar instead of vinegar and maybe there'd be nothing wrong with them!"

"I didn't use vinegar, I used lemon juice! Now, get back on that horse, dammit, before I lose my bleeding temper! You can fight me till kingdom come, but I'll see you take that mare around the field once by your own power if it damn well kills me!"

"Good, I hope it does!"

Deciding it was a timely moment to intervene, Brendan

took the white mare's sagging reins, looped them around his elbow, and cupped his hands. "Here, Eveleen. I'll help you up, all right? I'll be right here if anything should happen."

"And what good are you? You can't ride either!"

"Come on, let's go," he said patiently, keenly aware that one of Mira's dark brows had shot up in sudden interest.

Eveleen glared at him as though he were a traitor, gave Mira a look of pure venom, and favoring her crippled hand, grasped the pommel and allowed Brendan to boost her up into the saddle. There she sat, mutinous and angry and feeling as though the whole world were against her. "And furthermore," she sniffed, "this is not a proper sidesaddle, it's a *man's* saddle. She's insulting me by making me use it, and she knows it. She wants to ridicule me because I'm fat—"

"By the bleeding *Christ!*" In one quick, fluid motion Mira was off Rigel and stamping through the snow. "I gave you that saddle because I thought you'd find it easier to use! Another blasted word out of your trap about being *fat* and I'll yank the damned thing off and make you ride her bareback! But ride her you will, dammit, and I don't care if you sit out here and freeze your butt off before you do! Now, nudge her with your knees and make her *move!*"

"I won't!"

"You *will!*"

"No! No, no, *no*—"

Cursing, Mira slapped her crop hard against the mare's white rump.

Eveleen screeched, and Shaula's head jerked up in surprise.

"If you *don't* make her move, Eveleen, I'm going to take her away and put you on El Nath instead! And while I'm at it, I'll go get Matt so *he* can see how well you're doing!"

"You wouldn't!"

"I damn well would!"

Brendan crossed his arms and nodded. "She would."

"Just shut up, Brendan! Whose side are you on, anyhow?!" Eveleen shouted.

Her brother's brow shot right up to his tricorn in surprise, and even Eveleen gasped at what she'd just said. Were some of Mira's ways rubbing off on her? And Mira . . . She knew her hot-tempered instructor well enough by now to know that bluster and intimidation were her favorite weapons in her arsenal of persuasion. Still, Eveleen wouldn't put it past her to drag Matt out here to witness her complete and total humiliation. "You really would, wouldn't you, Mira?"

Mira gave one of her cat grins. "You can bet on it, Eveleen." She got back on Rigel and gestured with her crop. "Now, make her move."

"Do I *have* to?"

"Let it go, Mira," Brendan suggested.

Mira whirled on him. No wonder Eveleen was such a spoiled brat, with her own brother letting her get away with murder! "Look, one more word out of you, and *you're* going to be next; is that clear?"

His eyes widened and he backed up. "Oh, dear heavens—"

Eveleen seized upon the opportunity. "Make him do it, Mira; he can't ride, either!"

"Eveleen!" Brendan warned, growing nervous.

"Make him do it! Make him!" Eveleen cried, pitching forward over the mare's neck in laughter at Brendan's horror. "Make him—"

"Watch it, Eveleen!" Mira yelled.

But it was too late. Mira cringed as the girl lost her balance and, making a wild grab for the mare's mane, landed on her rump in the snow.

Mira leaped off Rigel's back and bent down, fully expecting to find the tears rolling down Eveleen's cheeks. She wasn't disappointed. Raising her head, Mira yelled, "Dammit, Brendan, do you know how much work you've just shot to hell?! It's taken me a long time to get to this point—"

But Eveleen's hand was on her arm, and as Mira looked down, she saw that the girl's tears were not ones of hurt and humiliation—but laughter.

"Mira?" she asked, getting to her feet and brushing the snow from her skirts. "We really *did* make progress today. I fell off for the first time, and it wasn't anything to

be afraid of, after all!'' Still laughing, she looked at her
astonished brother. ''Now I think it's time for Brendan to
have *his* turn . . . don't you?''

Two pairs of conniving female eyes fastened on him,
and Brendan felt the blood rushing from his face. ''Now,
wait just a moment—''

Mira caught him before he'd gained ten steps. He protested. He fought. But in the end, both she and Eveleen
succeeded in dragging him to the white mare, and Miss
Mira Ashton's School of Fine Horsemanship saw its second, unwilling student.

Chapter 19

''**A**ll right, ye can go.''
        Ephraim Ashton stood planted to the wharf,
swinging his watch and scrutinizing each and every lad
who passed beneath his nose. The present one gulped and
bolted, his flying feet carrying him down the wharf toward
the boat that would take him out to Matthew's *Proud Mistress.*

''Next,'' Ephraim grunted. Scowling, he ripped the cap
off the next boy, scowled some more when he saw it *wasn't*
his daughter, and gruffly waved the boy through.

''Next . . .''

With each hapless soul who *wasn't* Mira, Ephriam's impatience and annoyance grew. If she'd found a way to
sneak aboard Matt's ship again, he was gonna strangle her.

He never thought to look behind him—at the line of men
filing past him and into *Kestrel*'s boats.

And if he had, he would've found the lad he sought,
smirking and jostling her crew mates, thumbing her nose
at him—and cradling her brother's Brown Bess musket.

* * *

That had been two days ago; now *Kestrel* had got her wish and was at sea again, this time prowling the waters off Sandy Hook in company with *Proud Mistress*.

Her captain stood at the helm, casually balancing a sketchpad against his forearm and working on a drawing of Matt's ship, which ghosted along a cable's length to windward. The tiller bar lay alongside his leg, seemingly forgotten; every so often he nudged it with his thigh, and the schooner would turn her nose a half point into the wind, floating gently on a beam reach on the starboard tack.

Although it was wintertime, the wind was little more than a breeze. Gulls drifted quietly on the gray and brown sea, and *Kestrel*'s wake was a lazy, meandering ruffle that trailed far behind her. Nevertheless, there was a lookout aloft, another sitting out on the bowsprit, and both were scanning the horizon for a prize. So far, they'd turned up nothing but a few skittish fishing boats that had fled inshore at sight of the tall, majestic schooner and the battle-scarred brig that accompanied her.

Brendan wasn't worried, though. Rumor had it that a storm had blown the New York–bound convoy off course, and he was more than certain that royals and topsails would hove in sight above the horizon before too long. And when they did? He grinned to himself as he sketched in the intricate network of shrouds that supported *Proud Mistress*'s masts. He had an experienced crew, an eager ship, and Mr. Starr on his favorite gun, a trusty old four-pounder inscribed with a biblical verse and affectionately dubbed *Freedom*. Except now Mr. Starr happened to be some forty or fifty feet above the deck, clinging like a squirrel to the weather shrouds, a telescope to his eye, and his clothing—loose linen trousers, baggy shirt, and a tarpaulin coat that all but swallowed up his little body—fluttering in the breeze like a poorly set jib.

"Deck there!"

Brendan lowered his drawing and stared up into the misty pyramid of shrouds that pinnacled high, high above his head. How the lad could see anything through the fog was beyond him. "Report, Mr. Starr!"

"Make three sail off the larboard quarter, sir! Hull up and bearing away to the north'ard!"

"Flying any colors, Mr. Starr?"

At the rail the crew gathered, excitedly passing telescopes and straining to see off into the choking mists. In these waters, the ships were probably Tories, or better yet, Brits—either fat merchantmen or strays from the overdue London convoy. A prize either way, and ones that would bring a hefty sum once auctioned off back in Newburyport.

"Can't tell yet, sir!"

Grinning, Brendan looked back down at his drawing, already envisioning Mira's reaction when he and Matt brought three fat prizes back to Newburyport. She'd come galloping down to the waterfront on that wee gray colt, fight her way through the crowds, and fling herself into his arms. . . . She'd be all soft and warm, her kisses sweet and eager, her hair silky against his hands. . . .

His pencil moved over the paper, but he wasn't really thinking about the drawing, not really thinking about *Kestrel* even, which he guided by simple, unconscious movements of his leg against the tiller. Liam, however, noted how he played the schooner on the faint breeze as he might his own fiddle, making her sing, making her dance . . . except that Brendan sailed his ship without even looking up from his sketch. Liam folded his huge arms across his chest and watched his captain with fond admiration in his twinkling blue eyes. He'd known Brendan for some twenty-five-odd years—yet still his friend never failed to amaze him.

Despite appearances to the contrary, however, Brendan was keenly aware of Liam's presence. He tossed his sketchbook onto the deckhouse and grinned at his friend. "Faith, Liam, what're you just standing there for? Signal Captain Ashton before he tries to claim the honor of seeing those ships first! *D'ar m'anam*, I have a bet riding on this, you know!"

They laughed like a couple of conspirators, and seconds later, balls rose to *Kestrel's* sharply raked mast and broke to the whispering wind.

Mr. Starr's voice caught his attention again, fainter now

with height and distance. Brendan clapped a hand over his tricorn, tilted his head back, and looked up. High above, where the gaff and its tackle angled out from the mast, the lad had climbed, balancing fearlessly with one foot on the big spar, the other on a block, his arm laced around a line. It was a precarious position; had there been a strong wind, Brendan would've forbidden it.

"Looks like one's a cutter, sir, with two ship-rigged tubs in her lee!"

"Probably a Brit with her prizes," Liam commented, eagerly rubbing his hands together.

Brendan grinned and pulled out his spyglass. "Or a Tory shepherd guarding his flock from wolves like us." He strode to the weather shrouds, the glass under his arm. "Either way, they're *ours*, and so is she!"

The shrouds were stiff with ice and frozen spray, but he climbed dauntlessly, his boots slipping here and there, his hands numb and red with cold before he'd even reached the level of the mainsail's throat. There, he paused and looked up. The main topmast drove skyward above him, its sail fading into the gray mist. Mr. Starr was nowhere to be seen. Looping an elbow through the shrouds, Brendan briskly rubbed his hands together to restore their warmth, blew on them, and continued his climb.

He found the lad perched on the topgallant yard, feet swinging, felt hat clamped down over his eyes, and face turned toward the distant ships. His hair, dull with mist, was braided in a seaman's queue, the tip of it wafting in the breeze. Brendan tried not to think of the eighty some-odd feet between the end of that braid and the deck below.

"Brits, sir," the boy mumbled, yanking the hat even lower until Brendan wondered how he could see at all.

"You're absolutely right," he agreed, seeing the ships quite clearly up here above the mist and fog. He decided to test the lad. "But tell me how you know that, Mr. Starr. They're not flying any colors."

"That cutter's lighter-built than a Frenchie or one of our'n."

"Very good, Mr. Starr." He steadied himself against the slick topgallant yard, the dizzying sway of the mast below him. "Also, an American would have more dead-rise, more rounded curves, more rake to her bow, and a bit less depth and freeboard than that one yonder.''

"Ayup.''

As usual, Mr. Starr was not a man of many words. Brendan grinned and said, "I feel the wind starting to freshen. What d'you say to shaking out these topsails and going after them, laddie?''

The boy, wearing strange little spectacles with bottle green lenses, kept his face averted, although his captain's mood was as light, his grin as infectious, as ever. But no matter how friendly Brendan tried to be, Mr. Starr never met his gaze and avoided him as much as possible. Obviously he was terrified of his captain, and probably had a complex about his sensitive skin as well—yet Brendan didn't press him about it. No doubt the lad got harassed enough about it belowdeck, despite the popularity he seemed to enjoy with his shipmates.

Still squinting off toward the distant ships, Mr. Starr mumbled, "Maybe we oughtta set the t'gallants and fly the studders, too. Might get a couple more knots outta her, at least, 'specially if we get the wind dead abaft.''

Brendan stared. For Mr. Starr, that had been a speech. He lifted a brow. "Think so?'' he asked, testing him once again.

"Ayup. Oughtta be able t' run 'em down before dusk.''

"Very well then, Mr. Starr. Provided you can stand the cold, you may remain here until we come up on them, at which time I'd like you to come down and renew your acquaintance with *Freedom.*'' He tucked his glass into his pocket. "Carry on, then!''

Back on deck, Liam stood at the tiller, his brows knit in concentration as he peered at the compass. The fog was starting to lift, and watery sunlight managed to put enough glare on the water to throw a few diamonds back in her eyes. A seal bobbed just off the starboard bows, watched them for a while, then dived like a small whale. The splash it made was loud, almost eerie in the heavy stillness. Landing lightly on the deck, Brendan stamped his feet, trying to restore the circulation to his toes.

Dalby, bless his heart, had read his mind, and hustled toward him with a steaming pot of coffee and a dented pewter mug. Gratefully accepting it, Brendan wrapped his hands around the mug, letting the heat thaw his fingers and scald a path all the way to his stomach. "Ah, Dalby . . . you're ever the thoughtful one, aren't you?"

"Just thought you might appreciate something hot and bracing, sir." But Dalby himself was shivering.

Brendan frowned. "And how are you feeling today, Dalby?"

The moment the words were out of his mouth, he could've shot himself.

"Oh, not so good today, sir, not so good. I got up with a runny nose, and my head's all stuffed up." He pressed gnarled fingers to either side of his nose. "Right here, way down deep. Getting a cold, I think. Throat's scratchy, too. And I suspect I've got a fever." He held out one wizened hand. "See? I've got the shivers already—"

"That's 'cause it's cold, ye bonehead," Liam joked.

"Cold? I've a knit shirt, a waistcoat, a greatcoat, and a cloak on! Don't tell me I'm cold! I'm coming down with something, and that's all there is to it!"

From several feet away, Fergus McDermott, ex-atheist, ex-Christian, and now emphatic embracer of some Eastern religion Brendan had never heard of, nodded sagely. "I told ye, Dalb. It's *reincarnation.*"

Liam snorted. "Reincarnation, me arse! Ye've been listenin' t' that bloody furriner too much!" He threw a sharp glance forward, where a cloaked figure stood in the bows with a lead line in his hand. They'd picked him up out of one of *Kestrel*'s first prizes, and Liam rued the day they had. The man was an Easterner, with crystals hanging from his neck, the moon in his eyes, and strange ideas of where people came from. *Real strange.* The British were probably well rid of him, Liam thought. Anyone who went around proclaiming that Brendan had been a fox in his past life—*past life!* he snorted—deserved to have his head examined. It had been bad enough when Fergus had *seen the light.* But this reincarnation stuff? *God Almighty . . .*

Brendan went back to his sketch, hiding a grin.

"Well, he's right," Dalby sniffed. "Why else would I be sick all the time? Rama says it's because I'm paying for my sins in a past life. That my poor health is the price for the bad things I've done before.''

"God Almighty, we're all a-payin' th' price, havin' t' listen t' such bloody nonsense! Get up there an' make sure that dingbat calls out th' fathoms correctly!''

Dalby looked crushed, but he went anyway.

"Now, Liam, don't you think that was rather harsh?'' Brendan said reprovingly, but with a faint grin.

"I've nev'r heard such a crock o' nonsense in me life! Next he'll be a-sayin' that *Kestrel* was a bird in *her* former life!''

"Is that so?'' Brendan allowed himself to look serious for once. "Why, I'd have thought she spent it as a pine in the forests of Maine.''

They both laughed.

"Deck there!''

"Report, Mr. Starr!''

"Another sail, fine on the larboard beam! A snow, sir, with the Union Jack at her masthead!''

"Faith, this *is* getting interesting!'' Brendan said, mirth dancing in his eyes. "Four to two. *Wonderrrful* odds, eh, Liam?''

"Aye, but we 'ave *Kestrel*. They don't.''

"Nor will they.'' Brendan picked up his speaking trumpet, which he had salvaged from *Annabel* and which still boasted holes from that last fight. The metal was cold against his lips. "Hands to the sheets! Topmen aloft! Shake out tops'ls and t'gallants and up with jib fores'l! Lively now, laddies!''

Whooping and hollering, men flew to halyards and sheets. Grommets rattled, canvas thundered, swayed, and rose. *Kestrel* quivered in eagerness, swinging her bowsprit around, her sleek sides following. Beneath her the sea whispered and began to cream as she heeled over and found speed. Wallowing clumsily, *Proud Mistress* followed suit, her crew scampering up the shrouds to set her topsails. Brendan pulled out his spyglass and trained it on her quarterdeck. Sure enough, there was Matt, his red hair standing out in all directions beneath his floppy hat, his coat half-unbuttoned, his canvas breeches ragged and stained. He looked up, caught sight of Brendan, and touched his temple in a disgusted salute.

"Bet Ashton's steamin' about us seein' th' prizes first!" Liam cried, rubbing his giant hands together in glee, for prize sighting had become a friendly contest between the two captains.

Brendan adjusted his sketchbook over his arm. "Think so?"

"Don't you?"

"Well, I should think he's steaming more over the fact that *Kestrel*'s showing her heels to that ridiculously caked-up figurehead of his." He tipped his head back and yelled, "Mr. Starr! Come on down and prepare your gun for battle! We'll be upon them by eight bells!"

"Aye, Cap'n!"

High above, the topgallants snapped to attention, swelled mightily, and strained against their yards. *Kestrel* lifted her nose and pulled herself up in the water, higher and higher and higher. Beneath her sharp bows, the sea began to roar and fall away in great snowy blankets of white.

Brendan grinned.

"Tack on studding sails!"

Spray was driving over the rail now, freezing on shrouds and deck alike.

One of the Newburyporters muttered, "Jesus! There ain't even any wind and she's movin' like the hounds of hell are on her tail!"

"Aye, and I'd like to know how the blazes she's doing it! Gawd, we must be makin' six knots!"

"Seven when those studders go on!"

"But there *ain't no wind!*"

But Brendan, staring forward, paid no heed to the reverent looks the Newburyporters were throwing his way. The cutter was now speared on *Kestrel*'s bowsprit, the two merchantmen fleeing like sheep. . . .

And then the studding sails were on. Like the swift raptor she was, *Kestrel* folded her wings, dove through the mists, and swooped in for the kill.

A bucket of sand by her leg and a slow match in her hand, Mira stood beside *Freedom,* her heart racing, her mouth

dry, and her chest tight with that strange, nervous anticipation she always felt before battle. Just aft, Brendan clung
to the shrouds, looking resplendent and handsome in his
fine blue coat with its rows of gold buttons. His waistcoat
was as red as a cardinal's breast, his boots gleamed in the
gray light, and his tricorn was perched jauntily atop his
chestnut curls. From his wrist dangled his speaking trumpet, which he was swinging with uncontained excitement—and in his hand was his sketchbook.

She forced herself to look away.

The wind had backed, and *Kestrel,* close-hauled, was
catching it over her starboard bows. Her lofty bowsprit
rose up, down, up, down, in perfect rhythm, each downward plunge smashing the waves and sending big, hissing
blankets of snowy foam out and away from either beam.
The cutter, a Royal Mail packet with one tall mast stepped
well forward, was dead ahead now. Sporting a straight-
running bowsprit and carrying a cloud of sail, she would
be a fast sailor and armed to the teeth. She would also be
carrying the king's messages and cash, probably to the
British troops in New York. Mira imagined the guffaws
from her decks at the audacity of the little schooner sweeping down on them out of the fog.

Soon, she knew, they wouldn't be laughing.

"Mr. Wilbur! Ease the fore and main and prepare to
tack!"

Nope, they wouldn't be laughing at all. She smiled
smugly and blew on her slow match, her eyes still on the
cutter.

"Sheet in fore stays'l, fore and main!"

"Stand by the heads'ls!"

"Cast off the preventer on the fore!"

"Hard-a-lee!" Brendan's pencil was flying over the
page. "And *let fly!*" The schooner paced herself, gathered
her wings, and swung her bows neatly through the wind. The
great boom of the mainsail passed over their heads. Sails
filled on the opposite tack, and the deck heeled over.

"Pass jib and foresail!"

"Close haul for larboard tack!"

Up until that last moment, the cutter never expected the

schooner to attack. Surprise was with them, and taking full advantage of it, Brendan sent *Kestrel* swooping around the cutter's stern, and a broadside slamming through her windows that cut down everything in its path. Before *Kestrel* was even to windward of her, the cutter had lost her topmast, and with it, a good deal of her speed and agility. Brendan wasted no time. "Run out your guns, laddies! Hull her just below the waterline!"

Cupping the match with her hand, Mira lowered it to *Freedom*'s vent and quickly stepped aside. A puff of flame, a thunderous roar, and the four-pounder flung itself inboard against the breeching, its sharp bark lost beneath the angry, sporadic roar of the cutter's guns, which, in her crew's confusion, seemed to be hitting everything but her target. Or perhaps it was just that *Kestrel* was blessed with an Irishman's luck, for she moved like a dancer, teasing and flirtatious in one moment, flitting away on her heel the next.

And now Brendan was sending her right across the frigate's bows.

A voice, sharp with indignation and rage, roared out from the frigate's forecastle, sounding tinny and artificial through a speaking trumpet. "Damn you for an impudent dog! This is a king's ship! How dare you fire on us! Show your colors or I'll sink you where you stand!"

Brendan leaned out from the shrouds that supported *Kestrel*'s masts, lifted the speaking trumpet to his lips, and called back, "I invite you to try it!"

Those who had telescopes to their eyes saw the British commander go an angry red beneath his carefully powdered hair. "By God, what ship are you?!" he demanded.

For answer, *Kestrel* ran her thirteen-striped flag up the halyard and poured a broadside of chain shot into the cutter's rigging. The crew sent up a mighty cheer.

"Take that, ye bloody bunch o' British buggers!"

"Damn ye and yer prig-faced king!"

"Get a *real* ship! Ha, ha, ha!"

"Huzzah f'r *Kestrel!* Huzzah f'r *Kestrel!*"

Their raucous voices drowned out the sounds of cracking wood as the cutter's mast teetered and came whistling down in a hopeless tangle of cordage and spars.

"Think he knows who we are now, Cap'n?"

"Aye, Liam, I think that gave him a good idea."

"But he 'asn't struck t' us yet!"

"Nor do I expect him to. That's young Oliver Heathmore who commands her."

Brendan would know, of course, Liam thought. He remembered his acquaintances from his Royal Navy days well. "Not young Oliver Heathmore!" he said, jaw agape.

Brendan grinned. "An ambitious young pup if ever there was one. Oh well, we shall try not to do him too grave an injury. I want his dispatches and his money, not his ship."

"She'd make a nice prize, though. . . ."

"Not when Mr. Starr finishes with her!"

The little gunner and his team were already swabbing out *Freedom*'s bore with a wet sheepskin sponge attached to a flexible rammer. Seconds later, both charge and shot were rammed home and the gun run swiftly out on a squeal of tackle.

"Maximum elevation!" Brendan called.

Handspikes flashed, and *Kestrel*, now running down the cutter's beam and circling her stern, pointed her guns high. The wind took her, leaning her over. Farther.

And farther.

"Fire!"

The cutter disappeared in a wreath of smoke.

"Captain Heathmore! I invite you to strike while you're still afloat!" Brendan called, hanging out from the shrouds by his elbow, the sea sweeping beneath his feet. "If you do not, I shall sink you where you stand!"

The Briton's voice came madly through the trumpet. "Damn you to hell for this, you blasted rebel! I'll see you pay, so help me God!"

Brendan turned to Liam, his expression full of mock hurt. "Did you hear that? He called me a blasted rebel! Why, to think he doesn't even recognize me!"

"If he did, he'd strike for sure," Liam joked.

Gunfire was echoing across the water now as somewhere off to starboard, *Proud Mistress* engaged the other ship, a two-masted snow. Coughing and choking on the smoke, Mira strained her ears for her captain's next order. The smoke began to clear, and she anxiously peered through it, seized by a momentary panic that he'd been hit by the sporadic fire coming from the cutter. And then she saw him.

He was still clinging to the shrouds, his speaking trumpet dangling from his wrist, his drawing pad balanced on his arm. He was sketching wildly.

The man was insane.

At that moment he looked up. "Don't just *stand* there, Mr. Starr!"

She didn't—and the last shot did it. Dismasted and listing badly, the cutter was all but dead in the water. On her deck, her young commander squinted through the acrid haze and saw a handsome brig rounding up the two merchantmen who'd fallen in with him the day before, as well as the defeated snow. And then the smoke cleared, drifting away with the mists.

Captain Oliver Heathmore and his crew caught a collective breath.

There stood the schooner.

She was like nothing they'd ever seen. Graceful, but deadly. *Beautifully* deadly, like a sultry woman who knows her own power and wields it with a ruthless purpose. She wore her sails like a queen would her robes. Her two masts were sharply raked, as though swept backward by the pass of a giant hand. Her bows were keener than a butcher's knife, her bowsprit lean and long and haughty, her profile so low in the water, she seemed to be born of it, rather than to it.

Heathmore looked at the sea reflecting along her trim black sides, the giltwork picked out in red and gold at her stern.

Kestrel, he read. And beneath that, *Newburyport.*

And then he looked up and saw a slim figure, immaculate in the blue coat of an American privateer, standing above that lean stern and taffrail. He was holding up a book of some sort, his speaking trumpet hung from his wrist, and he was grinning.

Bringing his telescope to his eye for a better view, Captain Oliver Heathmore peered at that book and saw that it was a drawing of a sea fight; not just *any* sea fight, but the one he'd just lost.

The man raised the speaking trumpet to his lips. "Well, what d'you think, Ollie? D'you like it?"

And then Heathmore recognized the mirthful eyes beneath the jaunty tricorn of the American.

There was no mistaking that weightless grin, the Irish cadences in that lilting voice.

"The devil take me," he swore silently.

Chapter 20

Marine News

On Sunday last, the privateers Proud Mistress *and* Kestrel, *Captains Ashton and Merrick, of this port returned from a very successful cruise against the Enemy after sailing together in consort in the vicinity of Sandy Hook.*

From a reliable source we learn that the schooner Kestrel, *Merrick commanding, ran down and overtook the fast-sailing Royal Mail packet* Sussex, *bound from London to New York and carrying specie and dispatches to the Enemy which is stationed there. In company with said packet were two merchantman, the one carrying sugar, cotton, molasses, and some coffee, the other laden with 1,000 muskets and bayonets, 12 tons of musket shot, 100 rounds of grape shot, and several barrels of powder, all destined for His Majesty's forces, and a snow carrying 12 guns and 10 swivels, which Ashton engaged, the firing, by all accounts, lasting less than an hour. While the Royal Navy packet certainly gave a good account of herself before striking her colours to the schooner, her master hauling them down with his own hand, we have been told that the damage she incurred was so grave that Captains Merrick and Ashton deemed her unfit for sea and were thus forced to sink her. To all accounts, Captains Merrick and Ashton conducted themselves in a commendable, daring, but gentlemanly manner with the merchantmen, the latter even returning the private money and belongings to a lady passenger who was aboard one of the merchantmen.*

Ephriam Ashton cackled to himself and put down the newspaper. He'd read the account eight times; certainly enough to memorize it by now, which, of course, he'd done. From across the breakfast table Eveleen Merrick watched him, but so caught up was he in his private gloating, he was totally unaware of her perusal. Shoving a one-eyed tabby cat off his lap, Ephraim continued reading, his bushy eyebrows curling out over his nose.

With their three prizes in tow, Captains Merrick and Ashton, while in the latitude of the shoals of Nantucket, but many miles to eastward of them, spied a large British vessel having the appearance of a merchantman, and made towards her; but to their astonishment found her to be a frigate disguised. A light breeze prevailing, Captains Merrick and Ashton hauled off in different directions—one only could be pursued—and the frigate gained rapidly upon Merrick. Finding he could not run away, the wind favoring the frigate's square rig, Captain Merrick had recourse to stratagem—on a sudden he hauled down every sail, and had all hands on deck employed with setting poles, as if shoving the schooner off a bank! The people on board the frigate were amazed at the danger they had run, and to save themselves from being grounded, immediately clawed off and left the clever and more knowing Merrick "to make himself scarce," as soon as darkness rendered it prudent for him to hoist sail in a sea two hundred fathoms deep!

Ephraim threw back his head and roared with laughter.

Kestrel and Proud Mistress were welcomed into our port amid much celebration and rejoicing, the both receiving a 13-gun salute by ships in our harbour and the field guns on Plum Island. We have a fear that they have brought in so many prizes that there is not room for them in the river. For those who wish to view these two privateers who have done so much to aid the cause of Liberty, they are tied up at the wharf of Capt. Ephraim Ashton, where the gallant Captain Merrick informs us his ship is open to any who wish to go aboard her and count the shot-holes in her sails.

Ephraim slapped the paper down on the table and whooped until the tears ran from his eyes. Tripes 'n' bloody guts, what more could he ask? A son who brought him more and more glory every time he sailed, and now a future son-in-law whose cleverness and daring eclipsed even Matt's. That Brendan would marry Mira was not even an issue. Ephraim had it all planned out.

Suddenly he scowled. There was one thing he'd have to put a stop to, however, if his plan was to succeed—Mira could not get away with making any more jaunts aboard *Kestrel, Proud Mistress,* or any other ship, for that matter. Hell, no. When *Kestrel* next sailed, his daughter would be staying right here, where he could keep an eye on her. That would be *all* he needed, to have Mira make a mistake and Merrick find out she'd been deceiving him and going aboard his ship. Christ, if that happened, he'd *never* get her married off!

Aye, he was well aware of his daughter's whereabouts lately, though obviously *the gallant Captain Merrick* wasn't. No sooner had he brought his victorious *Kestrel* into port and fought his way through the cheering throng than he'd shown up right there on the doorstep, hat in hand, cheeks flushed with excitement, and looking every inch the valiant young sea captain that he was. He had asked for Mira, of course, and it had been tricky there for a moment, concocting an excuse that she was abed with a cold and wasn't receiving guests. It had also been an opportunity to force the ever-moving Merrick down in a chair, force some good hot cooking down his throat, and force him to relate every last, glorious, delicious detail of The Cruise.

There was no need for anyone to know, of course, that

the newspaper's informant—that *reliable source,* as it had been termed—was none other than Ephraim himself.

Ephraim gave a private hoot of laughter. With such triumphs, he could even overlook Matt's philandering (his son was presently holed up at Wolfe Tavern, paying court to that lady passenger he'd found aboard the merchantman) and pretend it didn't exist. Merrick, at least, was no rake. In fact, Newburyport's newest hero was upstairs in the east room, where Ephraim had dragged him following supper last night. That he was sleeping soundly, he had no doubt; he hadn't heard a sound from up there all morning.

Still cackling over his own shrewdness, Ephraim leaned back in his chair and folded his arms behind his white head. "Ah, Eveleen, that brother of yers is one helluva sea officer, ain't he? Never would've guessed it, that first day I met him. Looked like somethin' the cat brought in, by God!"

She glanced up from behind a plate of johnnycakes, ham, and a slab of cheese that would've kept a nest of mice in good spirits for a year. "Brendan learned to sail before he could walk. At least, that was what our da always told us."

"Yer papa must've been a seaman himself, teaching his son such things when he was just a babe!"

"He was." Eveleen stared down at her plate, lips curved in a winsome smile that made her look almost pretty. Especially since Ephraim had rarely seen her smile. She picked up a corn muffin and pasted an inch-thick cap of butter and strawberry jam atop it.

And then she put the muffin aside and looked at Ephraim. The smile was gone, her eyes sad. "He was an admiral in the Royal Navy when he was cut down on the decks of his own flagship."

Ephraim's jaw dropped. "An *admiral?* Ye mean to tell me yer daddy was an *admiral?* In the Royal Navy?"

"Yes."

Ephraim's throat was working. He was having a hard time digesting this. "Holy hell!" he expostulated, rising to his feet. "Don't that beat all! Abigail!" *Abigail!*" he roared, his voice shaking the very timbers of the house. "C'mon in here; I got something to tell ye!"

He couldn't wait to spread *this* around!

Upstairs, it was still quiet. Obviously that admiral's son could sleep through anything.

Abigail bustled into the room, wiping her hands on her apron. "Honestly, Ephraim, all that bellowing! You're going to wake the captain!"

He seized her by the shoulders. "Did you know that Merrick's papa was an *admiral?!* An admiral, Ab! How the Brits must be nettled to know that *we* have his son on our side now!"

"They have always been nettled," Eveleen said quietly, her eyes downcast. "Even when he was in *their* navy."

"What?"

The girl was rising, her long golden hair fanning out over her round shoulders. "Jealousy," she said quietly. "It has brought down many a man. My father included—and my brother, if he'd have allowed it."

She turned on her heel and shuffled out of the dining room, leaving Ephraim and Abigail to stare after her in disbelief.

Their gazes met. The johnnycakes, the ham, the cheese—and yes, even the muffin—were untouched.

"Well, I'll be damned. . . ." Ephraim said.

Things should've been quiet indeed up in the east room, for Brendan wasn't in it.

He'd allowed Ephraim to all but drag him in there last night, but he hadn't stayed long. Instead, he'd paced the floor and finished up one of his sketches while he waited for the old sea captain to retire, an event that had occurred at precisely 12:45 and not a second later, judging by the loud snoring coming from that area of the house. Before the nineteen clocks (it was up to that now—he'd actually counted) could finish tolling out the hour, Brendan had pried open the frozen sill of his window, hung out of it by his fingers, and dropped two stories down into several feet of snow.

It had taken only thirty minutes to make his way back to *Kestrel*.

He felt guilty about deceiving the old man, but Mira had been in the next room, and he no longer trusted himself around her. He'd seen the hungry looks she'd given him over supper, felt her dainty foot rubbing up and down his leg beneath the table, burning it even through his wool stockings. Thank God for the tablecloth that had hidden the evidence of his desire for her. Thank God for the elegant silver candelabra that he'd taken refuge behind so he wouldn't have to look at those impish green eyes, that wrinkly little nose, that luxurious, glorious hair. And thank God for a place to escape to—*Kestrel,* down in the harbor. If he'd stayed at the Ashton house last night, they would've ended up in Mira's bed or his. He was in love with the wee lassie, and it scared the devil out of him because he wasn't *ready* to fall in love, wasn't ready to give up the sea, wasn't ready to give up his beloved schooner.

He wasn't ready to be hurt again, and he didn't want to have to choose between Mira and *Kestrel*. That, and the nagging suspicion that Ephraim was up to something, had decided him.

That and the fact that he didn't like sleeping with cats.

He awoke in his bed aboard the gently rocking schooner, long after the sun heaved itself above the tip of Plum Island and shone lemon and gold upon the harbor. The cabin still smelled faintly of gun smoke; he could almost imagine the glorious thunder of the guns above, pounding away in fury, hear the shouts of battle-crazed men, feel *Kestrel* moving silently under his feet and gliding through the sea. . . .

He folded his arms behind his head and stared up at the deckhead, his lips curved in a faint grin. Footsteps sounded above him; Liam must already be escorting the first reverent visitors aboard. Abruptly his grin faded. They'd made him a celebrity, just as they had poor Matt.

Poor Matt? Ashton, at least, loved every minute of it!

The footsteps were moving toward the hatch now, too light to be Liam's, too solitary to be the throng he expected—and dreaded.

Dalby.

He shut his eyes. *No. Not Dalby.* Please God, not this morning . . .

The door creaked open and he let his jaw relax, pretending sleep.

Silence. Then footsteps coming slowly across the cabin, a hand touching his shoulder.

"Captain?"

His eyes shot open. It was Mira. He couldn't help himself; he blushed.

"I'm sorry to wake you." Her eyes were bright, and there was a healthy glow to her cheeks, as though she'd been out in the cold. "I didn't think you'd be sleeping."

"Er, actually, I wasn't."

She smiled saucily and touched his arm. "Sure looked it to me."

"I've grown very good at pretending it. You see, I thought you were Dalby . . ."

"Ah yes, that little man with the constant stomachache?"

"Yes, the very one."

She sat beside him, her eyes softening with humor, then love, as she gazed down at him. Contrary to his words, he looked like a man who'd just awakened; his rich chestnut hair was pleasantly rumpled, his face relaxed, his eyes heavily lidded. He smelled sweetly of the warm scents of sleep, and his nightshirt, looking as if it had seen better days, gaped open at his throat, revealing a wedge of golden skin and a light, curling mat of auburn hair. A delicious warmth spread through her belly and radiated into her thighs. He was handsome and desirable, and that delicious warmth soon became a delicious ache. Unconsciously Mira licked her lips and reached out to touch his unshaven jaw.

His own eyes darkened. "You look as good as breakfast after a three-day fast, lassie."

"Do I?" Her fingers traced the shape of his mouth. "Why don't you kiss me and see if I taste as good, too?"

He laughed and hooked an arm around her neck, pulling her down and kissing her long and hard. Then he released her, sank back against his pillow, and gazed lazily up at her in a way that quickened her heartbeat and sent tremors pounding through her blood. She took his hand, that fine, elegant artist's hand, and reverently kissed each finger, each knuckle, even the calluses that hardened his palm, before curling his fingers into a fist, placing it against her face, and rubbing it up and down her cheek. Presently that hand unfolded itself and pushed beneath the thick warmth of her unbound hair. Mira sighed and closed her eyes.

"I missed you, *Moyrrra.*"

Brief pictures flickered through her mind. Of Brendan, hanging out of the shrouds and sketching madly as the cannonballs and musket shot shrieked around him. Of Brendan, cleverly tricking the big frigate into believing they'd gone aground when they'd been in water over a thousand feet deep. Of Brendan, fidgeting madly as he'd brought *Kestrel* into port, dreading the fuss that Newburyport would make—and did make—over him. She had seen his haunted eyes, conspicuously absent of mirth, and known it was all he could do not to flee when the townspeople had set upon him in a frenzy of joy and admiration. And the look of misery on his face as they'd hoisted him up on their shoulders and paraded him through Market Square with all the fanfare due their most gallant hero . . .

Ah, Brendan. Her poor, humble captain!

She glanced outside, hiding a private smile. Sunlight gilded the cold river that flowed just beyond *Kestrel*'s stern windows, and she could see the hull reflections of the new prizes shining black and brown and white against the gold-painted water. Once again she remembered the sea fight, the English captain's indignation, and the cheers of Newburyport as *Kestrel* and *Proud Mistress* had herded those prizes through the river's mouth and into the harbor. . . .

When Mira looked back at him, her gaze was as reverent as the townspeople's had been. Taking both of his hands in hers, she gazed deeply into the laughing russet eyes she loved so well. "And I missed you, too, Brendan."

He grinned and looked away, as though her statement both pleased him and made him uncomfortable.

She ran her thumbs between his fingers, around his palms. "That was quite a haul you two made. I hear you were quite gallant."

He flushed and looked away. "And from whom did you hear that?"

"Mr. Starr told me," she said, with an impish glint in her eye.

"Oh? Are you two friends?"

"We . . . know each other."

"Hmm, that doesn't surprise me." He removed one of his hands from hers, lifted it, and let his finger rove down the curve of her nose and to lips as soft as rose petals. "You with your cats and Mr. Starr with his chickens."

"Chickens?" She cocked one dainty brow.

"Aye, *chickens!* Can you believe it? I caught him *talking* to one of the roosters we'd taken aboard as fare for the soup pot! Had the thing perched on his shoulder like a pirate with a parrot. A *chicken!*"

Laughter lit her eyes, and those little cat-wrinkles fanned out on either side of her nose. His heart gave a painful lurch. "Well, we animal lovers have to stick together," she chirped, lifting his hand and kissing his knuckles once more. And then, her eyes glinting with mischief, her tongue slipped out and lapped the little hollows between them.

He started and flinched. "Don't do that."

"Why not?"

His voice was tight. "Because."

"Because why?"

"Because I said not to, that's why."

"What, does it hurt?"

He tried to jerk his hand away. Faith, it hurt, but not in the way she thought! "No, it doesn't hurt, and you know it! I'm lying here burning up for wanting you, and you're doing your best to drive me to madness! Now, stop!"

His tone wasn't convincing. She put his whole knuckle into her mouth and swirled her tongue around it, all the while holding his gaze.

Desire, white-hot and hungry, lanced his loins. He jerked his hand away, terrified that he was losing control, terrified of the feelings she evoked in him.

"Moyrrra, this is unseemly!"

She used his comment as an excuse to vent what was really riling her.

"So is sneaking off in the middle of the night, Brendan! Do you think I didn't see the marks in the snow where you landed after jumping out the window? Or the tracks leading off across the lawn? 'Tis a wonder you didn't break your fool neck! And here Father thinks you're still abed!"

"I am." He was grinning.

She jerked his hand back toward her. "You care for me, don't you?"

"Of course I do."

And then, recklessly, "As much as you care for *Kestrel?*"

He paused in the middle of yanking his hand back.

"Be truthful now, Brendan."

"I care for you very much, *Moyrrra.*"

"That's not what I asked you. I asked you if you care for me as much as you do this stupid ship."

He missed the flippant, teasing note in her voice. All he heard were two words—*stupid ship*—and that hurt. Truthfully he said, "In a different way."

"How different?"

"Faith, lassie, you can't compare a woman to a ship! They're two different things!"

"Are they?"

She stared at him, her eyes challenging, her chin high. He couldn't fool her. She was a shipbuilder's daughter— faith, what did he expect?

Quietly she repeated, *"Are* they?"

He picked at a loose thread of his nightshirt and on a defeated sigh, said, "No . . . they're not." If only she understood. But no, she understood too well; that was the problem. *"Moyrrra . . ."* She was still holding his hand, her fingers now loose and growing cold. "A ship is made of wood and wind and canvas, a woman of flesh and blood. But both have a heart, both have a soul. Both sing when they are pleased, cry when they are not. Both call to a man's heart, draw him into their spell, bewitch him. Both are *lassies, Moyrrra!* Sultry and sweet and—"

"Brendan."

"—gentle, lovely and—"

"Brendan."

He paused, wondering why this strange feeling was twisting his gut.

"You don't have to explain. I . . . I know how it is with seamen." She gave a little smile she didn't feel. "Remember?"

"Are you angry?"

"No." Again that wan smile. "Besides, it wouldn't do me a blasted bit of good if I was, would it?"

He reached up and drew her down atop him, wanting to prove that she occupied as big a place in his heart as *Kestrel* did—it was just a different one. But would she be content with just a part of his heart? Or, like Julia, would she want all of it?

Julia.

Fear drove through him, cold, raw terror that froze his throat and made him want to jump up and flee. But Mira's hands were gentle and soft as she stroked his hair, his roughly stubbled chin, the lean muscles of his face and neck. Finally he relaxed, reminding himself that Mira was *not* Julia, that Mira would *never* be Julia, and that he had nothing to fear.

Did he?

And now she was running her finger over his mouth, tracing the contour of his lips. The guarded look left his eyes, and his smile regained its crooked charm.

"Brendan?"

"Huh?" Damning himself for what he was doing, he sat up, wrapped his arms around her, and buried his face in her thick hair. It was heavy and silken, and smelled like roses and the cold, fresh air outside. His teeth nipped her ear, sending delicious little shivers through her blood and up her spine. She shut her eyes, enjoying the sensation, her breathing growing heavy and strained. His lips grazed the side of her neck, trailing kisses behind her ear and along the satiny hollows of her throat. Sighing in contentment, Mira plunged her hands beneath his shirt, hungering for the touch of his skin. Her fingers explored the sinewy strength of his arms and shoulders, fluttered over his warm chest with its odd little scar.

Fire danced between her thighs and smoldered in her belly, stoked by his warm breath against her neck, the soft endearments he whispered in her ear. That they were in English, then a heavy Irish brogue, and finally Gaelic, didn't matter. The words were the same in every language. And oh, how she loved him. She loved him more than she loved Rigel and Shaula and El Nath put together. She loved

him more than every cat that God had ever sent her way
to rescue. She loved him more than she loved life even.

So what if he was a bit shy when it came to women.

So what if he loved *Kestrel* instead.

So what if *Kestrel* had the upper hand . . . for now.

Outside and beneath them, the water lapped gently
around *Kestrel*'s rudder. The cabin brightened, and a ray
of sunlight slanted across the floor planking, then the heavy
cotton quilt that covered the bed. Somewhere forward a
mast creaked and water splashed as someone, topside,
dumped a bucket over the side.

Ship sounds.

Wonderful sounds.

"We shouldn't . . ." Brendan was whispering, against
her neck.

"We should."

"Someone may come."

"Someone may not."

Shifting out from under him, Mira nuzzled aside the
folds of his nightshirt and pressed her lips to his lean, hard
chest. He was warm and sleep-scented, delicious and
golden. She wanted him. Oh Lord above, she wanted him.
She wanted him so badly, it *hurt*.

"But—"

She laid a finger against his lips, silencing him. If she
wanted this handsome, shy, humble sea captain, she'd just
have to seduce him again! Her heartbeat quickened and
her hands grew damp with anticipation and the delight of
the challenge. She passed her tongue over her suddenly
dry lips, then slowly, lightly, touched it to his sternum.
He tensed, and she felt the muscles in his arm jump. His
breath fanned moist and warm against the hair atop her
head. One hand caught in her hair, crushed it in his fist,
began to trail through it with quick, rhythmic strokes.
Again her tongue slipped out, this time to lick the hard
little buds of his nipples, the white, raised flesh of the
scar. He gave a mighty shudder and his heart thumped
madly beneath her lips.

He was responding to her. Just as she'd known he would.
Against his dampening skin, her mouth curved in a smile.

"*Moyrrra*, lassie—"

"Cripes, Brendan, why in *hell* do you wear this ridiculous old nightshirt? Even the buttons are hanging by threads! Do you know how hard it is to kiss you, having to deal with this foolish thing?"

And with that, she bit the first button off with her teeth.

The second.

Lower, and the third.

He was breathing harshly now, beginning to squirm. Her head dipped lower, moving toward his belly now.

The fourth.

He anchored his hand in her hair. *"Moyrrra . . .* Faith, you don't know what you're doing, lassie—"

"Oh yes I do," she said, and caught the last button with her teeth. It made a soft ping as it hit the floor and rolled away. She looked up at him, her eyes shining with impishness, her hair falling endearingly over her face. Then she straightened up, reached behind her, and undid what she could reach of her gown's fastenings. "I know very *well* what I'm doing, *Captain!* Now, help me with *my* buttons, would you?"

She gathered her hair and held it aside, presenting the sweet curve of her back to him. Obligingly he undid the rest of the buttons, his fingers trembling so badly, he thought he'd never complete the task. His eyes drank in the pale creaminess of her back, the striking contrast of her dark hair against it. Soon both gown and chemise were freed and fell to her waist. As she straightened up, that thick, glorious mane fell over one eye and streamed around her lovely breasts. Their soft, ivory globes drew his hungry stare. Their rosy nipples stood high and hard and beckoning. He groaned and reached for her, all thoughts of gentlemanly behavior, dreaded entanglements, and even *Kestrel* wiped from his mind.

"Why do you tempt me so?"

Her head fell back, and her eyes slipped shut in delight. "To see how far I can take you before you break," she murmured honestly.

"You have me quite close to the breaking point, *mo bhourneen.*"

"What?"

"Er . . . my love," he clarified, his lips moving down her throat.

She shivered. "Love? Then you truly *do* love me, Brendan?"

He didn't answer, instead dragging elegant hands roughened by sea salt and hard work through her hair and over the silken skin of her breasts. Sensations slammed through her, and heat burned in her thighs. But she was thinking only of his last words. Had she heard him right? Did he actually love her?! She caught one of those hands and asked him again.

Into the softness of her breast he murmured, "Yes, *grá mo chroí*, I do."

A joyous sob caught somewhere in her throat. Her heart lifted on a draft of hot air, buoyed up and up and up, and tears of love and gratitude burned behind her eyes. She placed both hands against his shoulders and gently pushed him back. His eyes were smiling, beginning to glaze with desire. Cupping his jaw in her palms, Mira looked deeply into his eyes. "And I love you too, Brendan."

He shut his eyes, struggling with something inner and private.

Beneath them, *Kestrel* rolled unhappily.

Images drifted back to her. Of Brendan, his voice warm and affectionate as he'd spoken of his ship. Brendan, passing a hand over her gunwales during the heat of battle as though to reassure the little schooner. Brendan, standing out in the snow that first day they'd taken her to sea, alone and in silent communication with her. Again Mira felt that stab of jealousy, and it was suddenly all-important to know that the love he had for her was as strong as what he felt for *Kestrel*.

But how?

She stared into his eyes and let the pads of her thumbs graze the rough sides of his cheeks. "You said that a woman and a ship are two different things," she said, carefully, knowing she was treading on fragile ground. "But we both know they're really not." There was a quick flash of something—vulnerability, perhaps?—in his honey-warm eyes, and then he swallowed hard and glanced away. "Oh, Brendan, *Kestrel*'s a lady, aye, but can she love you as I can? Can she take you in her arms and warm you, hold you, adore you? Tell you how special you are, show you how wonderful you are?''

He fidgeted slightly, obviously uncomfortable with the comparison.

''Can she do this—'' Mira slid her hands into the warm area between his gaping nightshirt and his chest ''—or this . . .''

His breathing grew shallow, ragged.

''Or—'' Her hand moved over the ridge of scarred flesh and pressed against his heart, now thudding wildly beneath her palm ''—this?''

''Moyrrra, lassie—''

She palmed the flat tautness of his belly, dipping her fingers tantalizingly lower. His eyes were half-closed, the curls growing damp around his brow. ''Can she make your skin burn and your heart race and your man-piece hard as rock, Brendan? Can she make you feel like this—'' she reached lower, teasing his hard shaft with a butterfly touch until his head fell forward against her shoulder ''—or this?''

She put her fingers beneath his jaw, forced his head up, and kissed him hard on the mouth. And when he responded with fierce passion, his tongue driving between her teeth and running along the insides of her lips, she finally tore herself free and looked deeply into his eyes.

''Of course she can't.'' Triumph edged her voice, for his arousal was hot and hard and thick beneath the loose folds of his nightshirt, making it stand like a tent between his thighs.

''You're right, *stóirín.* . . . You're absolutely right. . . .'' His eyes slipped shut in sweet agony and he bent his head once more, resting his brow on her shoulder and breathing hard.

Her arms went around him and clasped him to her. His breath stirred her hair, warmed her nipples, fanned the hot ache that burned in her thighs. She pressed against him and hooked her leg around his hips, barely managing to kick off first one shoe, then the other. They hit the floor with a soft thump, and she drove her stockinged feet beneath the heavy folds of the quilt. His arousal stabbed against her thighs and she rubbed herself against him, driving him past any hope of control. He was unable to resist her any longer, and indeed, no longer wanted to. His tongue slipped out and teased the hard peaks of her nipples. She sighed and stroked his rich, curling locks, letting her fingers trail in the downy hairs at his nape, around to his chest, and downward with titillating slowness.

From a distance, she heard her own voice. "Oh, Brendan . . . you can woo a ship, give her your heart, even your soul. A lady she'll be, but a proud and haughty one always. . . ."

He groaned as her fingers settled on his knee, began to move upward through the soft auburn hair on his hard thighs, and slowly, agonizingly, crawled higher . . .

"No warmth, just fire. No love, just beauty. Selfishness in place of generosity—"

. . . and higher.

"—possessiveness in place of love."

Her finger touched the tip of his manhood, and his breath burst out in a harsh woosh.

"Nay, your beloved *Kestrel* cannot love you as I can, Brendan." Her fingers were stroking his engorged manhood now, driving fire through his loins and making his world spin with sweet madness. "Can she do *this?*"

Her fingers closed around him, and his head fell back over her wrist.

Her thick hair lay across his hot belly, his burning thighs. "Or this?"

She bent her head. Her lips closed around him, and he sucked his breath in through his teeth. "By th' blessed saints, *Moyrrra . . .*"

She had him just where she wanted him. She had him fully in her power. And she had him where *Kestrel* could never put him—nor reach him.

He endured her maddening kisses and velvety lips for as long as he could, feeling the sweat pop out of his brow and seeing the deckhead reel above him. Finally he tore her gown off, heaved her onto her back, and raked her lovely face with hot and hungry kisses, trailing them down her breasts, her belly, and into the soft and moist curls of her womanhood. She arched beneath him, gasping, her fists clenching the damp sheets and her knuckles turning white. He throbbed, he pulsed, he *ached* for her. Slipping his fingers into her, he found her ready.

"Yes, Brendan . . . Show me you love me. Show me I mean as much to you as *she* does. . . ."

He parted her with his fingers, stroking the wetness between her thighs until her world blackened and spun and she thought she would die. She whimpered deep in her throat, the sounds guttural and primitive. Her head twisted on the pillow, her teeth caught on the soft linen and bit down hard. Back up her thighs, her belly, her chest, his head moved, and she felt his hair feathering against her hot skin as he took one breast into his mouth, then the other, suckling, tasting, nipping.

"Show me that you love me, Brendan . . ."

He dragged his mouth from her aching breasts and swept kisses down her gently curving ribs, her sleek belly, her—

"Show me—"

She gasped and cried out as his lips found the soft, rosy petals of her womanhood and opened her to his questing tongue. She balled the sheets in her fist and whipped her head back and forth on the pillow, sobbing in sweet, mad agony. The air grew too hot too breathe. She sucked in great lungfuls of it, feeling the sweat break out on her brow and beneath her back as his tongue darted between her hot folds, licking, tasting, loving. She drove herself upward, catching his hair in her fist, her mouth open in a soundless scream of ecstasy.

Thick, sweeping waves of heat drove through her. Higher and higher he brought her. Sobbing, she raked his back with her nails and bucked madly beneath him, his hot hand against her mound only inflaming her more as he pressed her down against the damp sheets and pinned her there. And then his tongue, his teeth, found the pulsing bud of her desire, and this time she did scream.

"Brendan!"

He lapped.

"Brendan, oh, oh, *God*—"

He suckled.

"Brendan, I'm going to—"

He drew back and drove his rigid shaft into her with

savage, primal force, impaling her with fire that tore a scream from her lips and a white-hot climax from her body that blinded her to everything but him. She felt his hot seed pulsing within her, filling her. It went on and on and on, and when he had finished, he brought her to the peak again and ruthlessly shoved her off it once more.

It took a long time for their breathing to return to normal, their heartbeats to slow, the last little tingles to fade into sweet, dying ripples of sensation. She lay in his arms, her silken hair spilling over his chest, her head tucked beneath his chin as he stroked her back, her buttocks, her soft shoulders. She loved him. She loved him, loved him, loved him—

"Moyrrra." His voice was strangely hoarse still, barely more than a whisper. Outside, a seagull called, and she heard the first sounds of hammering and sawing as the shipyard awakened.

"Aye, my captain?" She sighed and snuggled deeper with the curve of his arm, resting her head against his hard shoulder and gently nuzzling one tiny brown nipple. She could stay like this forever, pleasantly drugged with passion, blissfully content, satisfied, satiated. Her eyes slipped shut and she dragged her hand up to trace the odd little scar with her thumb.

He cradled her close, feeling strangely protective of her. *She loved him.* The trepidation, the terror? Gone. The fear that she'd try to make him choose between herself and *Kestrel?* Gone. She'd recognized it for what it was, had dispelled his worries with her words, her actions, her love. He stroked her soft hair and felt an inner peace that was so achingly beautiful, it made the moisture burn behind his eyes and a thick lump of emotion rise in his throat. Never had he been so happy. Never had he felt so . . . *safe* with a woman. She knew the dangers of loving a seaman and she knew how to deal with them. *She understood.*

He caught a thick, glossy length of her hair and rubbed it against his lips. "I . . . I think we ought to, er, get married."

She turned over onto her back and gazed up at him with sunbursts of love glowing in her lucid green eyes. And then she smiled, and the little cat-wrinkles crinkled at the side of her nose.

"When?"

"D'you mean you would? You *would* marry me?"

"Even if Father didn't have this stupid Ultimatum, I'd marry you, Brendan." She stretched and slid herself up against his chest, wrapping her arms around his neck and tilting her head back to gaze lovingly up at him. "You go on your cruise with Matt next week, just like you planned. And when you come back—"

"We'll start making plans?" he said, as excited as a little boy.

"Yes. *Plans.*"

"Oh, lassie . . ." He wrapped his arms around her and crushed her to him. "Oh, lassie, you don't know how much this means to me. God, how I love you, *mo stóirín,* my sweet. . . ."

"And how I love you, too, my Captain from Connacht!"

As they fell back to the bed together, the first footsteps sounded upon *Kestrel's* deck above.

The visitors had come.

Chapter 21

Ephraim had caught her just as she was slipping out the door this morning, garbed in her brother's clothes, carrying a ditty bag packed with a few belongings, and heading for *Kestrel.*

Obviously it hadn't taken him long to put two and two together, and all her screaming, yelling, and carrying on hadn't done a bit of good. Ephraim was adamant about keeping her off the sea, especially now that making a lady out of his disobedient daughter was all the more important

given Captain Merrick's interest in her. Furious and outmaneuvered, Mira found herself land-bound at last—and
a spectator to *Kestrel*'s glorious departure instead of a par-
ticipant.

She watched angrily from shore, where Plum Island's
frothy surf writhed around Rigel's hooves. The wind,
heavy and wet with the tang of the sea, tossed his mane
over Mira's hands and blew her hair into her eyes, across
her mouth, and around her shoulders. It was a cold wind
and it was taking *Kestrel* out past the river's mouth and
into open sea.

It was impossible to remember her anger when behold-
ing such beauty. Reaching up, she cleared the hair out of
her suddenly misty eyes and beheld the majestic sight.
Kestrel. The schooner was parading toward her, her topsails blossoming like a rose seeking spring. Water keened
at her bows, growing louder and louder as she approached,
passed, moved through the channel and into open sea, and
Mira caught bits and pieces of sound that only made her
heart ache more; Zachary Wilbur calling for more sail,
voices raised in a sea chanty, Liam's fiddle—and Brendan's
laughter. Sadness swept over her, then admiration. Sadness because Brendan was there and she was here; admiration because there wasn't anything else a person *could*
feel at sight of *Kestrel*.

The schooner rode high in her own bow wake, dancing
upon a sheet of white froth. She was a sight to steal one's
breath away as she swung her nose toward the wind and
showed her heels to the land. She was beautiful. Glorious.
And for this cruise, she would have her captain all to herself.

Mira shoved her hair out of her face and tried not to
think about it.

At least she had Brendan's love to sustain her. "Ah,
Moyrrra," he'd said as she'd lain in the hard curve of his
arm and watched Orion set beyond *Kestrel*'s stern windows
last night, "you *will* be waiting for me on the wharf when
I return, won't you? Nothing would make me hap-
pier. . . ."

But the sight of her rival, alone with the man she loved,
brought no ease to her heart, for *Kestrel* was as capable

of working her charms on the handsome captain who commanded her as any woman of flesh and blood.

Perhaps more so.

Sadness and admiration. . . .

Proud Mistress, sporting a freshly painted figurehead, was passing through the channel now, gliding in the schooner's wake like an attendant on a queen. Mira fished in her pocket, found her spyglass, and raised it. The brig's decks teemed with high-spirited Newburyporters, all waving wildly to her. So many years she'd sailed with these men. So many times Matt had led them into battle and glory, and still their excitement for a cruise made oldsters into boys, boys into hellions, men into heroes. And there was Matt, standing on the quarterdeck, coattails flapping in the wind, red hair whipping, scanning the shoreline and obviously looking for her. And then their eyes met, brother and sister, and she saw his teasing grin as he raised his hand in farewell.

Then the brig's courses filled with healthy wind and she leaned her shoulder into the waves, carrying Matt away from her. Far ahead, *Kestrel* spread her topgallants, a great, winged raptor of glory and pride, and Mira watched her until even the spyglass couldn't pick out the details on her deck any longer. Then *Kestrel* fell below the horizon. Sunlight glinted on those lofty topgallants, once, twice; then she was gone.

Around her, the wind sounded like dirge, and Mira trembled without knowing why.

And as she turned Rigel into the wind and headed back toward town, she realized she was more her father's daughter than even she'd thought.

In her hand was a watch, and she was studying it.

Counting the hours when *Kestrel* would bring the man they both loved back to her.

"That's it, Eveleen. Keep her going now, nice and steady. A little faster and we'll quit for the day."

Eveleen, clad in a plum-colored riding habit and wearing a hat with a feather sticking out of it, gave her instructor a sour look. But a combination of exercising her horse, shoveling the stall, and—at Abigail's gentle suggestion—

limiting her desserts to only the treats that Mira had made was beginning to have an effect on her figure. Eveleen no longer got winded when she walked Shaula around the field, the pink dresses were getting baggy on her, and the times when Mira would have to yell and scream and threaten just to get her to do something were growing few and far between. With every bit of ground she gained, Eveleen's confidence grew, and these days, there was something in her eyes that couldn't be quite hidden—the triumph of accomplishment. Today, however, was one of her biggest achievements to date; Shaula was actually trotting around the field. *Trotting!*

"But it *hurts,* and my stomach's starting to growl—"

Ignoring her halfhearted whining, Mira threw back her head in laughter. "Eveleen, if you can keep that mare at a trot for three more times around the field, I'll personally take you down to Wolfe Tavern and buy you a piece of pie big enough to feed Washington's army!"

The girl was jolted up and down in the saddle with every step the white mare took. But even Eveleen Merrick couldn't maintain an air of glumness when she'd just accomplished so much, and through knocking teeth, she managed a smile. In it, Mira saw something of Brendan, and her heart gave a little lurch. "You're doing well," she coaxed. "We're almost done."

"But by then my stomach's going to be so jarred and jostled, I won't *want* pie. . . ."

"Then post. Up and down, up and down. Let the mare's rhythm guide you. Watch her outside leg, and when it reaches out, rise in your stirrups." Caught up in the excitement of the moment, Mira sent Rigel ahead to demonstrate, thrilling, as she always did, to the raw, unleashed power of the colt beneath her. "Like this . . ." Up and down, up and down. "Just a little, enough to take the jostle out of it."

"Like this?" Eveleen rose out of the saddle so much that Mira could've flown a kite between her rump and the cantle.

"Not so much. You're working too hard. Let the horse do it for you."

They trotted side by side, instructor and student, so in-

volved in their mutual triumph that neither heard the bang
of guns down in the harbor as a ship was welcomed into
the river.

Not two ships, but one.

A privateer had returned.

Alone.

Mira heard the uproar all the way from Miss Mira Ashton's School of Fine Horsemanship and knew that Matt
was back, for the March winds carried Ephraim's angry
bellowing all the way across the paddocks, through the
woods, and into the field where she and Eveleen quietly
walked their horses.

"Damn ye fer a yellow-livered coward! How the bloody
hell could you let it HAPPEN! Traitor! Knavish son of a
bitch! I TRUSTED YOU!"

Eveleen, her pudgy face going white, pulled her mount
up short. Obviously she'd never witnessed the stormy re-
union between father and son when Matt returned from a
cruise. But Mira knew what all that hollering was about!
With a shout of glee, she gathered her reins and drove her
heels into Rigel's flanks. "Eveleen, c'mon! Matt's home!
Brendan's home!"

She sent Rigel tearing toward the house, his tail streaming behind him like a banner. Hard on their heels, a terrified Eveleen shut her eyes and clung to the pommel,
Shaula's snowy mane, and her courage as the mare broke
into a gallop in an attempt to keep up with her son. But
Mira felt only the wind on her face, the thrill in her heart.
She urged Rigel faster. Faster! *Brendan was home!*

And as the colt tore out of the woods, raced past the
paddocks in a blaze of gray, and slid to a stop on his
haunches, her joy faded and apprehension swept in like a
winter wind to take its place.

For there, filling the lawn, pouring up the driveway, and
racing in from the street, was an immense throng of people. They were shouting. They were yelling. And where
the women were concerned, they were openly sobbing.

And on the doorstep stood Ephraim, his face as white
as his hair, his features so twisted with agony that Mira
felt the icy fingers of dread crawling up her spine before

she'd even thrown herself from Rigel's back and hurtled across the lawn. Tears streamed down his craggy cheeks, and behind him, Abigail slumped against the doorframe, sobbing into her hands.

"Goddamned British *SCUM!*" Father was roaring, his voice carrying over the din of the crowd. "I wish I'd never laid eyes on ye! I rue the day I met ye and curse the day ye sailed into this town, ye miserable, rotten *COWARD!*"

Mira came up short. Horror tightened her chest, and her heart seemed to stop. She followed Father's gaze, and the blood drained from her face.

It wasn't Matt who stood there, but Brendan.

And he was alone.

He stood like a man on trial, the crowd behind him the jury, Ephraim, before him, the judge. He had his tricorn in his hands, and his eyes were filled with such horrible anguish that for a moment, Mira thought he was someone else, so different did it make him look, so much did the absence of the good humor that was so much a part of him rob him of who he was. Mira shook her head. *No.* Surely Father wouldn't be sobbing and raging at *Brendan!* Surely there'd be mirth in those tragic, haunted eyes if it truly was him—

And then it hit her, just below her ribs like a savage kick in the gut. Her brother was nowhere in sight. It *was* Brendan whom Father was raging at.

Blind, white panic seized her. *Matt.* And then, in a guttural scream of pure terror, his name was torn from her throat. *"Matt!"*

There was the thunder of hooves as Shaula came galloping up behind them, Eveleen still clinging, white-faced, to her back . . . Ephraim's bellowing, going on and on and on . . . the women crying, the young men shouting, the angry faces, the curses, the accusations—

And Brendan.

At that moment he turned toward her, and there was such a plea for understanding in his grief-stricken eyes that her heart constricted painfully in her chest. She flung herself into his arms, felt them go around her. Then she drew back. "Brendan, *where's Matt?!*"

He stood stiffly, as though afraid to move. A muscle

worked in his throat and he took a deep, measured breath. His eyes had an odd sheen, and blinking, he looked up at the clouds above. Then he took her hands in his own and squeezed them so hard, she felt pain in her fingers. His hands were freezing cold, as though the blood had ceased to move in his veins.

"Brendan, *where's my brother?!*"

He looked down at her, and she saw tears in his eyes. Raw, ugly terror filled her. He took a deep, shaky breath and gently set her away from him. And then he reached up to knuckle his eye. *"Moyrrra, lassie—"*

Panic seized her.

"Where IS HE?"

"Moyrrra, he's—"

Ephraim's grief-stricken roar pierced the air. "Dead! He's dead, and it's all the fault of this goddamned cowardly son of a bitch I should never've trusted in the first place!"

Brendan shut his eyes, and his fierce grip on her hands tightened, but he did not lower his head.

"I knew I should never've trusted ye, ye confounded spawn of the devil! Stinkin' deceitful, yellow-bellied traitor! The devil take ye, ye slinkin' dog! Traitor! Bastard! *BRIT!*"

Mira reeled backward, dizzily. From a great distance she heard the crowd's angry roaring, saw Brendan's stricken face. And then Abigail's keening wails began to close in on her, louder and louder and—

She pressed her hands to her ears. "No! Stop it, *stop it, all of you!*"

"But it's true. . . . Oh, Lord, it's *true*, Mira!" Abigail wailed, wringing a cloth covered with flour, dough, and the stains of her own tears. "Every last bit of it! There was a battle . . . they found the convoy from London . . . your brother stayed to fight, and this—this—*snake* slunk off and left him to do it *alone!*" Her sobs grew to hysteria, raised the hair on Mira's nape. Screaming, the housekeeper flung the wet cloth at Brendan. It hit him squarely in the chest, but he didn't move, merely standing there with flour marring the handsome perfection of his immaculate uniform. "Alone, Mira! Your poor dead brother *alone,* all by himself, to face the might of the British navy while this slinking dog crawled back here with not a scratch on his beloved, cursed ship! *That cursed ship!* That's what started it all in the first place! Would that we'd sunk it by the might of our own guns! Would that those drafts had never been resurrected! *Would that her creator had died with them!* Oh, Matthew. . . . *Oh, my poor, sweet Matthew. . . .''*

The servants managed to get her into the house, where her hideous wailing echoed through the rooms and flowed out over the lawns, the people, and Mira's heart, until it began to vibrate, to tremble, and then to rock wildly within her breast.

"Not Matt . . .'' she whispered, never hearing Rigel come up behind her to comfort her, as his kind had done for centuries. And though Brendan reached out to steady her, it was Rigel she fell against. "Not my brother . . .'' Hair tangled in her suddenly wet lashes and she clawed it free, shaking her head in denial and backing away from Brendan as he took a step toward her. "He was a good captain . . . the best. He's not dead, Brendan! I'd know it if he was! *He was my brother!* He's *not dead!* He's *not!* It's not true! It *cannot be!''*

Lucy Preble clawed her way to the front of the crowd. "It *is* true, Mira! You go down to the river and you'll see only one ship! That cursed schooner!''

"With nary a mark on it!'' someone shouted.

"Hauled himself off and let our poor Matt do the fighting! Didn't want to see his precious schooner harmed!''

"Newburyport's newest hero, eh?''

"Traitor!''

"Coward!''

"JUDAS!''

It became a chant. Louder. Stronger. Full of hatred and betrayal and a thirst for vengeance.

"Judas! Judas! *JUDAS!''*

An egg slammed through the air, just missing Brendan's shoulder and exploding against the side of the white Georgian.

"Judas! You *killed* him!''

And Brendan, just standing there, admitting nothing,

denying nothing, and no one ever considering that maybe he *couldn't,* for his own throat was working, and he was fighting a losing battle to repress his own emotion. But the fact that he didn't defend himself condemned him in the eyes of the townspeople, of Ephraim—and of the woman he loved.

She was looking at him as though he were a stranger, the tears sliding down her pale, freckled cheeks, one thick spill of hair tumbling over her eye. She pushed it away with a strange, jerky motion, and when she spoke, her voice was barely a whisper.

"Did you?" Her tip trembled, and she pushed a hand against it. "You didn't . . . didn't leave him to die. . . . Did you, B-Brendan?"

"*Moyrra*—"

"*DID YOU?*"

She didn't see his throat working as he tried to gain control. She didn't see the agony in his eyes as he fought to find the right words. And she never gave him the chance to explain. All she felt was a horrible, choking lump in her throat—and all she saw was *Kestrel,* glorious and proud and dancing, flitting away while *Proud Mistress* fought a valiant battle to her death. . . .

Her eyes filled with pain, Mira turned blindly away from Brendan and was on Rigel's back, bolting through the crowd, and thundering down High Street before anyone could stop her. Seeking escape in the mad pounding of hooves and sleek muscles beneath her, of wind in her face, her eyes, her head, her heart. Run away. Run far away. From the truth, from the grief, from the reality, from . . . from—

"Matt!" she sobbed, tears flooding her eyes as she tried to hold, tried to banish, the memory of that freckled face, that crimson hair, the spectacles that were always sliding down his nose—

Oh, God, Matt . . . "Please, God, not my *brother!*"

And then Rigel's thundering hooves hit a spot of sand and he stumbled, horribly, his forelegs crumpling beneath him. Mira was pitched headlong over his neck, her body hurtling through space until it was finally stopped by the Beacon Oak itself, there to lie crumbled like a broken doll at its base.

It was Brendan who found her. And as he picked her up, gently, reverently, his strong arms cradling her to his shot-scarred chest, his own tears ran at last, flowing like blood from the pieces of his own broken heart.

Chapter 22

Mira had never before awakened with tears in her eyes—as Brendan had never before fallen asleep with them in his, if one could call the dazed, exhausted stupor that claimed him sleep.

She opened her eyes to silence as deep and dark and ugly as the tomb. She was in her bed, the linsey-woolsey counterpane drawn up to her chin, the fine lace canopy above merging with the darkening ceiling. Twilight shone hauntingly through a window whose curtains were closed against it; beyond it, night approached.

Silence.

There was something alien in it, something strange, something not quite right. And then she realized what was wrong. What was terribly wrong. There was not a clock in the house ticking.

As though time itself had stopped.

Father? Father, *forget to wind his clocks?*

She came awake with a start.

Matt. Her choked whisper pierced the still silence of the darkening room. "Oh, Matt . . ." And then the tears came, slipping soundlessly down her cheeks to dampen the counterpane beneath her chin. She stared up at the familiar canopy and felt them stream from the corners of her eyes. Down her face. Tickling the hair at her temples, her ears, wetting the pillow beneath her head.

"Oh . . . Oh, Matt . . ."

She was not alone. In a chair drawn up to the bed, a

man with eyes that no longer laughed had kept a silent, tortured vigil, his long legs stiff and cramped from sitting there for so many hours, his unshaven jaw dark with stubble. He heard her anguished weeping and thanked the blessed God that she would be all right; he heard her weeping grow louder and reached for her hand in the darkness, never stopping to stretch his aching legs, never thinking of his own pain, but hers. He was there for her. He vowed he'd always be there for her. And he reached for her now as her sobs grew gut-wrenching and awful, shaking her little body to the very depths of its being.

And Mira, feeling those arms go around her, those hands stroking her hair, knew who that man was. Viciously she slammed her elbow into his ribs, his grunt of pain bringing her a savage satisfaction as she flung herself down and buried her face in the depths of the pillow, the thick tumble of her own tangled hair, and the memories of a brother she would never see again.

"Don't touch me!"

Yet still those hands, those damned, fine artist's hands. Hands that drove beneath her shaking shoulders, hands that pulled her up against a hard chest and a coat that was uncharacteristically rumpled.

Newburyport's newest hero.

Brendan.

She drove her palms against that chest and shoved herself backward, out of the warmth of those caring arms, away from the tortured heart that needed her as much as she needed him.

"Judas!" she spat, her voice low and terrible and ugly.

The room had grown too dark for her to see the stricken pain on his face, the grief in his eyes, but it wouldn't have mattered if she had—for at the moment Mira had never hated anyone more than she did Captain Brendan Jay Merrick.

She stared up at his shadowed features through eyes that were lucid and clear despite the anguish that ripped the tears from them and sent them falling down her pale cheeks. Her voice was a whisper, soft as a rattler's tail and just as deadly.

"Get away from me."

He swallowed hard and tried to take her hand.

"I said, get away from me—do you hear me?" The whisper took on voice, a voice clogged with tears and hatred and the smack of hysteria as she shrank away from him with teeth bared, a wild, wounded creature of savage fury. "Don't touch me with your filthy, traitorous hands—" the voice dropped to a whisper again "—you slime-sucking son of a bitch—"

"Mira."

She lay rigidly on her back, staring up at him through the darkness. "Slinking coward, gutless, wretched—"

"*Moyrrra.*"

She clawed the hair out of her eyes, and sickened by the sight of him, turned her face into the pillow, its feathery down muffling her sobs. Her shoulders shook, and she drew her legs up in a protective fetal position, as though she could curl herself around her grief, her very heart, and hold herself together with it. And over that fragile, huddled little body her thick, dark hair lay like a blanket, only the soles of her tiny feet peeking out from beneath. His heart broke at the wretchedness of it.

"*Moyrrra,* please . . . please listen to me. . . ."

"Where's my father?" she choked, into the depths of the pillow. "I . . . want my . . ."

He tried again to reach for her hand.

She slapped it viciously away and turned her face in to the damp heat of the pillow.

He winced as though she'd struck him across the face. And then he rose, went to the window, and stood gazing out over the street, the treetops, and toward the river. Ships drove their masts against a fading sunset sky. The ships of Newburyport. Except that one of them would never be coming home again.

Outside, a robin called good night to its mate, the sound lonely and sad in the twilight.

Quietly he said, "Your da is down at Wolfe's Tavern, *Moyrrra,* where he has been for the past day and a half."

Father. Losing himself in tipple, just as he'd done when Mama had died. *Oh, God, help me,* she thought, huddling closer to herself, *oh God, please help me . . . It hurts,*

*God. It hurts so much. . . . Please, God, make the pain
go away . . . Make him go away. . . .*

But he would not, his words coming quietly from across
the room. "Lassie, please . . . before you judge me, listen
to me. I *beg* of you. Give me a fair trial, at least. . . ."

She sobbed harder into the pillow, gripping its corners
in little, fish-cold fists and squeezing it about her head as
though it could muffle the pain and block out his voice.

He gripped the windowsill, his body silhouetted against
the last of that lonely light. "We had a strategy, your
brother and I," he began, quietly, not wanting to tell her
because of the pain it would cause, yet desperately need-
ing to, just to relieve his own grief, his own guilt, unjus-
tified though it might be. And as he began to speak, he
reached into his coat pocket and drew something out,
though Mira, her face buried in the pillow, never saw what
it was.

"A strategy we planned to try upon the convoy from
London." Swallowing hard, he closed his fingers around
the object in his hand. "I suppose I shall always wonder
if maybe it was all planned. That maybe someone *knew*
we would be there. You see, there were other American
privateers waiting to pluck prizes out of that convoy, too.
Yet none of them were touched. They wanted Matt, and
they wanted *me.*"

She sobbed something into the pillow, her voice incom-
prehensible.

"What was that, *mo stóirín?*"

"I said, I wish the bloody hell it *had* been you instead
of my . . . instead of my . . . b-brother!"

He turned back to the window, his heart feeling like a
sail that has thrilled to the strength of a hard wind, only
to have it sucked away to leave the canvas sagging beneath
its yard. He looked down at the object in his hand, biting
his lip, thankful that she couldn't see the pain, the tears
in his own eyes. But the lilting, musical tone of his voice
was gone, like an instrument out of tune, and through her
misery, she noticed it, and it broke her heart even more.

"We found the convoy ten leagues off Sandy Hook—a
huge convoy, Mira, of fat merchantmen and wallowing
ships, ripe for the plucking—and pluck them we did. It

was so easy. . . . Too easy. We'd stand off during the day, and when it grew dark, we'd take turns. One of us would distract the guard ships, and the other would dash in and cut out a prize. . . . Because it was dark, they dared not separate, and the guard ships couldn't be everywhere at once. Oh, they tried to escape, but with so many ships and only a few to protect them, there were many stragglers. . . . They were ripe for the plucking.''

He leaned his forehead against the cold windowpane. The sunset was just a gray glimmer now. Fading.

''We were fools. Too bold, too cocky, too confident—and too greedy. We took so many prizes, we barely had enough men to crew our own ships. And still we didn't stop. It went to our heads, lassie. We grew drunk on it. And you know that old tradition, about not returning to port until you have a prize to show for each of your guns. . . . And here *Kestrel* has ten, and *Mistress* had fourteen . . .'' He didn't tell her that returning to Newburyport with twenty-four prizes had been Matt's determined goal, not his. ''It was an insane thing to attempt, even for a couple of daredevils like us.'' He looked down at the object in his hand, feeling his eyes filling up, his nose burning. ''On the third morning, we anchored in the lee of an island to wait out a squall—''

He swallowed hard, steeling himself against the horrible memory, while his hands tightened around the fragile object. ''We woke to fog and rain, and a frigate bearing down on us from windward. A British frigate, with every sail set and a bone in her teeth. She caught us unprepared. I know now that she was waiting for us. Waiting until we didn't have the men to properly crew our vessels, having sent them off in groups on our prizes. Waiting until success blurred our caution. Matt and I signaled to each other—we'd worked out an elaborate flag code—and he asked me to use *Kestrel* as a lure, to try to lead the frigate away from himself and the prizes.''

He saw no need to tell her that the frigate had been HMS *Viper* and that its captain was a man named Richard Crichton. Instead, he told her of how he'd tried to lead that frigate away, for he'd been so secure in the knowledge that Crichton had wanted *him* that he didn't believe his old enemy would give Matt a second thought. But no. It hadn't happened that way. It was *supposed* to happen that way, but it hadn't. And as he'd hauled off to leeward and sent *Kestrel* on a smooth run, her sails set wing and wing and the American colors streaming saucily from her gaff like a flag tempting an enraged bull, *Viper* had chased her only long enough to ensure she would be safely out of the fight and then dashed back toward the solitary brig and her covey of prizes, quickly overtaking them and brutally opening fire with every gun. Matt had fought valiantly, with everything he had. But *Mistress* had been under-manned, with an island at her back and no room to ma-neuver. And fast as *Kestrel* was, she hadn't reached her sister ship in time. They'd returned to nothing but wreck-age floating on the gray waves.

"If only I'd known, lassie." His voice was flat and dead and emotionless. She heard him take a great, tremulous sigh. "If only I'd *known*. And if only Matt had a gunner like my own Mr. Starr . . ."

He winced as Mira curled herself up in a ball and let out one long, keening cry, her agony worsened by guilt that she'd been here on shore when her own skill on *Mis-tress*'s guns might've saved her brother's life.

"But the frigate had a skilled gunner. Or maybe just a lucky one . . ."

His hand tightened on the object in his hands. The twi-light gave a last, faint glimmer—

"His shot hit *Mistress*'s powder magazine, and she went up like a torch."

On the bed, Mira sobbed harder, the tears soaking into the very heart of the pillow, the pit of her soul. Horrible, wretched cries that showed no mercy, flooded the room with agony, caused Brendan to turn from the window and take a step toward her, two—

She raised her head, sensed his approach, and screamed, "Don't come near me! You should've *been* there for him! You should've stayed and fought! You bastard! *Don't you ever come near me again*, do you hear me?! I hate you! *HATE YOU!*"

He stopped.

"I don't ever want to see you again! *Ever!*" She struck

out, blindly, and her hand found something in the darkness. A blue and white bowl, commemorating the launching of the fine topsail schooner *Kestrel,* kept on her bedside table where it would always be near when she woke up in her lonely bed in the depths of the night, when she opened her eyes in the morning—

Her hand closed around it and she flung it with all her strength toward his voice, the piercing, agonized crash of glass against the far wall shattering the stillness.

"Get away from me! Filthy son of a bitch! Bastard! Coward! *Judas!*"

She fell back into the pillow, sobbing so hard she couldn't catch her breath, feeling as if she were suffocating in its wet softness, its damp heat, and drowning in the choking awfulness of her own grief.

"I hate you. . . . God, I hate you. . . ."

But it was really herself she hated, for if she hadn't been on shore, waiting for this—this *Brit,* she could've helped her brother.

But he couldn't know that. And neither could she.

"I hate you, hate you, hate you. . . ."

Silently Brendan moved across the darkened room. The object in his hand, found as he'd combed the beach of the island that had shuddered to the thunder of *Mistress*'s guns, and later, her death, was now warm in his hand. He ran his thumb over it one last time.

He thought of the broken bowl. Shattered, like *Mistress*. Like Mira's trust in him, and the love they'd shared.

Like *Kestrel*'s honor itself.

Quietly he reached out through the darkness and put the object on the table where that bowl had stood, and left the room.

There, alone, staring unseeingly up into the darkness, the metal growing cold once more, sat the spectacles of a dead privateersman.

They had no body to bury, but Captain Matthew Ashton's memory was laid to rest with full honors just the same, on a cloudy day with a mournful wind and a damp, oppressive rain that soaked through cloak and coat alike. Gray sky and gray river, gray faces and tears that mixed with the rain and went unnoticed. And a tombstone of granite, on which was painstakingly carved the likeness of a brig with the figurehead of a woman; a tombstone that reflected the mood of the sky, of the day, of the people.

It was a sad day for Newburyport.

The American flag flew at half-mast from the fort at Plum Island, and aboard every vessel in the rain-soaked harbor. A black coach carried the dead hero's family to St. Paul's Church on High Street, followed by a funeral procession and mourners of keening women, silent sea captains, weeping children, and a seventy-man detachment from the Newburyport militia. When the solemn ceremony was all over, the ships in the river fired their guns in solemn salute to one of their own, lost in the name of Liberty. Drums rolled, church bells tolled in lonely sorrow. And at the grave, and its reign of unbroken ground, the militiamen lifted their muskets and fired three volleys as the dead captain's sister tossed a single, blooming crocus to the earth and turned away to sob into her father's arms.

Apart from the group a lone figure stood, wearing his best uniform and clasping his tricorn to his heart. That uniform was dark with rain, and water streamed from his curling russet hair. He watched the girl in helpless misery, and when she lifted her face from the comfort of her father's chest, their gazes met across the rainy distance.

Brendan swallowed, and took a hopeful step forward.

The crowd huddled protectively around her.

And Mira turned her face away.

His heart broke. And as the ceremony ended and the townspeople looked up and saw him standing there, they cursed him, and turned away, leaving him to face alone the river that had brought him here—and the schooner whose name had become a curse.

Newburyport's newest hero.

Named by his Irish mother for a long-dead sea explorer, the patron saint of sailors.

In grief, the truth is often crushed.

Chapter 23

Being a man who viewed the use of excessive force as a necessary means of inducing information, Captain Richard Crichton saw no reason not to defy Sir Geoffrey Lloyd's demands for temperance and even less reason not to exercise such methods on his three Yankee prisoners of war.

They were a bedraggled, sorry-looking lot. With such ill-bred rabble to represent them, he wondered how the colonies could ever expect to win a war they were stupid enough to start in the first place. One, a salty old bloke with steady gray eyes and the honest face of a fisherman, had proved his Yankee idiocy by spitting in Crichton's face; now he was getting a taste of the lash he'd not soon forget. The second prisoner, also picked up from the wreckage of the privateer *Proud Mistress,* was a youth named Jake who wasn't old enough to put a razor to his fresh face. Even at such a tender age the boy refused to divulge any information about Captain Merrick, sobbing brokenly, even under Crichton's most *persuasive* methods, and insisting he didn't know a thing about him nor the schooner that had been wreaking such havoc upon British shipping. . . .

And the third—semiconscious, blinded by an exploding splinter, and lying slumped against the bulkhead in Crichton's fine cabin—was no help at all.

Captain Matthew Ashton.

No help at all, Crichton thought, with a cold grin . . . *yet.*

With controlled savagery, he drew back and kicked the blind man hard in the ribs. The Yankee captain doubled up in agony, his face paling beneath a spray of freckles that, coupled with his unruly shock of red hair and naked, owlish eyes, made him look boyish and defenseless.

Hard to belive this was the same man who'd fought his *Proud Mistress* with such doughty valor.

Crichton kicked him again.

"So, the brave Captain Ashton shows the same loyalty to his friends as he does his *country,* eh?" Crichton's milky eyes hardened, emphasizing their red-tinged lids and fair lashes, and his mouth tightened in a smile thinner than prison gruel. His blue uniform was freshly brushed, his shoes shone, his epaulets gleamed on his blocky shoulders, and the gold braid on his hat was almost decadent— yet his fine image was shamefully wasted on his blinded captive. But the Yankee's mind was lucid enough, and Crichton made full use of that fact.

"What, no answer, Captain Ashton? Do you think your silence will save you? Do you think it will save *Merrick* when I catch up to him?" He gave a short, brittle laugh. "The fox can only outrun the hounds for so long, you know. Sooner or later that fox, clever as he may be, will have to come out of his lair—and when he does, I'll be waiting for him."

"You're . . . wasting your time. . . . You'll never catch . . . that schooner. . . ."

Crichton's laughter was evil, awful and humorless. Chills danced up Matt's bruised spine, but he was in too much pain to bring on more by shuddering. Instead, he simply lay there in his own private darkness, gritting his teeth to steady himself as the laughter faded and the silky voice flowed over him like acid.

"Do you think me foolish enough to waste my time even trying? That schooner has given me ample demonstration of her speed. One does not try to outfly a *kestrel,* my good captain. But a kestrel can be netted—*and a fox can be shot.*"

"Captain Merrick is no fool."

"Precisely. He's a former officer of His Majesty's Royal Navy, and our navy does not breed *fools,* Ashton. Nor does it allow them to command our ships." Matt heard liquid sloshing into a glass, and pictured those glacier-cold eyes staring down at him as Crichton sipped his wine.

"Merrick entered the navy as a midshipman at age twelve, quickly proving himself and passing his lieutenant's exam at age seventeen. By his twentieth year he was commanding his first ship, by his twenty-third, a forty-four gun frigate, and by his twenty-eighth, was put in charge of Sir Geoffrey Lloyd's fleet as flag captain, a post that he deserted not a month after his appointment to it. Shortly thereafter he showed up in the service of the rebels, commanding a privateer named *Annabel*. A familiar ship to you, eh, Captain Ashton?''

Matt's lips thinned, and Crichton kicked him again.

"I asked you a question!''

"The devil take you,'' Matt wheezed, clutching his ribs.

Another kick, and the breath roared between his clenched teeth with a harsh whistle. Tiring of the game, Crichton went on, his voice calm and controlled. "In any case, there were those of us who felt that young Merrick's appointment to such a high post was politically based and largely undeserved—a favor on Sir Geoffrey's part. The old windbag was close friends with Merrick's father, you see. And Sir Trevor Merrick was an admiral himself, an autocratic old fire-breather with a stiff upper lip, but well respected and a particular favorite of the king. He moved in high places and intended his mongrel son to do the same. Of course, there are those who insist it was Brendan's own abilities that snared him the post of flag captain, but you know something, Ashton? I don't think so. 'Twas the influence of his sire and the luck of that damned Irish hussy he married, luck that Brendan seems to have inherited, God rot his bloody soul.'' A glass slammed down on a hard surface, and Matt heard the bitterness in Crichton's voice. "And that's all it was, Ashton. Luck. *I* should've had that position. *I* should've been promoted, not Merrick. Dammit, *I deserved it!*''

Matt looked blindly up toward that tight, hate-filled voice. "It seems that you are wrong after all, *sir,*'' he said, with a trace of his old fire.

"Wrong about what?''

"Wrong about your navy employing fools to command their ships. I think I'm speaking to one right now. You did say you're a captain, didn't you?'' He waited for another kick, but his brazen words seemed to have sent his tormenter into shock. "And furthermore, any man who thinks that Captain Merrick obtained recognition simply by being born the son of a British admiral—and not by his own intelligence, compassion, courage, and charisma, traits that I've yet to see reflected in *you*—is not only a fool, but a bleeding idiot besides."

"You dare insult me so?"

"I'll dare anything I damn well please, you treacherous whelp of a she-bitch." Matt glared sightlessly up toward that flat, emotionless voice, but inside he winced, waiting for another kick. It wasn't the blow itself he feared, nor even the pain; it was the fact that he couldn't see it coming, and couldn't see his enemy.

And perhaps that was best, for his last memory of the British captain was very clear indeed: that of Crichton standing on the decks of this frigate moments before she'd reduced *Proud Mistress* to a floundering wreckage. One of the balls had hit a gun, cut down its crew, and the exploding fragments of metal and wood had struck him in the face and left him in a world darker than the hide of Mira's black stallion.

Captain Richard Crichton. Arrogant and stout-shouldered, with a mouth hewn from stone and stamped with cruelty. Thatch-colored hair and a purposeful jaw. Crichton had been smiling as that last broadside had done *Mistress* in, and Matt didn't have to look upon that fair and emotionless face to know that he was smiling now. The thought chilled him, and again he fought a shudder. Not for himself. Not for whatever remained of his crew.

But for Brendan.

Crichton chose to ignore his last remark. "No, Ashton, I'm not a fool, nor am I an idiot. I'll prove that to you soon enough, when I shoot myself a fine fox and bring him home for my admiral to skin. And as for the schooner, she's the swiftest thing afloat for her size. Nothing but teeth and wings and claws. A most singular vessel, you'll agree, which is precisely the reason my admiral, and his peers back in London, want her. To study, to examine, to use her as a model so that our navy may improve upon its own designs." Matt heard the deck creak as Crichton moved slowly across the cabin, then back again. "And you must agree, 'tis only right that she ends up in our hands. I told you I'm no fool, Ashton—I know who designed her. And given that fact, I do believe that makes her *British* property. . . ."

Pain was shooting through Matt's ribs, sharp, lancing pain that made it hard to breathe, let alone talk. He clamped his jaws shut and ground his back teeth together to keep from moaning, and said nothing.

"No, the fox must be outsmarted," Crichton continued, as matter-of-factly as if he were moving pieces around on a chess board. "Outwitted. And you, Captain, are the one who's going to help me draw him out."

Gasping, Matt raised his head and stared sightlessly into the blackness. "Never, you son of a bitch . . . Nev—"

This time the kick did come.

Savagely Crichton drove his boot into Matt's temple and sent him into senseless oblivion. *Bloody rebel,* he thought, and drew back to kick him again. But at that moment Myles, his trusty first lieutenant, entered. There was a smile on his weasely face and his beady eyes were glinting.

"I delivered that missive to the Tory you asked me to find." Myles stepped over the sprawled, senseless body as though it carried the plague. "He'll see that it reaches Merrick, one way or another."

"Good." Crichton sipped his wine and stared disdainfully, then thoughtfully, down at the unconscious Yankee lying at his feet. Useless, he thought angrily. No help at all. *But he would be.*

He smiled thinly and met Myles's expectant gaze. "Douse our good captain with water—salt water, please, as it tends to *sting* more and I don't want to waste our fresh water on such vermin—and when he awakens, haul him up on deck. Blinded he may be, but he's not deaf. I want him to hear the screams of his men when I wring out of them what he won't reveal."

"And that is?"

"Every last, bloody detail of that schooner. Ashton's father built her, and Ashton knows more than he's telling me. I want to know precisely what I'm up against, Myles."

Myles smiled, drawing his lips back from his sharp teeth.

Crichton took another sip of his wine and prodded the lolling, red-haired head with the toe of his boot. "And when you get him up there, string him up to the grating. Young Midshipman Rothfield shows promise of making a fine officer someday. I should like him to witness the proper technique of stripping the flesh from a man's back."

"Yes, sir," Myles said, eagerly.

"Oh, and Myles?"

The lieutenant turned.

"Mind that you haul an extra bucket of that seawater up and save it for *after* the lashing. The good captain's back will probably need to be . . . washed." He returned Myles's sly grin. "These Yankees are a stubborn lot, you know. I have a feeling that if the boatswain's cat doesn't do this one in, the saltwater might. . . ."

Myles gave a slow, measured salute, thinking that if he hauled not one but several buckets up, his captain would be even more pleased. "As you wish, sir."

And as his faithful hound went off to do his bidding, the hunt master, still sipping his wine, looked down at his captive and smiled.

Tomorrow the scent would be laid.

Tomorrow the fox would sniff the wind.

Tomorrow the fox would run—and tomorrow the fox would be shot.

Eveleen was in the middle of packing her bags when Mira came in.

"What are you doing?"

Eveleen put down the skirt she'd been folding and looked down at her feet. Misery cloaked her features; not only had she lost her beloved Matthew, but now her adopted family as well. With Mira and her father so bitter toward Brendan, there was no way she could expect to stay here in the Ashton house. "I'm packing," she whispered, reaching for a plate that stood beside her bed. On it was a stack of cookies.

"Why?"

Eveleen looked up, her eyes tragic and filled with tears.

Mira, usually so perky and full of spunk, seemed no better; her features were pale and drawn, and there was a pinched look about her mouth. The two girls looked at each other for a long moment; then Eveleen put down the cookies, and they flew into each other's arms, hugging each other and crying bitterly.

"You can't leave, Eveleen," Mira sobbed into the other girl's hair. She clutched her desperately, unwilling to let her go. "You just can't!"

"But I'm not welcome here any longer."

"That's not true; you'll always be welcome here! You're the only real friend I've ever had, and I need you. Christ, Eveleen, we need each *other!*"

Eveleen drew back, and looked into Mira's tortured features. Her fingers were cold and bloodless, and in her eyes was something Eveleen had never seen before—terror. She knew that Mira was telling the truth, for she'd never been squeamish about her crippled hand, had never made an issue out of it nor allowed her to use it as an excuse to be miserable and full of self-pity. Mira had also taught her she didn't need food to appease the pain, a lesson that Eveleen, in her misery, was having a hard time remembering. Mira needed her as much as she needed Mira— but nevertheless, she didn't feel that she should stay in the Ashton house. "But I have to leave, don't you see? You all believe the worst of Brendan and—"

"I don't know *what* I believe anymore!" Mira sat down on the bed and dug the heels of her hands into her eyes. Then she looked up, the tears spiking her lashes and spilling down her cheeks. "Please don't leave me, Eveleen. I'm begging you. *Please . . .*"

Eveleen wiped her eyes with the back of her hand and stared miserably at her bag, her lower lip trembling with the effort it took to contain her own sobs.

"Eveleen, *please?* Can't you understand, I *need you. . . .*"

Mira reached for the bag and shook the contents out upon the bed.

Then she hurled the bag against the wall.

Eveleen made no move to stop her. "I need you, too,

Mira," she whispered. They hugged each other again, their friendship the only shield they had against the pain.

Reverting back to her old ways and burying the pain of the handsome Captain Ashton's death beneath apple pies, Indian pudding, tarts, scones, and any other confection she could get her hands on, Eveleen found the house strangely silent. Ephraim spent his days—and nights—locked in his library with his grief, a bottle, and a painting of his dead wife.

Mira had gone into an unreachable depression. Eveleen's riding lessons stopped, and the field that was Miss Mira Ashton's School of Fine Horsemanship grew thick and lush with spring grasses that heard only the footfalls of cats traveling on the silent paws of hunters. Inside the big Georgian the furniture grew dusty, the mourners came and went, and the rooms echoed with emptiness. Mira spent her days locked in the stable, and Ephraim spent his locked in the library, both emerging only to scream and shout at each other. At last, dejection overwhelmed them both. The fighting stopped. The neighbors across the street could sleep again. Abigail, miserable with grief, stopped cooking, and Mira started. But nobody ate.

And still the clocks remained unwound.

A week after Matt's funeral, Eveleen, lying awake in her bed with a piece of molasses cake balanced on her chest and crumbs sprinkling the sheets, heard Mira's muffled weeping coming from the big, empty room that had been Captain Ashton's. Putting aside the cake—and her own misery—she'd scooped up the gray cat from her bed and silently deposited it just inside the door, hoping that the little creature could ease Mira's suffering where her own efforts had failed.

Hoping for a miracle, she'd gone back to her room to wait for that wretched sobbing to stop.

It hadn't.

Hours later, Eveleen had finally crawled out of bed, gone to the window, folded both good hand and crippled one beneath her fleshy chin as she knelt in the moonlight—and prayed with all her heart for Brendan to come back from the sea to which he'd retreated.

* * *

Ships were the best link to the world, for they brought news of wars across the ocean, letters from loved ones, and as much gossip as could be digested. Realizing this, Richard Crichton made full use of the resources he had at hand. After making some inquiries, he learned that *Kestrel* was holed up in the privateering port of Salem; it was a small matter of getting his note to Brendan via the services of a fishing boat's captain, a man with suspected, but not confirmed, Loyalist tendencies.

Almost as if in answer to her prayers, Liam and Dalby showed up at the Ashton house with Crichton's note several days after Eveleen had knelt at her window. Brendan had refused to go to Newburyport, but under the pretense that he'd left his fiddle at Wolfe Tavern, Liam had managed to coerce his captain into bringing *Kestrel* into port.

Ephraim, who would've been furious had he known that *Kestrel*'s men were in his house, was drinking the afternoon away at Wolfe Tavern when Liam and Dalby arrived. But the big lieutenant had not come here to talk to the crusty old shipbuilder.

He'd come to talk to Mira. To beg her, if he had to, to make one last cruise aboard *Kestrel* so she could see for herself that Brendan was innocent.

Eveleen showed them into the parlor, read the note, discounted its contents as nothing but a ploy on Crichton's part to draw out her brother, and told Liam that Mira was not at home, but out riding the barren beaches of Plum Island, which was about *all* she'd been doing lately.

"I'll wait f'r th' lassie, then," Liam vowed, adding that he'd stay here all day if he had to—even if he had to end up *dragging* Mira back aboard *Kestrel* in the guise of Mr. Starr.

"Why do you need her so badly, anyhow?" Eveleen asked, suspicious.

Liam eased his great body down onto the sofa. "Because we're desperate," he said, spreading his hands. "Y'r broth'r's hurtin', lassie. He's no' t'imself. An' if he expects t' go aft'r Crichton, an' deal with him withou' gettin' himself killed in th' process, he has t' get his head on straight. An' Miss Mira's love is th' only thing t' do it."

Eveleen reached down, found her Irish temper, and let it take over. "What do you mean, Brendan's going after Crichton?" She commanded the Ashtons' parlor like a ruffled queen, her cloud of gold hair swirling about her shoulders, her eyes flashing, and a plate of gingerbread waiting on the tea table before her. "That boneheaded idiot! I wish he'd just straighten out Mira Ashton, not go chasing after Crichton! Doesn't he realize there's probably not a bit of truth to this note? Damn it all, sometimes I'd just like to strangle him!"

Liam spread his hands helplessly, grinned his great beamy grin, and glanced at Dalby, who sat in a fine Queen Anne style-chair with his hand, as usual, clamped over his gut. A piece of half-eaten gingerbread was set before him.

"Well, what d'ye think, Dalb?" Liam asked, folding his big arms across his chest.

Dalby eyed the gingerbread distrustfully. "I think, Liam, that there's something in that gingerbread that's upset my stomach."

"Nonsense, Miss Mira made it herself," said Liam, who'd never eaten at the Ashtons' house before. "F'rget abou' t'yer gut f'r once, would ye, Dalb? 'Tis a serious matter."

"So is my stomach. *And* my head, which is beginning to ache. I think I'm coming down with something. And I don't think it's a spring cold this time, Liam. I think it's something far worse—"

"Dalby, if ye don't shut up abou' t'yer ailments, I'm goin' t' remove both yer bloody gut an' yer head an' then we won't 'ave t' be hearin' ye complainin' about either one o' em!" His blue eyes narrowed as the little seaman pouted, fingering a strange ornament buried in the lacings of his shirt. "An' what th' bleedin' hell is tha' t'ye're wearin' around yer neck? Quartz?"

"A crystal," Dalby said sullenly. "Rama said it'll bring me good luck."

Liam screwed up his face. *"What?"*

"Good luck. I brought it because I think we could all use some right now," Dalby said, thinking of his captain's disgrace, *Kestrel*'s fall from favor, and the spunky little

Mira Ashton, whose skills at *Freedom* would be sorely missed if *Kestrel* made another cruise without her. And if Brendan went to hunt down Crichton without his most capable gunner, he'd be asking for suicide. They all would.

After all, the captain hadn't been himself these past weeks. . . .

Liam made a snort of disgust. "I want ye t' stop listenin' t' that Easterner, Dalby! He's already made a disciple out o' Fergus; th' last thing we need is f'r him t' be makin' one out o' you!"

"But, Liam, it makes sense—Fergus told me just today that the reason my stomach always hurts is because I was shot in the belly in a former life—"

Liam lunged from his chair, his hands outstretched and going for Dalby's scrawny neck.

"Gentlemen." Eveleen raised her haughty head and glared at the two of them. "As much as I despise the fact that Brendan is going after Crichton, I suppose it's inevitable. Therefore, I think that we should all be considering what *Richard Crichton* will be in his next life after my brother catches up to him," she said, eyes flashing.

"Yer broth'r ain't goin' t' catch up t' him if he doesn't get his head on straight an' stop hidin' from th' lassie."

"That's for sure," Eveleen declared, taking a bite of her gingerbread with regal elegance and just as quickly choking it out into her napkin.

"Well, ye know yer broth'r," Liam said, frowning in puzzlement as she wrapped up the gingerbread in her napkin and put it down, her unmaimed hand, like Dalby's, going to her stomach. "Brendan never does anythin' halfheartedly. An' when it comes t' lovin' a woman, he does it with every shred o' his soul, his heart, his bein'. As he does with *Kestrel.*" His voice grew hard. "As he did with Julia."

The silence hung heavily between them.

"As he's done with Mira," Eveleen said quietly.

The silence deepened. Liam was right; not only did *Kestrel* need the skills of her best gunner if she was going to face HMS *Viper*, but her captain needed the love of Mira Ashton if he expected to be on his toes when it came to dealing with Crichton's treachery. It didn't matter if

Mira revealed herself as Mr. Starr or not; what mattered was that she forgave Brendan as *Mira*.

And if she didn't see or interact with Brendan, that just wouldn't happen.

Eveleen thought of her brother's pain when the people of Newburyport had turned against him at Matt's funeral. Not only had they turned against him—the man they'd hailed as their new hero—but also against the magnificent schooner they'd built with their own hands, sent off with their blessings and prayers, and welcomed back as a heroine, then a traitor. Pride had become shame. Admiration, disgust. No one in town mentioned the schooner's name; indeed, they went to great lengths *not* to. She was an embarrassment. She was evil. She was anathema.

And, as Liam, Dalby, and everyone else had so vehemently declared, she was innocent.

It wasn't fair.

As much as she hated the ship for the attention Brendan lavished on it, Eveleen loved her brother too much to allow him to suffer such undeserved treatment. She was not alone in her defense of him; *Kestrel*'s faithful core crew of Irishmen was so incensed that the lot of them were planning to storm Wolfe Tavern with balled fists and fury on the morrow if apologies were not made to their captain.

God help the town if *that* happened.

But there was still Crichton to be dealt with. Always Crichton, Eveleen thought bitterly. And who more capable of doing it than her own beloved brother? No Yankee knew Crichton as Brendan did. No American knew the British navy as he did. And no ship could run down *Viper* as *Kestrel* could.

Crichton must be dealt with.

And Mira Ashton must be in place on *Freedom,* must be made to believe the truth, must find it in her hot little heart to forgive Brendan so he could get his damned head on straight and get on with the business that had to be done.

In Liam's hand was a missive, dirty and crumpled and stained from being passed through so many hands during its journey here from *Viper*.

A missive from Crichton, which some might've said was

a ransom note—for a Yankee captain who was not dead at all—and an invitation for the Captain from Connacht to come and get him.

Chapter 24

Crichton was right. The British Royal Navy didn't breed fools.

And it had bred Captain Brendan Jay Merrick.

The wily half-Irishman was not about to put much hope in his nemesis's claim that Matt was alive, nor was he rash enough to endanger his ship and crew by honoring Crichton's request to meet at a time scheduled by the Englishman at a small island off Machias, that lonely Maine outpost where the first naval engagement between Britain and her rebellious colonies had, ironically, taken place several years before.

If anyone was a fool, it was Crichton for believing that he would.

No, Brendan had shaken the dust of Newburyport from his shoes, buried his heartache over Mira Ashton beneath a vow to avenge her brother's death, and gathering his surly Irish crew, had let the tide carry *Kestrel* downriver and into the Atlantic. With a spring southerly filling her sails, she'd leapt through racing seas with the spray hissing and breaking high over her beakhead, arriving silently in the waters off Machias a full day and a half before Crichton's scheduled meeting with him.

Such a premature arrival was no coincidence, for Brendan was taking no chances and had no intention of letting himself be drawn into a trap. He'd kept track of Crichton's whereabouts for a good eight and three-quarter hours by the time he made his move. With Mr. Starr perched on the topgallant yard, silhouetted against the clouds and

ready to call the alarm should *Viper,* anchored unsuspect-
ingly in the bay on the other side of the island, notice
them, he'd again relied on the element of surprise. And
surprise had been a mild word to describe the reaction of
the frazzled-looking British landing party as they came
trudging out of the woods where they'd been foraging for
fresh water and seen the rakish schooner sweeping around
the island's lee.

Astonishment and awe were more like it. And terror,
for *Kestrel* had effectively cut off their escape route to the
frigate.

They looked at the schooner's yawning gunports, and
their faces went white. A young lieutenant screamed and
pointed. Seamen dropped their water casks and fled back
into the woods. But Mira was oblivious to their terror, to
Brendan's triumphant grin, to the fact that she was sitting
atop a hard-braced yard some eighty feet or so above a
rolling deck as comfortably as though it were Rigel's back
beneath her trouser-clad rump.

For there, standing on the beach and surrounded by a
group of red-coated marines, were Jake Pillsbury and old
Hezekiah Simmons, friends of hers since she'd been old
enough to know how to coil a line.

She swayed and almost fell off her comfortable perch.

They had been part of *Mistress*'s crew—a crew that had
supposedly perished.

Their torn, soot-stained shirts were blackened with
blood, their faces gaunt and unshaven, their eyes haunted.
Yet when they looked up and saw *Kestrel* sweeping around
the headland with the spray bursting from her bows and
the sea creaming beneath her keel, the look in their eyes
was worth every hour Mira had stayed up there in the
biting wind, every doubt she'd had about letting Liam talk
her into coming aboard *Kestrel* once again. She leaned her
face against the mast and let the tears roll down her cheeks.
And as her chest heaved in a single sob of relief, of hope
that her brother might also live, she saw Brendan standing
on the deck far, far below.

His slim form blurred behind her tears. To Jake and
Hezekiah, he must look like a hero. At the moment he
sure looked like one to her, splendid and achingly hand-

some in a tailored blue coat that spanned his elegant shoulders and showed off his crimson waistcoat with its rows of gold buttons glittering in the sun. His hair was neatly queued with a black bow and hung beneath the shadow of his jaunty tricorn, his stock was pristine and white. And he was swinging his speaking trumpet by a lanyard looped around his wrist, grinning rakishly, and taking it all in with an air of humble triumph that made her tears of relief come even faster.

Single-handedly he was bringing his little schooner to face the might of one of the king's frigates, and the hatred of a man who, Liam insisted, was bent on killing him. *Oh God*, she thought, feeling something huge and painful welling up in her chest. *Was I wrong about him? Did I misjudge him after all?* Was he truly innocent, as his crew, and even Eveleen, so vehemently proclaimed? Her throat constricted, her chest tightened. *Was he?*

She drove her hand into her pocket and touched Matt's spectacles. She'd kept them close since finding them beside her bed that awful, ugly night. Now they were no longer cold, but warm with the heat of her body.

"Oh, Brendan . . ." she murmured. And then, *oh, Matt*. She squeezed her eyes hut. "Oh, Matt, dare I *hope* that you're alive, too?"

But Brendan, despite appearances, was far from relaxed or triumphant as *Kestrel* glided through the shallows with confident majesty, folded her wings, and turned her lofty nose into the wind. He wore a grin, yes—but beneath it his jaw was clenched, his throat dry, his nerves shroud-tight. For bringing up the rear of the landing party was Lieutenant Andrew Myles, whose weasely face Brendan remembered, and cared not to, from his sailing days with these very men—and Crichton himself.

Something twisted in his gut, and he recognized it for what it was. Fear.

He put the speaking trumpet to his lips to hide his strained grin. "Ahoy, Captain Crichton! Fine day to be at sea, isn't it? I'm surprised that you're not!"

The Englishman looked up. And then he saw *Kestrel* perched in her reflection, her great sails luffing in the wind, her gunports all open, and every one of her four-pounders run out and staring at him. His jaw hardened to iron and his eyes went flinty.

"Please forgive me for being so early for our *meeting*, Crichton, but I do believe you denied me the opportunity to agree to a time that was convenient for *me!*"

"Damn you, Merrick!" Whirling, Crichton grabbed the two Yankees and drove a pistol into the ribs of young Jake.

The boy managed to scream, "Captain Merrick! You gotta help us! He's got Cap—" before Crichton cuffed him sharply across the face.

"Shear off, Merrick! You'll not make a mockery of me again!"

"God Almighty," said Liam, standing faithfully beside his captain and gripping the rail. "Now what, Brendan?"

Brendan stared at the drama unfolding on the beach. He took a deep, steadying breath, and when he spoke, his voice was quiet. "Liam, please call Mr. Starr down and put him on the swivel at the after rail."

He felt his chest knotting, as though the old gunshot wound itself were aching, and unconsciously pressed his fingers to the scar hidden beneath his clothing. There was Crichton, angry, desperate, and yes, *afraid.* One blast from *Kestrel's* guns and the nightmares would end. One blast and the evil in those translucent, milky eyes would be no more. He had Crichton right where he wanted him, right where he'd wanted him for the past four years, and his men were as eager as *Kestrel* herself to avenge Matthew Ashton, his crew, and the brig he'd been so proud of.

But Brendan could not fire. Not only would that one blast kill Crichton, it would kill the Yankees, too—and Crichton knew it as well as he did. Stabbing his pistol into Jake's side, Crichton yanked him close and faced Brendan across the short gulf of breaking waves. "Bring that ship in any closer and this brat's a dead one, Merrick! Shear off now or I'll execute him where he stands!"

"He won't do it." Liam's knuckles were white, his huge hands gripping the rail. "He's bluffin', Brendan! Th' lad's his insurance against us!"

But Brendan wasn't so sure. "Faith," he muttered, all but slamming the speaking trumpet against his lips. He felt the eyes of his crew weighing heavily on him, the restless surge of *Kestrel* beneath his feet. "Crichton! How about discussing this like gentlemen? Come aboard my schooner and we shall do so. You'd like to see her up close, wouldn't you?" He walked to the rail and stood there, elegant shoulders thrown back and the wind lifting his coattails, his queue, the lace at his wrist. "Well, here's your chance!"

High above him, Mira shut her eyes and leaned heavily against the foremast. Wind sang in her ears, but her heart was hammering so loudly, she was aware of nothing else. She wondered if she was going to faint. If she did, they'd be scraping her off the deck with a shovel.

But the controlled rage in the British captain's voice steadied her. This was the man who'd commanded the frigate that Brendan had tricked onto the bars at the river's mouth last summer. This was the man who seemed determined to avenge that humiliation. This was the man who, Liam had told her, had crippled Eveleen—and *this was the man who'd killed her brother.* And seeing the soulless mind behind those pale and milky eyes, the cruel cast to the lips, she realized, with dawning horror, that if he got his hands on Brendan, he'd show him no mercy, for she'd seen snakes with more feeling in their stares. Less poison in their bites.

Yet Brendan was determined to face Crichton with nothing but his wits, his men, and the little *Kestrel.*

In that moment, Mira knew for sure that she *had* misjudged him.

The knowledge, bare and raw and awful, slammed her between the shoulders and almost sent her tumbling down from the yard on which she sat. She dug her fist against her mouth. Had her faith in Brendan been so shallow—or, more appropriately, her jealousy of *Kestrel* so intense— that she'd actually *believed* what the rest of Newburyport had? That the little schooner had come out of her engagement with Crichton's ship unscathed because Brendan didn't want her to get marked up by an enemy's guns?

A sob caught in her throat and she gripped a line to keep from falling.

"Oh, dear God, Brendan . . . forgive me. . . .

"I'll not bargain with the likes of you, Merrick!"

Crichton was shouting. "Nor will I come aboard that schooner till *my* flag streams from her gaff! Do you hear me, Merrick? Now, haul off or so help me God, this boy's death will be on your conscience!"

Brendan's resolute stance never wavered, though he was swinging the speaking trumpet around his wrist a bit faster. Again he brought the instrument up. "Now, Crichton—"

"I said I won't bargain! Shear off, *now,* Merrick!"

Brendan felt dampness between his shoulders. His mouth was so dry, he could barely speak. Gravely he turned to Liam. "Do as he says."

"By the count of three!" Crichton shouted.

Young Jake began to sob.

"Now, Liam," Brendan said tensely.

"But, Cap'n, 'twill take more'n three seconds just t'—"

"I said do it!"

Too late. A shot rang out in the tense stillness. Birds rose shrieking from the trees, and a great cry of horror went up from *Kestrel's* deck as the boy collapsed at Crichton's feet, his young body twitching once, twice, before going still.

Silence. Someone bit back a sob. Brendan shut his eyes, and Liam saw his lips moving, as though in prayer.

"Brendan—"

"Go ahead, Merrick!" Crichton grabbed Hezekiah, drew another pistol, and shoved it against the seaman's temple. Tears streamed down the old man's leathery cheeks as he stared at the dead boy, and in his eyes was the quiet acceptance of a man with no hope. "Stay here as long as you like! This one's next, and then it'll be Ashton!"

No one except Abadiah Bobbs, climbing the rigging, heard Mr. Starr's cry from high above.

Brendan raised the speaking trumpet, slowly, as though it were of great weight. He was no longer swinging it. His eyes were hard, his elegant shoulders rigid with fury. "I don't believe you have Ashton any more than you believe I'll be content to let the matter rest here! I'll haul off, but only to spare the life of Mr. Simmons. Yours, Crichton, *I will not spare* when next we meet!" Only Liam, standing beside him, saw his captain's hand trembling as he brought his speaking trumpet down, the savage anger with which he thrust it into his pocket to hide its shaking from his crew.

"Mr. Wilbur!" he called loudly, so that Crichton could hear him. "Up jibs and main! Trim for close haul on the starboard tack!"

"I'll kill him, Brendan," Liam swore, slamming his meaty fist into his palm. "By God an' Mary, I'll see him in th' hell where he b'longs—"

"Easy, Liam."

Onshore, a triumphant Crichton breathed a sigh of relief, watching with awed fascination as sails blossomed on the schooner's nose and her great mainsail began to rise. She turned gracefully away, her sleek underside showing and her guns pointing toward the clouds as she heeled. She was beautiful. Magnificent. Crichton's hands grew sweaty on the pistol and his heart hammered in his chest. Sweat broke out beneath his arms and he stared at her as a starving man would a wedding feast. And then he remembered Sir Geoffrey's promise of flag rank, and saw that promise fading to dust as the schooner drew away. . . .

"Merrick!"

Another second and the breeze would push her around the headland, send her out of reach—

"Merrick!"

Her captain turned, every inch the capable commander he'd been four years ago, except now the stamp of experience had replaced the reckless optimism of youth. No longer the mirth in those Irish eyes; now nothing but the steely determination and hard anger of a man who'd been pushed too far.

A man who would seek revenge.

Crichton cupped his hands around his mouth. "I've changed my mind! I'll make a deal with you, Merrick, on *my* terms! You don't believe I have Ashton? Let me show you aboard *my* ship and I'll prove to you that I do!"

Brendan raised an elegant hand, as though to control the schooner's moves, and her crew, in the midst of hauling the jib sheet over, paused.

"Don't listen to him, Brendan!" Liam warned, desperately gripping his captain's sleeve.

Challenge burned in Crichton's milky eyes. Triumph. "Come aboard *Viper* at eight bells and speak with Ashton yourself! He's been asking about you! And after you've seen that he still lives, I'll return him in exchange for one of your own. A prisoner of war for a prisoner of war, Merrick!"

"Brendan, *don't*" Liam cried, for he knew who Crichton wanted.

High above their heads, Abadiah was fighting with Mr. Starr and trying to hold onto the lad and keep him from scurrying down the rigging. But Brendan was oblivious to the struggle so far above. He thought of the girl he loved back in Newburyport. The girl who believed the worst of him, the girl who had turned her heart against him. He looked at Crichton, standing there on the beach with a pistol against a Yankee's head and a dead boy at his feet, and saw the only way to win that heart back.

What did he have to lose, besides his life? A life that would be meaningless without Mira Ashton. . . .

He turned back to the rail. Even *Kestrel* seemed to have guessed his intent; now, she protested violently, trying to take the wind in her teeth and run with it before he could respond to Crichton's invitation.

"Your decision, Merrick!"

Kestrel was moving farther away, as though on her own.

Brendan stared hard into those translucent eyes. Then he grinned and turned jauntily to his lieutenant, his hands steady now as he unbuckled his sword belt, removed his pistols, and handed them to his horrified friend. "You always wanted a ship of your own, Liam," he joked. "Well, here you go. Take good care of her for me."

"Brendan, I beg o' ye, *don't do it!*"

"She's a bit spirited with the wind across the beam. Mind you don't set the topgallants when it shifts or she'll give you a devil of a time—"

"*Brendan, don't!*"

"Jesus," someone muttered.

"What is he, insane?!"

Forward, Dalby collapsed in a dead faint.

But *Kestrel*'s captain was already striding past the helm, past his horrified crew, past the guns that could've sent

Crichton to the hell where he belonged. Beneath the shadow of the schooner's great mainsail, he paused. "Ready the launch, and dress it out with full ceremony. I'm going across to the frigate."

A silence like the tomb fell over the ship.

Woodenly the men did as they were asked. Not because they wanted to, but because their captain commanded it.

Mira felt mad, desperate hysteria rise up in a scream in her throat, but again, Abadiah gripped her arm. "Let him go, Mira!" he said hoarsely. "The man has his pride! You go down there and reveal yourself, you'll strip him of the last shreds of it!"

They watched as the boat was swung over the rail, lowered to the skipping waves.

Sickened, Liam slammed below and, in the privacy of his cabin, buried his face in his great, hamlike hands while the tears leaked between his fingers. High aloft, Mira turned her cheek into the sunlit wood of the mast and cried bitter tears of helpless agony.

In the depths of her keel, in the song the wind made as it whined mournfully through her shrouds, in her own proud and lovely heart, *Kestrel* wept, too.

And many miles away, the great Willard clock in the Ashton's front hall stood silent.

Chapter 25

What *Kestrel*'s anguished crew saw as their captain left the schooner's deck was a tall and handsome man, laughing and confident and unafraid, who made a joke or two as he walked to the gunwales, and stopped there—briefly—to doff his hat to them, the ship, and her second-in-command for what all of them knew to be the last time. He was going to his death, they said, and Lieutenant Doherty had ranted and raved in pure Irish fervor, begging him not to trade himself for Captain Ashton and put himself at Crichton's mercy. Dalby, huddled in the bows and clutching his chest, sobbed openly; Fergus McDermott waved crystals around and profoundly proclaimed that when the captain returned, it would be in a different life form; *Kestrel*'s marines grouped around the rail as though determined not to let him pass; and *Kestrel* herself bucked and writhed on the choppy seas, fighting John Keefe's steady hand as he forced her closer and closer to where *Viper* stood anchored in mist a scant mile away.

Mira, standing miserably on deck with a chicken that had been destined for the soup pot perched on her shoulder, stroked the rooster's sleek, irridescent feathers and bit back a sob as Brendan turned his back on them and resigned himself to his fate. *Stop him!* her mind screamed. *To hell with his damned pride! Stop him now, before it's too late!* She started to remove her hat and reveal her identity; she took a step forward, the tears rolling down her face—and caught Abadiah's eye. Her friend was right. Brendan had his pride. If she stopped him, she'd not only make him look like a coward in front of Crichton, she'd deny him the chance to redeem *Kestrel*'s name in Newburyport's eyes.

It never occurred to her that he was going to redeem himself in *her* eyes.

And so she pushed her fist against her mouth and watched him climb down the Jacob's ladder, her heart breaking into a thousand pieces. He was sacrificing himself for the sake of a schooner. Yet she also knew that no one was more capable of rescuing Matt than this gallant captain with the elegant British shoulders and the winsome Irish grin. No one knew Crichton as he did. He was the only chance her brother had.

A group of seamen waited in the boat below, their faces long and solemn; as one, they took up the oars and rowed him away. From his silent crew. From his ship, still fighting the helmsman's hand. From *her*.

"God bless you," she whispered brokenly as she stood alone at the rail. The wind caught her braid and ruffled the thick tuft at the end. "Oh, Godspeed, Brendan. . . . I—" her voice caught on a sob *"—I love you."*

Liam joined her, his eyes hopeless and haunted as he watched the little boat carry his friend and captain farther and farther away. He reached out, silently took her hand, and gripped it so hard, she felt pain. She looked up and saw that his eyes were misty.

"Crichton'll kill him, ye know," he said quietly, his throat working and his gaze fastened on the departing boat. Brendan never looked back, and Mira swallowed hard to keep from crying. Oh, God, *why* hadn't she said the hell with Abadiah's advice and revealed her identity? *Why hadn't she apologized for her treatment of him?* Would she ever feel those sinewy arms around her again, look up into those laughing Irish eyes, hear sweet Gaelic endearments whispered in her ear . . .

Would she ever see him alive again?

"Oh, Liam . . ." She looked up at him, the tears magnifying her eyes in her pale face. "Does this schooner mean so much to him that he'd throw his life away for her sake?" Her fingers bit into his brawny arm. *"Does she?"*

Above, a yard creaked in protest. The deck moved restlessly beneath her feet. And the big Irishman squeezed her hand and stared once more at the now distant figure in the boat.

"No, lassie. You do." He turned then, looked down at her. *"He's doin' it f'r you."*

She bit down hard on her lower lip, squeezed her eyes shut, and turned her streaming face skyward. Her jaw trembled; her hands fisted at her sides. And then, unable to hold back the emotion any longer, Mira buried her face in her hands, propped her elbows on the rail, and sobbed brokenly.

Clouds rolled in from the east and swept toward the mainland on a freshening wind, promising rain by nightfall. *Kestrel,* restless and uneasy, began to drift toward the island as though she sought to dash herself against the shoals that girded it. With a curse, Liam ran aft, bawling orders to the boatswain. It didn't sound quite right to hear him doing it when it should've been Brendan.

"Hands aloft t' loose th' tops'ls! Right lively now, here comes th' wind! Hold her steady, Mr. Keefe!"

Kestrel moved uneasily, reluctantly answering her helm and fighting them every step of the way.

"I said *steady* John! God Almighty . . ."

Mira raised her head. She could almost sense the schooner staring after her creator and captain like a faithful dog, trying desperately to swing her bowsprit on the now distant boat. She heard John Keefe swearing, then Liam, as he pounded forward to take the tiller himself; she heard the angry slatting of lines above, the protesting creak of spars and masts. Head bowed, Mira gripped the smooth rail in trembling hands, and felt her soul, her own agony, traveling down through the fingers and merging with that of the schooner.

And for the first time, she felt a strange kinship with this other woman of Brendan's—this other woman of wood and canvas and wind. The tears stopped, and bewildered, she closed her eyes and allowed herself to feel the presence, the soul, of the ship around her.

His ship.

"*Kestrel*," she said softly, wiping a tear from her eye. "Oh, *Kestrel* . . ."

Above, the wind hummed, caught the topsails, and sang a poem through lines, shrouds, and stays.

"We can't let this happen," she whispered, slowly stroking the damp rail and staring off in the direction where Brendan had gone. "You see, he's . . . my captain, too. And I . . . I love him."

High overhead, the wind cried hoarsely through stays and shrouds.

But you deserted him. Were faithless when I remained true.

Mira froze.

He's going to his death. Not because of me. Because of you . . .

Because of you . . . You . . . You . . .

With a sob, Mira jerked her hands from the rail and fled below.

The welcome that *Viper* gave the Royal Navy's long-lost flag captain was a mocking one, and Brendan, emerging through the entry port and stepping onto her deck, knew it. Lines of spit-polish marines with immaculate red coats, blue-and-white-clad officers, pigtailed seamen; all watched him with awe, for he was something of a legend. The thought merely increased his uneasiness. Through long habit he doffed his hat to the quarterdeck, turned, and faced Captain Richard Crichton as his old enemy came forward, his hard smile triumphant, his eyes translucent with a strange light, his epaulets emphasizing the blockiness of his shoulders.

"Captain Merrick." Crichton hadn't changed much over the past several years; he was a bit broader through the waist, his harsh jaw was a bit more so perhaps, but that was all. "How *nice* of you to join us. I see you had the foresight not to bring your sword. Always such a clever one, weren't you, *sir?*" His eyes gleamed as he glanced off toward where *Kestrel*'s lights glimmered on the waves. "And noble, too. Imagine, sacrificing yourself to save a friend. My, my, what is this world coming to?" Again that hard grin. "Myles! Please see to it that my steward brings a pot of tea down to us in my cabin. . . . My former flag captain and I have *much* to discuss. . . ."

"And Captain Ashton?" Brendan said tightly, gripping his hands together behind his back.

"Oh, I'll have him brought up shortly. He's been a spot of trouble, you know. Typical Yankee. Hotheaded and quite difficult to handle. But I have my methods for dealing with recalcitrants, Captain Merrick. Just as I have them for dealing with *deserters*. . . ."

He let the threat hang on the wind. Brendan shivered and his nails bit into his palms, but he allowed Crichton to see only a fleeting grin.

"Myles? Please bring the Yankee up and send him back to the schooner. Both of them, in fact. The old one isn't worth the time it takes to restrain him. Captain Merrick and I shall be in my cabin. Please see that we're not disturbed."

With an elaborate motion, Crichton swept his hand before him. "After you, Captain." He gave a humorless grin, and when Brendan hesitated, drove his pistol brutally into his spine and shoved him forward. "Oh, and Myles? One last thing. Please, rig up a halter to the foreyard, would you? I feel that a lesson in the punishment of deserters is forthcoming."

Myles, ever protective of his captain's image in his admiral's eyes, protested, "But, sir? I thought Sir Geoffrey wanted Captain Merrick delivered to him alive. . . ."

"Who said anything about *killing* him, Myles? Please, do not put words in my mouth. Just do as I say, would you? You know I don't like to be kept waiting." He smiled his thin smile, eyes glinting beneath his carefully powdered fair hair, and turned to Brendan. "As *you* have kept me waiting for four long years, Merrick."

Wordlessly Brendan glanced a final time at *Kestrel,* anchored so close, yet so far. Desperate fear rose up in him. Then Crichton's pistol was jabbing into his spine again and they were moving. Down the hatchway. Down into the depths of the ship.

Down, he knew, into hell.

With a grim resolution, Liam had carried out his captain's last order and brought the schooner to windward of the anchored frigate, where her chances of escape were far greater than if she'd lain helplessly to leeward of the swift square-rigger. Not that Liam hand any intention of fleeing if it came down to a fight—and neither did *Kestrel,* who showed him her sweet side as she glided to a new anchorage a quarter mile away from the bigger ship and settled down for the night to await her fate.

But if a fight ensued, nothing short of Brendan's absent Irish luck would save them, for *Viper,* built of solid Sussex oak and boasting thirty-two guns on her deck and twin nines mounted in her forecastle as chasers, was the little schooner's superior in both stoutness and firepower.

But not spirit.

Twilight passed, and the sky glowed red on the horizon. Waves slapped endlessly against the hull, and timbers, masts and yards creaked as they settled for the night. Someone started a chanty to try and raise the gloomy spirits, but one sharp glance from Liam and the voice went dead.

And so the decks lay quiet, the glow from a pipe here and there the only spot of light in the gloom. Another hour passed. Two.

And still they waited.

The watch changed. Fergus carried a lantern aloft and hung it in the shrouds; Liam ordered the gunports silently opened and *Kestrel*'s little four-pounders run out. The schooner fidged uneasily. Then, from across the water, they heard sounds. Oars biting into waves, lifting, dripping, biting again. Grunts and curses and voices. As one, the crew ran to the rail and stared out into the darkness of the night.

"Boat ahoy!" Liam called, his voice wavering with apprehension.

"*Kestrel!*" came the reply. "Stand by for Captain Ashton!"

Mira collapsed against Abadiah Bobbs and would've fallen if not for his steadying hand beneath her elbow. "Matt," she cried, the night wind cooling her wet cheeks. "Matt!"

The Jacob's ladder was lowered amid frantic activity and excited voices. Muffled curses drifted up to them, and groans as someone wrestled with a great weight down there by the glow of a feeble lantern. Mira clapped her hand over her mouth to quell fearful sobs and tried to see.

"We're bringing him up!"

"Matt!" Desperately she tried to get past Liam's brawny restraining arm. "Let me go, dammit! He's my brother!"

"Stay back, lassie, till we get him aboard," the big Irishman said, not wanting Ashton's little sister to see the possible extent of Crichton's cruelties firsthand.

"But, Liam—"

As they hauled Matt over the rail, it took both Liam and Abadiah to restrain her, for the limp, lifeless form they laid out on *Kestrel*'s lantern-lit deck bore no resemblance to the brother she'd known and loved.

"Matt!" she shrieked.

He'd been harshly beaten, his face so battered, bruised, and swollen that she almost didn't recognize him. By the lantern's glow his freckles stood out on his pale cheeks like shot on parchment. Blood matted his hair and crusted his upper lip. Someone thrust the lantern closer, its soft glow falling over his face, and as he turned his head, she saw that his eyes were sightless, staring, and dead.

"Matt!"

"Mira? That you, sis?"

Blind.

"Catch her, she's goin' t' fall," Liam said tonelessly, his face like stone as he stared off beyond the black spiderweb of *Kestrel*'s shrouds to where *Viper*'s distant lights glowed upon the water like evil beacons from hell. And Mira, taking her brother's hand and sobbing over it, thought of the laughing man who'd gone to that devil-ship to trade himself for him.

Crichton had nothing against Matt, and look what he'd done to him.

But Crichton hated Brendan.

Liam's words echoed over and over through her mind: *"No, lassie. He's doin' it f'r you."*

"No!" She lunged to her feet and dove toward the rail, toward that distant ship, hearing her own screams coming from farther and farther away. Dalby caught her before she went over, and the memory of *Viper*'s lights was her last thought before her world went black.

The wind freshened during the night, and by the wee hours of the morning, waves were glinting white in the darkness and breaking over *Kestrel*'s plunging bows in great sheets of hissing spray.

High, high above the surging deck, Mira turned her face into the teeth of the wind, licked the spray from her lips, and stared off into the night, where *Viper*'s lights shone like a beacon as she tacked on a southerly course. Against the lightening horizon Mira could just make out her yards braced hard around and hear the wind thundering in her acres of canvas. And the only reason she could hear it was that *Kestrel*, in hot, silent pursuit, glided as soundlessly as a nighthawk on the hunt.

She laid her hand against the thick spar on which she sat. This time she felt no animosity from her jealous rival, just an overwhelming sense of camaraderie. They had made their peace. They were united, she and *Kestrel*. United for a single, desperate cause.

To save the man they both loved.

Far below, the crew conversed in hushed tones, and even the sea spoke in whispers as it creamed back from *Kestrel*'s sharp bows and fell away in a great, swirling wake of moonlight behind them.

The rain had held off all evening; now low-hanging clouds raced past the masthead, letting the moon shine through here, the spring constellations there. Looking up, it seemed that the tip of that lonely spire was all that held the storm clouds at bay. But now they were gathering in force, rushing in from the south, snuffing out the stars and casting an eerie, blackened pall over the rising waves. The storm would be upon them soon, Dalby had predicted with his usual doom and gloom. But they were desperate men in a desperate ship, and Mira, thinking of her blind, semi-iconscious brother lying in Brendan's cabin below, dared not imagine the fate of the man who had sacrificed so much to get him there.

When I see you, Brendan, I'll tell you. Her nails dug into the spar and she set her jaw, resolute and determined as she stared ahead. *I'll tell you all—beginning with how much I love you.*

A gust of wind caught the pennant high above her head and snapped it like a whip-crack. Dauntless, *Kestrel* added another knot to her swift pace, heeling hard over and driving her shoulder into the waves as she kept her plunging bowsprit trained on the frigate's lights.

Her hand stroking the spar, Mira felt the schooner's nose come up, heard the sea's song rise in pitch as *Kestrel*'s speed increased and the wind drove her through the waves.

Plunge and dip . . . Plunge and dip . . . Ever forward. Ever faster.

"Pray that we're not too late," she whispered.

Beneath her, *Kestrel* lifted her bows in answer and added yet another knot.

Brendan, stumbling painfully out of *Viper*'s hold the next morning under heavy guard, would never forget the glorious sight of his schooner rising up from the waves and filling every inch of the horizon behind them, stacking a mountain of sail that glowed white against black storm clouds, the sea parting beneath her bows, and her colors streaming in the wind.

And neither would Crichton. He took one look, dropped his telescope, and roared, "Man the braces! Stand by to wear ship! *Wear ship!*"

The British, staring in openmouthed awe at the magnificent vessel bearing down on them with her rail awash and every gun run out, were slow to react. When they did, there was only frantic activity, panic, and confusion.

And *Kestrel*, coming on like a glorious, winged angel of vengeance.

For Brendan, time and place slipped away. The horrors of last night faded . . . of Crichton, stringing him up to the gratings and laying his back open with the whip, then tearing him down and furiously kicking him in the ribs because he'd refused to cry out. There was only *Kestrel*— and nothing else. His heart sang, and despite the pain that burned through his ribs, his back, and his jaw, he laughed out loud—and gauged the distance between himself and the rail.

"Wear *ship!*" Crichton yelled, seizing the boatswain's rattan and laying it across a seaman's straining back.

Men ran to the braces, and slowly, ponderously, the frigate began to respond. And Brendan, left alone, limped calmly to the gunwales, saluted Crichton as he whirled around, and dove over the rail.

He struck out through the icy seas, blinded by waves and choking on seawater so cold, it sapped his breath and left him numb and gasping. But his Irishman's luck was with him. Or maybe one of Mira's fifteen some-odd cats had donated a life or two. One moment and the waves were closing over his head; the next, and *Kestrel* was coming on, faster and faster, passing. . . .

He lunged out of the water, tried for the dolphin striker, managed to grab a line that someone threw, and nearly ripped his fingernails out. It was so cold, he never felt the pain. The bow wake thrust him down and back, but he held on, desperately. And then Liam was throwing the Jacob's ladder down.

He caught it and clung there, the bitter wind ripping the breath from his lungs. With the last of his strength he hauled himself upward, his hands bleeding, his limbs frozen, every rib screaming in agony. He was almost to the rail of his beloved schooner. Water rushed from his clothing. Hands seized his arms, grasped his shoulders, and hauled him aboard. Someone tore off his coat and threw him a dry one; someone else wrapped a blanket around him. Cheers thundered in his ears. And then he was running to take the tiller, teeth clenched beneath a strained grin, hoping no one would see him stumble and almost fall as agony brought a blackness that came and went.

"Faith, these decks are slippery!" he managed, hoarsely, to cover it.

His hand closed around the wood, and the schooner's life sang up through keel and rudder and tiller, suffusing him with its vitality, restoring him. The wind began to shift, to veer, to back with the mad approach of the storm—

"Ready about!"

Viper had completed her turn and, with the wind behind her, was coming on like a charging bull.

"Sir, she's runnin' out her broadside!"

"Then run out ours, Mr. Wilbur! *Lively, now!*"

And *Kestrel,* singing, dancing, swooping to meet her.

"Stand by to come about!"

Bowsprits aligning, swinging around . . .

"She's comin' over!"

He shoved the tiller hard, hard, *hard.* Jibbooms crossed, passed, and touched like the fleeting kiss of two lovers. Two enemies. Fat sides slid against sleek. Stays caught, held, parted. Somewhere a gun cracked out, and the schooner yelped in surprise.

And then she was past, showing her heels to her enemy as *Viper*'s broadside cracked into empty air and the first raindrops began to fall.

"Huzzah! Huzzah! Three cheers for our captain!"

"Three for the Captain from Connacht!"

Aft, *Viper* was staggering, hauling her yards around, unwilling to give up.

"Mr. Keefe!" He had to get aloft, where Crichton could see him, where his *men* could see him. He coughed, the effort of yelling too much for him, and grabbed the speaking trumpet from Liam. "John, take the helm, *now!*"

He leapt for the shrouds, the pain ripping a cry of silent agony from his lungs, his feet finding a toehold, his hands pulling him aloft.

"Sir, are you all right?"

Higher and higher he climbed.

"Sir?!"

The rain slashed against his face and the wind rose, thundering in his ears as he climbed higher . . . and higher. . . .

Forty feet above deck he paused, the wind whipping his hair into his eyes, the rain streaming down his cheeks. He saw Crichton standing rigidly on that plunging deck. He saw that the frigate would never catch them. Laughing in triumph, he lifted the speaking trumpet to his lips.

"Mr. Doherty, run out *Freedom* and put Mr. Starr—"

The dizziness struck, dark speckles dancing across his vision as the speaking trumpet fell from his hand, down, down, down to the plunging deck so far below "—on it. . . ."

Kestrel swung through the wind, leapt across the waves, and turned to face her enemy. Blindly, Brendan grabbed for the crosstrees, thinking only to reach them before he passed out—but found nothing but empty space.

He'd misjudged it. *Misjudged his own ship.*

The luck of the Irishman had finally run out.

And then he felt himself falling, heard the screams of the men below, felt lines snapping beneath his back as he tumbled down and down and down. He heard a woman's voice, shrieking . . . and then he knew he was fading, because it sounded like Mira's. . . .

Mercifully, he was out before he hit the deck some forty feet below.

"Captain!"

"Jesus!"

"By God and Mary—"

Sobs, screams, cries—

"Here comes Crichton!"

And then the storm struck with savage wrath. Leaderless, *Kestrel* was left to face it—and Crichton—alone.

Chapter 26

Mira would never forget it. The storm, roaring down in full fury; chaos, as she'd raced back to the helm to get *Kestrel* out from beneath *Viper*'s guns; Liam, sobbing as he picked up Brendan's broken body and cradled it in his huge arms—and the long sail back home.

It had taken *Kestrel* a good three days to reach Newburyport. She'd had to beat against angry, shifting winds left over from the storm, her sails reefed and her bowsprit buried under foam. Giant combers had lifted her high, rolled beneath her keel, and left her staggering in the troughs, where she barely had time to catch her breath before having to lift her bows and crest the next mountain of water. Perhaps if her captain had been at the helm, they might've made the journey in two days; with a distraught Liam standing in his place, it was a wonder they even made it back to port at all. But Brendan had never regained consciousness from that awful fall, and *Kestrel*'s escape from *Viper* without his leadership, her survival of the storm without him at the helm, had been nothing short of miraculous. Yet somehow, someway, the little schooner had done both, solemnly bringing both fallen warriors back home to Newburyport.

The doctor, a squat, dapper little man with a red nose and white hair rolled beneath a tricorn, came often. Matt would recover, the physician said, especially with such a capable and attentive nurse as Eveleen Merrick tending to his every need. Bruises faded, cuts mended, and swelling went down. And his eyesight? Only time would tell.

But Brendan was another story, and the doctor did not

smile as he examined his inert body and straightened up from the big four-poster where he lay. "There is nothing I can do for him, Miss Ashton," he said sadly. "He is in God's hands."

And he was. God's—and Mira Ashton's.

She refused to accept that he was dying, that the likelihood of him regaining consciousness dwindled with every passing day, that his lilting, musical brogue would never put goose bumps on her arms, tingles up her spine, laughter in her heart, again. About the only thing she could accept was that it was her fault that he lay dying in this big bed.

If only you'd told *him who you really are . . . You could've stopped him.*

But she hadn't. God help her, she hadn't.

She shut her eyes in silent agony, remembering their anxiety as Liam had carried him below and laid him out in his bunk. They'd stripped away his clothing, and there, dark and ugly and awful, had been the evidence of Crichton's brutality. . . .

Now the bruises on his torso had faded, his bound and broken ribs were healing, and the angry lash-welts on his back no longer oozed blood.

But he was still in a coma.

A tear slipped from Mira's eye. With laughter and a grin, he'd mustered his crew and got *Kestrel* to safety as best he could; yet the pain he'd silently suffered had been so intense, he'd misjudged the layout of a ship that *he* had designed. And now it was too late. If only she'd had faith in him. If only she'd *believed* in him . . .

If only she'd told him.

But no. She hadn't. She'd allowed him to seek Crichton out, allowed him to go to his death thinking she hated him. He'd proclaimed his love for her; she'd proclaimed her hatred for him. What was there in this world for him to come back to, except a lonely schooner down in the harbor and a crew who thought he could walk on water?

That crew visited often. The people of Newburyport, however, stayed away, too ashamed and embarrassed over their earlier treatment of him to even make an appearance, though in his senseless state, he would never have known

whether they were there or not. One or two made brief
visits to put their consciences at ease, and Abadiah Bobbs's
five-year-old daughter, eager to visit the tall captain who'd
grinned, teased her, and given her a drawing of her father
standing with Mr. Starr at *Freedom*, brought him a cluster
of wildflowers; but when she approached his bed with them
clenched in her little fist and he did not awaken, did not
thank her for them—and did not laugh and grin and lift
her up high—her face puckered and she began to cry,
frightened and confused.

And after that, she did not come again.

Mira spent her nights sleeping in the chair beside Brendan's bed, where the heavy silence was broken only by his
shallow breathing. She spent her days reading to him from
naval books borrowed from Ephraim's library. She held
his hand and talked to him, praying that her words would
penetrate his consciousness and get through to him—
though he never twitched a muscle, never made a sound,
and his fine hand lay heavy and lifeless in her own. She
cared for him, forcing liquid down his throat, flexing his
arms and legs so they wouldn't stiffen, washing his face,
and tenderly kissing the sensitive, fine features she loved
so well: the elegant brows, the sculpted cheekbones, the
now-faded laugh lines around his lax mouth. She had Eveleen help her turn him so he wouldn't develop bedsores;
she combed his hair and queued it with a neat black bow.
And one night when it grew too hard to hope, too hard to
pretend to hope any longer, she went to the waterfront and
boarded the silent *Kestrel*. There, she sobbed out her anguish to the little schooner, who listened quietly and shared
her grief; there, she lifted her face to the stars perched
above the dark, crossed yards and learned how to pray
again; there, when she could cry no more, she lowered
the shot-torn American flag with her own hands and, with
it filling her arms, brought it home and hung it on the wall
so that if he awakened—*when* he awakened—that proud,
glorious banner would be the first thing he'd see when he
opened his eyes, and he would *know* he'd more than re-
deemed himself to her.

And he'd know she loved him.

But he didn't awaken. And the banner began to droop from the pegs that held it up.

Days and nights passed. Spring faded to summer, and the peeper frogs no longer chirruped in moonlit ponds and swamps. Grass grew tall and sweet in the meadows, on the lawn, in Miss Mira Ashton's School of Fine Horsemanship. Pink and red roses burst upon picket fences, wildflowers spread perfume to the sea wind, robins stole the hair that Eveleen combed from Shaula's mane and tail and threaded it through their nests.

Down in the harbor, the weed began to grow on *Kestrel*'s tallowed bottom.

Up in Maine, the British invaded a little peninsula called Bagaduce.

And in a quiet bedroom in a morgue-silent house, the Captain from Connacht lay silent and still.

Guilt and tension took its toll on everyone. Shadows appeared beneath Mira's eyes, and a haunted look appeared in their green depths that had Abigail sick with worry. The housekeeper, who'd taken Eveleen under her wing when Mira had sneaked off aboard *Kestrel*, got into a squall with the girl over who would cook and care for Matt, a squall that Eveleen eventually won—and only by the persistence and loyalty she'd shown in nursing her patient. Ephraim, with his son laid up, his daughter a ghost of her old self, and no one to fight with, grew so bored and irritable that he wound every clock in the house tighter and tighter until the big Willard piece in the front hall finally broke a spring and the clockmaker had to be hastily summoned (at precisely 2:17 A.M.) to fix it. And when the man nervously twittered there was simply no way it could be repaired by 2:30 A.M. (precisely), Ephraim toured the house in a fit of rage, bellowing at the top of his lofty lungs that he'd had it up to his bleedin' ears with incompetent asses who were supposed to be professionals and a family that didn't give a damn about his peace of mind, something that could only be had by the smooth workings of his clocks.

Mira was indifferent to the activities of the rest of the house's occupants. Once in a while she visited Matt's sick-bed, where Eveleen had set up her own vigil and Matt seemed to be enjoying all the attention the girl heaped upon him. By the way that Eveleen blushed and fidgeted when Matt paid her a compliment, and the way Matt grinned and preened when Eveleen was near, it was obvious that things were finally heating up between the two. Maybe Matt didn't need his eyesight to see that Brendan's sister was a more attractive person than any of the women who'd wanted him for his money and status alone. But Mira's heart wasn't into encouraging their relationship. It wasn't into anything.

The mutual frustration and helplessness they both felt as Brendan faded before their eyes, and Mira's spirit died with him, only strengthened the growing bond between Matt and Eveleen, for it brought them together out of necessity, as well as need.

On a day when Eveleen was spooning clam chowder to Matt as the two sat lamenting the situation, Eveleen finally decided she'd had enough of Mira's self-pity and despair. Her friend had pulled her out of the misery that had been hers since Crichton had left her a cripple; now it was time to do the same for her. Eveleen waited just long enough for Matt to finish his supper, carried the bowl back to the kitchen, where, oddly, she was able to pass by a plate of Abigail's sugared almonds without taking any, and marched back up the imposing mahogany staircase and into Brendan's room.

And there was Mira, still glued to the chair, head bent, Brendan's hand clenched in her own, and the *Essex Gazette* spread across her lap. Her voice was muffled through her thick hair, and her words were strained, hoarse, and ragged, as though she'd been crying.

Eveleen frowned.

Sunlight slanted through the window, backlighting Mira's rumpled muslin gown; her hair fell down over her eyes and across the page from which she was reading. Doggedly she put the newspaper down, shoved the hair over her shoulder, and never relinquishing her hold on Brendan's hand, continued on, forcing a cheery note to her voice that, combined with the choking brokenness of it, was absolutely pitiful to listen to.

'' 'Yesterday—' '' *sniff* '' '—the privateering sloop *Yankee Lady* defeated the British brig-of-war *Worcester* in a brief but intense exchange in the waters of Nantucket Sound, where the enemy hauled down his colors to the sloop after losing his main topmast.'' *Sniff.* She passed a knuckle under her eye, shoved her hair back again, and turned the page. '' 'By the intelligence of well-placed informants, we learn of a plan by the British to fortify Penobscot Bay'—*Penobscot,* Brendan, that's in Maine!—'and establish a haven for loyalists who've been driven from their homes. It is feared that the Enemy may construct a fort here, and talk abounds as to the best way to drive them out before they do. . . .' '' She paused, for that was *not* good news, and she'd given the order herself that nothing but good news must reach Brendan, whether he appeared to hear it or not. Hastily she flipped to the front page. ''And here, Brendan, listen to this—'Spain has now allied itself with France, who's agreeing to help her recover the Bay of Honduras, Florida, Minorca, and Gibraltar from the Brits in return for military and naval aid.' *Spain is in the war!* Now, *that's* good news, isn't it?''

He didn't move.

She wiped another tear away, drying her finger against skirts that were already damp. Another tear trickled down her cheek. Another.

The skirt grew damper.

''And here, something about the brave General Washington. And wait! Look at this, Brendan.'' The page was dog-eared and worn, for Ephraim had had the newspaper first. ''This is about you! It says, and I quote, 'And the people of Newburyport continue to pray for the brave and gallant Captain Brendan Merrick, who was treated most shamefully at our hands before setting out to rescue Matthew Ashton from the hideous brutalities of Captain Crichton of His Majesty's Royal Navy. . . .' '' She paused, the tears filling her eyes, her nose, her throat, and making it impossible to read the blurry print. With a sob, she set the paper across her lap and buried her face in her wet hands.

And then she jerked her head up and viciously clawed the hair out of her eyes. "Dammit, Brendan, did you hear me?! I said they've forgiven you. . . ."

He didn't move.

Heartache swelled her chest, threatening to burst it. *"Forgiven you!* What more do you want?! Patrick Tracy and Mr. Johnson were here this morning, and Michael Dalton's penning a letter to General Washington commending you, telling him all you did—" She gulped back the tears, her voice catching on sobs. "N-next thing you know, the general will be b-b-begging you to lend *Kestrel* to the Continental navy—" *Sniff.* "Next thing you know, he'll—" *sob* "—be asking you t-to give up privateering and join the n-navy instead." *Sniff. Sob. Sniff.* "N-next thing you know, they'll be making you a c-commodore. A . . . f-*flag captain.*"

Bursting into tears, she hurled the newspaper to the floor and buried her face in her hands. She didn't know if the American navy had flag captains or not—but she did know that Brendan would never be one.

And that he'd never be a commodore.

And that he'd never be a privateer again, either, for he wasn't going to be doing any sailing. Not today. Not tomorrow.

Maybe not ever.

In the open doorway, Eveleen, regal in pink and gold silk, set her jaw and put her hands on her hips as Mira's voice, barely discernible through fingers, tears—and hair—shattered the quiet of the room.

"Oh, Brendan . . . you never cared what Newburyport thought, you only cared what *I* thought. If I'd believed in you from the very start, you'd never have made that last cruise, never would've set out to rescue Matt. I could've told you that I loved you when you most needed to hear it, but I didn't. I was too busy wallowing in my own grief, looking for someone to blame Matt's death on, never realizing that *you* carried more hurt and pain than any of us because you had to bear our condemnation, our accusations, our *hatred.*" Her voice broke and the tears rushed like April rain, darkening her muslin skirts and wetting her hair, her anguished sobs drowning out the chirps of baby sparrows just outside the open window. "Oh, Brendan . . . I *know* you love Matt as a brother! I *know* you're not a coward, not a traitor, not a . . . not a *Brit!*" She raised a red and puffy face, clawed the tears from her cheeks, and screamed, "You're a goddamned . . . Irishman! You're a d-damned *American!* You're a cussed, bloody, stupid, gallant *FOOL!*"

Angrily she flung his hand back across his chest, her muffled sobs wracking her body and making her chair creak as she rocked miserably back and forth, her head in her hands. "Stupid, bloody *FOOL!* You've had your revenge on us, now, *WAKE UP,* damn you . . . Damn, damn, damn . . ."

Huddled there with her arms wrapped around her knees, she missed it: the twitch of his finger; the shift in the rhythm of his breathing; the slight roll of his eyes beneath lax lids.

"God d-damn it all. G-God damn you. . . ."

And Eveleen, standing in the doorway. "Really, Mira. You disappoint me."

Mira raised her head, glared at her, and let her face fall back to her wet palms again. "Go away!"

"He needs your spirit right now. Not your self-pity."

"Get out!"

Eveleen arched a haughty brow. "Excuse me?"

"You heard me; get *OUT!*"

Eveleen was not intimidated by the rage of a woman she outweighed by nearly thirty-five pounds. She also understood the frustration that governed her friend's actions. With regal grace she swept into the room, shoved the window open as wide as it could go, and pulled up a chair, where she faced Mira from across the bed. Eyes clashed; calm gold against glittering green. Serenity against rage.

Knowledge against ignorance.

"Well?!" Mira shouted, swiping at falling tears and glaring at the other woman from over the top of Brendan's blanketed legs. "You came here to say something, so say it and then get the hell out!"

Eveleen looked thoughtfully down at Brendan's still face and adjusted her gown, which kept sliding down her shoulder and exposing the pretty chemise beneath. She frowned and, forgoing hauteur, finally yanked it back up and said something under her breath that sounded suspiciously like a curse before facing Mira with an apologetic smile. Mira did not smile back.

"When I first met you," Eveleen began quietly, "I admired you because you had everything I didn't, everything I wanted—and yet you never struck me as a vain person. But lately I've begun to believe otherwise."

Mira's eyes hardened, and she clenched tiny fists at the sides of her chair.

Dauntlessly Eveleen continued, "What gives *you* the right to sit here and hate yourself for what my brother did?" Reaching out, she brushed her fingers against Brendan's pale cheek. "Do you honestly think he could've let what Crichton did to Matthew go unavenged? What Crichton did to *me?*" She thrust her maimed hand toward Mira for emphasis. "This has been going on for four years, Mira. *Four years.* And it isn't finished yet. Oh, no, not by any means. When my brother recovers, he'll go back out there and he won't stop until he finds Crichton and puts an end to his cruelties."

Mira sniffed back angry sobs. "Your brother isn't going anywhere, Eveleen, except to a plot behind St. Paul's Church!"

"I beg to differ, Mira. And so does John Keefe, and Fergus McDermott, and even Liam Doherty—"

"Liam Doherty!" Mira leapt to her feet, slamming her tiny fist into the wall so hard that outside, the sparrows stopped chirping. "What the bloody hell does he know?! And Fergus waving crystals around like a sachet of perfume every time he comes here! You and Liam and the rest of those bloody Irishmen are making me sick! *'He'll be just fine, Mira; you wait and see,'*" she mimicked. "None of you can face reality! None of you see him wasting away before your eyes as I do! Or maybe you don't bloody well care! Damn you, damn all of you, *he's DYING,* Eveleen!"

Shoulders shaking, tears pouring from her eyes, she pressed her damp face to the wall and beat against it with tiny palms, making a pastel drawing of a brigantine tremble on its hook. The artist's signature was the same one as that affixed to *Kestrel*'s drafts, framed and hanging in a place of honor in Ephraim's library.

Brendan's.

"Dying, Eveleen," she sobbed, brokenly. *"Dying . . ."*

Eveleen shrugged and stroked the loose fingers of her brother's hand. "I've seen him worse," she said with a little smile.

Mira whirled. "Any worse and he'd be dead. *DEAD!*"

"Mira, there are a few things you don't know about my brother. You see, he's always tended to be rather . . . accident-prone. He's also cursed with our mother's Irish luck. I say cursed, because there have been times he's wished himself dead, times he *should've* been dead—but no." She leaned across the bed, picked up the coverlet, and gently drew it back from Brendan's chest. "Come here, please."

Sniffling, her face pale and angry and wet, Mira did.

"See this scar?" Eveleen indicated the circle of white skin. "Brendan got it the *first* time he and Crichton came to blows. I know Liam told you about what Crichton did to me, but I'll bet neither he nor Brendan told you about what Crichton did to my brother." Eveleen looked up, her eyes level, her voice almost hard. "Crichton shot him in the back when he was trying to save an innocent man— Dalby, incidentally—from the lash."

Mira's tears stopped abruptly.

The silence hung heavily in the room.

Outside the window, the baby sparrows shrilled as their parents flitted in on whirring wings.

"The ball passed through his body and out through his chest, right here." Eveleen ran her thumb over the circular ridge of scar tissue. "It should've killed him—but it didn't. Another shot hit him a half inch away, right . . . here, driving him over the rail and into the sea. *That* one should've killed him, but it didn't." She gently drew the coverlet up, her eyes filled with the pain of remembrance. "But I'll tell you what almost did. . . ."

Mira, sniffled and wiped a tear from her eyes.

"Julia," Eveleen said quietly.

"Julia?"

Eveleen gazed out the window, her eyes distant. "She

was the daughter of an American army officer in Boston. She was also the one who found Brendan washed up in the surf there after he fell overboard from *Halcyon*. A pretty young thing, with dark hair like yours and violet eyes that looked deceptively innocent. Like you, she cared for my brother and nursed him back to health in her father's own house. The Americans used to come and go; it was somewhat of a gathering spot, and Brendan heard enough of their political opinions, saw enough of their suffering, that eventually he came to believe he'd been fighting for the wrong side, the wrong cause.'' She smiled slightly, and squeezed his limp hand. ''Of course, my brother always *was* something of a rebel. Our mother's Irish blood, Da used to say. . . .''

The door swung open and shut in the breeze, and Rescue Effort Number Forty skittered nervously in, glanced around, and jumped up on the bed. Purring loudly, he rubbed himself against Eveleen's wrist and finally nestled in the curve of Brendan's feet.

''In any case, to make a long story short, Brendan fell in love with Julia. And I mean *love.* They were going to get married, and all the time, my brother was entertaining this idea of designing a schooner to combine the best of American craftsmanship and British standards of perfection. He was a fine naval architect, you know. But it never occurred to him that his precious Julia couldn't have cared less about his dreams, would only see the ship as something to take his attention away from her . . . something to *compete* with. He thought she'd love it as much as he did. He thought she'd be proud of him, as he intended it to be a privateer in the service of his newly adopted country. But no. He didn't see that. Didn't see that Julia was nothing but a spoiled, selfish little brat. Love is blind, they say. Julia wasn't about to share him with the sea, the navy, and certainly not a ship, no matter how lovely it would be, no matter how heralded, no matter how much General Washington himself praised its design. . . .

''Well, one day Brendan came back from an appointment with the general and found a note from Julia, propped up against the drafts. 'Choose the ship or choose me,' the note said. But Julia never *gave* him a choice. She left him, and ended up marrying some army major not three months later.'' Eveleen ran her thumb over the back of her brother's lax hand, squeezed the loose fingers, and looked up. ''She broke his heart, Mira.''

Outside, the baby birds quieted, while inside, the silence in the room grew oppressive. Mira felt like something was pressing down on her chest and squeezing her heart up through her throat, and choked back the bitter taste of the truth. Quietly she said, ''So that is why he was always running from me. . . .''

''Yes. That *is* why.'' Eveleen gazed down into her brother's face, her smile a bittersweet one of remembrance. ''You see, Mira, Brendan has been in love with you from the very beginning. He came to me in Portsmouth and told me about this girl he'd met who'd run him down on a horse and went around dressed in breeches. And when I met you, and saw you pounding the pudding out of that scruffy hooligan down on the docks—and the admiration in my brother's eyes as you were doing it—I knew in my heart it was true. That he loved you. And while he loved you, at first I hated you—not only because you were thin and pretty when I wasn't, but because I saw you as another Julia. I love my brother, too, Mira. And I didn't want his heart to be broken again.''

Eveleen was the image of serenity as the sunshine streamed in through the window and gilded her pale hair. ''You've always wondered why I didn't tell Brendan who Mr. Starr *really* was, haven't you?'' She gave a little smile. ''It had nothing to do with your promise to get Matthew interested in me, because honestly, I never thought that could happen. No, I had a very different reason for keeping your secret. That very first time you defied your father and stole aboard *Kestrel,* I realized you were as different from Julia as Brendan is from . . . from Crichton. I saw that you loved the sea, loved ships, as much as he did. That he could have with you what he'd tried so hard to have with Julia. Love. Happiness. And so I held my tongue. You see, Mira, when Brendan loves a woman, be it a person or a ship—'' she smiled and folded his loose fingers in her own ''—he does so with every bit of his heart. Every bit of his *Irish* heart, Liam would say. And he loves you. He's just afraid to show it, afraid to trust you. Afraid of being hurt again. And so he places that trust in *Kestrel* instead, because to him she's safe. Because she's not a threat. Because she'll never desert him as Julia did . . .''

Mira raised her head and met the other woman's gaze. *"As I did."*

Silence. But there was no condemnation in Eveleen's eyes as she rose with stately grace, squeezed her brother's hand a final time, and gently placed it over the scar on his chest. She looked at Mira and smiled. "He's not going to die, Mira, because you're going to tell him how much you love him. Somehow, someway, he'll hear you. He'll *know*. And death itself won't be able to hold him once he learns that *you're* here waiting for him.''

She yanked up the loose shoulder of her gown a final time, her smooth brow furrowing in confusion, and turned toward the door.

"Eveleen, wait! We have to talk!''

But the other woman was eager to get back to her own patient.

"Eveleen, please! You must tell me more! About Crichton. About Julia. About *Brendan!* I'll even have Abigail bring up a pot of tea and some of those cookies she baked earlier—''

But Eveleen was shaking her head, smiling. As she paused in the doorway, wrinkles fell from the silk at her plump waist—wrinkles that hadn't been there when Mira had last seen her in the dress. "Know something, Mira?''

"Eveleen!"

"Between you and me, I'm glad Brendan's here with you and not aboard that schooner.'' She winked, never looking as much like her brother as she did in that moment. And then, from behind the side of her hand: "I hate ships as much as Julia did.''

Brit.
Damned Irishman!
She was shouting at him, swearing at him, her voice ringing through his head, fading in and out on giant, rolling combers that glittered and danced in bright sunlight—

Bloody, stupid, gallant, FOOL!

That hurt.

"Faith, lassie," he said, but she didn't seem to hear him, only going on with that awful yelling.

His back hurt. His chest hurt. His head hurt.

He hurt.

And Eveleen . . . Was that her voice? What was she doing on *Kestrel?* She hated ships. He *was* on *Kestrel*, wasn't he? Yet that sounded like Ephraim's big Willard clock, and heaven help him if they'd dragged *that* aboard his lovely schooner. . . . And why was the ship rocking so? He hadn't designed her to wallow like a tub. Didn't remember the bunk being so soft. Didn't think birds chirped out in the middle of the ocean. He *was* in a bunk, wasn't he? Or had they dragged a bed into his cabin? But that didn't explain the sparrows. They were sparrows, weren't they? Sparrow hawks? *Kestrels?* Good heavens—

"Faith," he said, and opened his eyes.

He saw a cat, a black and white and orange one, against the great backdrop of *Kestrel*'s shot-holed flag. It was nestled against the curve of his feet and staring at him in alarm.

He blinked, wondering what it was doing on his ship.

The cat fled. He looked up.

And saw her.

A wall of thick, tumbledown hair that was in desperate need of a combing. Green eyes peeping out between and beneath it, sparkling oddly despite the dark shadows beneath them. Freckles peppering an impish nose—and a jaw that had come unhinged.

"Moyrra?"

Faith, why was she staring at him so?

"Eveleen!" she screamed.

And Eveleen, just coming into the room—faith, had she actually lost weight?!

She merely gave him a serene smile and turned away, heading down a hall he recognized as Ashton's, her steps in time with clocks he knew were Ephraim's, two cats in her wake he identified as Mira's, that wasted no time in jumping upon the bed.

And Mira?

''Brendan!'' she was screaming, at the very top of her lungs. ''Oh God, Brendan! *BRENDAN!*''

He shut his eyes. She was smothering him with thick hair and the scent of roses. Silky locks and kisses, raining over his face, his eyelids, his scarred chest. Arms that wound beneath him, tears that wet his chest and ran down the little grooves between his ribs and tickled his armpits. She was squeezing the life out of him. Pain lanced through his ribs. *Squeeze any harder, lassie, and I'm going to pass out,* he thought.

She drew back only long enough to yell, ''You're awake! *AWAKE!*'' and then she was vaulting up on the bed, bare feet first, making the supports creak, making the cats bounce, making his teeth snap together—

''Faith, lassie—''

''Awake!'' she shrieked, *''AWAKE!''*

She fell, sobbing, atop him, giggling and crying and shouting all at once, her arms around him, her wall of hair suffocating him, her kisses and laughter filling his soul.

''Mira! What the goddarned bleedin' tarnation's goin' on in—''

She paused. Drew back. Swept her hair aside and gave him an unhampered view of a doorway that was quickly filling with people. Matt, staring sightlessly at the wall behind him, but grinning as he leaned against Eveleen; Abigail, wiping floured hands on her skirts; Liam, John Keefe, Amos Reilly, Abadiah Bobbs. Dalby, clutching his chest. Fergus, clutching his crystal.

And at the forefront of that formidable pack, Ephraim—clutching his watch.

''The British have invaded Maine,'' the old sea captain snapped. *''Kestrel* sits rotting in the harbor. And *yer* sittin' here taking a goddamned nap!''

He snapped open the watch and shoved it in Brendan's face.

''It's about bloody *TIME* ye woke up!''

Chapter 27

Early the next morning, Eveleen climbed from her bed and, from her seat atop the window cushions, watched the sun come up over the harbor. Above the buildings of Market Square, she could see ships' masts silhouetted against the pink and gold sky; the distinctive rake of a pair of them marked them as Brendan's schooner. Mist rose from the river, and down in the harbor a cloud of seagulls raised their raucous voices, no doubt fighting over some fishy morsel washed up by the overnight tide.

Eveleen closed her eyes, treasuring these early dawn moments before the rest of the household awakened. Formerly a late riser, she'd never appreciated the beauty of the sunrise, the songs of warblers, cardinals, and sparrows.

The birds would not have been enough to drag Eveleen from her bed. But Matthew Ashton, who got up with the sun, most certainly was. Now she awakened when the morning was still gray and shadowy; now she perched herself here on the window seat every morning and eagerly waited for him to pass beneath her window as he took his morning walks. She hugged her arms to herself. Oh, what would it be like to be kissed by his handsome mouth, to be enfolded in his strong arms, to lay her cheek against his leather vest and listen to the beat of his heart?

She carefully pushed the curtain aside. He was out there now, returning from his walk, his shoes leaving darker trails through the silvery morning dew that carpeted the grass. Sunlight glinted off the spectacles he no longer needed and turned his brilliant red hair to flame. In his hand was a long stick, which he used to carefully chart his course. But his steps were sure and confident. She wondered if he'd lived his life as a privateer the same way: daring, fearless, and unafraid to take risks.

Craning her neck, Eveleen strained to catch a last glimpse of him as he passed beneath her window. She heard the front door open, then slam shut, making the floor tremble beneath her feet. Ephraim shouted something, Matt shouted something back. And then every clock in the house chimed the hour in perfect symmetry and the door slammed again as Ephraim, tight-lipped and hard-eyed and clad in a fashionable brown coat, left for his shipyard.

Downstairs, she heard Matt moving about, then a loud crash as he walked into something. His good-natured curses wafted up to her. *Oh, Matt,* she thought, *you're so brave, so noble, never complaining about your blindness, never bitter. . . .* Yet how well he'd tried to hide his pain when the news about the British invasion of Penobscot had swept Newburyport. The town had been so eager to take part in the Expedition to rout the enemy that some thirty sea captains had volunteered to go to Maine as common seamen. But Eveleen had seen the raw, naked pain on Matt's beloved face that *he* couldn't go, too. Not so long ago he'd been Newburyport's most celebrated hero. Now he was left behind, a forgotten invalid, when his country needed him most.

A forgotten invalid. Just like her.

Except that Matt had never drowned himself in self-pity, as she'd done. Matt had risen above it.

The stairs were creaking now. Eveleen's heart begin to race, and her stomach filled with butterflies in anticipation. Soon Abigail would be sending a servant upstairs with a breakfast tray, and Eveleen, as she did every morning, would be there to take it from the girl and bring it in to Matt herself. Lately he'd even been asking her to stay and talk to him while he ate, listening with rapt attention while she'd·relayed developments about the Expedition, and the war itself.

Tiptoeing across the room, she went to the door and put her ear to the white-painted paneling. Matt had reached the top of the stairs; she could hear him murmuring to Luff, and the happy *thump, thump, thump* of the dog's tail.

Eveleen closed her eyes and smiled. She could just picture Matt scratching the dog's ears, perhaps offering him something he'd filched from the kitchen earlier. Then the floor creaked, and the door across from her banged shut.

She stood there, chewing her lip and leaning against the wall, her heart thumping madly in her chest. Blind or not, in her eyes he was perfect. Wonderful. But while he'd probably ask her to stay and talk to him again, did he truly enjoy her company as much as it appeared he did?

No one, aside from her dear brother, Brendan, had ever really cared about her—but as she and Matt had gotten to know each other during his convalescence, he'd begun to ask her questions, encouraging her to talk about herself. He'd asked her what her life had been like in England, and later, Ireland. Last night he wanted to know what sort of pictures she used to paint, and why she no longer painted. And when she'd told him, the unseen tears slipping down her cheeks, that it was because of her crippled hand, he'd merely taken a bite out of his cornbread and casually asked why she just didn't paint with the other one.

How easy he made it all seem. And how much he cared, sensing her tears when he couldn't see them. . . . She could still hear his quiet voice, soft with compassion and understanding as she'd stood by the window last night and hugged that awful, ugly *thing* that used to be her hand to her breast.

"Tears, little Evvie?"

"Oh, Matthew, don't pretend you've never noticed my hand! You were just too polite to ever call attention to it! I'm a *cripple!*"

"So am I. We make a good pair, huh?"

"But my hand's no longer good for anything," she whispered, shoving it as far down into her pocket as it would go when he'd moved to stand behind her.

"Give it to me, Evvie."

She'd panicked. "No, Matthew . . . I—I can't! It's hideous! It's awful—"

"It's part of you. Give it to me, Evvie."

His arms had gone around her, and she'd felt the lanky, hard length of him pressing against her shoulders, her spine, her rump. Fearful tears had slid down her cheeks, tears that, upon such close scrutiny, he'd find her disfigurement so hideous, he'd turn away. Shivering, she'd bitten her lip to contain the tears as he'd gently touched her shoulder and followed the length of her arm, roving lower and lower until he'd found the scarred, shattered hand at the end of her wrist and, ignoring her struggles to pull away, brought it up to his lips.

He'd gently turned her around to face him then, holding her gaze with a sightless one of his own. Then, tenderly, lovingly, he'd kissed her hand again and told her how beautiful she was. How brave she was for standing up to Crichton. And then he'd brought her hand up to his cheek and closed his eyes, and Eveleen had cried for all she was worth.

Matthew had not found it hideous. Matthew did not find *her* hideous.

And Matthew, despite the brave front he presented to his family, his friends, and the town itself, needed her as much as she needed him.

Oh, if only she were as bold and brassy as Mira; she'd go into his room and tell him that she loved him, had always loved him. But no. Although she had Matt's friendship, she dared not ruin even that precious bit of him that she could claim. What if he, like every man since that awful day upon *Halcyon*'s decks, rejected her? Matthew Ashton, Newburyport's favorite son, had been the hotheaded rake who could've had—and probably *had* had—any woman he chose. Friends were one thing; lovers, another. Why would he want *her,* fat old Eveleen Merrick who only had one hand and a closet full of pink dresses? What would he see in her?

She walked past that hated cheval mirror and stuck out her tongue.

And then she stopped short, stared, and took a hesitant step closer.

"What?" she said aloud.

The image reflected there seemed to belong to someone else. Swallowing hard, Eveleen stepped closer to it. There were bone-points in her elbows and knees, cheekbones had surfaced out of the roundness of her face, and the figure beneath the sagging pink dress had passed the median and begun to gain a few inward curves instead of outward ones. Her breasts had shrunk, no longer able to hold up the pearl-encrusted bodice of her pink gown, and one of her chins had melted away to nothing.

Transfixed, she stared at the mirror, seeing the changes in her body for the very first time. Sudden tears filled her eyes, and the image grew blurry. But they weren't tears of shame or self-hatred; they were tears of awe and reverence and humility. Slowly, as though the image might fade, she ran her hands down over her belly, her waist, her hips, where she could just feel bones coming up through the flesh.

The tears began to roll down her face in earnest now. What had happened to her? How had she lost weight? Had it been her involvement with the horses while Mira had been away on *Kestrel?* Mucking stalls and grooming their hides until they shone?

No. The horses had helped—but they weren't the *real* reason at all.

Suddenly she knew what was.

She'd been so intent upon helping Matt with his meals that she'd barely thought about the food growing cold on her own plate. Indeed, she'd been so concerned about *someone else's* welfare instead of her own that she'd not even thought about filling her own stomach, and satisfying the emptiness in her heart, for with Matt around, there *was* no emptiness in her heart. There was no reason to eat until she was stuffed, and then go back for more and more. . . .

There was no emptiness.

Her sobs came harder. The woman who looked out of that mirror was really she, Eveleen Merrick. Not a stranger, not a fairy image that was going to vanish in the blink of an eye. It was the girl she'd been before Crichton's shot, and the woman that girl had become. It was a woman who had learned how to stop feeling sorry for herself, thanks to a hoyden who talked like a sailor and dressed in breeches. It was a person who, in caring for someone else, had thrown off the protective cloak of obesity to become someone capable of giving, and receiving, love. A woman who was capable, and deserving—of the very best.

Matthew Ashton.

The woman in the mirror was smiling through the tears now, her eyes shining with brightness.

Slowly Eveleen ran her fingers through her hair, shaking her head until it spilled down her back in a glorious display that shone with the beauty of the morning sun. She stared at that cloud of gold floating around her shoulders and framing her shrinking waist, until it was all she could do not to run to the window and shout out her joy for all the world to hear.

"I'm here!" she wanted to sing. *"I'm here, I'm here, I'M HERE!"*

Hugging her arms to her breasts, she glanced at the mirror once more. Oh, she still had a ways to go, but the woman who looked back at her was no longer fat.

She was no longer bitter.

And she was no longer ugly.

That morning in June was the last time Eveleen Merrick ever wore a pink gown again. She pulled every one from her closet and spent the next half hour shredding them with a pair of shears. Then she slipped into the simple homespun dress that Mira had made her buy last winter, a dress that was too big for her now but far more flattering than pink silk would ever be. She tore off her jewelry and tossed it to the bed, shook out her curls a final time. There were no pockets to tuck her hand in, but suddenly she didn't care if anyone saw it or not. There was nothing left to hide.

Grinning triumphantly at the mirror as she passed it, Eveleen swept from her room.

The reflection in the mirror grinned back.

And so did the red-haired man across the hall when his door opened and she slipped inside.

Brendan groaned and threw his arm over his forehead.

Traffic moved smartly on the street below: handsome coaches belonging to wealthy merchants, farm carts pulled by plodding horses, an older couple out taking the air. It was that time of night when the shadows are long, the sunlight rusty and orange, the heat, left over from the hot summer day, oppressive.

That heat seemed to have concentrated on the second floor of the Ashton house, although Abigail had thrown open every window in an attempt to relieve it. Brendan lay propped up in a stack of fluffy pillows, the sheets no longer crisp but now wilted against his damp skin. A glass of cool water freshened with a slice of lemon stood in a circle of condensation on the table beside the bed; a supper tray was balanced across his legs. He had no spirit to muster an appetite, although the fare certainly looked, and smelled, delicious: fine lobster chowder, accompanied by piping chunks of crusty bread still hot from the bake oven, a dish of peas and carrots, and a golden square of gingerbread smothered in fresh cream. For lunch, Abigail had sent up codfish cakes, clam fritters, and sour milk biscuits generously spread with wild strawberry jam. He hadn't touched that either.

He'd been awake—if one could call his state of half consciousness wakefulness—for a week now. His memory of the time was hazy at best; he had dim recollections of Mira spooning clear broth down his throat those first few days after he'd woke from the coma, her arm beneath his back and head to support him. By the third day he'd been eating oatmeal, and more broth, thickened with finely chopped meat and vegetables. He'd struggled to sit up in bed and had fallen back in a faint; but that hadn't stopped him from trying again, and again.

Now he could sit up in bed, swing his legs out, and, if he took several deep breaths and clutched the bedpost, stand. Of course, following the doctor's orders of stretching his limbs every chance he got had helped; so had healing sleep and meals, which now consisted of solid food. Such therapy had done wonders; just this morning, he'd been able to exercise his arms and legs without feeling as if he might pass out.

That accomplishment, however, did little to lift his spirits.

He stared dejectedly out the window, his heart heavy and his soul sad. No, he didn't remember much of this past week, and even less of those few moments just before he'd fallen from *Kestrel*'s rigging, though the doctor assured him that his short-term memory would be a while in returning. Now, however, he was beginning to wish he'd never woken up, if only to have spared Mira this latest distress.

Last night he'd made the decision to bring *Kestrel* to Maine to join the Penobscot Expedition.

"Penobscot?!" She'd nearly deafened him with her re-action. "What the hell is *wrong* with you?! You've just come out of a bleedin' coma; you can't go traipsing up to Maine—"

"Moyrrra—"

"I won't have it, Brendan, you hear me?! I just won't have it!" she'd cried, bursting into uncharacteristic tears. "I've come so close to losing you, and now you want to go and endanger your life all over again!"

"Lassie, you have to understand—"

"You can't go; you're not *well enough!* Something will happen to you. I just know it!"

He'd pulled her down on the bed, hugging her and stroking her hair while she'd soaked his nightshirt with her tears. "Massachusetts needs every privateer it can get, *stóirín,"* he'd explained as gently as he could. "I built *Kestrel* for a reason. It would be a shameful waste to have her laid up in harbor when she could be of use to America in the most ambitious naval effort the colonies have un-dertaken to date. . . ."

Mira had cried even harder, the sobs wracking her little body until he'd thought his own heart would break.

"Moyrrra, lassie, I didn't build her just to *look* good. . . ."

She'd raised her head, flung the hair out of her eyes, and cried, "You and your bleedin' honor! Sometimes you're so damned *gallant,* I want to choke you! I don't care about *Kestrel,* I care about you! If you go up to Pe-nobscot in your condition, you're going to end up getting yourself killed!"

She'd fled the room then, and all day he'd waited for her to return so that they could talk the matter over—but she was obviously too upset to want to see or speak to him.

His spirits had been on a downward plummet ever since. He shut his eyes. Maybe she'd been right—perhaps he *was* too honorable for his own good. But how could he live with himself if he just lay here in bed, when his new country needed both him and his legendary schooner?

He broke off a piece of the bread and tried to eat it. It had gone cold and tasteless, but he forced himself to swallow that one token bite for the sake of sparing poor Abigail's feelings, before putting it back on the tray.

Mira . . . please come back, lassie. . . . I never wanted to hurt you.

Shifting position in the bed, he felt a lingering, dull ache in his ribs that only reminded him of Mira's demands to know where the now-faded bruises had come from. He'd laughingly made up some story about slipping and falling on *Viper's* decks when he'd gone aboard the frigate, but judging by the way her green eyes had narrowed, she hadn't believed him for a moment. He'd seen no need to tell her the truth—that Richard Crichton, frustrated by his blithe responses to his questions about the American forces, had become a bit . . . overzealous in his attempts to force the information from him.

He shuddered, remembering the whipping and the awful beating that Crichton had given him the night he'd traded himself for Matt. That hadn't been all that Crichton had planned for him. An ominous, terrifying picture of the noose, swinging from *Viper's* foreyard with the roll of the ship, rose up in his memory, and the sweat that sheened his body turned cold. Thank God *Kestrel* had come when she had. He would never forget the sight of his valiant little ship, sweeping down on *Viper* with every sail set, every flag streaming, every gun run out, and the sea bursting over her bows. She'd been magnificent. She'd been glorious. And, he thought with a sudden frown, she'd come about a hairbreadth from oversetting herself in her determination to reach him.

He would have to speak to Liam about that. Such recklessness at the helm would not be tolerated.

But even thoughts of *Kestrel,* waiting for him down in the harbor, could not make the pain of hurting his beloved Mira go away. There'd been a time when *Kestrel* was all that he'd needed; or all he'd thought he'd needed. What a fool he'd been. He needed *Mira*. Not only her love, but her acceptance of all that made him the man that he was.

He *had* to go to Penobscot—not just because Massachusetts had asked him to go, not just because of his desire to see *Kestrel* in the glorious role he'd designed and built her for, but because of his need to restore Newburyport's faith in him . . . and his little schooner.

The shadow of *Proud Mistress* still hung over his head. He stared dejectedly at *Kestrel's* magnificent red and white privateering flag, dominating the entire wall opposite the bed. *Ah, Liam,* he thought sadly, *bless your heart for putting that there.* . . . But he'd failed that flag. Failed to save *Mistress,* her crew, and her captain from Crichton's cruelties. He'd failed to redeem himself in Mira's eyes, and in those of the people of Newburyport. A cruel irony, that flag.

He placed the tray on the bedside table, peeled the sheets from his damp skin, and taking a deep breath, rose from the bed. His limbs felt as though the bones had been removed and water poured in their place, and the room spun around him with such force that he had to grab the bedpost just to keep his balance. He was in no condition for heroics, no condition to command a ship.

Not yet, anyhow.

But by tomorrow, maybe he'd feel better. . . .

He stood there for a moment on unsteady, shaky legs, praying that no one would come in and see how sick he *really* was. Leaning his head into the curve of his elbow, he shut his eyes against a sharp wave of dizziness that came and went. Tunnel vision closed in and his body trembled violently. Determined not to pass out, he took several deep breaths, his fingers tightening on the smooth wood of the bedpost. Finally his senses stopped swimming and he could stand upright once again. And as he did so, he heard Mira's soft weeping coming from outside, from the direction of the stables.

"Ah, *mo stóirín,*" he whispered, his heart going out to her. "My poor little treasure . . ." He staggered to the window, but he could only see the darkened barn and the shadowy outline of the fenced paddock. Mentally praying for her forgiveness, he tipped his head back and stared miserably up at the plastered ceiling, listening to the distant weeping until he could take it no longer. And then, his legs buckling, he let his back slide down the wall until he sat on the floor, his head bent, his hands over his ears, and his eyes shut against the visions that sad weeping evoked.

Go to her.

He couldn't.

Faith, laddie, go down there and take her in your arms! She needs you!

Needed him, yes . . . but couldn't accept his need to do what he had to do.

He could face the might of a man-of-war from *Kestrel*'s decks. He could face battle with a sketchpad in his hands as the iron flew above his head. He could face Crichton's calculated cruelties even.

But he couldn't face his own failure to save Matt and his crew.

And couldn't go comfort Mira until he came to terms with Crichton—and himself.

He sat there huddled on the floor, head buried in his hands, his rich chestnut hair falling over his elbows as he tried to block that awful sobbing.

In the end, he couldn't take it anymore. Without a word to anyone, he got up, wrapped a few precious belongings in his coat, and very, very carefully, stumbled out the door and downstairs.

Sea-ready or not, *Kestrel* was leaving Newburyport.

Chapter 28

"**G**od Almighty, Brendan, ye can't be serious! What d'ye mean, ye want t' go join th' Penobscot Expedition? Are ye out o' y'r bloody mind?!''

Brendan swayed and braced his shoulder against the wall, hoping that Liam wouldn't notice how much difficulty he was having just standing up. But the dizziness didn't go away. He was in Wolfe Tavern—or at least he thought he was—though how he'd managed to get there, he didn't know. He remembered leaving the Ashton house, had recollections of lurching drunkenly down the street. Dirt smudged his knee breeches, and there were angry scuff marks on his palms. He must've fallen, but he didn't remember it.

"Out of my mind?" He managed a faint grin, noting how Liam's bright blue eyes were assessing him with blatant disapproval. "I don't think so. What's wrong with wanting to lend *Kestrel*'s support to a patriotic cause, eh?"

"Patriotic me arse!" Liam snorted. "Ye took a forty-foot fall, f'r God's bloody sake; ye can't be expectin' t' go commandin' a warship. In fact, I wouldn't be trustin' ye t' take out a laddie's sailboat with th' way yer lookin' now!"

Brendan shut his eyes and leaned his head back against the wall. If he looked as bad as he felt, it must be terrible indeed. He had the shakes. He was sweating fiercely beneath his shirt, his legs felt like jelly, and the room was spinning around him. And worst of all, the other patrons of the tavern were all staring at him. He clawed at his stock, his fingers fumbling. A dark tunnel began to snuff out his vision, and a roaring started in his ears. Faith, he had to get out of here before he passed out!

"Liam . . . Liam, help me—"

"Easy there, lad." He felt Liam's hand beneath his elbow, the strength of his massive arms holding him up. "I've got ye. . . ." Shakily Brendan mopped his brow and, as Liam eased him down, collapsed into a chair.

Faith.

He was aware of something wet and cool on his forehead and realized he'd slumped forward, his brow resting in a puddle of moisture from Liam's ale mug. Cursing, Liam dragged him back up. The chair pressed against his spine, and the room swayed sickeningly as his head fell back over the top rung. He opened his eyes and saw the weathered beams of the ceiling, spinning above.

"F'r God's sake, Brendan—"

"You all right, Captain Merrick?"

It was the tavern's owner. "He's fine, Moses!" Liam declared, holding Brendan upright by his immaculate lapels. "Just a bit too much t' drink, eh, Cap'n?"

He shut his eyes, nodding weakly.

"Fetch him up a cup o' hard cider," Liam said. "He'll not be thankin' me f'r it in the mornin,' but he could sure use it now."

The innkeeper hurried off, frowning, for he'd never known Captain Merrick to be a drinking man.

"Now, ye listen t' me!" Liam yanked him forward, snapping his neck, until his blue eyes bored into his captain's hazy sienna ones. "I'll not have ye makin' a spectacle o' y'rself. Y'r not takin' *Kestrel* t' Maine f'r the sake o' helpin' the Americans drive th' British out—y'r runnin' from somethin'! Wha' 'tis it *this* time, huh? Or need I ask?"

He took a moment to answer. "Miss Mira Ashton."

"God Almighty, when're ye goin' t' *stop* runnin,' Brendan, an' let th' wee lassie catch ye? She loves ye, she does, an' if only ye'd f'rgit about that bloody Julia an' see Mira f'r who she is an' not f'r who she ain't—"

"She's angry with me, Liam. .. .."

"So, she'll get o'er 't! I told ye, she loves ye; 'tis the only reason she's riled! Th' lassie stuck by y'r bed f'r the entire time ye were lyin' in it! She took care o' ye when ye couldn't, bathed ye an' washed y'r hair, made ye drink, an' fixed ye up real handsome-like when ye had visitors—"

"*Visitors?*" he said, mortified.

"Aye, *visitors!* Some o' the townsfolk dropped in t' pray f'r y'r recovery."

Some of them, Liam had said. Weakly Brendan waved his hand. "If they were dropping by, it was probably to see Matt. Poor, blind Matt . . ." He shut his eyes, reliving the pain of *Proud Mistress*'s death all over again.

"Poor *blind* Matt, eh? Huh! Well, let me tell ye, Brendan, he c'n see well enough t' note just how pretty y'r sister is of late! Those two 'ave become thick'r th'n peas in a pod since ye brought him home! Maybe his eyesight's a bit hampered, but I bet he could take a ship t' sea if he had t'! But nooo! He's too busy feigning how blind he is so y'r sister c'n dote on him! I've seen th' way his eyes follow her when her back is turned, an' there ain't no trace o' blindness a'tall! This mornin' he asked her t' paint his picture, an' unless I miss me guess, the next thing he'll be a-doin' is askin' ye t' design a ship f'r him with a figurehead that looks like our Eveleen!''

"Faith,'' Brendan murmured, stunned. He shook his head, trying to clear it. Matthew? And *Eveleen*?!

"So if our fine Cap'n Ashton c'n let y'r sister get *her* claws int' him, well, ye c'n let Miss Mira get hers int' you. Ye go a-sneakin' off withou' tellin' her y'r goin' an' she's goin' t' come aft'r ye wi' those claws bared.''

Brendan looked away. "I *must* go to Penobscot,'' he insisted, trying to keep his thoughts from spinning. "Newburyport has already sent four other ships. . . . 'Tis only right that I bring *Kestrel*, too. Massachusetts has called on every privateer . . . and a spell of dizziness shan't stop me from going, too. I'm an American now, aren't I?'' He grinned. "Besides, Matthew tells me that Paul Revere himself is up there, in charge of the artillery for the land forces. I've always wanted to meet the lad!''

"Brendan—''

"It *is* an amphibious effort. Why, I could get *Kestrel* to Penobscot in less than two days. . . .''

"Brendan—''

"Well, I'm not much good here, mopping your ale up with my forehead!''

"Ye go t' Maine an' th' Brits'll be moppin' *you* up off o' *Kestrel*'s deck!''

Moses was coming back, carrying a tray with two pewter mugs balanced on it. Liam quickly exchanged his empty mug for Brendan's full one, so that to all appearances his captain had consumed the beverage and not him. Then he gripped his immaculate sleeve and stared desperately into his eyes. "Listen, Brendan. Th' Americans 'ave been up there f'r nearly a month an' still 'aven't made a move t' rout th' British, thanks t' some bloody impasse b'tween th' general in charge o' th' land forces an' th' commodore commandin' th' sea forces. That commodore is Dudley Saltonstall, Brendan, an' ye know as well as I do tha' t'he ain' t'a pleasant person t' serve under, let alone deal with!''

"But, Liam, I *have* to go." The dizziness was returning. Desperately Brendan bent his head to his arms and gripped the edge of the table. "Don't you understand? I *have* to. To restore Mira's faith in me. To restore this town's faith in me—"

"F'r God's sake, Brendan—"

"To restore my own faith in me!"

He stood up, staggered, and almost fell.

"Brendan!"

His knee hit the chair, toppled it. He reeled off the table, drew the stares of a group of seamen. Two men looked up from their game of backgammon, their brows raised.

"Brendan!"

It took every bit of his strength to walk through that smoky, crowded room, but he did it, pulling his tricorn low over his eyes so no one would see how pale and sick he really was.

And then he felt Liam's hand on his arm.

"God Almighty, Brendan, ye can't be goin' off—"

Brendan raised his head, squared his elegant shoulders, and slowly turned. He personified the hauteur of the British Royal Navy, from the braid on his tricorn to the buckles on his shoes to the very way in which he stood. "In future, *Mr.* Doherty, I'll thank you to remember yourself. I am your captain. Please address me as such!" Then, grinning to soften the remark, he pushed open the door and stumbled off into the night.

Wolfe Tavern was abuzz; to think that after a nearly fatal injury, the Captain from Connacht could come in here, drink with the rest of them, put the big, strapping lieutenant in his place, and then saunter off to war, as right as rain!

Except that no one but Liam knew that his captain *wasn't* as right as rain.

No one but the captain himself knew that he passed out three times on his way to the waterfront.

And no one but *Kestrel* knew that he never made it to

his cabin, but collapsed upon a neatly coiled pile of rope on the foredeck, and there, spent the night.

The Penobscot Expedition. It was on everyone's minds, everyone's tongues. News filtered down from Maine, trickled up from Boston. The redcoats had entrenched themselves on the little peninsula of Bagaduce, and undaunted by the huge American fleet sent to rout them from their stronghold, merely swapped their shovels and picks for muskets and prepared to defend their little fort. Captain Henry Mowat, that hated Briton who'd laid waste to Falmouth several years past, had drawn his three sloops-of-war up around the fort to protect it, and according to reports, the most action the Maine woods had seen was some minimal gunfire between the British and the American fleet. A bit of territory had been gained on nearby Nautilus Island, assisted by fire from Newburyport's own *Pallas,* but that was all. Despite the American's superior forces, the British were still in Maine.

And expecting reinforcements any day.

In Massachusetts, tempers were strained. In the Ashton household, where those tempers usually ran rampant, the explosion came as Mira went down to breakfast.

Unfortunately, it was set off by an innocent-looking blueberry betty that she'd made in the hopes of showing Brendan just how well she was learning to cook—and therefore, keeping him home. But Brendan, unfortunately, was still upstairs, and so it was Ephraim who had the misfortune of taking the first bite.

"Jesus—bloody—Christ!"

Pieces of blueberry, topping, and other unspeakable ingredients shot across the table like grapeshot from a cannon. Blackened dough hit Eveleen's cheek. Cream spattered Matt's spectacles. Tears streamed down Ephraim's face; and then, reddening with fury, he picked up his plate and flung it, food and all, across the room, where it smashed against the elegant wainscoted wall and left a sticky, dripping mess of blueberries that slid, in great, ugly chunks, toward the floor.

Luff, who'd been quietly begging two feet away from

where the plate hit, fled the room with his tail between his legs.

"Cripes an' GUTS, this god-awful shit is gonna put me in my grave! Man can't eat a decent meal without it bein' booby-trapped! What the bloody hell did ye put in it, Mira, a whole goddamned lemon?!"

Mira slammed down her own fork. Across from her, Matt, his lips twitching, removed his spectacles and wiped them with his shirttails, unaware that he was smearing cream all over the lenses and making the mess worse. He put them back on, his kind brown eyes blank and sightless as he stared at the wall and the shapeless purple mess oozing down it. Beside him, Eveleen wordlessly dished up a plate of fried eggs and ham and set it before him, her hand lingering on his as she placed a fork in his hand and guided it to the plate. "As a matter of fact," Mira snapped, hurt that her father found fault with a treat that had taken her all morning to make, "I put *two* lemons in it. *And* a cup of vinegar *and* a cup of sour milk, *and*—"

"Sour *milk?! You put sour milk in it?!*"

"I couldn't find any butter!"

"What the hell does butter have to do with sour milk?! Any woman worth her salt'd know not to put sour milk in a blueberry betty, let alone two friggin' lemons—"

"I thought the sugar would balance out the sourness!"

"What sugar? There ain't no sugar in this *CRAP!*"

"I think she forgot to put it in," Matt speculated, trying not to laugh.

"I didn't either! I just didn't have enough, so I substituted something else!"

"What?!"

"The extra lemon!"

"I ain't bloody surprised! Ye'll never make a good wife fer anyone, ye hear me? No man'll have a woman who can't cook, can't bake, an' brings home enough bloody animals to start a bleedin' zoo! He won't put up with it! *I* won't put up with it! Thank God that Ultimatum is almost up and I can git ye out of my hair *and my kitchen!*"

Mira lunged to her feet and flung her own plate. Ephraim ducked just in time, but a shower of blackened crust fell like rain into his snowy hair. Enraged, he leapt to his feet.

"Merrick!" he roared, at the top of his lungs.

Matt jumped to his feet. "For God's sake, keep your voice down; the poor fellow's sleeping!"

"He ain't sleepin' no more! I want him down here and eatin' and gainin' his strength back so he can take that cussed schooner outta here and git it to Maine with the rest of the fleet!"

Matt slammed his fork down. "That's what's really eating you, isn't it?!" he raged, his spectacles fogging up behind flecks of cream and smeared blueberries. "The fact that you have nothing to brag about to your old cronies down at Davenport's!"

"Two privateersmen under my roof and the finest schooner the Commonwealth has ever seen, and none of 'em are in Penobscot! Damned right I have nothin' to brag about! Cripes, I ain't never been so humiliated in my whole life!"

"You lower your voice before you wake Merrick!" Matt shouted.

"I'll raise it till he gits himself down here and takes that schooner outta here!"

Eveleen grabbed Matt's arm, hoping to prevent a fight. But it was too late. Mira, green eyes blazing, had leapt onto a chair and was screeching down at her father in a voice that would not only wake Brendan, but half of Newburyport as well. "Matt's right! You just want *Kestrel* in that Expedition so you'll have something to read about in that stupid newspaper! Something to brag about to your stupid friends in that stupid tavern!"

"Don't you talk like that to yer father, ye hear me?!"

"You just want to impress everyone with that schooner! You want everyone to know *you* built her! You don't care about kicking the British out of Maine, you don't care about Brendan—"

"I do, too, and it don't matter to me *who* takes her, long's she's a part of that Expedition!"

"Which you see as nothing more than a damned *showground* for your masterpiece!"

"*Kestrel* speaks for herself; she don't need me to brag about 'er!"

"And she's not asking you to! And I'll tell you this, neither Liam Doherty nor me nor God himself are going to take that schooner anywhere! She's *Brendan's*, do you hear me?! Brendan's! *He is her captain!* And no one, I repeat, *no one,* is going to take her anywhere!"

"She oughtta take her rightful place in that Expedition!"

"She will when her captain is well enough to command her!"

"She'll take it whether I have to go and command her myself!"

"That'll be the bloody day!" Mira leapt from the chair, let loose a string of curses, and stormed from the room, trailed by Rescue Effort Number Forty and Ephraim's loud bellowing. No wonder Brendan felt obliged to go to Maine! Damn Father and his stiff-necked pride! She was sick of him controlling other people's lives! Furious, she raced up the stairs, tore down the hall, and flung open the door to Brendan's room.

She came up short, her mouth hanging open. The bed was made as neatly as a seaman's berth, and the room was empty.

She clenched her fists at her side. *No . . .*

And then she saw that *Kestrel*'s huge red and white striped flag was gone.

Damn him! She was too late! Without breaking stride, Mira raced from the room. There was no time to lose!

Chapter 29

"Oh, there was a proud schooner, her name was Kestrel, and no Brit could catch her when she spread her tops'ls! Sharp-hulled and lovely, a lady she be, she's sweet and she's pretty, she's Queen of the Sea! Singin', down, down, down Derry down!"

Drifting along under shortened sail, *Kestrel* left a long, lazy wake of foam winding back among pine-studded islands and coves. She'd left Newburyport several hours before, in the dead of night; now morning light burst over the ocean, touched upon streaming pennants some eighty feet above deck, raced out along topsail yards, and dragged brilliant orange fingers down the length of her masts to flood the decks below. It glinted on sleepy guns, turned varnished woodwork to gold, sharpened stays and ratlines against the bright blue sky, and painted the deck in myriad variations of color, light, and shadow.

"Oh, her decks are of white oak, her masts of Maine spruce, of the might of the Brits, oh we don't give a deuce! Be it gale or dead calm, the sweet Kestrel will fly! For freedom from tyranny we're willin' to die! Singin' down, down, down Derry down!"

The smell of fresh coffee and frying fat stained the air. Galley smoke crept from the foredeck area and was snatched away by the wind. Men, throwing long shadows across the deck, were coming topside now, carrying their breakfasts. Some took one look at the barefoot figure standing atop *Freedom*'s homely old barrel and dropped their plates of biscuit and fried pork; others gulped and shot apprehensive glances toward the hatch—where any moment now, the captain would be coming topside.

Mr. Starr wasn't wearing his tarpaulin hat. He wasn't

wearing his odd little "sun" glasses. And he wasn't wearing his breeches.

He was wearing skirts.

And they were tucked up into his waistband and showing a very fine, very pretty pair of curvy, well-shaped legs.

The guise was over, then. The day of reckoning had come.

"Well, her captain's a man bred from old Cornwall way, but the luck of the Irish goes with him this day! Not afraid of the Brits, oh he's brave and he's bold! And under his hand, Kestrel's wings'll not fold! Singin' down, down, down Derry down!"

And now a black tricorn was coming up through the hatch.

Liam put down his fiddle.

Fergus produced a crystal.

And Dalby clutched his stomach.

As immaculate as ever, the captain, walking with the assistance of a cane, made a fine sight as he emerged on deck. He wore a red waistcoat over a bright white shirt, and his breeches, trimmed with gold embroidery, were molded to his long, handsome thighs. Sunlight glinted from his sword hilt and shoe buckles, and his tricorn sat jauntily atop his rich chestnut hair, boyishly tousled from sleep and caught in a loose queue. Spying Liam, who stood at the helm with a very pale-looking Dalby, he snapped off a brisk salute. *"Dia dhuit ar maidin, Liam!"*

"Good mornin' y'rself, Cap'n!"

"Fine day to be at sea, eh? If the wind kicks up, we'll raise Penobscot Bay by sundown, I should think."

"Aye, Cap'n." There was a suspicious twinkle in Liam's eye, but Brendan, preoccupied, missed it. Crossing the deck, he wandered to the weather rail and gazed out over the sparkling sea, watching *Kestrel's* frothy wake as though he could follow it all the way back to Newburyport.

"He doesn't see her," John Keefe whispered.

"Give 'im a moment," Liam predicted.

Dalby clutched his stomach, his voice full of doom. "Well, if he doesn't see her, he'll certainly *hear* her. . . ."

"Well, a Brit boxed us in b'tween island and shore, and

our bold Captain Merrick said 'fear ye no more! Hoist out those old oars even though it is deep, we'll fool that old Briton and Kestrel we'll keep!' Singin' down, down, down Derry down!''

But Brendan, deep in thought, was oblivious to the singing. Propping his elbows on the rail, he sipped his coffee and watched a gull wheeling high above. The sea rolled before him. Spray hissed at *Kestrel*'s bows, cooled his cheeks, made his coffee mug sticky and damp in his hands. He felt pretty good this morning. A bit weak, but at least he could see straight. Think straight.

Mira.

What had her reaction been when she'd arisen this morn and discovered him gone?

Perhaps he shouldn't have left so hastily.

Maybe when he reached Penobscot he could convince Commodore Saltonstall to lift the siege and make the long overdue attack on the British; maybe in doing so, he could give *Kestrel* back her glory; and maybe, just maybe, he could return to Newburyport and make Mira his wife.

Make her his wife.

He smiled and shut his eyes, envisioning it. . . .

The wind began to freshen, whipping up froth on the azure sea, driving over *Kestrel*'s stern and sending wave-chop slapping against her hull. Thousands of little pockmarks dotted the ocean's surface. Above, blocks and tackles swung, wind hummed through taut shrouds, and masts creaked as the schooner rolled on the long swells.

Forward, the wind caught the end of Mr. Starr's braid and made it dance a jig around his little rump.

"Well, the Briton was fooled by our captain's bold plan, figured it was too shallow, so off they did stand! No sooner had they bore off and a-way, Kestrel spread her great wings and we laugh till this day! Singin' down, down, down Derry down!''

He shook his head, trying to clear it. Odd, that voice . . . strange, but familiar. Shrugging, he fished his sketchbook and a pencil out of his pocket and studied the gull hovering just beyond the tip of the fore topsail yard. But he couldn't think. Couldn't concentrate. Kept remembering soft, rose-scented hair tumbling down in his face. Bare fairy-feet springing up and down in his bed. Green eyes alight with joy, salty tears washing his face . . .

"Well, the Kestrel, she's huntin' those Britishers down, she's a thorn in the side of His Majesty's crown! But our captain's a sly one, a bold one he be! Sails Kestrel on a course marked Li-i-ber-ty! Singin', down, down, down Derry down . . .

He leaned the sketchpad against the rail and kneaded his temples. The sunlight hurt his eyes. The sea reflected against the launch, vibrated against shimmering waves, and hurt his eyes even more. Faith, maybe he ought to get some of those—what were they called?—ah yes, sunglasses that Mr. Starr had. Irritated, but not knowing why, he turned from the rail.

And saw his men staring at him as though he'd grown a third arm.

"For heaven's sake, string up that mainsail and let's make some time!" he snapped. Faith, what the devil was wrong with everyone this morning?!

Seaman ran to the sheets. Up went the gaff on its bridle, like some giant sacrifice to the blinding sun above. Inch by inch it climbed, the proud mainsail rising with it, and finally the boom, swinging gently in the wind. Canvas shook itself out, fluttered, and hardened in a tight curve of brightness against the azure sky. Brendan's momentary irritation dissipated instantly, and a thrill went through him at the sheer majesty of the moment. Laughing out loud, he wrapped his hands around his coffee mug and called, *"Maith go leor,* laddies! Good enough! Now look lively and hoist the foresail!"

Kestrel kicked up her heels like a spring filly, and the water beneath her began to sing. Eyes watering in the intense sunlight, Brendan gazed up at the giant mainsail, watching its reef points dancing and flirting in the wind. And then, blinking away the sunspots, he turned his head, suddenly realizing what was making him feel so devilishly irritated. . . .

That god-awful singing.

He lowered his pencil, looking for its source. And then he saw a figure standing atop *Freedom,* head thrown back, bare feet braced on the cannon's long breech, and rooster perched on his scrawny shoulder.

It was Mr. Starr.

Brendan dropped his coffee cup.

"And so we head seawards with a stiff wind a-beam, hanging fores'l and main, and our heels kicking clean! With Doodle as music and guns as our sting, as we headed to sea all the bells they did ring! Singin' down, down, down Derry down!"

"Up staysails and jibs . . ." Brendan heard himself saying. And then—*faith, what the* devil *was Mr. Starr wearing?!*

"With a gale blowin' hard through our shrouds and our stays, Cap'n Merrick he said, 'Lads, now don't ye belay! There's a Brit lurkin' well off our starboard bow—and we'll ne-e-ver catch him if we stay here and row!' Singin' down, down, down Derry down!"

Skirts.

His eyes bugged out and his mouth opened and closed. *Skirts!*

And beneath them, long, curvy legs, kissed by sunlight and glowing like honey. A doll-sized waist, and a shirt that did nothing to conceal the sweet valley between her even sweeter breasts. He stared into her eyes. She stared back. And then she saluted, smiled, and a fan of lines crinkled the sides of her impudent little nose like cat whiskers.

"Well, the Kestrel, being such a right fine la-dy, she opened her wings and she took to the sea! With the spray in her teeth and her guns aimed low, our captain he shouted, 'Fire on the uproll!' Singin' down, down, down Derry down!"

He dropped his pencil. The sketchbook slid from his limp fingers and fell into the sea.

"Liam!"

He reeled and caught the rail for support.

"LIAM!"

And then she threw back her head, laughed, and in a loud, ringing voice, belted out, *"Well, a broadside like that you just ne'er did see, on the Britisher's decks there was death and melee! Our Cap'n he nodded and then he*

did grin, 'Now let's see ye load up lads and do it again!'
Singin' DOWN, DOWN, DOWN DERRY DOWN!''

Liam appeared, his mouth twitching with laughter.

"Aye, Cap'n?"

They were all staring at him, even the rooster. They'd known all along, every last one of them! Brendan took a deep, steadying breath, and pulling out his speaking trumpet, agitatedly rapped it against his thigh. He never took his eyes off his little gunner. "Tell me, *Mr. Doherty,* just *who* was at *Kestrel's* helm the day you rescued me from Crichton?"

Liam stared at him blankly, pretending ignorance. "The helm, sir?"

"Yes, Liam, the helm! H-E-L-M, helm! *Tá ainm diobhal,* what are you, deaf?! It wasn't Mr. Keefe, it wasn't Mr. Reilly, and it most certainly wasn't you! What I want to know is, *who the devil almost overset my ship!''*

"Er . . . uh, why, th' gunner, sir, but he 'ad th' ship well und'r control—"

"The gunner!" He felt a muscle twitch in his jaw. It could've been a controlled grin. It could've been anger. It was neither. "You mean *Mr. Starr?!''*

"Aye. Ye see, Brendan, there was really no one else t' do it. . . . Keefe, well, he 'ad three sheets t' th' wind, 'n' Dalby was complainin' about his stomach—Mr. Starr made supper that night, ye see—'n' poor Reilly, er . . ."

"Mr. Reilly *what,* Liam?!"

"Got his eye blackened by Mr. Starr, sir . . ." Liam said, lamely.

"And why, pray tell, did Mr. Starr blacken his eye, Liam?!"

"Well, uh, he was threatenin' t' 'ave his rooster f'r supper, sir."

"I see." Brendan shut his eyes. And then he grinned, a hard, exasperated grin mixed with admiration. He almost wanted to wrap his hands around her neck and strangle her! Sunglass, eh? *Albino?!*

"Where ye goin', Brendan?"

"Below." He removed his tricorn, raked a shaking hand through his hair, and set the hat back on his head. "I think I need to . . . to lie down for a spell."

"You all right, Cap'n?"

He kept walking, his back stiff and straight, his elegant shoulders thrown back. But no one saw that those shoulders were shaking with mirth.

She had followed him. *Followed him!* And, by the looks of it, forgiven him.

"Cap'n?"

Brendan paused, turned, and met his lieutenant's questioning gaze. "Liam—" he grinned and swung his speaking trumpet once around his wrist "—I've never felt better. Please see that *Kestrel* doesn't get into any mischief, would you? And then send *Mr. Starr* down to me so that I can put an end to *his!*"

Liam's eyes lit up. Slyly he said, "But, Cap'n, I thought ye were goin' t' be lyin' down. . . ."

Brendan shoved his tricorn back. His eyes glowed like honey in the morning light, and his smile was dazzling, bright, and completely roguish.

"I intend to be, Liam," he said. Still grinning, he turned, and went below.

He did not expect her to appear looking sheepish, worried, or contrite, and indeed, she didn't disappoint him. The door banged open and she swaggered in, the rooster perched insolently on her shoulder with its iridescent feathers shining in the sun. Still humming that awful tune, she shoved her forefinger beneath the bird's breast until it climbed up on it. Then she walked to one of the chairs surrounding the table and deposited it on the top rung.

The rooster stood there, looking discomfited.

It cocked its head, looking at the shiny buttons of Brendan's waistcoat.

And then it tensed, shuddered, and squirted out a wet dropping that splattered the varnished floor.

The gunner snapped off a crisp salute. "Mr. Starr, sir, reporting for duty!"

"Please sit down, Mr. Starr."

She shrugged, sauntered to the window seat, and draped herself atop the cushion, idly playing with the end of her long braid and letting her eyes rake appreciatively over his face, his chest, and the front of his breeches. He felt the fabric begin to tighten across his loins. Carefully sidestepping the rooster's mess, he pulled out a chair, steepled his hands, and tried to regard her thoughtfully. Laughter bubbled up in his throat, threatening to wreck his composure. The little imp!

His lips twitched. "Mr. Starr," he said calmly, "please tell me what you know of our role in this so-called Penobscot Expedition."

"Aye, sir. To lend our assistance to Commodore Saltonstall's fleet and kick the damned Brits out of the Penobscot."

He gazed at the tantalizing display of flesh blatantly revealed by her loose shirt. "Very good, Mr. Starr."

"But it's all a big secret, because we don't want the British to find out and send for reinforcements."

"That's right, it *is* a big secret. You're very good at keeping secrets, aren't you, Mr. Starr?"

"Oh, aye, Cap'n." Her eyes gleamed. "Very good."

He stared at her intently. "Have you one you'd like to share with me, Mr. Starr?"

She twisted her glossy braid around her wrist, never taking her eyes off him. "Only if ye'd like to hear it."

His gaze traveled over her curvy body, her gently flaring hips, her skirts, and the shapely calves beneath them. "I think I should very *much* like to hear it."

"Ye sure?"

He smiled, leaned back, and crossed his arms behind his head, waiting. "Very sure, Mr. Starr."

She jerked her thumb toward her pet. "See that there rooster? He always shits in threes."

Slumping forward, Brendan leaned his brow into the heel of his hand to hide his laughter.

"Sir, you all right? I can come back another time when you're feeling better."

"I'm feeling just fine—Mr. Starr."

"Are you sure, now? We wouldn't want you to overexert yourself after that injury and all."

He looked up, his eyes mirthful, his lips twitching. "Mr. Starr, please get up off of that window seat, come over here, and take your shirt off."

"Sir?"

"And your er, breeches, too."

"I'd rather not, sir."

"And why is that, Mr. Starr?"

"I find the window seat quite comfortable. Why don't you come over here and let me take *your* shirt off?"

His brows shot up.

"And your breeches, too," she mimicked.

They stared at each other. Her nose wrinkled with humor; he grinned and got to his feet. Then they both burst into helpless laughter.

"I ought to have you keelhauled for your deceit, *Mr. Starr!* To think, all this time that I've been missing my wee Newburyport lassie, and here she is, manning a gun right under my very nose!"

Laughing, she lay back on the cushions and folded her arms behind her head. Her shoulders crushed the rich velvet, and she felt the thrum of tiller and rudder vibrating against her spine. Boldly she let her gaze travel down the handsome length of his body, until it rested on the telltale bulge at the front of his breeches. "Missing me, huh? You mean you're not going to *run* this time, Cap'n?"

"Run?" His warm sienna gaze slid over her body, caressing her. "I wouldn't dream of it . . . *Mr. Starr.*"

"Ye dreamt of it last night."

He leaned over her, unlatched the stern windows, and threw them open. Sea wind, salty and full of tang, danced into the cabin and shivered over her skin, mixing with the deliciously clean scent of his shaving soap. "Last night was different." She looked up at him, and he leaned his forearms against the sill, hung his head, and gazed lovingly down at her. "I had a reason for running."

"And what was that, Cap'n?"

"Because I couldn't stand to see how upset I'd made you."

"I was only upset because I love you."

"Love me, *Moyrrra?*"

"Aye. But I think you need to be convinced of it," she said, smiling as she reached up and touched his cheek. She put her finger to her tongue and licked it, grinning wickedly as his eyes darkened and his pale lashes lowered. His breathing quickened. The room grew quiet. His head drooped slightly, and she ran her tongue around her finger until she knew she had him burning against the taut fabric of his breeches. Then she withdrew her finger and touched it to his lips, gently tracing their sensuous shape, painting them with her own moisture. His eyes grew heavy, unfocused.

"You should know that *Kestrel* and I have settled our differences. I am quite willing to share you with her—under one condition."

He sighed, his lips moving against her finger. "Anything, *stóirín*."

"You must share her—with *me*."

"That's a lot to ask. . . . You nearly let her broach to."

"Like hell I did."

He smiled lazily, and taking her hand, rubbed it over his cheek and down his chin. "All right. You had her well in hand. Why should I have doubted you?"

"You shouldn't. I've been sailing almost as long as Matt. Besides, *Kestrel* and I had a common goal that day. We were depending on each other. She wouldn't have let me down. She wouldn't have let *you* down."

"Neither of you would have. . . ."

"That's for darned sure! So are you going to let me take her out once in a while?"

"Er . . . well, maybe."

He was leaning heavily against the sill, his forearms supporting his weight. Above his head a tin lantern swung with the roll of the ship.

"I'm not going to prove how much I love you till you give me a 'yes' answer, Brendan," she said, slowly thrusting the buttons of his waistcoat through their holes, one by one. Her other hand drifted downward, grazing his manhood through his breeches. His eyes slipped shut and he leaned his brow on one arm, allowing her the pleasure of seducing him.

" 'Yes' to what?" he asked, distantly.

"To taking *Kestrel* out." She drove her palm against him, rubbing hard. "Didn't you hear me?"

"No . . . Yes . . . Faith, I don't care. . . ."

"Is this too much for you?"

"No, take her out. . . . I really don't care."

"No, Brendan, I'm talking about *this* now." She squeezed him through the breeches and ran her fingernail down his thigh. "Am I pushing you too far? Can you withstand a rigorous afternoon of making love to me without fainting in my lap?"

He managed a quirky grin. "The day I cannot love a wee lassie is the day I'm dead and buried."

She stared up into his mirthful eyes. Then, playfully, she reached up, jerked his arms down, and squealed with delight as he fell atop her. In one quick motion she flipped him onto his back, her laughter ringing out and filling the cabin with joy. Her soul sang. Tears of happiness dampened her cheeks.

"Let me up, lassie," he said, half-convincingly, as she sat on his belly.

Wantonly she rubbed her cheek, then her breasts, against the buttons of his waistcoat, teasing him and reveling in the power she had over him. "In time, *sir!* I'm not through . . . *convincing* you yet!" She straddled his chest and pinned his arms down with her knees. His waistcoat gapped open; she drove her hands beneath it and caressed his chest with her thumbs, feeling his heart thumping madly. He struggled once, twice, and then lay still, completely at her mercy.

Mira didn't waste the moment. She bent her head and kissed the lean curve of his jaw, the planes of his cheeks, the tip of his nose. She curved an arm around the back of his neck and dragged the waistcoat from his elegant shoulders until only his crisp white shirt separated his heartbeat from her hand. Pressing her palm there, she let her fingers curl in the springy hair that matted his chest and linger on the little burst of scar tissue. Slowly she rubbed it, occasionally letting her hand drift downward toward the flat of his belly. Then she sat back. Beneath her rump, she felt his rock-hard arousal.

"Am I proving my love for you well enough, Brendan?"

"No, *stóirín* . . . I fear you must try harder."

"Will you allow me all afternoon to do so?"

"And half of the night if you need it . . ."

Smiling in feline promise, she slowly unbuttoned his

stock. With her teeth, she drew it from his neck and let it fall to the floor. His neck was warm against her lips, the woodsy scent of his shaving soap heady and clean. She buried her face against the base of his throat, unbuttoning his shirt with her lips and teeth and letting her tongue slip beneath the closures to lap at his salty, lightly furred skin.

"Faith," he murmured, shutting his eyes in dizzy, tortured delight.

She laughed against his neck, sending shivers up his spine.

"Sunglasses . . . that floppy hat . . . albino . . . A clever disguise, Mr. Starr."

"And what gave me away, Captain?"

"Three things." He managed to get his arm out from beneath her knee, and smiling lazily, ran his hand up her sleek thighs. She shivered as he caressed her calves, the sensitive skin at the back of her knees. "One, that awful singing . . ."

"Awful?!"

She dragged him up and pulled the shirt over his head. "Two, that rooster."

"A fine cock, eh, Cap'n?"

He groaned as she moved onto her side and swept her hand over the hard bulge in his breeches.

"But it was Dalby's reaction to your cooking that did it. . . ."

"My cooking!"

"Yes, *mo stór*. 'Twas a dead giveaway, I'm afraid. Did you bake him one of your apple pies?"

"Well, I tried. . . ." She was opening the flap of his breeches now, her hand roving against him. "I'm not very good at shipboard cooking, you know."

He laughed, then gasped as her hands cupped him, pressing on either side, gently rolling his staff between her palms until he thought he would die.

"Faith, lassie!"

She lowered her head, rubbing it against his arms like a cat begging to be stroked. Thick, glossy hair tickled his belly, caught in the nest of hair in which his manhood was rooted, and felt like silk on his skin. Her tongue flicked against his belly, and his skin went drum-tight. And now she was peeling the breeches from his hips, dragging them down his thighs. Her hands pushed against his shoulders, holding him down. Her lips circled his manhood, branding him with their heat, their love. His vision blurred and began to spin and he shut his eyes, gripping the side of the bunk to anchor himself in consciousness. And when he opened his eyes, he saw her gazing down at him in triumph, licking her lips and slowly untying the leather thong from her braid.

Mesmerized, he watched her fingers thread through that glorious, thick mane, until it spilled over her shoulders, down her back, and over his jutting manhood.

Her hands followed, then her mouth, and his head twisted on the pillow. *"Moyrrra,"* he said weakly.

She let her tongue flick over him. Sweat broke out on his brow, beneath his back.

"Moyrrra, I beg of you, please stop. . . ."

"But, Brendan," she said impishly, raising her head, "I'm not through convincing you." She caught one of his fine, artist's hands, dropping kisses over the long-boned digits, the gentle rise of his knuckles, and the hollows between each finger. She turned it palm upward and kissed it, once, twice; then her tongue slipped out and traced little circles there, around and around until he shivered and moaned and shut his eyes in torment.

"You are about to make me lose control of myself, *stóirín!"*

Laughing, she dragged her fingernails down the indentation of his chest and through the soft hair there, past the taut hardness of his torso, into the hot rug of chestnut and gold curls, and along the inside of his thighs. He gritted his teeth, holding himself together with a strength he didn't know he had. She untucked her skirts, unfastened them, pulled them tantalizingly across his chest, and let them slide to the cushion. Beneath, she was stark naked. *Oh, faith,* he thought, desperately. *God help me.* His blood went thick and hot. The sheets grew damp beneath his spine. His vision began to spin. Dragging his hand out from beneath her, he blindly slid it up her leg and to the inside of her thigh, finding her ready for him, hot and sweet and moist. She let him touch her for a brief, teasing moment, then caught his hand, grinning wickedly.

"Patience, sir," she purred huskily, "is a virtue."

Then she traced his thighs, cupped the fruit of his loins, stroked his tumescence with her palm. He filled her hand with hot, hard desire, and slowly, tantalizingly, she dragged his swollen tip toward her molten core, teasing him with her slick sweetness, rubbing herself with him. He reached for her, but again she pushed his arm away, preferring to make him suffer this sweet torture before succumbing to his fiery caresses. He gripped the edge of the bench seat, his knuckles whitening, his breath coming hard and fast.

"*Moyrrra . . .*"

She rose up on her knees, and he had a glorious view of rich, glossy hair tumbling over proud breasts, down her stomach, and around the dark, curling hair at the junction of her thighs. She held his gaze, then looked down at him, licking her lips. Slowly, agonizingly, she lowered herself atop him, straddling him.

"Are you sure this isn't too much for you, Brendan?"

He'd sooner die than admit that perhaps it was, for she was fading in and out of his spinning vision. But the dizzying effect only heightened the pleasure. And as for her taunting, teasing ways . . . well, he'd had enough of that! Gripping her hips, he began to raise her up and down, slowly sliding her along the length of him until her triumphant smile faded and her rosy lips parted with desire.

"Ah, *grá mo chroí,*" he murmured, sinking into her luscious moistness.

For a long moment he held her poised on the tip of his rigid manhood as he drank in the lovely sight of her. Then he slowly lowered her, filling her completely and touching upon the highest reaches of her hot and moist cavern. Her head fell back in sweet pleasure, sending her glorious hair spilling down her back. Her hips began to move, to rotate, to slide up and down over him, riding him in timeless rhythm. Impatiently he slid his hands beneath her shirt, finally pulling it over her head until her breasts were bared to his hot palms. He stared at the pale, sweet globes, so perfectly formed, like twin melons capped by dusky little rosebuds; and then he swiftly lifted her from himself, set her on her back, and, quivering with hungry, waiting desire, suckled her hard-nippled breasts until she was whimpering and writhing beneath him.

"So . . . is this my punishment, Captain?" she breathed.

"Just the beginning of it, lassie. No one deceives the captain and gets away with it." He caught her hands above her head and took each breast into his mouth in turns, licking and sucking the taut, budding peaks until her head began to thrash on the cushions beneath him.

"Brendan, please . . . please, take me."

"Not yet, *mo bhourneen,*" he murmured, against a tight nipple.

His lips burned the valley between her breasts, his hand roved down her stomach and parted her thighs. His fingers tickled the soft curls of her womanhood, finding her slick and ready. He teased the stiffening bud of her desire until she was sobbing, crying, begging—then he locked his arm over her hips and held her pinned to the cushions while his mouth moved into those moist, fragrant curls.

"Brendan . . ."

His lips, then his mouth, fastened upon the plump, sweet folds of rosy womanhood. She spasmed upward, her mouth open in a soundless scream. His tongue flicked in, flicked out, lapping, licking, sucking, and drawing her sweet honey. She cried out in sweet agony, feeling his tongue laving her, pulling her into his hot mouth. And still she couldn't move, pinned like a butterfly beneath his sinewy arm.

"Brendan, oh, Brendan, oh, oh, *God!*"

The room whirled, then blew apart in a blinding burst of color that sent her spinning out over the edge and into darkness. When she opened her eyes, he was kissing her, his mouth hot and moist against her neck, his hands rough and gentle in her hair, over her breasts.

Still throbbing from her explosive release, she wrapped her legs around his hips, her arms around his back, and with a fierce sob, drove herself up against his shaft. And when he finally slammed into her, filling her with his seed, she climaxed again and then again, her cries muffled beneath his lips.

They lay together, breathing hard, slowly drifting down from the heights. As they stroked and touched and gazed into each other's eyes, it took them a long time to realize that there was a voice coming from high, high above.

"Deck there!"

Brendan raised his head, one arm locked possessively around her waist, a thick lock of her hair draped over his neck.

"Brendan!" Liam was there, over the skylight, his body cutting off the sunlight streaming down from above. "Come topside, laddie! There's a strange sail in th' lee o' one o' these here islands! She's flyin' British colors an' runnin' with 'er tail b'tween 'er legs!"

Brendan sighed and lay back, staring up at the deck beams above. He let the silence stretch on, his hand absently stroking Mira's hair. "Well?"

"Well what?" she asked, cuddling up against him and kissing his chin.

"Shall we take her, Mr. Starr?"

Their eyes met. Hers gleamed; his danced; and beneath them, *Kestrel* whispered softly to herself.

Take her.

The tension built. Then, Mira leapt from the bed. She grabbed her clothes and raced naked across the cabin, hopping into them as she went. Laughing, she snatched Brendan's sword from the bulkhead, and pirouetting on bare fairy feet, raced from the cabin.

He was not far behind.

And when they emerged on deck, no one noticed that their wee gunner's hair was loose and unbound, her lips swollen from kisses, her eyes gleaming with feline contentment. No one noticed that their captain didn't look so immaculate, his coat half-unbuttoned, his tricorn slapped atop curls that were rumpled and tousled.

And neither did *Kestrel*.

For there, speared like a moth just beyond her surging bowsprit, was a schooner, with the Union Jack fluttering from her mast.

Brendan took one look and cupped his hands around his

mouth. "Trim for starboard reach! Tack on topsails and topgallants, Mr. Wilbur! Faith, d' you expect to catch her with *Kestrel* half-dressed?! Better yet, rig the studders, and be quick about it!"

Topmen raced up the shrouds, out along the yards. Sails spilled down and were sheeted smartly home. *Kestrel* rose on her tiptoes, the water washing through her ports as she began to come across the wind.

Brendan took the tiller, thrilling to the feel of the wind driving against that giant canvas and sending its raw power thrumming down the masts, through the deck, and right up into the soles of his feet. *Kestrel* leaned her shoulder into the sea and swung her jib-boom around, past a rock-rimmed islet just off her bow, farther and farther still, until the wind was coming over their starboard beam and heeling her well over on a course that sent her plunging toward the other vessel.

He felt a certain sadness that their quarry was a schooner, but quickly drove the feeling from his mind. The British ship and *Kestrel* were night and day, one short and stubby, bluff-bowed and unwieldy, the other sleek and dark, dangerous and beautiful.

"To stations, gunners!"

He saw Mira race past on her way to *Freedom*, and groaned inwardly.

Kestrel was closing in now, swallowing her prey's foamy wake as it changed tack and tried to dart behind an island. Unconsciously Brendan slid his hand into his pocket and found his sketchbook missing. He swore beneath his breath and grabbed the speaking trumpet that Dalby, wheezing, thrust toward him. "Will you strike?" he yelled.

A solitary gun boomed out in reply, slapped through *Kestrel*'s jib, and hissed into the sea.

"Very well then." Shrugging, Brendan raised the trumpet once more, and caught Mira's gaze from where she stood waiting at *Freedom*, her gun crew holding rammers and sponges.

"Gunners, cast off tackles and breechings!" he called.

One by one, the commands were fired off with swift precision and obeyed with equal smartness. At last, every gun captain and every crew stared aft, awaiting the word—

"Run out!"

He saw Mira fling her hair over her shoulder and crouch down beside *Freedom*'s ugly snout.

"Point your guns . . ."

"FIRE!"

Kestrel heeled over beneath the force of the broadside, then quickly righted herself. Blindly she drove on through thick, billowing gray smoke, bursting free of it and into open sea once more.

Guns were sponged out, loaded. Again *Kestrel* loosed her broadside, and a great cheer went up as the other schooner's fore topmast shuddered, leaned, and fell in a tangle of rigging and sail to her decks below.

It was enough to send the British captain racing aft to haul down the colors with his own hand, for the identity of his attacker was no mystery to him. There was only one schooner in these waters, indeed anywhere, that looked like this one did. Lean, rakish, and lithe, she could only be the Americans' legendary *Kestrel;* and that blue-coated figure, framed against the great, undulating backdrop of the glorious red and white flag of the privateer, could only be Brendan Merrick.

Captain Edward Sorrington was no fool. Let *Kestrel* have his little schooner. It would probably be the last prize she'd ever take.

For Sorrington was on his way to Penobscot himself, and he carried information that might've saved the American forces had they known it.

Just one day's sail behind him were the reinforcements that the British general Francis McLean in the Penobscot was expecting, a powerful fleet of British warships led by Sir George Collier in the sixty-four-gun *Raisonnable.*

But Merrick didn't need to know that. He'd find out soon enough, anyhow.

Let him go to Penobscot. Let his legendary vessel join the other American ships already there. Let him, and the cocky Americans, think they could reclaim Penobscot Bay.

They were in for a big surprise.

And so was Merrick, he thought wryly, for in company

with the British fleet was HMS *Viper*, with Captain Rich-ard Crichton in command.

Chapter 30

‷*That seat of Science, Athens, and Earth's proud mistress Rome! Where now are all their glories? We scarce can find a tomb! Then guard your rights, Americans! Nor stoop to lawless swa-a-y! Oppose, oppose, oppose, oppose, for North A-mer-i-kay!*''

Mira, clad in a blousy, white cotton shirt, tucked her pretty green skirts up into her waistband and, laughing off the crew's lewd comments about her bare legs, danced barefooted atop *Freedom*'s barrel to the rollicking tune of Liam's fiddle. It was a new day, a glorious morning, and they were going to meet the American fleet!

A brisk wind chased *Kestrel* steadily up the bay. Her prize, with just enough Americans aboard to sail her, fol-lowed, its crew locked in *Kestrel*'s hold. Islands slid past, densely wooded with pine and cedar, their shores rimmed with pebbled beaches strewn with green, purple, and brown seaweed. Sapphire blue water surrounded them, and *Kestrel*'s streaming wake glittered foamy and white in the sun. High overhead, an osprey circled her proud mainmast and played chase with the streaming pennants.

''*We led fair Freedom hi-ther, and lo, the desert smiled! A paradise of plea-sure was opened in the wild! Your harvest, bold Americans, no pow'r shall snatch a-wa-a-y, preserve, preserve, preserve your rights, and free A-mer-i-kay!*''

''*And free A-mer-i-kay!*'' the crew echoed.

At the helm, the captain grinned and moved the tiller to compensate for a slight shift in wind. Amidships, Dalby, clutching his ribs and complaining about a stitch in his side, worked to repair a small tear in one of the sails. At the rail, the crew eagerly crowded for their first glimpse of the mighty American squadron.

And *Kestrel,* caught up in the excitement, lifted her bows and began to dance.

"Torn from a world of ty-rants, beneath this western sky! We formed a new do-min-ion, a land of liberty! The world shall own we're free men here and such we'll ever be-e-e, huzzah, huzzah, huzzah, huzzah, for love and lib-erty!"

They rounded an island, caught the breeze in their faces, and saw, in glorious, magnificent array, the American fleet spread out before them.

Mira's first glimpse of it filled her eyes with tears. There they were, so many vessels she could've played leapfrog from deck to deck. Nearly a score of armed warships drawn up in a crescent, with the storeships and transports tucked safely behind them. The pride of America. The might of their new country!

"Brendan, look!" she cried, hopping up and down atop the cannon's sun-warmed barrel.

But her breath caught in her throat. Tall and straight and handsome, the buttons of his blue uniform gleaming in the sun, he captured her heart in a way the glorious American fleet could never do. Her chest swelled with emotion, and she thought her ribs would burst.

He was her captain.

Kestrel was her ship.

And they would do what they had to do for their proud young country.

Now she fully understood how Brendan had felt, why it was so important to him to be a part of this mighty and glorious effort. Filled with an overwhelming sense of unity and joyous elation, Mira curled her fingers around the fore-shrouds and let the tears roll down her cheeks. And the crew felt it, too. They laid fond, possessive hands on their little ship, touched her gunwales, raised her magnificent red and white flag to the wind. The fleet was mighty, but *Kestrel* was *their* ship and they were *her* crew. And as they sailed boldly into the midst of that immense gathering, a thunderous welcoming cheer echoed across the water and filled their ears.

Liam put down his fiddle. "God Almighty, would ye look at that," he said hoarsely, his blue eyes strangely moist.

Abadiah Bobbs wiped his nose with the back of his hand. "Aye, a fine, purty sight, ain't it?"

"They're cheering us," Dalby said, glancing aft at his captain.

But Brendan saw only the stubborn British flag that still flew from the fort—and Captain Henry Mowat's three sloops-of-war snugged pugnaciously in the harbor's entrance. Catching Dalby's eye, he leaned on his cane and raised his speaking trumpet. "Mr. Wilbur! Lower those sails else we end up in Bangor! Mr. Doherty! Have your gun captains give the fleet the traditional thirteen-gun salute! And Mr. Starr! I mean, er, Miss Ashton!" Laughter greeted his momentary error. "Let *Freedom* lead it off!"

"Aye, Cap'n!" She leapt down from the gun, the wind lifting her skirts and tempting him with a view of suntanned legs and bare feet. A moment later, she was lowering a slow match to the gun's touchhole. One by one, *Kestrel*'s guns shattered the peaceful stillness. Deep reverberations rang out across the bay and echoed around heavily wooded islands and mainland alike. Seabirds winged away, screaming. Smoke rings billowed across the water.

Drawing his spyglass, Brendan trained it on the fleet. There was Commodore Saltonstall's handsome Continental flagship *Warren,* her thirty-two guns making her the most powerful vessel here. Nearby lay the Continental sloop *Providence,* formerly commanded by the plucky John Paul Jones, and now the capable, no-nonsense Captain Hoysted Hacker. The Massachusetts brigs *Hazard* and *Tyrannicide,* both of sixteen guns, were anchored off the flagship's stern, and Connecticut's *General Putnam* was visible just beyond her network of spars and shrouds. New Hampshire's contribution, the twenty-gun *Hampden,* lay nearer shore, her tall masts almost indistinguishable from the spruce, cedar, and white pine of a nearby island.

Good God, he thought, moving the glass and recognizing others by the shape of their bows, the cut of their sails, the number of guns they carried. And then he saw the privateers. They were the ones who had the most to lose should this heroic expedition fail. Ships like the beautiful *Black Prince,* Salisbury-built and Salem-owned, one of the finest of her class and commanded by Captain Nathaniel West. And there, swinging at their anchor cables, three Newburyport vessels that had been among the first to volunteer for the Expedition: the sixteen-gun *Sky Rocket* and the ships *Vengeance* and *Monmouth,* both mounting twenty guns. Their crews were thick at the rails, wildly waving to *Kestrel*'s crew and yelling greetings across the water. He lowered the glass. There were just too many to recognize, too many to count.

Gunfire boomed out over the water, and he realized that *Warren* herself was firing her mighty cannon in thunderous salute to *Kestrel.* Signal flags soared to her masthead and broke to the wind.

"Orders from Commodore Saltonstall, sir." John Keefe craned his neck, his silver hair roiling about his face as he tried to see above the heads of his shipmates. "He wants you to repair aboard the flagship with all possible haste."

Brendan grinned, sighed, and thrust his hand though the lanyard of his speaking trumpet. He swung the instrument once around his wrist. "Just as I expected." He saw Mira watching him from where she still stood atop *Freedom,* her green eyes shining with love and pride. What was she thinking? What did she expect of him? He nodded to her and turned smartly to his lieutenant. "Liam, I'm leaving you in command. See that you take good care of *both* our fine lassies. Hopefully the commodore will be merciful and not detain me for too long."

Liam, who knew his captain was a restless man not inclined to waste time in a social call, predicted, "Well, he'll probably be expectin' ye t' join him f'r supper. He'll detain ye, all right, if ye let him."

But Brendan was grinning his rakehell's grin and rubbing his elegant hands together. "Well then, I shall have to make certain he does not, eh?"

Liam raised his brows. "And why don't ye be a-tellin' me how ye plan t' do that?"

"Certainly." Brendan's eyes were deceptively innocent, like a wayward youngster playing a prank on his schoolmaster. "I shall bring him a . . . contribution. Something for supper, I think. Mr. Starr! I mean, Miss Ashton!"

"Captain?!"

"Do you have any more of those blueberry pies you, er, baked last night?"

"Sure do! Got a whole mess of 'em!"

"Ah, *wonderrrful!*" Liam and Brendan exchanged knowing grins. "Please fetch one and bring it to me immediately!"

Beaming with pleasure, Mira raced across the deck and ducked below.

Liam's face went dark with foreboding. "Ye're askin' f'r it this time, Brendan. This *ain't* the way t' get on Saltonstall's good side, ye know. . . ."

But Brendan only laughed and tossed him his speaking trumpet. He had his own worries—and Saltonstall's reaction to Mira's blueberry pie wasn't one of them.

Seated in *Warren*'s great cabin amidst the other captains of the fleet, Brendan read the urgent letter that anxious members of the Navy Board in Boston, some one hundred seventy miles away, had rushed off to the commodore urging him to either capture or destroy the three English sloops-of-war—immediately.

"But I can't send in my ships until Lovell's forces reduce the fort!" Saltonstall protested, his face reddening as he faced the *Providence*'s pugnacious captain, Hoysted Hacker, from across a table laid with silver and crystal.

"If we do not stop procrastinating and destroy those ships, the British reinforcements that General Washington has warned us about are going to arrive and take care of *us!*" Hacker barked.

"Would ye have me risk your vessels at the guns of that fort?!"

"I'd rather take my chances with the fort than with British men-of-war! They come up that bay and trap us in, and it's all over for us!"

"I think we should go in," Brendan said, piling a sizable helping of roast chicken on his plate. "From what you've told me, you've been having these councils of war nearly every night, and *still* haven't taken any action. Either you or General Lovell must make a move! Hoysted's right. I've read his proposal of attack, and find it sound. If you do not do something, and do it soon, those reinforcements will arrive and trap *all* of us in the bay!''

"Ah, what do you know, you're just a bloody Irishman!'' Saltsonstall growled.

"Who made quite a name for himself in His Majesty's navy before defecting to *our* side!'' Hoysted roared, in Brendan's defense.

Captain William Burke of the Newburyport ship *Sky Rocket,* leapt to his feet. "Aye, that schooner of his holds a record all of us envy and none of us can match!''

"You ought to be right proud of him!'' snarled Captain John Edmonds, of the *Defense.* "We're lucky to have him, and so soon after his near-death at that bloody knave Crichton's hands!''

"Aye, it ought to be Merrick leading this farce!'' Hoysted snapped, gripping his fork.

Brendan, uncomfortable, cleared his throat and dabbed at his mouth with his napkin. "Here, now,'' he said, holding up his hand. "We'll not accomplish anything if we fight amongst ourselves.'' He poured himself a glass of buttermilk to wash down a bit of ship's biscuit. Normally the bread was almost inedible, but after Mira's cooking, it was like ambrosia. He eyed the yet-untouched pie that sat ominously on the far end of the table. "And think of it. Lovell's militia is ill trained and skittish. They were lucky to take the western part of Bagaduce as it is, what with those banks being so steep. Give Revere credit, 'twas no easy task. Now morale is dropping and men are deserting. *We,* on the other hand, are experienced naval officers and capable commanders. Let us go in and take out Mowat's three sloops. 'Twill hearten Lovell's militia and give them courage.''

"He's right. Listen to him, sir!'' said Titus Salter, commander of the *Hampden.*

"Aye, the *bloody Irishman* knows what he's talkin' about!

"Englishman,'' Burke said, grinning.

Saltonstall's face darkened and he set his jaw. Even his own captains were against him. Lovell ought to attack first, not him! Let *him* and his precious Paul Revere go in and take the fort, *then* he'd send his ship captains in!

Benjamin West, captain of the *Black Prince,* poured himself a glass of claret and spoke for all of them. "Sir, we depend upon the swiftness of our vessels and miles of open ocean for our very survival. Read the blessed letter from Boston," he pleaded. "Consider Washington's warning. *We're sitting ducks up here.* Hacker's right, Merrick's right, *everyone's* right. Let's just get in there, destroy those three ships, and hightail it out of here. I've no desire to be penned into this bay, twenty-five miles from the ocean, like a cat treed by hounds with nowhere to go but up. And if those British reinforcements arrive—"

"That's just what'll happen!" Hacker barked.

"Aye!"

"Do something *now!*"

"Get on with it!"

They fought. They quarreled. Lovell and his officers were called in, and after much discussion, the general accepted Captain Hacker's plan on how his ragtag militia could occupy and hold a position behind the British fort. The ship captains agreed to force their way into the harbor; after all, their vessels were superior to those of the British, and destruction of Mowat's three sloops was essential. Without their protection, all aid and provisions going into the British fort would be stopped—and the British General McLean would have no choice but to surrender.

An agreement had been reached. But the next couple of days would bring about further disagreement, no action— and a powerful British relief squadron from New York.

On the third day of August, eight ships under the command of Vice Admiral Sir George Collier had left port, turned their prows north, and headed toward Penobscot to relieve the besieged General Francis McLean and Captain Henry Mowat. British spirits were high, confidence strong. In the lead was the vice admiral's powerful sixty-four-gun flagship *Raisonnable;* in the midst were several large men-of-war; and in the rear was a sullen frigate named *Viper.*

The squadron, hampered by fog, rendezvoused off the entrance to the great Penobscot Bay on the evening of August 13, where their presence sent a panicky American vessel on picket duty fleeing upriver to warn the American commodore Saltonstall and his fleet. But Sir George Collier, in command of His Majesty's naval forces in American waters, was not worried. Although the rebels had more ships than he did, his men-of-war could withstand far more abuse than the fragile privateers, or even Saltonstall's thirty-two-gun *Warren.* The American militia was raw and ill trained; he, on the other hand, had more than two hundred guns and some fifteen hundred well-trained and enthusiastic men.

He went to bed that night confident of victory. He had heavy, powerful ships manned by the finest navy in the world. He had the element of surprise. And he had one of Sir Geoffrey Lloyd's—since retired to his fine home in Kent—most ambitious captains, a man he bore no liking for, but a man who was desperate enough to go to any lengths to prove himself after several past disgraces. . . .

Captain Richard Crichton of the frigate *Viper.*

That Friday, Brendan paced his cabin, going over the agreement that had finally been reached between Lovell and Saltonstall. Upon a favorable tide in the afternoon, they would make a coordinated attack. Lovell himself would lead some four hundred of his men to a position behind the British fort, where his presence would sever contact between McLean and Mowat. Once that had been done, Saltonstall would send in his ships and destroy the three sloops-of-war.

Five of Saltonstall's ships were anchored at the harbor entrance, waiting for high tide. Above, Brendan could hear the crew quickly readying *Kestrel* for impending battle. His fingers tightened on his cane and he tried in vain to shake the heavy, overwhelming feeling of doom. Just beyond the stern windows the sea swelled and surged and danced in the noon sunlight; beneath him, *Kestrel* rolled at her anchor cable, unhappy that *she* was not one of the lucky ones being sent in against Mowat's sloops. He really should go topside; by now, Lovell would be in position and ready. Any moment now they'd get the signal that the American forces had taken position at the rear of the fort.

But this waiting . . .

His hands were sweating.

He was dizzy, light-headed, faint. Was it the heat? His weakness? The tediousness of waiting? As Ephraim might've done, he drew his watch, shoved it restlessly back into his pocket, and tried to keep his mind off his poor health by recalling Saltonstall's reaction to Mira's pie. His mouth curved in amusement. Pleading a stomachache that had "hit him in the gut like a ball from a six-pounder," the surly commodore had cut short last night's council of war and sent them all back to their ships with curses ringing in their ears.

So much for blueberry pie. And, he thought wryly, lengthy meetings where nothing got accomplished. He was back aboard *Kestrel* by six bells.

But as he'd held Mira in his arms last night, staring into the darkness and listening to the owls hooting off in the woods, the ominous feeling of pending disaster had grown so strong, he'd finally had to rise from bed and go topside. There, he'd spent the rest of the long night watching the lights from the fleet glowing upon the silent waters, his Irish heart filled with dread. If only he could find a way to get Mira off the ship . . . He'd thought of Saltonstall's incompetence and unpopularity. He'd thought of the poorly trained militia. He'd thought of the British reinforcements they all feared—and then he'd thought of Mira's blueberry pie.

Tired and sad, he'd forced a grin as he gently shook her awake early this morning.

"Moyrrra, lassie! Wake up, *grá mo chroí!* I've a task to occupy you while we suffer another day of waiting!"

He, of course, knew that today there'd *be* no waiting. Today they would attack. Stretching like one of her Rescue Efforts, Mira opened her eyes. She looked up at Brendan through a tangled curtain of thick, silky hair, smiling as he reached down and cleared it from her cheek.

"Dia dhuit ar maidin," he said, grinning to cover his own sadness, his apprehension.

"Good morning to you, too, Captain," she said, wrapping her arms around his neck. Her shirt gaping enticingly open, she pulled his head down to hers and kissed his cheeks, his nose, his brow, his lips, until hot desire flared tightly in his loins. "And what is this task that is so urgent you can't let me sleep?"

He smiled down at her, hiding his hands behind his back so she wouldn't see them shaking. "The commodore was quite impressed with your blueberry pie," he said, hating himself for lying. "I think it would please him if you baked him another. Would you like to go ashore and gather some more blueberries, *mo stóirín?"*

Her eyes lit up like a little girl's. "You mean the commodore liked my pie? He actually *liked* it?!"

"Oh, most assuredly. He was . . . he was, er, raving about it!"

She was out of bed in a flash. He caught her up in his arms and managed to swing her around without collapsing, his heart lurching painfully in his chest. Her feet hit the table and spilled a bottle of ink all over the drafts he'd been working on of Matt's new ship. Her hair swirled around her creamy shoulders and scented the air with the sweetness of roses. But by midmorning, she was safely off the ship and accompanied by two well-armed backwoodsmen who served as *Kestrel*'s marines, and her ever protective friend, Abadiah Bobbs.

With a heavy heart, Brendan watched her go.

And then he joined Liam on the deck and waited.

It was afternoon when the first warning shots thundered up the bay.

Liam, munching a handful of wild strawberries, wiped the back of his juice-stained hand across his mouth and stared to the south. "What th' bloody divil was *that?!"*

Brendan had been making notes in the log, squinting in the blinding sunlight. Now he calmly put his pencil in his pocket, shut the book, and handed it to Zachary Wilbur. He allowed none of the trepidation he felt to show in his eyes as he clasped his hands behind his back and gazed nonchalantly to southward.

"God Almighty, Brendan, that sounded like—"

"Shh!"

He cocked his head, listening. A strange silence had settled over the bay, and he pictured the other captains grabbing their spyglasses, training them in the direction of the distant gunfire, fighting back these same butterflies of thick, ugly dread.

There, it came again. A far-off noise like thunder.

Except he knew in his heart that it wasn't.

"Gunfire, Liam," he finished. He forced a grin, hoping to bolster the men's confidence. They'd need every bit of it, and then some. "I believe the enemy has finally arrived."

Liam passed a huge, shaky hand through his spice-colored curls, leaving them stained with strawberry juice. And then he glanced at the commodore's flagship. Moments ago, signals had risen to her mast, telling them that Lovell was in place at the rear of the British fort and the attack could begin; now flags streamed aloft once more.

"Message from *Warren,* sir," said John Keefe quietly. The helmsman's face was white, and growing whiter. "He has *Diligent* in sight. She reports eight strange sail coming up the bay."

"Go hálainn," Brendan said, already reaching for his sketchpad. "Lovely."

"Think it's really th' British relief forces?" Liam asked.

"Oh, no doubt about that. Certainly not *American* relief forces, my friend!"

Liam looked at his captain, and the two gazed at each other in silent communication, one thick and brawny and solid, the other tall and elegant and refined. They had shared many trials together. They had come through many a storm. And they both knew that this would be the worst one yet.

The gunfire came again, closer this time.

"Are ye up t' it, Cap'n?" Liam eyed his friend's pale, drawn features, the arms that had yet to regain all of their sinewy strength.

"As ready as I'll ever be, Liam."

"Is *she* up t' it, d'ye think?"

"*Kestrel?*"

"No, th' wee lassie. Miss Mira."

Brendan took off his tricorn and stared down at its gold braid. "I don't know, Liam. Nor shall I. She won't be here for me to find out."

"*What?!*"

"I sent her ashore—to pick blueberries."

"*Blue—*" Liam's mouth dropped open. And suddenly he understood. They didn't need blueberries. They didn't need another pie that no one dared to touch. Brendan had sent the lassie ashore for her own protection, knowing intuitively that today something would happen. Liam shook his head. "Ye're a clever one, y'know. Always said it an' always will."

"Not so clever, Liam. Would that I could protect all of you like I can my Mira." He eyed the forlorn and empty *Freedom*. "I may well regret my decision to send away my best gunner."

"And ye may well regret y'r refusal t' tell ol' Sir Geoffrey the *real* reason ye switched loyalties. About what Crichton did t' ye so long ago—"

"Enough of that, Liam. Let bygones be bygones. And let Sir Geoffrey enjoy his retirement in Kent without the blemishes of the past to haunt him. He's earned it. Besides, there are other matters that demand my attention right now."

Liam knew he was still worrying about Mira—and what her absence might cost them. "At least ye have y'r oth'r fine lassie," he said, stroking *Kestrel*'s sleek rail.

"Aye. Would that I could protect her, too."

The distant ship's guns thundered again, followed by others that weren't her own.

"Well, Liam, shall we ready our lassie for whatever fate holds in store for us?"

"Aye, Brendan. I'll take care o' 't. You go down an' 'ave yerself a bit o' refreshment." He eyed his captain's pale, sensitive features, worrying about the glazed look in his eyes that seemed to come and go like a foggy mist. Their leader was not well, and every man on the ship knew it. "An' put on that fine coat o' yers, too. If *she's* a-watchin' from shore, she'll think ye look right dashin' in it.''

Brendan nodded. Oh, he'd put on the coat, all right. If not for Mira's benefit, then for his crew's. They'd need a strong, inspiring leader to follow today. They'd need a capable commander at the helm.

Dizziness washed over him, and he pinched his arm, hard, to quell it. But *was* he strong? Was he capable?

Liam was staring at him, his blue eyes dark with worry. Fergus and Rama were hauling out those foolish crystals and chanting about past lives. Dalby, holding his gut, was frowning. And some of the men were eyeing him uncertainly.

He couldn't have that.

''Good heavens, laddies, what are you all staring at, eh? We've got company coming for dinner!'' Laughter greeted his light joke and dispelled some of the tension. ''Faith, I've never seen such a hesitant bunch of do-nothings. You'd think we were waiting for a funeral!''

He grinned, playfully punched Liam's shoulder, and without a further look at the advancing British squadron, went below. No one noticed that he'd stuffed his hands beneath his coattails to hide their trembling. No one noticed how he leaned heavily against the bulkhead at the bottom of the hatch until his vision righted itself. No one saw him wipe the sweat from his brow with the back of his shaking wrist.

But everyone saw him glance a final time toward the deep, choking woods where somewhere, a pretty little lassie was out picking blueberries for a pie that would never be made.

He donned a snow white shirt over his damp skin, a red waistcoat, and his tailored blue coat with its red facings. His knees were weak and he was sweating heavily, a cold, ugly sweat that had nothing to do with his apprehension about the growing battle and everything to do with his body's weakness. Coming up through the hatch, he yanked his coattails down over his hips, straightened his stock, and pulled out the ruffled lace at his wrist.

Liam met him as he came up through the coaming, his face grave.

"Today's the day, Liam," Brendan said, with more cheerfulness than he felt.

"Aye, Brendan." He handed Brendan his sword and pistol. "Don't push y'rself too hard, eh?"

"No harder than ever, Liam. But as hard as I must to see us out of this."

"Well, just don't ye be thinkin' about that lassie. She'll be just fine, right where ye put her."

He nodded, and mustered a grin. "Yes . . . Why, she'll have the best seat in the house, won't she?"

As he emerged on deck, over fifty worried faces turned toward him, and some of the men began to cheer. More and more joined in, inspired by the sight of their dauntless young captain, until the whole ship rang with the wild thunder of their voices.

"Huzzah! Huzzah!"

"Three cheers for our captain!"

"And for the *Kestrel,* too!"

But he merely nodded, gave a fleeting, embarrassed grin, and drawing his spyglass, went to the rail. Bracing himself against the shrouds, he trained the instrument off the starboard beam toward the choking wilderness and held it there for a long time. Finally the glass began to shake in his fine hands. Somewhere out there was a little green-eyed lass with hair that wouldn't stay out of her eyes, and a skill with a cannon that he'd never need more. But she would be safe.

And then he swung the glass aft.

There was *Diligent,* storming up the bay with signal flags streaming from her mast. On the horizon he could just make out tiny puffs of clouds, like a squall coming in from the sea.

Except they weren't clouds at all.

Little Dalby pressed close to his elbow, and in a voice filled with doom, relayed the awful message. "The enemy's in sight, sir."

Brendan lowered the glass. Unbidden, his gaze went to *Freedom,* standing alone in her red-painted carriage. High above, the raking masts rose into the sky, swaying and creaking as *Kestrel* rolled uneasily at her mooring. Aft, the proud American flag billowed in the wind.

He laid a comforting hand atop the schooner's gunwale. *Kestrel* was nervous. The men were nervous. *He* was nervous.

Again he eyed that empty gun, suddenly wishing he'd have Mr. Starr by his side for their most desperate fight yet.

Chapter 31

"If ye'd stop eatin' them berries, Bobbs, the lady'd be able to gather enough to make a pie out of! How the hell's she supposed to do that if ye keep stuffin' yer face, huh?''

Abadiah scratched at his mole. The captain had told him to keep Mira out here as long as possible. He'd seen the desperate look in those russet eyes, the tension that tightened that laughing mouth. Oh, he'd keep her out here till hell froze over if he had to. Their captain had never steered them wrong yet. If he anticipated something bad, then Abadiah would trust his judgment. "Why don't ye just shut up, Stan? You're eating more than I am.''

"Am not!''

"Are, too!''

"Keep it up and the two of you'll be out behind the rocks with the shi—''

"Really, Miss Mira, if your father could hear such language!''

"My father's the one I learned it from,'' she announced, grinning saucily. Her hair fell down over one eye, and impatiently she tossed it back over her shoulder. She was hot, sticky, and growing tired. "Let's go back now, Bobbs. I think we have enough blueberries now.''

"Not enough to make a pie with," he said hastily.

"So? I'll fill up the space with something else."

"Like what?"

"Oh, I don't know. Hardtack? Raisins? Some of that fish chowder—"

"Fish *chowder?!*"

Well, there's milk in fish chowder, and you're supposed to drizzle milk over the crust, aren't you?" she snapped defensively. "If you can put it over the crust, I don't see any reason why you can't put it in the pie! And further-more—"

Bobbs's grizzled head suddenly jerked up. "Jee-zus, what was that?!"

"What was what?"

"That noise! It sounded like thunder!"

"Probably a storm coming in," growled Stan, leaning on his rifle.

Mira yanked her hair free of a pricker bush and placed berry-stained hands on her hips, listening. And then she heard it, too. Her face blanching, she clawed the hair out of her eyes and stared at Abadiah Bobbs. "That's not thun-der, Abadiah!"

He lowered his pail. "Nay, girl, I don't think it is."

The other marine, clad in buckskin and a beaver hat, slapped at a mosquito and popped a blueberry into his mouth. " 'Tis, too, thunder. I've been out in enough storms to know thunder when I hear it."

"That ain't thunder; it's gunfire, and you know it!" Mira cried. "I'll bet the British reinforcements have ar-rived!"

"God help us," Stan whispered, blanching.

Abadiah grabbed at her sleeve and caught only a branch that slapped him across the face. "Mira, *wait!*" But she was already tearing through the thick brush, stumbling over roots and rotten stumps, her hair catching in thick branches, and her boots sliding on boulders slick with moss. Grabbing his pail, Abadiah tore after her, crashing through the woods with the two marines close behind. "Mira!"

"Brendan!" she cried. "Oh God, we have to reach the ship!"

They tore out of the trees, raced down the beach, and slid to a halt on the slimy, seaweed-covered rocks. Mira's heart skipped a beat and filled her paralyzed throat. Dread froze the blood in her veins. There, coming up the bay, was *Diligent,* the ship that Saltonstall had posted as a lookout twenty-five miles away at the entrance to the bay. Far behind her was the other lookout, *Active.* And far, far off in the distance, almost indistinguishable in the haze, were the sails of a mighty fleet.

"For God's sake, hurry up!" Mira screamed, dropping her pail and running for the little boat they'd dragged up on the beach. Already the tide was coming in, lapping at its keel. "Brendan needs us! *Kestrel* needs us!"

"No, Mira." Abadiah grabbed her arm. "Look."

She flung the hair out of her eyes and followed his gaze. The color drained from her face. There was the American fleet, some of them already weighing anchor. There was *Warren,* signal flags soaring up her masts and calling a halt to the attack.

Attack?! What attack?!

And there was *Kestrel.*

Sail was blooming at her nose, climbing her sharply raked masts, and filling with clean, strong wind. Guns poked from hastily opening gunports. She was not dropping anchor like the others, but turning her face south—toward the enemy.

"*Brendan!*" Mira screamed at the top of her lungs. "*Damn you, don't leave me!*"

Water reflected off *Kestrel*'s glossy black hull, then her tallowed underside, as she heeled gracefully and moved quietly downriver in stately, majestic hauteur. Away from the fleet. Away from *her.*

Tears racing down her cheeks, Mira cursed and swore and screamed until her voice went raw in her throat. It took Abadiah and both of the marines to hold her down. And as she watched the little schooner sail bravely away to face the enemy, Mira vowed that if *Kestrel* survived, it would be the last time Brendan would ever run away from her again.

"What the bloody deuce is that damned Irishman up to now?!" Crichton thundered, grabbing his glass from a

stunned Myles and training it on the oncoming schooner.
"What is he, crazy?!"

Myles sniffed and dug at his pockmarked face. "I would
give him more cleverness than his peers, sir. At least he's
going to try to make a run for it. They, on the other hand,
will be sitting ducks when Sir George's ships move in."

"If I know Merrick, he's not running, he's up to something! And I don't give a damn about the rest of the fleet!
I want that schooner and I want Merrick! You think I really care about those other cursed rebels? You think I per-
suaded Sir Geoffrey to assign me to this squadron just for the
jolly hell of it?" Crichton slammed the glass shut and
thrust it into his lieutenant's hand so hard, it nearly broke
the man's finger. "I joined it because I *knew* Merrick
would be a part of it, and I wasn't mistaken! This time he
won't escape me!"

Myles, who was inclined to let bygones be bygones after
their last humiliating brush with the Captain from Connacht, shrugged and picked at the cuff of his sleeve.
"Honestly, sir, perhaps we should forget about this one
little schooner and one privateersman when there's the
whole American fleet just sitting—"

Fuming, Crichton spun around and cracked the back of
his hand across Myles's face. "Dare you question my
wishes? That one little schooner is my ticket to flag rank!
That one privateersman is the reason I never got it in the
first place! He *owes* me, Myles! And this time he's going
to pay up!"

"Yes, sir," Myles said, sullenly rubbing his cheek.

"Now, get forward and run out the bow chasers. Have
the men beat to quarters and load every gun with grape.
Should Merrick try to get past me, I'll blast him and that
damned schooner to kingdom come!"

His milky eyes glowing with a fanatical light, Crichton
gripped the rail, set his jaw, and waited.

"Make five . . . six . . . *seven* enemy sails, sir, standing up the bay!"

"Thank you, Mr. Reilly." Looping the lanyard of his
speaking trumpet over his wrist, Brendan calmly pulled

out his sketchpad. So be it, then. Seven British ships against Saltonstall's twenty. Ought to be a good fight. Drawing his knife, he sharpened his pencil and made a test mark on the clean white paper. This was definitely one battle he wanted to save for posterity!

Liam was at his elbow, his face going purple. "God Almighty, Brendan, don't ye think ye ought t' be mindin' th' ship just this once, instead o' playin' artist?!"

"Minding the ship? Faith, Liam, that's *your* job. Tell Mr. Wilbur to see to that foresail, would you? She's luffing a wee bit. I don't want the vice admiral to think I've lost my penchant for perfection. And oh, Liam, while you're at it, do get your fiddle out and strike up a lively tune, would you?"

Liam stared at him. "Somethin' Irish?"

"No, something American, I think. Like . . . oh, I don't know. 'Yankee Doodle'? 'Derry Down'? Actually, I think 'Free America' might do quite nicely."

Fergus McDermott, clutching a crystal in one hand and a Bible in the other, nervously eyed *Freedom*. "But we don't have Miss Mira to sing it for us!"

"And we don't know all the words," added George Saunders.

"Fine, then make them up as you go." Brendan grinned and tapped his pencil against the sketchpad. "That's what *she* would do!"

He turned away, pretending blithe indifference when, in truth, he was anything but blithe, and anything but indifferent. He swallowed hard. There was an ache in his chest that had nothing to do with his old injury as he looked at the forlorn and lonely *Freedom*. Mira. At least *she* would be safe. Furious with him, yes—but safe.

Hurriedly he put pencil to paper and sketched out the admiral's flagship, unaware of the whispered comments of his crew.

"Cap'n's ailin'. Look at the way his hands are shaking. He can barely hold that sketchpad of his, let alone draw on it."

"And he's leaning against that mast as though he's trying to hold it up!"

"He ain't recovered yet, Reilly. He ought to be abed, not on the deck of a warship. . . ."

"Think he's up to it?"

"Nay, he's not up to it! But there still ain't no captain in this here fleet I'd rather be with than our Brendan!"

They watched as he went to the rail, pretending not to notice the way he hooked an elbow through the shrouds to keep his balance, the way he braced a hip against the gunwale, the way his gaze kept straying to the woods where they'd left Miss Mira.

"Makin' three knots, sir," Liam said gravely.

"Hoist the fore topsail and let's try for five."

"Might need the t'gallants f'r that, sir."

"Fine, Liam, then hoist them, too." Pulling out his spyglass, Brendan trained it on the vice admiral's flagship, studying her lines, her sail set, the way she cleaved the water. Finally he lowered the glass, his hand quickly and expertly putting to paper what he'd seen. The man-of-war's big courses were bloated, her topsails clewed up for battle, her mighty stem plowing the water. She had sixty-four guns against *Kestrel*'s ten. A crew of hundreds against his fifty. He pitied Saltonstall. And an experienced admiral against a cowardly commodore.

He wondered if he'd survive long enough to get a taste of the infamous Mill Prison—and decided he'd rather die first.

"I don't hear your fiddle, Liam!"

"God Almighty, Brendan, wha' t'about th' commodore?"

"The commodore shall thank me for diverting the enemy long enough for him to think out his next—and only— move! Mr. Keefe! We *must* make it look like we're trying to escape to sea, do you understand? The entire British navy is after our little *Kestrel*. 'Tis a gamble, but if we can lure them to follow us, then it might allow Saltonstall the time he needs to gather his forces and prepare to meet the British fleet!"

"That's gambling a lot, sir!"

"I know it, Mr. Keefe, and we're going to take a beating doing it! But we're the only chance the commodore has. Let's hope he's a survivor and takes the opening we shall give him! Now, when I tell you to swing to larboard, I want you to go to *starboard!*"

"Aye, sir!"

"Hands to the sheets and prepare to come about! Gunners, to stations and load up with grape, double-shotted! Mr. Saunders, you may take Mr. Starr's place on *Freedom!* No singing, please! Mr. Wilbur, send topmen aloft and shake out the fore topsail! And, Dalby, please let go of my sleeve!"

"But, Captain, my stomach—"

Liam was there, hauling Dalby away. "Leave th' cap'n be, Dalb! Ye know he hates t' be bothered when he's doin' a sketch. . . ."

But Brendan was no longer sketching. Dividing his attention between the oncoming British ships and his men, he directed his crew with brisk gestures of his spyglass. "Run out the starboard battery, Mr. Doherty! I want to fool Sir George into thinking we'll loose the starboard guns when, in truth, 'twill be the *larboard* ones! And larboard gunners, keep down lest our fine British friends see you! Get that topsail hung, Mr. Wilbur! Lively, now! Faith, you people are slower than molasses today!"

Men, bare-backed and barefooted, raced each other up the shrouds and streamed out along the yards. Aft, the schooner prize they'd taken earlier was left wallowing in *Kestrel*'s foamy wake as she lifted her bows, spread her wings, and gathered speed, her pennants snapping and streaming in the wind.

Above, the topsail made a noise like thunder before being sheeted home.

Brendan stroked the schooner's sleek rail, feeling her determination, her apprehension, her trust in him. "A wee bit faster, lassie. 'Tisn't much I ask of you. . . ."

Beneath the bows, the keen of water grew higher and higher in pitch as *Kestrel* answered his gentle plea. Wind sang in the rigging, and the great foresail curved like a drum against the bright blue sky. Spray hissed at the bow, drove back in the wind, flecked Brendan's cheeks with a damp mist. He licked his lips and tasted salt.

"Six an' a half knots, Brendan."

"*Go hálainn*, Liam, but I want seven!"

He'd be lucky to get it. Not in this wind. He put his hands behind his back and braced himself against the gunwale, the dizziness striking with swift and sudden force.

Another three minutes and they'd be in range of *Raisonnable*'s guns.

"Seven knots, sir!"

Two minutes.

He hung his head, fighting to stay on his feet. "Sheet in foresail and main!"

The crew stared at the oncoming man-of-war. Every breath caught in every throat. Panic widened frightened eyes. Liam wrapped his big, brawny hands around the mainsheet. *Kestrel* quivered in fear, driving closer and closer to the mighty two-decker, now rising above her like a fortress. . . .

"Our father, who art in heaven . . ." Fergus was chanting.

Dalby, pale with terror, clutched his gut and whispered, *"Hallowed be thy name. Thy kingdom come, thy will be done—"*

"On earth as i' 'tis in heaven!" Brendan slammed his speaking trumpet to his lips. "Larboard your helm, Mr. Keefe, and let fly. . . . *Now!*"

The tiller went over, hard. The big mainsail boom skated over their heads and to the other side. *Kestrel* danced across the wind, her bowsprit sweeping over the rippling water, toward the oncoming flagship, past it, farther and farther, aligning now on the hazy mainland, the islands. . . .

"Straighten her out, John! For the love of God, *now!*"

Kestrel nosed back toward the wind, her sails a-thunder, her rigging shaking—and then the man-of-war's horrible broadside crashed out, around, above, and beside them. Iron slammed into her flanks and ripped through rigging and sails alike. Debris rained down on the deck, splashed into the sea. *Kestrel* shuddered, lurched, hesitated—

"Come on, lassie, you can do it!"

—and dove through the hole in the thick black smoke.

"Four knots!" Liam was screaming. "God Almighty, Brendan, we lost th' fore tops'l mast—"

Dimly Brendan heard *Raisonnable*'s broadside crash out

again. The deck trembled beneath his feet, and the world seemed to explode as his own guns bellowed in impudent reply. Thick, choking smoke drove back in his face. Spent powder burned his nose. Masts swayed and yards shook as *Kestrel,* pitching and yawing, fought valiantly to make headway.

Dizzily he staggered to the tiller and wrestled it out of Keefe's hands, its solid support the only thing keeping him on his feet. "We're almost through, lassie! *Don't fail me now!"*

Kestrel, shuddering, clawed upward, trying desperately to regain her balance. Gathering her courage, she answered her captain and bravely swung herself back toward the mighty flagship. Moments later, she was safely past the huge two-decker and showing a fleet pair of heels to the vice admiral's flag.

Kestrel's crew went wild, cheering and tossing their hats in the air.

"We did it! *We did it!"* Liam was jumping up and down, pounding his great fist against the rail in triumph. "God Almighty, Brendan we did it! She'll follow us, right out t' open sea if we want her to! Now let's take on th' rest o' the British fleet! The commodore'll be a-thankin' ye up 'n' down when he sees wha' 'tye've done f'r him! Brendan?'' He raced aft—''Brendan! Easy there, laddie!''— and caught his captain as he fell, supporting his elegant shoulders in his massive, brawny arms.

His head spinning, Brendan raised his arm and pointed with his spyglass through the parting smoke. "Not yet, we haven't, Liam. . . .'' He shut his eyes and fell back against his friend's chest. "Look . . .''

Liam's gaze followed his captain's arm. His eyes bulged, and the triumphant grin froze on his face.

For there, blocking the way to the open sea, was HMS *Viper.*

At midnight the American general Solomon Lovell, several miles north of *Kestrel,* gave the order to evacuate the peninsula. The panicky militia were put aboard the transports, and these were protectively herded behind the swift and well-armed warships. Ammunition was hastily loaded, artillery gathered, supplies collected. By eight o'clock the following morning, the mighty American fleet was headed up the narrowing river, where Lovell hoped the British fleet, with their deeper-drafted men-of-war, would be unable to follow. But follow they did, and thwarted by an ebb tide, the Americans finally dropped anchor and prepared to face Sir George's ships.

At noon Commodore Saltonstall made his most decisive move since the Expedition had arrived in Penobscot.

Calling off his defenses, he signaled for every ship to fend for itself.

From shore, Mira, Abadiah, and the two marines watched in stunned horror as a southerly breeze drove the British squadron closer and closer. But the Americans didn't turn and fight. One by one the warships and skittish privateers weighed anchor and raised sail.

"Bloody hell, Saltonstall's giving the order to *retreat!*" Stanley yelled. "C'mon, we have to follow them!"

"There ain't no place to retreat *to*—but upriver!" Abadiah cried.

Frantic, they raced along the heavily wooded shoreline, terrified of losing sight of their ships and desperately trying to keep pace with them. Seeing the Americans' flight, the British piled on more sail, and even Mowat's three sloops came out of their lair and joined into the fray.

What had been a pursuit was now a downright rout.

Chaos reigned. Screams and shouts and gunfire shattered the quiet of the great woods, echoed over the bay. Defenseless, the heavily laden transports wallowed like tubs as the fleet warships that were supposed to protect them crowded on all sail and, with the British in hot pursuit, fled upriver, passing them one by one and leaving them to the mercy of the British. It was a sight that the helpless militia aboard them—and the little party of stranded mariners on shore—would never forget.

Swift Yankee brigs, their sails spread to catch the wind at their sterns, bolting upriver with their tails between their legs. Mighty square-riggers, their wakes streaming behind them. Privateers and state ships and Continental vessels— and *Warren* herself, with Saltonstall's flag fluttering shamefacedly at her mast.

All fleeing.

The utter humiliation and disgrace of it wrung the tears from their eyes. Sobbing, Mira sunk down and buried her face in her knees. Why didn't they turn and make a stand? Why, why, *why?!* She stood up and clenched her fists at her sides. Clawing her hair from her streaming cheeks, she screamed, "Damn you, Saltonstall! You cowardly bucket of spineless slime! Turn around and *fight!*"

Sunset came and went, and darkness cloaked the Maine woods. One of the transports fell into enemy hands; another. And then, out in the river, a mighty explosion lit up the night in a horrible, spectacular display of disgrace. A great sigh went up from Mira's little band. The Americans were setting the transports afire to prevent their seizure by the enemy. By the light of their funeral pyres, the militia waded dejectedly ashore and watched mutely as their ships went up in flames.

And then the proud warships and privateers began to follow suit.

One drove against the far shore and, seconds later, exploded into flames as its crew torched it. Off to the right another blew up, belching a fountain of orange sparks into the tall pines and scorching their fringed branches. The horrible scent of burning pitch, tar, and canvas filled the air as the privateers died. Tears raced from Mira's eyes, tracing paths down her smoke-blackened cheeks and reflecting the sad flames.

Oh, Brendan . . . She pushed her hands against her mouth and sobbed brokenly, unable to bear the sight. *Oh, thank God you made it to sea and don't have to see this. Oh, thank God, thank God, thank God—*

Abadiah Bobbs grabbed her wrist and pointed downriver. Through the glowing orange smoke. Through the tangle of American and British warships, and the fires that lit up the night. Toward the south.

There, charging upriver, her black hull reflecting the flames, every sail set and her proud colors streaming from her gaff, was *Kestrel.*

She hadn't gone to sea after all.

And then Mira's heart lodged in her throat and her blood

turned to ice. In hot pursuit was a frigate, her very size dwarfing the little *Kestrel.*

Mira fell back against Abadiah's arm.

That frigate was *Viper.*

Some tried in vain to get past the British squadron and out to sea.

None, save Newburyport's *Pallas,* succeeded.

The brigantine *Defense,* of Beverly, went aground. New Hampshire's *Hampden* engaged one of the men-of-war, lost the fight, and was surrendered. Headed off as she tried to scoot between Long Island and the mainland, the eighteen-gun *Hunter* lurched ashore and was abandoned. With the exception of *Kestrel* and her prize, the rest of the American fleet fled upriver.

Brendan stood solemnly on the varnished deck of his little ship, surrounded by his crew. His plan to save Saltonstall had been for naught. And now they were trapped with the rest of the Americans.

Faces were long and sad in the flickering orange light of the flames. Eyes were haunted; tears stood in devastated eyes.

Beneath his feet, *Kestrel* rolled uneasily.

Ahead, the river narrowed and would grow impassable. Behind, their escape was prevented by three men-of-war and the frigate *Viper.* There was nothing more to do, nowhere left to go.

Near shore, an American ship went up in flames with a terrible, rushing roar, and then a mighty explosion as the fire found her powder magazine.

Brendan swallowed hard. He touched the rail and felt *Kestrel* trembling all the way down to her keel.

I can't, Brendan thought. He stroked the rail and swallowed the hard, burning lump in his throat. *You're my lassie. . . . I can't destroy you. . . .*

But he couldn't allow the British to have her either.

To larboard, *Defense* blew up, screaming like a live thing as the flames roared up her masts and, in seconds, consumed her sails and swallowed them whole. Sickened, Brendan turned away, unable to watch the awful death.

"I can't," he said aloud.

No one spoke. *Kestrel* surged restlessly beneath him, fearful, suddenly wary.

The British ships moved closer.

He took off his hat and raked shaking hands through his hair. His vision swam and his heart was burning a hole in his chest. The old scar ached. Tears burned behind his nose and he straightened his shoulders, careful to keep the emotion out of his eyes. But to muster a grin was too much. He looked at the ships dying around him, the smoking remains of the once proud American fleet—and knew what he had to do.

"Liam," he said quietly, "bring me some hemp and a lantern from belowdecks."

Kestrel was shaking. Pleading. Begging.

"Brendan . . . what're ye goin' t' do?"

"The only thing I *can* do." He shut his eyes in agony, his nails biting into his palms. "Torch her."

Aft, the prize pressed close to *Kestrel*'s flank as though seeking protection. His jaw clenched, Brendan stared past her, out over the smoke-clogged water and into the night. Tears stood in his eyes and he hastily turned his back so the crew wouldn't see.

And then Liam was there, solemnly holding the lantern and a thick piece of hemp.

The time had come.

With trembling hands, he reached for the lantern.

A mile away, Mira and her little party huddled together onshore and watched another blazing hulk come drifting down the river in a thundering wall of bright orange flame and billowing smoke.

A horrible, keening cry of grief rose in her throat, and she turned her sobbing face into Abadiah's arms to block the sight.

It was a schooner.

Chapter 32

What was left of the mighty American fleet gathered together and, on foot, made the long, exhausting trek back through the Maine wilderness to Portsmouth. Many died in the lonely woods. The true losses were never counted. Starving, dejected, and footsore, they followed the coast and returned to their homes.

On the day that Mira wearily pulled open the Ashton front door, the sun was glowing with that melancholy late afternoon burnish that painted the sides of the house in rust and cast long shadows over the lawn. She was greeted by a sobbing Abigail, a jubilant Ephraim, and a new sister-in-law.

In her absence, Matt and Eveleen had gotten married.

She passed the table, set with fine silver and polished crystal. She waded through some twelve or thirteen cats, clapped her hands over her ears at the sound of Ephraim's great, chiming Willard clock, and retreated to her room without a word to anyone.

She'd never felt so lonely in her life.

And with each hour she was home, the pain only worsened.

Two days after her arrival, she wandered out to the stable and watched her three horses grazing in the paddock. Rigel, his dappled coat shining like gunmetal. El Nath, looking over the fence with his long, inky forelock hanging in his eyes. Shaula, prancing along the perimeter, her white tail raised like a glorious flag.

Once, they had meant everything to her, those horses. Now she could not have cared less about them.

In several of the Market Square stores, merchants displayed brilliantly executed sketches of sea battles and got the high prices they asked for them. Mira, dejectedly buying some flour several days after her return, happened to glance up and see one. She knew who the artist was without even having to look at the signature.

She didn't go into the store again.

Across High Street their neighbors, no doubt tired of the unreasonable amount of noise coming from the Ashton household, had long since moved out. Now Matt, who'd regained the sight of one eye, and Eveleen, soft and lovely and growing as willowy as a weed, lived there.

And down in the Ashton Shipyards, a new ship was taking shape on the ways, not far from where the legendary *Kestrel* had been born. She would be a brig, sleek-sided and graceful, with a jaunty nose and a tapered tail and miles of masts holding up the sky above. Her figurehead would be a blond maiden with soft eyes, and the name across her counter was *Eveleen*. And her drafts, carefully locked in Ephraim's office, had been drawn by a naval hero named Merrick, an Anglo-Irishman who'd met his end in the wilderness of Penobscot.

A week after her arrival, Ephraim, uncomfortable with, and unable to bear, Mira's dejection, took matters into his own hands. No daughter of his was going to pine her life away in loneliness. Obtaining Abadiah Bobbs's consent, he plotted and schemed and announced that she would marry Abadiah's thirty-year-old son Roger, a man who was more proficient at quoting poetry than setting a sail.

He'd expected—and hoped—for a show of resistance from his daughter, but Mira's spirit had died somewhere up in the wilderness of Maine. She didn't care what Ephraim did anymore. She couldn't have cared less about anything.

The wedding was set two weeks later, much to both Matt's and Abigail's disapproval. But Ephraim was adamant. Mira needed a husband to take her mind off her recent loss. Roger Bobbs was a decent man; a bit insipid, but he'd have to be to put up with the likes of Mira.

The wedding was set. The day drew closer. Mira wilted and drooped like a dying flower, but for her, there was nothing left to live for. Roger was a good man. She'd try to be a good wife. Thoughts of the puppyish Roger touching her body never occurred to her. There was no room for thoughts of the future . . . just the memories of the past.

The church filled rapidly, despite the heat of the day and the short length of time since the couple had made their announcement. The Reverend Edward Bass sweated in his long robes. The groom fidgeted and looked paler than a ghost. Guests sat in the hard pews: sea captains wearing their best uniforms, mariners in freshly washed shirts and homespun vests, merchants in silk and velvet with the sweat pouring out of their powdered hair. Men scratched beneath their wigs. Ladies fanned themselves and daintily dabbed at their brows.

And then the bride entered.

Escorted by her father, she was resplendent in a soft cotton gown of plain blue. White ruffles bordered her décolletage, frothed at her wrists. Matching petticoats shone through her split skirts, and a lacy mobcap covered her glorious hair. Her green eyes were pale and distant, as though drugged. Her mouth was colorless, her cheeks sunken.

Ephraim, wearing his watches like war medals, had never looked prouder.

And Matthew Ashton, escorting his own lovely young bride, looked angrier than a maddened hornet. His brilliant red hair stuck out in riotous disarray from beneath his tricorn. His brown eyes snapped behind spectacles fogged with steam. His lips were set in a tight line, and his snarled whispers were heard by everyone. "Father, you can't do this! She's not herself! This is unfair, do you hear me?! Unfair!"

"Shut up, Matthew, do ye hear me?! Just shut up! The one fine moment in yer sister's life and yer tryin' to wreck it for her!"

"Goddammit, Father—"

"You shut your mouth; this is a *church!*"

"With its own cussed sacrifice!"

The Reverend Bass cleared his throat. Roger Bobbs looked about to faint. Somewhere in the back, a baby yowled and split the tense silence with lusty cries.

"Dearly beloved. We are gathered here today . . ."

Mira heard the words through a foggy, pressing daze. She saw poor Roger through glazed eyes and actually felt sorry for him. He looked miserable. She didn't blame him.

Reverend Bass droned on. The shadows grew long. The baby screamed louder and had to be carried out. Outside, a wind came up and the trees rustled, and from far off came the distant roll of thunder.

"Captain Ashton, do you give this woman to Mr. Roger Bobbs. . . ."

Ephraim stuck out his chest and puffed, "I will."

"Miss Mira, would you please repeat after me . . ."

From outside came the mad approach of flying hoof-beats.

The doors of the church burst open and a horseman, breathless, tore off his hat and pressed it to his heaving chest. "Come quick! Two ships're coming into the river's mouth! There's gonna be one helluva battle off of Plum Island, mark my words!"

The pastor blanched at the horseman's rough language. In dismay, he watched as a sea captain grabbed his hat, strode toward the doors, and breaking into a run, bolted outside. Another followed. Another.

"Gentlemen, this is a *wedding!*"

But that didn't seem to matter. The Tracys, privateers and shipbuilders themselves, were hard on their heels. One by one every sea captain in the church raced out the door. Then the seamen went, the fresh-faced boys, and finally the women. In moments, the big church was empty.

Not even Mira's family remained.

And then the Reverend Bass put down his Bible and, with long robes trailing behind him, hurried down the center aisle and out the door.

The groom relaxed and, shrugging, faced his prospective bride. He stood shifting his weight from foot to foot, his face reddening. "Guess I'd better go, too. . . . You don't mind, do you, Miss Mira? We can get married when everyone comes back."

"Fine," she whispered, sinking down into a pew.

He left and she was alone.

Then, and only then, did she cry, as off in the distance,

some ship engaged another and brought back sad, grief-filled memories. On and on it went, each distant report tearing a little piece of her heart out. It went on forever. And then the deep reverberations stilled and from far off, probably down along the riverfront, she heard a wild cheering.

She put her face in her hands and sobbed in bitter agony. Whatever the identity of the victorious ship down there, that glorious welcome should've been *Kestrel*'s.

She cried harder.

The cheering was getting closer now. A carriage raced past in a clatter of wheels and thunderous hooves, the driver yelling something she didn't hear. Strands of thick, heavy hair drooped from beneath her mobcap and she pushed them off her damp cheeks. Damn them all, why didn't they cheer Brendan when he'd gone off to war, taken his little ship into battle and faced Crichton, returned home with Matt—

The cheering grew deafening, just outside the church now. Out of the corner of her eye she saw the swelling crowd, numbering in the hundreds, surge past the window, with a man lifted to their shoulders. She heard their voices, raised in excitement and glee. "Let's get on with this wedding! We've waited long enough and we won't wait any longer!"

"Get on with it!"

"Now! Now! Now!"

And Father: "Blast it all, 'bout time ye showed up, and in the nick of time, too! Another moment and poor ol' Roger here wouldda been consigned to a fate worse than death! Now, git up there an' take yer place next to her, dammit! I want a son-in-law and I ain't waitin' no longer, you hear me?!"

"Marry her! Marry her! Marry her!" the people cried.

It became a chant, growing louder—

"Marry her!"

And louder—

"Marry her!"

And louder, until the doors exploded inward and the voices spilled into the church.

"MARRY HER!"

Light streamed red-orange across the varnished wood of the pew before her. It slanted through the still open doors and picked out striations in the wood. And then that light was cut off.

Mira looked up, the sob catching in her throat. She turned.

There, framed in the doorway with the crowd behind him and pushing him forward, was a tall, immaculately dressed man with a jauntily set tricorn and a weightless grin.

He was holding a sketchpad.

A drawing depicting a frigate with a British flag at its masthead, and a little schooner with sharply raked masts.

The schooner, victorious, was chasing the frigate. And the frigate was sinking.

He grinned, and their eyes met across fifty feet of space. . . .

"Mira," he said.

And it came out, *Moyrrra.*

Epilogue

The *Essex Gazette*, September 15, 1779.

"After setting his prize—not his ship—afire, and using it to cut a hole through the British fleet at Penobscot and therefore making his escape, the brave Captain Merrick gallantly brought his sharp-sailing schooner Kestrel *off of Newburyport, where he engaged in a heated battle, and a race, with Captain Richard Crichton in His Majesty's frigate* Viper.

"Being that the battle was a fight, and the race a flight, we are happy to report that Kestrel *won the BATTLE—and* Viper *won the RACE!"*

There was no mention of the brave Captain Merrick's collapse following his ingenious escape from Penobscot, nor of Lieutenant Liam Doherty's taking over command of *Kestrel* and keeping her out to sea for several weeks, long enough for his captain to recover. But that didn't matter.

The *important* details were all right here.

Cackling with glee, Ephraim Ashton, shipbuilder, picked up the paper and read the passage a final time.

And then he licked the jelly from his fingers so as not to get any on the Marine News section, carefully rolled up the paper, and made his way to Davenport's Wolfe tavern, chuckling all the way.

Avon Romances—
the best in exceptional authors and unforgettable novels!

WARRIOR DREAMS Kathleen Harrington
76581-0/$4.50 US/$5.50 Can

MY CHERISHED ENEMY Samantha James
76692-2/$4.50 US/$5.50 Can

CHEROKEE SUNDOWN Genell Dellin
76716-3/$4.50 US/$5.50 Can

DESERT ROGUE Suzanne Simmons
76578-0/$4.50 US/$5.50 Can

DEVIL'S DELIGHT DeLoras Scott
76343-5/$4.50 US/$5.50 Can

RENEGADE LADY Sonya Birmingham
76765-1/$4.50 US/$5.50 Can

LORD OF MY HEART Jo Beverley
76784-8/$4.50 US/$5.50 Can

BLUE MOON BAYOU Katherine Compton
76412-1/$4.50 US/$5.50 Can

Coming Soon

SILVER FLAME Hannah Howell
76504-7/$4.50 US/$5.50 Can

TAMING KATE Eugenia Riley
76475-X/$4.50 US/$5.50 Can